Giaime Alonge is a screenwriter, novelist, and an Associate Professor of Film History at the University of Turin. He has also served as a visiting professor at the University of Chicago.

Clarissa Botsford studied Italian at Cambridge and Comparative Education in London. She currently teaches English and Translation Studies at Roma Tre University. Her translations from the Italian include Sacha Naspini's *Tell Me About It* and *The Bishop's Villa*, *Sworn Virgin* by Elvira Dones, *The Game* by Alessandro Baricco, and the prose poems of Valerio Magrelli.

THE FEELING
OF IRON

Giaime Alonge

THE FEELING
OF IRON

*Translated from the Italian
by Clarissa Botsford*

Europa
editions

Europa Editions
8 Blackstock Mews
London N4 2BT
www.europaeditions.co.uk

Translation by Clarissa Botsford
Original title: *Il sentimento del ferro*
Translation copyright © 2025 by Fandango S.p.A.

A catalogue record for this title is available from the British Library
ISBN 978-1-78770-583-8

Alonge, Giaime
The Feeling of Iron

Cover design by Ginevra Rapisardi

Cover photo by Frederick Wallace/Unsplash

Prepress by Grafica Punto Print – Rome

The authorized representative in the EEA
is Edizioni e/o, via Gabriele Camozzi 1, 00192 Rome, Italy.

Printed and bound in Great Britain by Clays Ltd, Elcograf S.p.A

CONTENTS

PART ONE
Human Material - 13

PART TWO
Operation Berserker - 173

PART THREE
The New World - 357

And you shall destroy all the peoples that the Lord your God
will give over to you, your eye shall not pity them
—*Deuteronomy* 7:16

What is needed is a new drug which will relieve
and console our suffering species.
—ALDOUS HUXLEY, *The Doors of Perception*

THE FEELING
OF IRON

PART ONE

Human Material

1

F ar away on the horizon, Leningrad was burning. The German air force had dropped more than six thousand incendiary bombs over the old center the night before. The air that morning was crisp and the columns of smoke rising from a massive fire at the Badajev Warehouses could be seen from miles away. The vanguards of the Northern Division were already in Ligovo, a southern suburb. An artillery observation post had been installed on the tower of the Pishmac plant and cannon fire was raining down on the main Leningrad Road, jammed with fleeing civilians. From the Baltic to the Black Sea, the Wehrmacht had swept across the immense Russian plains—*Lebensraum*, or "living space," in the language of the Party—like a tsunami of flesh and steel. The Eastern lands were *Raum*—a surface, an abstract place, geometric—because they were *empty*, without a cultural dimension, without a people in the true sense of the term. They were inhabited only by *Untermenschen*, savages the Aryan race was on a mission to subjugate. After the war, the natives would be deported somewhere and replaced by German colonists: peasant-soldiers who would guard the Asian border and finally bring History to these desolate steppes. The East was a blank sheet of paper on which Germany could write whatever it pleased. According to Heinrich Himmler's directives as Reich Commissioner for the Consolidation of German Nationhood, the landscape itself was to become German.

In the diaphanous dawn, a Ju 52 tri-engine towing a Gotha tactical transport glider flew toward the Red Army lines. The double tail and large glass roof of the cockpit made the glider look futuristic, a warning to the enemy that there would be no point in resisting. The two aircrafts were accompanied by a pair of Messerschmitt Bf 109 fighters. The Luftwaffe had almost entirely eliminated the enemy air force in that sector, but an escort had nonetheless been assigned. Orders had come directly from Berlin. The operation was top priority. The formation flew over a column of tanks rumbling through a wheat field. The farmers had not had time to harvest their crops and the tanks flattened the sea of ripe stalks in their wake. The planes were flying low. The pilot could see the commander of the leading tank, his whole torso sticking out of the turret of his Panzer, his arms resting on the sides of the hatch as if he were on parade at the Unter den Linden. Then the Ju 52 began to climb in altitude, dragging the large glider behind it, the escort fighter planes swift on their tails.

It was still summer, but at an altitude of two thousand meters it was cold in the fuselage of the Gotha. Lieutenant Kurt Steiner shivered and hugged himself to keep warm. Eyes closed, chin on his chest, he was on the verge of falling asleep. Sergeant Vogt, sitting beside him and chewing on a pretzel, calmed him. The man always ate before any action. Vogt had been his companion since the beginning of the war, as had several other members of the platoon: about twenty men in all. Many, however, were new, recently-arrived replacements and their tension was palpable. Only a year earlier there had been a feeling of invincibility. On May 10, 1940, they had captured the Belgian fortress of Eben-Emael, whose cannons might have blocked Field Marshal von Bock's troops on their advance towards France. With a spectacularly daring action, seventy-eight *Fallschirmjäger* had captured a garrison of more than a thousand soldiers in a few hours. Then came Crete. The Australian and New Zealand Army Corps, along with what remained of the Greek Army, had valiantly held their positions on those rocky plateaus, shattering the myth that German paratroopers were invincible. Manfred Grüber, whom Steiner had known since childhood, had been killed there. They had been together since primary school and enlisted together. He had met his fate on a barren, windswept mountain overlooking the blue sea in Suda Bay. In Crete, the 7th Airborne Division had suffered such heavy losses that it had been unable to take part in the subsequent attack on the Soviet Union. The *Fallschirmjäger* were only now being brought to the front line, three months after Operation Barbarossa was launched. Vogt's light elbow-dig forced the lieutenant to open his eyes. They were almost directly above the target. The Ju 52 released the glider, which continued its silent course flanked by the Messerschmitts.

The pilot was clearly skilled. He made a perfect landing on a small field between a stream and a softwood forest, which were invisible from the position they had been ordered to attack. As they clambered out of the plane and prepared to march, Steiner saw that the Ju 52 and the two fighters were returning to base, where the second formation was already supposed to have taken off.

Hidden in the tall grass, Lieutenant Steiner peered through his binoculars at the NKVD men loading large wooden crates onto a truck. The agents of Stalin's Secret Service were working fast. They knew they were running out of time. The greenhouse was only a few yards away from the other buildings, which could present a problem. He had received orders to avoid damaging any plants or specimens at all costs. He was happy to have brought an extra machine gun rather than the mortar. He cocked his MP40.

"Fire!" Steiner shouted.

The parachute platoon was arranged in a semicircle, with the two machine guns at either end. They fired from under cover, calmly and accurately. Most of the bullets hit the mark.

Major Remizov had thrown himself to the ground after the

first shots and crawled to the truck. He was shocked to find a wood and leather mask with a long, pointed beak right in front of his nose. He had seen masks like these in a newsreel report on Siberian and Central Asian populations. It must have fallen out of one of the crates. Remizov and the mask stared at one another, then the NKVD officer jumped into the vehicle. Revving the engine, he realized the bullets must have punctured the tires because the truck was not moving. He got out, crawled under the vehicle, and aimed his machine gun at the Krauts, who were starting to emerge from the bushes. They moved forward in small groups, covering for one another. From the sides, the two machine guns were furiously sweeping the ground with bullets. Remizov pulled his trigger. The shot hit one of the paratroopers, who fell down dead. He saw the man's lips part. He may have uttered a cry or a curse, but the Major did not hear it. The din of gunfire drowned out any other noise. It may simply have been an ingenuous expression of astonishment, which was fitting considering the childlike features of his face. Remizov inserted a new magazine and fired again.

Lieutenant Steiner ran toward the enemy, firing blindly. Vogt, as always, followed. Bullets sprayed from less than a meter away.

Remizov was about to adjust his aim, but one of the *Fallschirmjäger* spotted him hiding behind the large, deflated tire. The major's last thought was not for his wife, or for the newborn son he would never meet, or even for comrade Stalin. The last image that flashed through his mind before he died was that strange bird-shaped mask.

Steiner had reached the main body of the laboratory. The Russians seemed to have abandoned all resistance. The bodies of NKVD agents were strewn haphazardly here and there. Steiner reloaded his machine gun and entered the building. He thought he heard the rumble of a car engine in the distance.

The second glider, with the *Kübelwagen* and the SS team, must have landed.

The large laboratory was bathed in shadow. The lieutenant's footsteps echoed sharply on the wooden floor. To the left, a counter ran along the wall, covered with scientific equipment and test tubes. When he reached the back of the room, he spotted a white shape under the table, pressed against the wall. Steiner bent down. A woman in her early thirties was clutching her knees to her chest and staring wide-eyed from behind a pair of round lenses in a metal frame. Steiner lowered the barrel of his machine gun and held his hand out, inviting her to come out. A polite, restrained gesture. The woman hesitated for a moment. As soon as she emerged from her hiding place, Steiner was stunned to see that she was brandishing a semiautomatic. He opened his mouth to say something, but never got the words out.

Vogt ran into the laboratory. The lieutenant was lying on the floor. A few steps away, the woman was pointing the gun in the air, the muscles in her arm and hand contracted, an expression of disbelief on her face. A thin swirl of smoke rose from the mouth of the weapon. Vogt let out a deep animal-like groan and emptied his entire magazine on the woman.

Two paratroopers burst in. At the sight of their commander's lifeless body, they fell silent. The event was unfathomable and they waited for their sergeant to enlighten them. Vogt turned to the counter. There was a glass jar filled with small brownish seeds. The SS had recommended not touching anything. Orders were for the *Fallschirmjäger* to limit themselves to eliminating the defenders and securing the laboratory. The sergeant sank a hand, greasy from the machine gun, into the container, grabbed a fistful of those brown kernels, and let them slip through his fingers. Were these what Lieutenant Steiner had died for?

Suddenly, the two soldiers snapped to attention. The sergeant looked up. A clutch of SS officers had come into the laboratory. The silver skulls on their caps gleamed in the dimness of the room. They studied the specimens lined up on the counter without deigning the paratroopers, alive or dead, with so much as a glance. Against his will, Sergeant Vogt clicked his heels and gave them a military salute.

Merida, southern Mexico, June 25, 1982

Mr. Johnson and Mr. Huberman wandered lazily through the deserted halls of Yukatan's Museo Histórico y Arqueológico. In the dusty display cases with handwritten labels, a range of artifacts represented the history of the region from the Mayan civilization to the twentieth century. The way the collection was organized attempted to convey the idea that progress was a guiding principle in the world, despite all the pain and suffering. However, the long sequence of foreign invasions and revolts repressed with bloodshed made for a very different story. In any case, the two gringos appeared uninterested in either the splendor or the misery of the people here. They threw occasional and distracted glances at the cabinets, talking quietly as they did so. Johnson was tall, in his early forties, with a puffy, pale Anglo-Saxon complexion. With his white shirt and Regimental tie, he could have been a bank clerk. Beside the short, dark-skinned custodians, he looked as if he hailed from an entirely different species. Huberman stood out less. He, too, had marked Nordic features, but his brightly-colored, locally-made shirt, the white ponytail that fell down his back, and the copper bracelet with a Sanskrit engraving gave him the air of a beat poet who had found a safe haven in an exotic corner of the world. Huberman was over seventy, but his stance was unyielding and his step assured.

"This meeting is off protocol, to say the least," Johnson said.

"I don't give a damn about protocol. The Agency is dumping me."

"It's gone a long way. Too far, some say."

"If they had provided me with the funds I asked for, this wouldn't have happened."

Johnson paused and eyeballed Huberman.

"You don't realize. The Agency's resources are limited. And our sector is by no means a priority."

"I know, Central America is insignificant. The important business takes place in Europe and the Middle East. But if the Reds take El Salvador, everyone at headquarters is going to start squawking."

"We have a very solid position in El Salvador."

Huberman started pacing.

"For the moment, Mr. Johnson, for the moment," he commented through gritted teeth.

Emerging from the cool museum rooms, sheltered by thick walls, the dusty, sun-baked city streets felt unbearable. The air was so dense and sticky you could almost touch it. Johnson's forehead was instantly slick with sweat. The gringo dried his brow with a handkerchief and slipped on the pair of mirrored Ray-Bans he kept in the breast pocket of his shirt.

"Do you know a place to eat without getting food poisoning?" he asked.

"There's a *taquería* somewhere back here. I was there last night. It's not bad."

Johnson made a guttural sound, unconvinced.

"Come on, Mr. Johnson. Let me introduce you to that mysteriously alluring world beyond McDonald's."

Johnson grunted again and followed Huberman down the wide staircase.

In front of the museum, sprawled on a bench in the shade of a tree, a man appeared to be sleeping with a wide-brimmed panama over his face. As soon as Johnson and Huberman turned the corner, the man lifted his hat, stood up, and started tailing them.

The place was small and well-kept. Half a dozen Formica tables, almost all free. A short wooden counter festooned with strings of chili peppers. A noisy old Coca-Cola refrigerator. The owner emerged from the kitchen with a tray of tacos stuffed with meat and pineapple and a dish of *puerco pibil*, which he deposited in front of the customers with two bottles of Corona. Johnson cast a suspicious glance at the pork marinated in banana leaves. Huberman ignored him and picked up the tableware wrapped in paper towels. As he unrolled the bundle, the fork fell out. He stooped to pick it up. At that very moment, the man in the panama hat appeared at the door of the restaurant, lobbed something in, and ran out. It was an M26 fragmentation grenade.

Perfect aim. The hand grenade exploded right above the table occupied by the two gringos. Johnson was hit by a cascade of shrapnel that shattered his face. All around him, chunks of hot metal ferociously mowed down everything in their path.

The *taquería* was shrouded in smoke. Huberman tried to get up but couldn't. The table had collapsed on him with Johnson's body on top of it. He could hear the proprietor screaming from somewhere. The cloying stench of burnt human flesh covered everything like a pall. It was a smell that Victor Huberman knew well.

Litzmannstadt, Wartheland, October 18, 1941

S hlomo Libowitz was running at breakneck speed down the street, zigzagging among passers-by, who stared at him in amazement. The bag with the potatoes and lard he had bought on the black market banged against his side. The regular thumps gave him a pleasant feeling: a physical certainty that his family would have food, at least for a couple of days. He cast a glance over his shoulder. The corporal from the *Ordnungspolizei* was still hot on his tail. He looked at least forty and pretty heavy. The chase had been going on for about ten minutes. Shlomo estimated that the Kraut would be able to keep it up for another two or three blocks at most. Of course, if he had decided to stop and aim his rifle at him, things could have turned ugly. But the boy counted on the fact that the policeman would not open fire on a street full of people. Many of them were Poles, whose lives were almost as worthless as the Jews'. The city was no longer even on the map. Łódź had been renamed Litzmannstadt and annexed to the Reich along with the rest of western Poland. But there were also a few off-duty Wehrmacht officers taking a stroll, not to mention the *Volksdeutschen*: ethnic Germans—descendants of ancient colonies that had emigrated to various parts of Eastern Europe, from Latvia to Romania—who, over the centuries, had built small islands of German culture in the interminable Slavic sea and who, at the end of 1939, had been "repatriated" to Germanize the newly annexed Polish territories. In Nazi racial taxonomy, the *Volksdeutschen* were inferior to the *Reichsdeutschen*—who were born within Germany's historical borders—but, in any case, they could not be mown down in the streets with impunity.

Shlomo hoped the policeman would bear this in mind and accelerated, the strength of a sixteen-year-old pumping through his legs. He dodged an elderly couple, leaped over a lady's lap dog, turned left, and found himself in the large round square dotted with kiosks and stalls where he had often been with his father. Before the war, he and Baruch often used to come to town to sell geese and eggs. Shlomo used to love making the trip and always looked forward to it. His father had liked it, too. For both of them it was a precious chance to escape for a few hours from the *shtetl* where the Libowitz family had lived for generations, a miserable settlement lost in the boundless expanse of mud that was the Polish countryside. Two communities lived there: one Jewish and the other Catholic. They had always ignored one another, but they had been part of a shared medieval existence, shrouded by the mist of an archaic and bigoted culture, whether it was Orthodox Judaism or the superstitious Christianity of the peasant world. As a boy, Baruch had wanted to emigrate to America but his parents had opposed the idea. Then he had taken a wife, and Miriam had wanted to stay by her elderly mother's side. Once the old mother had died, the children had arrived: first Shlomo, then Esther, who had died of diphtheria at the age of three. Miriam had never really recovered from the loss. Under the burden of responsibility and misfortune, Baruch Libowitz's dreams of escape had faded. But somehow, they had been passed down to Shlomo. And this had forged a silent but steadfast allegiance between father and son.

Shlomo crashed into an itinerant knife grinder who was sharpening a kitchen knife on a whetstone mounted on his bicycle frame. In the collision, the knife flew out of his hands, nearly injuring its owner, the proprietor of the corner street-food kiosk. Shlomo looked back. He caught a glimpse of the policeman's green coat in the crowd. The Kraut was stubborn. Amid insults from the grinder and his customer, Shlomo got up and started running again. He darted into an alley which took him to the next square. Perched on a lamppost in January

1938, he had listened to Vladimir Ze'ev Jabotinsky, the great leader of the Zionist right, speaking at a rally there. The man had been introduced by a fanatical-looking young functionary, Menachem Begin, who had not drawn much applause. Jabotinsky, on the other hand, had been awe-inspiring. The short man, wearing a pair of spectacles that gave him an air of a provincial high school principal, had mesmerized the thousands of people crowding around the stage with his eloquence. One phrase in particular had struck Shlomo: *Liquidate the Diaspora before the Diaspora liquidates you.* At the time, he hadn't grasped the meaning of those words. Now he understood it all too well. He crossed the square. The policeman was losing ground. Shlomo dove into a street that led to the Ghetto. That day, Mr. Gottlieb, who ran one of the city's most prestigious law firms, had sent his cook out to pick up a goose for a dinner the attorney intended to offer his Warsaw associates. When Baruch heard that Shlomo had been wasting time at the rally instead of doing his delivery rounds, he had gone personally and dragged him away by his ear. The dent to their reputation with the Gottliebs was indefensible but, more importantly, Baruch voted for the Bund, the General Union of Jewish Workers, and therefore opposed Zionism. Both the Bund and the Zionists wanted to break with the past and erase the traditional image of the devout and submissive Jew. They both saw an opportunity for a new way of being Jewish, at ease in the modern world and filled with courage. The Bund, however, felt that the transformation should take place in Europe rather than in the middle of a desert where no Jews had lived for two thousand years. In Baruch's eyes, Jabotinsky was doubly suspect. Not only was he a Zionist, but he was also the founder of a revisionist current which bore disturbing affinities with fascism: a passion for parades and military uniforms, anti-trade-union practices, and a loathing for socialism. As Shlomo kept running, his eyes scanned the sidewalk for the manhole cover. Finally, he saw it, a few yards ahead. He quickened his pace and got there in a flash. *Liquidate the Diaspora before the Diaspora liquidates you.*

Shlomo was struggling to lift the iron cover when, out of the corner of his eye, he saw the exhausted, red-faced, panting *Ordnungspolizei* corporal. The German slipped his rifle off his shoulder and aimed it at the boy. Shlomo stared at him for what felt like eternity, paralyzed like a cat dazzled by headlights. The bullet flew too high and crashed into a votive shrine of the Black Madonna. The policeman pulled back the bolt. The cartridge case popped out in a cloud of smoke. The sharp click of the second cartridge being inserted into the chamber echoed despondently in the alley. Shlomo summoned what strength he had left. With the sleeve of his pastern, the German dried the sweat dripping into his eyes from under his helmet and took aim. Shlomo threw the manhole cover to one side and dropped into the void. The shot whistled over his head. *Liquidate the Diaspora before the Diaspora liquidates you.*

The impenetrable darkness of the sewer shrouded the beam coming from Shlomo's pocket flashlight but, after numerous forays out of the Ghetto, he had learned to grope his way through that blind, slimy world. He worked his way through the tunnels cautiously, looking for the marks on the wall that he, or others like him, had left as sign-posts. There were bullet holes, too. Occasionally, the Germans would rappel themselves into the sewers to teach a lesson to Jews who dared break the laws of the Reich. But it didn't happen very often. It was so disgusting down there that even the fetid air of the Ghetto smelt good as he emerged from the manhole.

Shlomo walked resolutely down the teeming street. The crowd was immense: a rag-tag, foul-smelling multitude, begging for alms, bargaining, arguing, scheming, or cursing. Everyone had something to sell, but hardly anyone had the wherewithal to buy. Less than an hour earlier, Shlomo had been walking down streets filled with streetcars and lined with movie theaters.

Merchandise had been on show in store windows and people had been sitting in cafes. It already felt like a dream. Shlomo stepped over a corpse on the sidewalk. The man was naked, wrapped in sheets of newspaper. A fee had been introduced to bury the dead—the Jewish cemetery had been incorporated into the perimeter of the Ghetto, on the eastern border—and many families could not afford a burial. Once the body was on the street, the Jewish Council was forced to deal with it. Besides, clothes were precious. The dead had no use for them.

All of a sudden, he was surrounded by a pack of barefooted children. Two boys distracted him by talking, while a third tried to open his bag. Shlomo turned abruptly and grabbed the little thief by the wrists. They were unbelievably thin. The boy gave him a challenging look. Shlomo shoved him. Another older boy tried to grab him and received a backhanded slap for his efforts. They all ran off, squawking like a flock of pesky birds. The Łódź Ghetto had been the first to be established by the Germans, inaugurated in April 1940. At first, it had housed only the 160,000 local Jews: about a third of the city's inhabitants. Later, more had arrived from all over Wartheland. Among them were Shlomo and his parents, who had been deported in May 1941. Recently, convoys had arrived from other countries including Germany, Austria, and even Luxembourg. Some didn't speak Yiddish and could almost pass as *goyim*. By then, 250,000 Jews had been crammed into the Ghetto. The occupation authorities had set a per capita ration of 700 grams of bread a week. Starvation and rampant disease led to a death rate of around 2,500 people per month. But the Malthusian accounts never squared up. There were still too many people alive compared to the available space and resources.

The Libowitz's living quarters comprised one room. The bathroom was shared with five other families, which caused constant tension and fights. As soon as Shlomo came in, his ravenous father snatched the bag out of his hands. Shlomo had let him take it, but Baruch was ashamed of his feral gesture and returned the bag to his son.

"Next time I'll go," he muttered.

He said this after every expedition to the Aryan zone, though he knew full well that he would never make it. When it was time for the next foray, it would be the boy's turn again. Shlomo nodded and his father smiled back, grateful for his complicity in that little lie.

"Lard has gone up to seventy złoty a kilo," Shlomo said as he emptied the contents of the haversack on the table.

Baruch began to peel the potatoes. Shlomo took off his jacket and hat and went to sit next to his mother. Miriam was lying on the straw mattress, as usual. The day they had arrived in Łódź, after a long and tiring journey, she had taken to her bed and never gotten up again. The boy took her hands in his to get her attention.

"I brought food," he said softly.

The woman nodded, but there was no telling whether she had understood, or even recognized her son. She was lost in a world of shadows, her skin tight and jaundiced, her gaze vacant. Sometimes she called out to Esther. More often she would start a long conversation with her mother or with her sister Ruth, who lived in Białystok, about whom they had had no news since the outbreak of war. She would complain about their neighbor, Mrs. Zuckerman, who was a gossip. Or, she would describe in great detail the outfit she had had made for Shlomo's Bar Mitzvah. It had been quite expensive, but the goose business had been doing well and they had been able to afford it. Baruch had also bought himself a new suit. She had been lucky to find a good husband, an honest, hard-working man who had never beaten her and had never let her lack for anything.

Shlomo shifted his gaze to his father, who was sitting at the table in a ray of gray light filtering through the small window. He was peeling the potatoes extremely slowly, both because he was determined not to waste a single sliver and because, every now and then, his hands started shaking and he had to stop. He was only forty-two and already looked like an old man, with stooping shoulders and graying hair. Money was running out. And even if they had more, sooner or later the Krauts would catch Shlomo, and that would spell the end for his parents. Shlomo felt his throat constrict. He wondered if anyone in the outside world knew what was going on. The British, the Polish government in exile, the Zionist leadership in Palestine. They needed to be warned. They needed to do something about it. As soon as possible.

Liquidate the Diaspora before the Diaspora liquidates you.

4

Mérida, southern Mexico, June 28, 1982

The fan hummed tediously and uselessly in the hot air. From the street, beyond the large inner courtyard, snatches of the city's sound-track could be heard. A firefighter's siren. A jackhammer. A church bell ringing. After a long interval with no noise at all, a truck passing by. Victor Huberman conjured up an image of a rickety vehicle, its cab decorated with saints and Virgin Marys, the windshield plastered with promising captions such as "Jesus is my co-pilot," or "The Virgin of Guadalupe is watching over me." His thoughts were sluggish and the images were struggling to surface. Huberman was sinking back into sleep when he suddenly felt a presence in the room. It was not the usual nurse, a silent indigenous woman he only noticed when she changed his IV bag. There was someone awkward and threatening, desperately trying to get his attention.

"I'm a journalist."

Huberman was awake but ignored the nuisance, determined to wait until the journalist gave up on him. He wondered why they had let him in. The man had probably tipped someone. Damn Hispanics. They were all like that, from the Rio Grande to the Tierra del Fuego. And the reporter seemed intent on putting his investment to good use, as he leaned over him and raised his voice at the same time.

"I am a reporter for the *Diario de Yucatán.*"

He was so close that Huberman could smell his eau de cologne.

"We have picked up some information and would like a statement from you on this matter. Can you confirm that the US consulate official Andrew Johnson, who was in your company when the bomb went off, was actually a CIA agent?"

Huberman didn't move a muscle. His eyelids still closed, he whispered, "Did he die?"

"On the spot. The explosion blew his head off. It took the police two days to identify the body."

The police. Shortly after Huberman had arrived at the hospital, some officers had made an appearance. They had asked to interrogate him, but the doctors, who were about to extract shrapnel from his back, had flatly refused. The officers had insisted. Huberman had uttered a few meaningless and slurred words. The officers had relented, promising to return as soon as the patient was able to answer their questions.

The reporter waited for the old man to open his mouth again. Faced with his silence, he pressed him, "Is it true that you took part in Operation Condor?"

Victor Huberman's opened his eyes wide. The journalist was a light-skinned Mexican, a twenty-year-old with the wan look of a seminarian. His editor can't have considered the story very important if he had sent this rookie. Still, the fact remained that someone who was not the Mérida police, or even the federal police, seemed to be taking an interest in him. Huberman struggled to focus. He had to act fast, but he feared his body would not respond. He tried pulling himself up. It proved easier than he expected. He yanked the needle out of his arm. The journalist gawped. "Mr. Huberman . . . ," he stammered.

The old man got out of bed and went to open the closet. His clothes were a sodden bundle of rags covered in blood and dust. He took his passport and wallet out of his pants pockets. The cash had gone, but the traveler's checks were still in place. He closed the cupboard door again and turned to appraise the kid. They were about the same size.

"Strip," Huberman ordered. His tone was not aggressive. He said the word with the chilling calm of someone used to issuing orders.

"Excuse me?"

"Take your clothes off."

The reporter had no time to reply. With a snap movement that was surprising enough in a man of his age, but even more so considering he was also wounded, Huberman kneed him in the testicles and, when the Mexican doubled over in pain, struck him on the back of his head with his clasped hands. The journalist collapsed to the ground.

The acrylic shirt stank of sweat, but it was much better than walking around in pajamas. Huberman left the room, reached the elevator, and pressed the button. If that reporter had been telling the truth and Johnson was dead, the Agency may hold him somehow responsible. The killing of an operative is always complicated, especially if it comes out in the media. He had to get away quickly. The elevator reached the ground floor and Huberman was about to get out, but a painful twinge in his back prevented him from moving. His head was spinning. He leaned against the elevator wall, blocking the door with his hand. He took a deep breath. He could hear people coming from the corridor. He forced himself to move. Looking reasonably casual, despite his shuffling steps, he managed to reach the lobby and slip out of the hospital.

Outside there was the same heat and dust on the streets of Mérida that he had experienced a few days earlier in the company of Andrew Johnson. He had only known him superficially, and had never liked him that much, but he was still a fighter who had fallen for the cause. He deserved respect. He cast a glance around, looking for a cab stand. Why had the reporter asked him about Condor? That was old hat. Perhaps it was just good guess-work and the man simply didn't know there were more interesting things on his resume. He clambered into the battered green Ford and slumped into the seat. He had only walked a few yards but he was exhausted. He wiped the sweat from his forehead with the palm of his hand.

"Where to?"

He drew a blank. Huberman couldn't even remember the name of the hotel.

"Where to?" the driver asked again.

Huberman concentrated. "Imperial," he exclaimed with relief. The car pulled away from the curb and went to join the slow and noisy procession of afternoon traffic.

There wasn't anything very imperial about the hotel. It was an anonymous, cheaply built construction for locals and tourists of limited means. The man at the front desk greeted him with an astonished look. He had heard on television that he would not be recovering any time soon. But there he was, already on his feet. He congratulated him. Huberman cut him short and asked him to cash a traveler's check. The taxi driver watched dubiously, but when he saw the bills change hands, he smiled with satisfaction.

Huberman told the receptionist he would go to his room to get his luggage. The doorman replied that they had given the room away, imagining a long hospital stay. But there was no need to worry about his belongings. Everything had been packed into his suitcase by one of the housekeepers and safely stored in the manager's office.

"Did the police come?" asked Huberman.

The man said that two officers had shown up the day after the bombing. They had wanted to see the room. They had stayed for half an hour. He did not know if they had taken anything.

"Bring me my luggage."

"Right away."

To be honest, there had been nothing valuable or particularly compromising that might have attracted the cops' interest aside from a modest quantity of dried peyote mushrooms, which had indeed vanished from the suitcase. They had been high-quality mushrooms from the state of Coahuila, but he could not call it a serious loss. Victor Huberman snapped the suitcase shut.

"Call me a cab."

The car arrived at the Imperial ten minutes later. The driver put the suitcase in the boot and hurried to open the door for the pathetic old gringo. He looked as if he might keel over at any moment. The taxi driver hoped he didn't pee his pants or worse.

"To the airport," Huberman said.

The driver nodded and started the car.

"Back home?" he asked distractedly.

"Yes, to Los Angeles," Huberman lied.

From Mérida there were no direct flights to Tegucigalpa. He had to go all the way to Mexico City. It was going to be a painful trip, especially with a freshly sutured wound and metal shrapnel still lodged in his legs. Victor Huberman gritted his teeth and told himself he had been in worse situations.

The cab left the city center and took the road to the airport. The driver made a comment about the beauty of the surrounding landscape, which Huberman ignored. When the car stopped in front of the boarding area under the large Aeroméxico sign, it was almost seven o'clock in the evening. Huberman bought his ticket with a traveler's check and boarded the last flight of the day to the capital. He fell asleep before the plane had lifted from the ground.

5

Protectorate of Bohemia and Moravia, October 18, 1941

At the head of Convoy 9228 was a three-cylinder loco-motive manufactured by Škoda, the acronym of the Czechoslovak State Railways hidden by a hasty coat of paint but still legible on the side. The engine had more than thirty cars attached to it and was making slow progress. The stoker took one last greedy drag on his cigarette, staining his lips with the black charcoal coating his hands, and tossed the butt out of the cab. They were approaching a level crossing. The bars were already down, a bus and a peasant's cart waiting to go through. The driver pulled the siren cord, and for a few seconds the train workers' ears were pierced by the steam whis-tle. It was the first time they had served on what the Germans called a "special train." Colleagues had advised them to take the work and not ask any questions.

In many respects, 9228 was indeed special. Its travelers had been boarded at gunpoint after a methodical operation had de-prived them of most of their material possessions and stripped them of all the rights granted by liberal society over the past century. By March 1939, after the Munich Conference, the Wehrmacht had occupied what was left of Czechoslovakia. The following day, the Führer had arrived in Prague in person. He had stayed at the Castle, the historic residence of the Bohemian kings, and in one of its halls, Hitler had signed a decree establishing the Protectorate. With immediate effect, Jews had been expelled from professions and businesses, had their bank accounts frozen, and lost homes and businesses, which had been "Aryanized," that is, assigned to new owners with Germanic bloodlines. The follow-ing step had been forced labor and relocation to the ghettos.

But in other respects, Special Train 9228, which had departed from Prague bound for Litzmannstadt at 7:50 A.M., was absolutely ordinary. Like any other train convoy, it had been arranged by employees of the Ministry of Transport. The folder had been passed from one office to another, and little by little the 9228 had been prepared. One official had studied the route, another had worked out the timetable, a third had determined the number of wagons, and a fourth had selected the engine. Any risk of last-minute mishaps or impediments had been preempted by phone calls and telegrams bounced between different stations along the line. And as for any other train, a ticket was charged for the 9228: the Reichsbahn charged the basic third-class fare of four Pfennigs per kilometer. Children between the ages of four and twelve paid half. Any child under four traveled for free. Tickets were one-way for Jews, and round-trip for the fifteen or so guards per convoy. If at least four hundred people were traveling together, a group fare could be negotiated. Unsurprisingly, a travel agency, the Mitteleuropäische Reisebüro, was known at times to play a role in the operation. As well as handling special trains, they offered visits to historical cities and vacations on the Baltic Sea. The bill for the whole operation was submitted to the Reich Central Security Office, headed by Reinhard Heydrich, who had also been appointed deputy protector of Bohemia and Moravia in September 1941. The Office settled the payment by drawing on funds requisitioned from Jews.

The 9228 stopped at a town just before the German border to board families that had been rounded up in the vicinity and to let a military convoy through on its way to the front. While the train was at a halt, a boy managed to jump out and run into the woods, the sound of his footsteps covered by the clanging of open cars loaded with Panzers and cannons on the parallel track. Two men from the Ordnungspolizei tumbled out of the guards' carriage swearing, as their comrades set about hammering the wooden planks back onto the narrow windows of the cattle cars. The boy flitted like shadows against the backdrop of the damp fields. After three attempts, the soldiers hit their target.

More than a hundred people were crammed into a few square meters in the cattle car. Sitting down was impossible. The tin bucket in the corner that served as a toilet was already overflowing. People dug their elbows into one another in a desperate attempt to carve out some space. When three gunshots echoed through the carriage, for the first time since they had left the station, there was silence. Every futile attempt to find a comfortable position by struggling against neighbors or with their own body, came to a halt. They waited in a frozen silence. When there were no more retorts, the shouting and fighting resumed more urgently.

In the midst of the crush, Anton Epstein was straining to shield his sister Greta, a slip of a girl who was looking around with a bewildered expression. Anton was in his twenties but he looked younger, and his habitual good manners were of no use in that terrifyingly new situation. A little farther over, his father David, former chief of surgery with a chair at Charles IV in Prague, the oldest university in Central Europe, was holding his wife Rachel round the waist as she pressed a handkerchief to her nose, making an effort to keep calm. Professor Epstein exchanged a few discreet but eloquent glances with Fischer, an attorney who was also attempting to hold his spouse in an upright position. They had been patrons of the same café and knew each other superficially, after occasionally playing billiards and engaging in a few political discussions in the swirling cigar smoke. The object of their attention was the group of Hasidic Jews the Germans had just rounded into the car. Superstitious rag-tags with greasy beards, with a horde of brats trailing after them. Neither of the burghers had said anything, but Anton knew the word his father had on the tip of his tongue: *Ostjuden*, a term the family used with a mixture of awe and pity to indicate everything that Professor Epstein had always striven to get away from, ever since, to his great good fortune, he had been sent to study in the city. "Eastern Jew" was a byword for the primitive rules that governed *shtetl* life. As soon as he had moved to Prague at the age of fifteen, David Epstein had abandoned Yiddish for German, stopped worrying about turning lights on during the Sabbath, and dived enthusiastically into the effervescent lifestyle of his epoch. He had been a loyal subject of the emperor and had served honorably during the Great War as a medical officer, first in Serbia, then on the Italian front. When the Empire had dissolved, moreover, he had become a staunch supporter of the newly born Czechoslovak Republic. David Epstein had believed in science, the press, and the free circulation of ideas. He had believed that in the twentieth century, at least in civilized nations, the concept of citizenship had replaced that of family lineage or tribe.

In turn, the newly-arrived Hasidim gawped at the inhabitants of Prague's wealthy quarters with an astonished, almost embarrassed air. A little boy with long curly locks at his temples addressed Anton. He spoke articulately in a string of subordinate clauses. Anton understood some of it because Yiddish and German were close. Indeed, Yiddish could be said to be a parody of German: Goethe and Schiller's language ruined by an ignorant vernacular. But the overall meaning had escaped him. He shook his head to let the boy know that he had little or no command of their language. The kid looked at him with a serious expression and sounded out the syllables. This time the phrase was short and centered on a word Anton knew: *goy*. And it was framed as a question. Anton hesitated. Before the Nazis came along, neither he nor his sister had ever thought of themselves as Jewish. One summer before Greta was born, when his parents had gone on a trip alone, his grandmother had made him memorize the *Shema Israel*. But that was as far as his religious education went. They didn't go to synagogue, they didn't eat kosher, and at Christmas they decorated a tree.

Of course, in many ways they were not even Czech. His father had grown up in Bohemia and kept a portrait of President Masaryk in his study. And his mother, who came from a family of merchants with ramifications across the continent, had been born in Amsterdam and was as perfectly at home in a theater in Paris as in a hotel on the Venice Lido, or in a London tearoom. Rachel and her children were primarily Europeans, and Germany was at the heart of their idea of Europe. Now, the nation that had nurtured them with its music and literature was imprisoning them in a cattle truck and condemning them to a new, incomprehensible Babylonian exile. They had been told they were being sent to the East to contribute to the victory of the Reich. But what task could Greta possibly perform for the Wehrmacht? Her tapered fingers knew only the discipline related to ivory piano keys. The young Hasid was still waiting for an answer. Anton shook his head. "I'm Jewish." The child looked reassured, though the glimmer of doubt in his eyes had not gone out.

The carriage swayed, and the convoy set off uncertainly in a screech of connecting rods and wheels. A tremor of both fear and relief ran through the crowd. They feared what awaited them in Łódź, but they longed for the terrible journey to come to an end. As Convoy 9228 picked up speed, a voice rose from the back of the carriage. At first it was barely a whisper, but when the general hubbub had subsided, the voice gained strength. "Listen, Israel: the Lord is our God, the Lord is one." Anton stretched up on his tip-toes and tried to catch a glimpse of the man who had begun to recite the *Shema*. He was an old man with a prayer shawl on his shoulders, and phylacteries tied to his arm and forehead. Anton turned toward his father. His eyelids half-closed, his features relaxed, David Epstein was muttering to himself. On that motionless face, his lips looked like they were acting independently of the rest of the body. They were uttering ancient sounds that their people had been repeating for centuries. "You shall love the Lord your God with all your heart." Others in the car had joined the old man: "And you shall put these words that I send you today into your heart, and you shall teach them to your children." Anton looked around at a loss. The prayer was completely foreign to him and yet it offered him a promise of comfort. He struggled to remember: "If you truly listen to the precepts I prescribe today, loving the Lord your God and serving him with all your soul, I will give rain to your land." The sharp whistle of the train's siren intruded on the chanting. Anton sang louder: "Thus I will reap your wheat, your must, and your oil, and I will give grass to your field for your cattle: you shall eat and be satisfied." The train pulled into a tunnel and the lines from Deuteronomy were swallowed by the darkness of the mountain.

6

London, June 30, 1982

The water was cool and smelled a little brackish. Harry Dobbs reached the buoy, touched it with his fingertips, and immediately turned around, colliding with another swimmer coming in fast who was the owner of an East End dry cleaner's. He and Dobbs were among the oldest members of the club and had known each other for years. They had joined the Serpentine Swimming Club when George VI was king, but in all those years they had never said more than a few "good mornings," "goodbyes," or the odd exchange regarding swimming techniques. They stared at one another from under their rubber swimming caps and mumbled a few words of apology. Dobbs set off in a backstroke, while the other man paused to catch his breath. The clear blue sky was streaked only by the thin wake of a jet plane. Dobbs swam steadily amid high splashes. A boy doing the front crawl darted past him. Beyond the line of buoys, a pair of swans looked on in amazement as these human specimens rippled the surface of the lake with such extraordinarily graceless movements.

Harry Dobbs hoisted his belly with its thick pelt of white hair onto the dock and pulled himself up into a sitting position. Although it was before seven A.M., there were a dozen people in the water. It was summer, after all. True passion would be measured in January and February when the banks of the Serpentine froze over. Dobbs had joined the club in 1947. Since then, he had gone swimming almost every morning before work, as well as on weekends. It was a habit he had formed as a child. When he was eight years old, his parents had sent him to a Scottish boarding school, where the days began with an obligatory dip in the murky waters of the freezing lake. Life had been hard up there in the Highland fog for little Harry Dobbs, especially in the early days. He was a shy child, and short for his age. The dorms were drafty, the food terrible, the teachers strict, and the older pupils perennially on the hunt for a newbie to bully. In retrospect, however, Dobbs was glad he had attended King James College in Inverness. It had been a ruthless but valuable initiation. Having survived the experience, nothing struck fear into his heart, not even war. That was what these schools were for. To prepare members of the British ruling class to forge their character and prepare them for the challenges they would encounter out in the world. If Mummy tucked you into bed until you were eighteen, you would never be able to stand up to a horde of Zulu warriors or a mob of striking factory workers. He took off his cap, shrugged into his bathrobe, and walked toward the low building that housed the club.

Dobbs buttoned his batiste shirt, fastened the cuffs with a pair of mother-of-pearl cufflinks, performed a flawless four-in-hand with a perfect dimple under the knot, right in the center of the tie, donned his cool, dark-gray woolen jacket, and exited the dressing room.

The waiter arrived as soon as Dobbs had sat down. He served him at least three or four times a week, and Dobbs always ordered the same thing, but he took his order in a detached tone, as if it were the first time he had seen him.

"What would you like?"

Dobbs ordered a full English breakfast. Eggs, sausage, bacon, black pudding, grilled tomatoes, sauteed mushrooms, baked beans, toast, and a cup of tea. He opened the Times. Straight to the financial pages. The stocks in which he had recently invested were doing well, but the profits were nothing to get excited about. He played the stock market more for the pleasure of the gamble than for the gain. The system was cumbersome: there were too many checks and balances, rules introduced after the 1929 crisis, which was irrelevant nowadays. However, it looked like the present American president was intent on changing things with the magic word 'deregulation'. Dobbs was curious to see if he could pull it off.

The waiter served his breakfast. Dobbs turned back to the front page, put the newspaper on the table, and began buttering a slice of bread, casting distracted glances at the headlines. There were the usual articles covering the ongoing war in Lebanon and the Falklands campaign, which had just ended. He popped a strip of bacon into his mouth along with some crispy-edged egg white. He went to the inside pages. An interview with the navy commander who had defeated the Argentines. New speculation on the case of the Italian banker found hanged under Blackfriars Bridge. A detailed analysis of the British Airways flight that had crashed into the ash cloud of an Indonesian volcano. The black pudding was delicious: moist and pungent. Dobbs started an article about the tensions between the Thatcher government and the civil service unions but gave up after the first paragraph. He took a gulp of tea. Hidden at the bottom of page five, there were two columns describing the assassination in southern Mexico of an American embassy official who may have been a CIA agent. It was still unclear who had been responsible. No one had come forward to claim the act. The diplomat had been in the company of another US citizen, who had also been wounded in the attack. The man had been hospitalized but had escaped and was still missing three days later. A local newspaper claimed he was a Nazi war criminal. It also mentioned what the man's real name was purported to be. Dobb's fork was suspended midair, a dangling slice of bacon dripping grease onto the Times. He read the article again, more carefully. The Mexican press claimed the missing man was a former SS officer who had been enlisted by the Americans after the end of World War II. They also alleged that he had taken part in Operation Condor, the CIA's grand plan to cleanse Latin America of communists and leftists back in 1975. Harry Dobbs put down his fork and asked for the bill.

He strode across the park to Kensington Road. As always, his driver was waiting for him at the corner of Rutland Gate. The owner of the dry cleaner's walked by on his way to the Knightsbridge Underground station. His fellow swimmer politely touched the visor of his cotton cap in greeting. Dobbs walked straight past him and climbed into his car without responding to the salute.

7

Berlin, October 18, 1941

The lobby was imposing, as befitted the city's finest hotel, inaugurated by Kaiser Wilhelm II himself in 1907. Vaulted ceilings adorned with stucco and frescoes, thick Persian rugs, twinkling lights, a red-carpeted marble staircase leading to the first floor. Baroness Carlotta von Lehndorff slipped through the lobby, checked her fur coat into the cloakroom, and walked down the corridor leading to the restaurant. The maître greeted her with the big smile reserved for regular customers and immediately entrusted her to an eager waiter, who led her to a table set for two in a discreet corner of the room next to a window overlooking Unter den Linden and the Brandenburg Gate.

"May I bring you an aperitif?" the waiter asked with a bow.

The lady pulled off her black gloves.

"A champagne cocktail."

"Very good."

The baroness took a bright-green jade cigarette holder out of her purse and lit a cigarette. Konrad was late. She was still not used to having to wait for her lovers. In the past, they had been the ones waiting for her, for hours. Once, an American writer had waited an entire afternoon.

But now, at fifty-one, she was aware that it was her turn to do the waiting. And that was the least of it. More humiliating was the fact that she often had to pay. Not directly. She would never stoop to leaving money on the bedside table, even though she sometimes thought it would be more honest. And cheaper, for sure. Bribing the military doctor who had exonerated Konrad from military service had been a considerable financial commitment, despite the baroness's vast wealth. Not to mention the legal risks.

The waiter arrived with a silver tray and left the cocktail on the table. The pink liquid in the chilled flûte promised immediate relief for the anguish that had been tormenting her for days, ever since Wilhelm had been put under house arrest. The first sip was always the best. Champagne and Cointreau were a perfect, yet unlikely, marriage: the altar, a sugar cube soaked in angostura melting at the bottom of the glass. Carlotta took another sip and began to feel better. She had married Wilhelm very young, against the wishes of her entire family. Her father, an industrialist from Munich, a Catholic with modern ideas for the time and for his milieu, harbored a deep distrust of the Lutheran and military traditions of the Prussians exemplified by the von Lehndorffs. Despite her parents' woeful predictions, the early years had been splendid. The couple had led a colorful and carefree life of soirees and trips abroad. In addition to being an army officer, her husband was a member of the national fencing team, which meant they traveled throughout Europe while Wilhelm and his teammates took part in international competitions. But sometimes they would also take a private trip. Her fondest memory was their first visit to Paris, in 1912. The teeming theaters and boulevards had thrilled her. Compared to the French capital, Berlin felt provincial. One evening, after attending an exotic and sensual performance by the Russian Ballet, which Carlotta had never even imagined could be staged, Wilhelm had attracted the stares of the entire bar at the Ritz by drinking champagne out of one of his shoes. Then the war had come. Wilhelm commanded a regiment and had set off full of enthusiasm, confident of victory, but with each leave his silences had grown longer. He had spent four years at the front. He had been wounded several times and had earned countless medals. When he had finally come home, he was a different man. He was somber and resentful. They had tried to have children but had been unlucky. After the second miscarriage, they lost hope. Her in-laws, who had never loved her, disliked her even more. In the stern eyes of the two Prussian aristocrats, Carlotta was too free, too cultured, too metropolitan. And now the ultimate insult. She had failed to give them an heir. Wilhelm's brother had died on the Somme without marrying and his sister had only had daughters. The von Lehndorff name was in danger of dying out, thanks to a Bavarian whore. Gradually, she and Wilhelm had begun to drift apart. He had shut himself off in the gloom of the barracks and the family estate. Carlotta had turned their Berlin home into one of the city's most fashionable salons, where she received artists and show people. Marlene Dietrich had visited once. When Hitler had become chancellor, Carlotta had taken to traveling with increasing frequency, eventually spending most of her time abroad. Until Germany had unleashed a new war.

Konrad crossed the hall and joined her. Carlotta held out her hand to him. He kissed it with exaggerated affection, which annoyed the baroness.

"My being late is inexcusable."

"Sit down," she replied coldly.

The waiter brought the menus. The lady's copy had no prices on it. Carlotta appreciated the delicacy.

"The *pâté de fois gras* is excellent. It came in yesterday from our suppliers in France," said the waiter.

"Fantastic," Konrad exclaimed cheerfully, as he shook his napkin open and put it on his lap.

"Let's start with the *fois gras*, and a bottle of Saint-Émillon," said Carlotta.

"And after that?"

The baroness scanned the card distractedly.

"The *coq au vin*," she replied.

The waiter wrote everything down in a small notebook. "And you, Sir?" he asked Konrad, who was poring over the menu. He lingered over each item, his brow furrowed, evaluating and comparing the proposals in order to be sure to choose the one that would offer him the greatest pleasure. There was something childlike in his seriousness and the baroness was softened by it.

"The *Sauerbraten* with red cabbage and potatoes, please," Konrad said in a hurry, as if afraid that the magic that had brought him to in the Hotel Adlon restaurant might suddenly vanish.

The waiter took the orders and disappeared.

Carlotta stared at the young man sitting opposite her. He had a delicate profile, with a small, upturned nose and fleshy lips. As if to counterbalance his feminine features, he wore his hair very short, in a military-style. But thanks to the Baroness's intervention, the Wehrmacht had not called him up. It would be a shame to ruin that pretty face with a bullet. Everyone said the war would be over soon. It could well be. But Carlotta remembered all too well the summer of 1914 when they said that Germany would win the war in a few weeks and the soldiers would return home for Christmas. Konrad stretched one leg out under the table and began gently rubbing one of her calves with his ankle.

"You're going to put a run in my stockings," Carlotta said coyly.

Konrad smiled and continued.

Carlotta smiled, too. She was excited at the thought of what awaited her in the suite she had booked. After which, she would never see him again. She had made the same promise before and had never kept it. But now things had changed. Wilhelm had attracted the attention of the ever-vigilant Gestapo. Carlotta considered it her duty to stand by him. There were still so many invisible threads binding them. However, this last night would be hers and hers alone.

"You are beautiful," Konrad whispered.

The baroness stroked the skin under her chin, once firm and supple, and now, despite all the creams and massages, slightly sagging. She knew the boy was lying, but she allowed herself to believe him.

8

Rome, June 30, 1982

Monsignor Witold Grabski turned off the faucet and rinsed his face with the hot water that had collected in the sink. The radio croaked the morning news from a shelf above the mirror. It was a dilapidated old wireless that had belonged to the previous tenant, a Spanish prelate who had been sent to head the apostolic nunciature in Buenos Aires. The cardinal dried his hands and tried to improve reception by fiddling gently with the knob.

Clashes between the Israeli army and Palestinian militias continued throughout the day in Beirut. The city, under siege since last June 13, has suffered heavy shelling from the Israeli armed forces, both from the air and from the sea.

Monsignor Grabski wet his shaving brush and turned it in the soap dish. "The Jews never give up," he hissed between his teeth.

Supplies of electricity and water have been interrupted, causing serious problems for the civilians who have already been put to the test by the heavy fighting.

The prelate lathered his face slowly and picked up his razor.

This morning, Treasury Minister Beniamino Andreatta will report to the Parliament on developments in the investigation into the collapse of the Banco Ambrosiano and the role played by the IOR, the Istituto per le Opere di Religione, *the Vatican bank headed by Monsignor Paul Marcinkus.*

Grabski shrugged his shoulders. What did they expect? That they would get by with donations from the faithful? The Church was a vast institution with branches everywhere in the world: like Coca-Cola, only instead of selling soda it saved souls. But it had to operate in a hostile environment, where the competition was often at an advantage, especially in Western countries. For millions of people, the Holy Father now counted far less than rock stars or movie actors. One had to adapt to this new world, learn to master its tools and technologies. And then one had to support those who were in the front line in the battle against Marxist atheism: Lech Wałęsa's union in Poland, the Contras in Nicaragua. This required substantial funds. As Marcinkus had once told him at the end of a meeting of the IOR's board of governors: you can't run the Church on Hail Marys alone.

He heard a knock at the bedroom door.

"Monsignor, it's ten past eight. Remember your meeting with the congressman."

"Yes, Sergius, I remember," the cardinal answered rudely. His secretary was a bright and meticulous young Jesuit, but sometimes his pedantry irritated him. Besides, the appointment was almost an hour away. The Italian prosecutors seemed intent on getting serious about the Ambrosiano affair. Not only were the usual left-wing newspapers supporting them, but there were also areas of the political spectrum, including representatives of the Christian Democrat party like that horrible Tina Anselmi. The cardinal thought there was something unnatural, corrupt even, about a woman who preferred getting elected to Parliament to caring for her home and children. Perhaps, however, there was still room for maneuver. That was what he needed to talk to the congressman about. He finished shaving, washed off the soap, and rubbed his cheeks with aftershave: a delicate lavender lotion, a welcome gift from the wife of one of the Holy See's financial advisers.

In the southern Mexican city of Mérida, a US Embassy official has been killed in an assassination attempt.

The cardinal did not react immediately. He was about to turn off the radio when the speaker mentioned the other individual involved in the attack. The perpetrators were still unknown.

Left-wing terrorists. Or perhaps a Jewish organization, given the survivor's background. The news also mentioned what appeared to be the man's real name. Witold Grabski sat on the edge of the bathtub and passed a hand over his balding skull, his gaze lost in memories. He knew that name. Many years earlier, he had added it to a list.

9

The ashtray on the bedside table was full. After making love the previous night, they had talked at length. Konrad had begged her to call him, or at least write when she could. He had told her that not seeing her would be agony but that he wanted to hear her news at least. Carlotta, however, had been adamant. She had never provided Wilhelm with direct evidence of her affairs. Her husband knew but, in his presence, she had always been the perfect wife. It was the most important clause of the tacit agreement they had made many years before. And she was not about to break that rule now that Wilhelm was in such difficult circumstances. Evidently the young man hoped to exploit her a little longer, but he should consider himself more than satisfied. Without her, he would be marching across the Steppe by now, or buried, perhaps, in the graveyard of some godforsaken hamlet. She put on her pearl earrings and looked in the mirror. She saw a civilized, middle-aged woman: a face lined with wrinkles, black bags under her eyes, and a few gray wisps in her once blond hair. She shuddered. She powdered her face, touched up her lipstick, applied mascara to her eyelashes, donned her mink coat and hat, and pulled down her veil. Now she felt better. She went back to examining herself. She could pass muster, without looking too closely. But the thought of not being looked at closely was hateful to her.

Wrapped in the blankets, one arm hanging off the bed, Konrad snored softly, his mouth half open. In that disheveled sleep, he looked even younger than he was. Carlotta pulled a fountain pen out of her purse and wrote a few lines on a sheet of hotel letter paper. She put the note on the wooden console near the door, along with her silver lighter. Then she turned the doorknob and left without looking back.

The baroness settled the bill, hinting obliquely that a gentleman was still in the room and that the housekeeping would have to wait. The receptionist narrowed his eyes, signaling that he understood.

"I need a cab," Carlotta said.

"Certainly, Baroness," the receptionist replied, indicating the uniformed doorman standing to attention on the other side of the revolving door. A young bellboy carried the baroness's suitcase out and handed it to the doorman, who hurriedly blew into a metal whistle around his neck. The cab arrived instantly.

The taxi made its way slowly through the morning traffic. The streets were cluttered with cars, trucks, horse-drawn delivery wagons, buses, and military vehicles. At the end of the avenue, a highline train came to a stop at the station. A mass of passengers poured out of the cars, others quickly took their seats, and the locomotive puffed away in a hurry. Red flags with a white circle and a skewed black cross were fluttering everywhere, on the balconies of houses and public buildings, on the roofs of department stores and in the parks. Not a single block was without at least one. Men in black or brown uniforms and polished leather boots marched down the sidewalks, Baroness von Lehndorff looked away and rummaged in her purse for a cigarette. She would not miss Berlin. It was no longer her city. It was the capital of the Third Reich.

Konrad woke up when the sun was already high. He looked around. The old woman had left. He jumped out of bed cheerfully and went into the bathroom. A good shower would wash away the stench of flaccid flesh he could smell on himself. He lingered under the jet of water for a long time. He dried himself and got dressed. He was about to leave when he saw the small metal object on the console. It was Carlotta's Dunhill. He had always liked it. Next to it was a farewell note, which was not over-sentimental. His cigarette case was empty and Konrad had to look in the ashtray. He lay down on the bed, his shoes on the white sheet, and lit the cigarette butt with his new lighter. All in all, it had worked out well for him. Carlotta was of a certain age, but she was not to be trifled with. And she had plenty of experience, for sure. In his career as a gigolo, Konrad had had far more unpleasant tasks to perform. Besides, the baroness was a generous woman. He took one last drag, slipped the lighter into his pocket, and exited the room. "Wilhelmstrasse 102," Konrad said to the driver.

When he heard the destination, the Reich's Central Security Office, the taxi driver hesitated for a moment before shifting into gear and setting off.

10

Haifa, June 30, 1982

The clock radio had been spewing rock songs alternating with the DJ's inconsequential comments for at least twenty minutes, but Rivka was unable to muster the strength to reach out to the bedside table and turn the infernal contraption off, however much she wished the racket would stop. *And now, a blast from the past.* She should already have been at the bar, helping her husband out, but instead she was lying there staring at the ceiling. *We got no choice, all the girls and boys.* Music blaring from the stereo speakers in their son's room had been the source of frequent, exhausting discussions when Eli was still living with them. Rivka could never have imagined that one day she would miss Alice Cooper. *And we got no principles, and we got no innocence.* The cadence was cut off by the DJ's voice repeating the title of the song and saying goodbye to his listeners until the following day. A string of commercials followed. A brand of diapers. A dishwashing detergent. A new Volkswagen model. When the news came on, the headlines were all about Lebanon. A retired general commented on how the maneuvers were going. The New York correspondent explained the ongoing debate at the United Nations. Prime Minister Menachem Begin declared that capturing Arafat's headquarters in Beirut had the symbolic significance of taking Hitler's bunker under the Chancellery. Indeed, it was the *equivalent* of taking Hitler's bunker under the Chancellery. Various leftists and cultural figures objected. Begin was using the Holocaust to justify a policy of military aggression at odds with the spirit of Israel and the tradition of the Jewish people. A concentration camp survivor had begun a hunger strike in protest. Rivka's arm reached out and silenced the radio. She lay there listening, frozen in place. The garbage truck was emptying the bins. Upstairs, Mr. and Mrs. Goldfarb were arguing, as usual. Doors slamming, screaming, sobbing.

On the street, a dog started barking. It must have been Mrs. Kaufmann's mutt, on his morning rounds with his mistress.

Rivka held her breath and waited. The seconds ticked by. Fifteen, twenty, twenty-two. Finally, she opened her mouth.

Upstairs, Mrs. Goldfarb was yelling. "I'm going to kill you. I swear if I find you with that bitch, I'll kill you both!" Her husband was silent. There was a crash of broken plates. Rivka drew a deep breath and pulled herself up onto one elbow. The room was still there, just like the day before. She went to the kitchen. Shlomo had laid the table for her breakfast. He might seem cold and distant at times, but Rivka knew he paid attention to detail and lavished small attentions on her. After almost forty years, they still loved one another. But now there was this unfathomable pit between them that made her dizzy and felt like it was about to swallow everything up. Mechanically, Rivka began to make coffee.

Eli was gone. He had been killed on the first day of the invasion. The Israeli command had called it "Operation Peace in Galilee." Along the roads leading north, columns of tanks and military vehicles had snaked for miles. Fighter jets had streaked the sky since the first light of dawn. It was June 6. He had been shot in the throat by a sniper hidden behind a boulder. He had died on the spot and hadn't suffered. At least, that was what the army people had told them. The enemy fighters had barricaded themselves inside an ancient Crusader castle. Although it had been built in the twelfth century, the walls were thick enough to withstand the blows of modern artillery fire. The Golani Brigade had struggled to conquer it but had eventually succeeded. Those who hadn't died. Begin had traveled to the battle site by helicopter to congratulate the living in person. In order to form an anti-Islamic alliance between the two nations, that irate, dried-up old Pole had decided to drive the Palestinians and Syrians out of Lebanon and put Gemayel's Christian Maronites in power, all in one fell swoop. Who was Rivka to interfere with an ambitious strategic vision like this? She poured herself a cup of coffee, dropped a teaspoon of sugar into the cup, and stirred slowly. He had been their only son, just two years younger than Israel. He had come into the world when the Jewish state was still an uncertain entity, a raft to which survivors of the carnage in Europe had clung. Now Israel was a powerful and respected country with modern cities, industry, trade, transport infrastructure, aqueducts, and the most efficient army in the Middle East. And yet, all this had not been enough. Once again, the angel of History had come knocking on the door of Rivka Libowitz, née Berkovits.

She finished her coffee and went into the living room. Eli stared at her with a smile from inside a silver frame. He was clutching his senior thesis to his chest. Dark blue binding and gold lettering. *Features of Reinforced and Lightened Cements for Bridges.* She picked the photograph up from the shelf and stroked it gently. He had been the first member of the family to graduate. Shlomo had burst with pride. The telephone rang. Rivka ignored it. She put the picture back and went to the bathroom to get ready.

11

Berlin, October 20, 1941

Time, measure, speed. The three fundamentals. *One must seize the proper moment to execute an action, combining the choice of time at due speed, and aiming for a sufficient measure to touch the opponent.* The master, Bernard Simon, taught these rules in the Lincoln Square fencing salle. *Haste and force are capital enemies in fencing. Anyone who employs force will only delay their speed and haste will make every movement precipitous.* In class, or in a textbook, these lessons may have sounded convincing enough, but on the piste, there was no way to think. The body needed to act before the mind could elaborate a strategy. The foil was faster than the intellect. That is what training was for: to produce an automatic reaction and fuse theory with instinct.

SS Major Hans Lichtblau parried and attempted an advance-lunge but his opponent had already retreated and deflected his blade. Lichtblau paused for a moment to catch his breath. He was leading four to three but running out of strength. Fatigue made him less agile and accurate. He advanced, stabbing haphazardly, ignoring the en-garde lines. Colonel Saito grabbed his opportunity and came forward with a flawless counter-attack

"*Quatre partout,*" the referee announced at the end of the bout. He signaled the combatants to take up their positions. "*En garde. Êtes-vous prêts? Allez.*"

For several months now, Lichtblau had been fencing every Friday afternoon at the SS clubhouse with Colonel Saito, the military attaché at the Japanese embassy. Knowing your enemy was only useful up to a point. Each bout was an experience in itself. Saito was a kendo master who had discovered fencing in Europe.

He was a dogged opponent—and left-handed to boot—but despite years of practice, he still did not understand an essential principle of Western fencing, or perhaps refused to understand it. This was because it went against his innermost convictions, not only in terms of the art of handling a blade, but also in terms of life in general. In kendo, the aim was to follow a precise and rigidly formalized pattern with perfect strikes, responding to canons of harmony as well as effectiveness. For warriors like Saito, brought up with the precepts of Bushidō—"The way of the warrior" that fused martial arts and Zen Buddhism—there was no victory without beauty. In Western fencing, by contrast, there was always room for improvisation and individual initiative within a set of rules and principles. A hit that scores a point, no matter how clumsy and unsightly, no matter how far-removed from the ideal, will not be disallowed by the referee.

Saito disengaged his foil from a *tierce*-bind with a perfect *dérobement*. His wrist movement was rapid and tight, and his fist had not moved a millimeter from its center of operations. Excellent. Crystal clear. The Sturmbannführer readjusted his measure and panted inside his mask. Sweat was dripping down his forehead and making his eyes burn. He had to do something. Victory belongs to those who truly desire it. Saito stepped forward. Lichtblau executed a *quarte* parry, then a *seconde*, and thrust down violently, clumsily. He touched Saito on the thigh.

"*Halte! Touché à droite*," the umpire called. "*Cinq-quatre. Victoire à gauche*."

The two fencers took off their masks and shook hands at the center of the piste.

"Thank you," Lichtblau said.

Saito smiled vaguely. "East is East, and West is West," he murmered.

The SS officer stared at him in amazement, delving into his memory. Saito was an educated man and, considering he was Japanese, very outspoken. Lichtblau smiled back. "And never the twain shall meet," he added.

Having broken the spell of the match—for the duration of which the outside world becomes a blurred backdrop, not only because the mask muffles sounds and limits visibility but also because the tension of the competition reduces the entire universe to the few meters of piste and the white shape dancing in front of you—Major Lichtblau realized there was a strange silence in the weapons room. He looked around and spotted the stern figure of Obergruppenführer Reinhard Heydrich, supreme head of the Reich's Central Security Office, responsible for counterintelligence, the Gestapo, and the criminal police. After Reichsführer-SS Himmler, Heydrich was the most powerful man in the entire SS apparatus, and he was narrowing his eyes and staring straight at Major Lichtblau.

"A hard-fought assault," Heydrich said approvingly.

Lichtblau immediately switched hands in order to extend his arm in a salute.

Colonel Saito bowed and disappeared in the direction of the locker room.

"I have very little time," Heydrich said.

Lichtblau wiped his face with his sleeve. The black diamond with the SS symbol stood out on his chest against the white outfit. He followed the Obergruppenführer toward the buvette. The secretary at the Reich Central Security Office had arranged to meet at the clubhouse but their appointment was supposed to be almost an hour later. Heydrich was known to be a tireless worker. And he was also known to act on his own initiative when it came to selecting a candidate. He trusted his own impressions more than staff reports. Evidently, he had arrived early to assess Sturmbannführer Hans Lichtblau's talents on the piste. The major regretted his mediocre performance. Heydrich was an excellent player, with both épée and saber, though he had a predilection for the latter. In addition, he excelled in athletics, riding, and swimming. But still, Lichtblau consoled himself, he had shown character with Saito. The Obergruppenführer must have appreciated that.

"Have you been fencing for a long time?" Heydrich asked as they sat at a small table.

"I started when I was ten, in Chicago."

Heydrich had read in his file that Lichtblau had been born in America, in 1911, to a German immigrant family. His father had made his fortune on the New Continent, but the 1929 Depression had wiped out his business. When his parents died, he had returned to his homeland, where he had completed his university studies, going on to earn a doctorate in plant chemistry, thanks to which he had obtained a position in the Bayer laboratories. He had joined the Party in 1937 and been accepted into the SS the following year. In 1940, Lichtblau had fought in Norway and France, earning himself a second-class Iron Cross. After that, the Party had discharged him. His skills would be invaluable to the Ahnenerbe, the scientific branch of the SS.

"Do they have good teachers in the United States?" asked Heydrich.

"Mostly Germans. We brought modern fencing to America."

The answer seemed to satisfy the Obergruppenführer.

"I saw your report on the capture of the Soviet experimental station."

"Unfortunately, some of the documentation had already been taken away by the NKVD. I was able to study the material we managed to get hold of. They were working in different directions. The most important research for them was developing plants that could withstand the cold. I do not see this as a priority for the Reich. At the end of the war, we will have plenty of temperate areas available for cultivation."

Heydrich nodded almost imperceptibly.

"Luckily," Lichtblau went on, "the scientists working at the laboratory were not disciples of Lysenko."

"That is?" the Obergruppenführer asked dryly. He did not appreciate being led into areas where he had no expertise.

"Stalin's favorite agronomist. A charlatan who rejected Mendel's laws of genetics."

Heydrich relaxed. He had wanted to meet Lichtblau in person precisely to make sure that he had not fallen prey to Himmler's mystical irrationality, with his circle of astrologers, diviners, and occult scholars. People who wasted the Reich's resources searching for Shangri-La. Heydrich had never uttered a word against him in public, because his career was inextricably linked to the Reichsführer-SS, but in private he despised the esoteric nonsense his boss was so full of. Himmler was convinced that he was the reincarnation of Henry the Fowler, the Duke of Saxony, who had defeated the Magyars at the Unstrut River in 933 AD Germany needed patents, not magic spells. A project with interesting potential had been launched. Heydrich wanted to make sure that a man of science would lead it. His initial feeling had been positive. Athletic, Aryan profile, fighting temperament. The comment about Russian agronomy confirmed his first hunch.

"In what direction do you plan to move?" Heydrich asked.

"I know that the Reichsführer is very interested in research on a plant that promises to make humans infertile. If we could synthesize the substance, we could solve the Jewish problem within a generation."

The head of the Reich's Central Security Office maintained a deadpan expression. The Sturmbannführer was in possession of outdated information. The hypothesis of mass sterilization had been set aside, as had the idea of shipping all the European Jews to Madagascar. The time was ripe for something much more radical. They could not wait a generation, nor challenge the British fleet in order to build a huge African ghetto. The war offered a unique opportunity for the Aryan race. It should be seized as soon as possible. Nevertheless, Lichtblau's response had been shrewd. First things first. Always meet Himmler's demands. "And then?" Heydrich asked.

"I think that a very important area to work on, where the Russians have made some progress and on which we should build, is that of analgesics. This would provide our troops with great comfort."

Heydrich nodded. The sharp, pointy nose in the middle of an impenetrable face was a rostrum on the prow of a ship waiting to be boarded. "The laboratory will be housed on the estate of Baron Wilhelm von Lehndorff in East Prussia. The baron has been placed under house arrest." The Obergruppenführer lowered his voice and moved closer to his interlocutor. "Career officer. At the beginning of the war, he commanded a mechanized brigade. A good soldier. After Poland capitulated, his unit was still stationed in the East." Heydrich paused briefly, only to resume in the hushed tone of someone telling a story that was hard to believe. "And von Lehndorff started flooding the desks of his superiors with letters criticizing the treatment of Polish prisoners and Jews. Sentimentality that belongs to the past." Lichtblau nodded mechanically. "He hasn't been deported to Dachau because he is a hero of the other war, and because he is a personal friend of Field Marshal von Kluge." Lichtblau imagined that there was another reason why the baron had not ended up in the concentration camp. Von Lehndorff had been a champion fencer. Lichtblau knew that Heydrich had helped Jewish fencer Paul Sommer leave for the United States. And that he had protected members of the Polish national team after the country had been occupied. Among the many positions he held, Heydrich was also Reichsfachamtsleiter: head of Reich fencing. Fencing represented the one area of his existence where ideology did not take precedence.

"The Baron has a wife," Heydrich continued, "who is also hostile to National Socialism. A decadent whore who poses as a woman of the world. She is currently in Berlin but will soon be joining her husband. They will be confined to a wing of the castle. Should they cause you any trouble, do not hesitate to let me know."

The major assured him that he would.

Heydrich studied Lichtblau's face. A scar traversed his right eyebrow. "War wound?" he asked.

"Duel. I almost got expelled from university."

The Obergruppenführer smiled inside. He had been dis-barred from the Navy for failing to honor a promise of marriage to a high society girl. He decided he liked Hans Lichtblau.

Heydrich glanced at his watch and sprang to his feet. He was slightly behind schedule for the day.

"Keep me informed," he said.

The farewells took a few seconds. In the blink of an eye, the Obergruppenführer was already gaining the exit. As he watched the official stride out of the room, Lichtblau was surprised at how small his retinue was. A single secretary. No escort, no lackey. The head of the Reich security services was traveling alone, in an open car. A truly rare individual. He could even fly an airplane. In July, he had fought with the Luftwaffe on the Eastern Front. During an attack on a bridge over the Dnestr, his fighter plane had been hit and he had had to make a crash landing beyond the German lines. He had been picked up by a Wehrmacht unit. The press had reported on it at length. In his synthesis of ancient heroic virtues and mastery of modern tech-nology, Reinhard Heydrich was the perfect embodiment of the "romanticism of steel" that Goebbels spoke of to describe the essence of National Socialism. Sturmbannführer Lichtblau felt proud to belong to an organization led by a man of his caliber.

12

Haifa, June 30, 1982

Markets had always existed, ever since humans had emerged from their caves and founded cities. In the slow merry-go-round of kingdoms and empires, conquerors had come and gone—Phoenicians, Persians, Romans, Byzantines, Arabs, Crusaders, Ottomans, the British—but markets had remained a crossroads of trade, peoples and languages. On display in the stalls that lined crowded aisles filled with voices were multicolored carpets, with hues ranging from the white of braided garlic to the black of olives, via the pale yellow of melons, the streaked green of watermelons, and the bright red of chili peppers. A sweet smell of mint hovered in the air around the Arab vendors, alongside a pungent scent of cumin from stands selling Aleppo spices and soaps. In a pavilion lined with blue-and-white tiles, fishmongers called out to potential customers, showing off the fresh fish still flipping in ice-filled Styrofoam boxes or plastic bowls brimming with water. At first glance, it might have looked like any Mediterranean market but the Ashkenazim had brought *gefilte* fish and strudel from the heart of Europe, lined up next to falafel and baklava in the deli windows.

Halfway down an alley that led to the sea was the café that Shlomo Libowitz and his wife had taken over many years earlier, a cramped place with a tiny counter and only two tables, which served mostly market workers. A boy ran back and forth almost non-stop between the café and the stalls carrying trays laden with small glasses of Turkish coffee or mint tea, large glasses of orange juice tinkling with ice cubes, snacks of pita and hummus sprinkled with paprika. Shlomo was in the back room, on the phone. The signal rang free, but no one was picking up. Rivka must already be on her way. Or, she hadn't gotten up yet. He sighed and hung up. At the counter, a couple of tourists with cameras around their necks and polite smiles signaled that they were ready to order. Behind them, an old Arab was sitting at one of the small tables. He was sipping his coffee slowly and working his way through a wooden rosary. He was the owner of the carpet store opposite, one of the few Arab residents of Haifa who had not fled in 1948. In part under threats from the Jews, and in part following orders from the Palestinian leadership that counted on making life in the city impossible, almost all of them had fled across the border, convinced that they would return to their homes in a few months, once the united armies of Egypt, Iraq, Syria and Jordan had pushed the Zionists back into the sea. Out of sixty-two thousand Arab residents, only five or six thousand were left. Entire neighborhoods had been emptied. But the city had survived. New Jewish residents had replaced them.

Shlomo stooped under the counter, taking two small Coca-Cola bottles out of the refrigerator for the tourists, and when he resurfaced, a third person was leaning on the Formica counter. The woman was petite. The stool she was sitting on was not high, but her feet did not touch the ground. She had a slightly oversized skull compared to the rest of her body, and a broad forehead. It was impossible to tell her age. The wrinkled face was that of an old woman, but the short raven curls without a single gray hair were those of a girl. Shlomo knew perfectly well how old she was, however. They had met many years before, in a place that was not only bleak and terrifying to think about, but literally inconceivable here, in the midst of all these people chatting, eating breakfast, buying and selling quietly, peacefully.

Shlomo and the woman stared at one another without saying a word.

The tourists downed their Cokes and went out to look for picturesque views.

"I heard about your son," the woman said.

There was something childlike even about her voice, which was high-pitched and shrill. The obnoxious little voice of the teacher's pet.

Shlomo arched his eyebrows but betrayed no other emotion.

"And how is Rivka?"

Shlomo's face was a mask of stone.

"She's always been strong, she'll make it," the old woman-child answered her own question.

She was ashamed of the cliché. How could Rivka get over the death of her only son? Besides, what did she know about what it felt like to lose a child? During the war, three surgical students from the University of Königsberg had removed her ovaries for practice. As they prepared for the incision, while she was still conscious on the operating table, they talked among themselves about this and that. The quality of the canteen, a visit to the brothel, a letter from a friend at the front. They had not mistreated her. They would not have mistreated even a lab rat. They were not sadistic. They just needed practice, for the sake of science and their careers. Sometimes she thought she had been lucky after all. If she had had children, every caress, every drop of milk from her breast, every goodnight kiss, would have communicated her immense grief, and an unquenchable thirst for revenge. Grief, like debts, should never be bequeathed. But sometimes life is too short to settle all your accounts.

"What do you want, Sara?"

The old woman-child cast a suspicious glance at the Arab, who continued to slide wooden beads along the leather cord, keeping an eye on his store and distractedly watching the people passing in front of the café.

"There's an assignment for you," she whispered, and pulled a brown envelope out of her bag. She put it on the counter, covering it with her wrinkled hand, the large bluish veins bulging under the skin.

"You know I'm done."

"This one is different."

"They're all the same."

"I'm telling you this one is different."

"You're wasting your time."

The old woman-child paused and enunciated clearly, "Lichtblau."

Shlomo let a few seconds go by, poker-faced, then he took the envelope.

13

East Prussia, October 22, 1941

Baron Wilhelm von Lehndorff was already on his feet when the first rays of the sun had begun to filter through the mists of the Vistula after the dark night, revealing the trees and tinging them green and auburn. He had started to sleep less and less as he got older, almost without noticing it. That morning he had gotten up even earlier than usual. He had washed, shaved, trimmed, and combed his mustache carefully. He had tightened the black patch over his right eye, which he had lost in the Third Battle of Ypres in 1917. And he had put on a Shetland sweater under an old tweed jacket, worn-out at the wrists and with velvet patches on the elbows, an Anglophile affectation that Prussian high society frowned upon. In any case, he no longer saw anyone, neither members of the aristocracy nor townsfolk. He had even stopped going to mass on Sundays. He had become a prisoner in his own home long before the Gestapo had put him under house arrest.

As he walked along the corridor leading to the stairs, the baron passed his wife's room. Carlotta had arrived the previous evening. Von Lehndorff knew how much she detested country life, especially life in that countryside, and was grateful to her for being there when nobody had forced her and there was no real reason for her to be. The baron reached out and opened the door a chink. A beam of light penetrated the room bathed in shadow. The baroness's bedroom was the only one with thick curtains, unusual in northern Europe. Unlike von Lehndorff, his wife still managed to sleep late. The curtains were a blue and gold brocade, which Carlotta had purchased in Venice on one of her trips. A strong smell of cigarettes hung in the room, mingled with a hint of Coco Chanel. Under the snow-white comforter, framed by the slender twisted columns of the four-poster bed, the baron glimpsed the outline of the woman he had married in a bygone era, before the world had descended into chaos. He stood and watched her sleep for a few moments, then he closed the door and went downstairs.

Albert, the butler, was in the kitchen. He had been in the service of the von Lehndorff family for more than forty years, the spirit and brain behind the estate, the man to whom everyone—servant or master, guest or employee—turned for any problem related to the castle and its vast lands, which stretched for miles from the Allenstein road to the river, and which included a small hamlet inhabited by the farmworkers, a windmill, and a forest, as well as fields and pastures. They greeted each other with both confidence and formality, owing to their long acquaintance and the knowledge, ingrained in both of them, that there were some barriers that neither time nor mutual regard would ever overcome.

"Would you like some breakfast, Herr Baron?" Albert asked.

"I'm not hungry, thank you. I'll just have coffee."

"Then I'll tell the cook to make you something to go." The Baron took a seat in a corner of the dining room, a vast space designed for a large family. He filled his pipe and lit it. After the first few puffs, Albert arrived with coffee.

The stables were in the west wing, the most recent addition. The oldest part of the property was to the north. That was where the von Lehndorff family had built the initial core of the castle—a large square tower—when they had come from Thuringia in the fourteenth century, after the crusades that the Teutonic Order had promoted to convert and subdue pagan populations living on the eastern shores of the Baltic. The building had been restructured several times over the centuries, creating a strange amalgam between the simplicity of medieval military architecture and the whimsy of Rococo. The groom brought out the baron's favorite horse, a sturdy, dark bay, and held him steady as he threw the leather saddlebags over his neck. Von Lehndorff set off at a calm pace along the driveway he had ridden down thousands of times. He would have been able to do it even with the only eye he had left closed. He crossed the stone bridge over the stream and skirted the little wall enclosing the small family cemetery. The von Lehndorffs had been buried there since before the last grand master of the Teutonic Knights joined the Reformation in 1525 and secularized the Order, thus laying the foundations of the Prussian state. Some of the tombstones also belonged to German officers who had fallen during and immediately after the Great War while defending that faraway piece of Germany, first from the Tsarist armies and then from the Bolsheviks.

The baron gave a light kick with his spurs, together with a snap of his tongue, to increase his pace. The horse responded and went into a trot. He rode past the barn where, as boys, he and his cousin Friedrich would rape the farmer's daughters in a rite of possession as old as the foundations of the castle, and headed straight for the woods. The sun had now driven the fog away, and the green hills were shimmering. He went into the woods. The trunks of some of the pines had curved into the shape of a treble-clef. They had begun to take on that bizarre shape a decade earlier. Agronomists who had studied the phenomenon had not yet been able to agree on the cause. The peasants believed it was an ill omen, a sign from the ancient gods who had dwelt in those forests and who had been felled by the missionaries' swords. The original inhabitants of the region, the Prutenes, were both barbaric and proud and used to worship thunder, animals, trees, and ancestor spirits. They had doggedly resisted conversion, despite the evident superiority of the invaders, who had pillaged and slaughtered until the last Prutene was either christened or dead. Legend had it that in that very grove, a tribal chief had been put to death by warrior monks in a particularly heinous manner. They had gouged out his guts, nailed them to a tree, and forced him to run. The forest smelled of moss. The sun lit up the treetops but failed to reach the ground, which was still dappled.

The baron stopped in a clearing, dismounted from his horse, pulled off the saddlebags and sat in the bend of one of the curved trees, as if it were in an armchair, eating rye bread and lard. The bay grazed at a bush just past him. Suddenly, a gust of wind rustled the leaves. The horse lifted its head sharply and looked around tensely, as if in fear of an unseen enemy. The baron had no difficulty believing the truculent legend. Immediately after Warsaw had surrendered, in fact, the massacre of the Polish ruling class had begun. Officers of the armed forces, intellectuals, members of the clergy, and the aristocracy had been killed without even a trumped-up charge. They went straight in front of the firing line. They had called it "extraordinary peacemaking action". Their other target had been the Jewish community, with three million people and centuries of history to their name. The baron had personally witnessed an SS unit lock about fifty Jews into the village synagogue and set fire to the building, mowing down those who tried to leave with their machine guns. Von Lehndorff was no stranger to the ferocity of war. In the Great War, he had fought in the trenches on the Western Front. Stuck in the mud, amid the stench of rotting corpses in no man's land, he had seen first-hand the Moloch of modern battle. But what Germany was doing in Poland was on a different plane. Von Lehndorff had protested. He had telephoned and written. To begin with, they had listened to him, but only because the old generals had not completely surrendered to the Nazis and were trying to hamper the rise of the SS by denouncing their lack of professionalism and sense of proportion. His exposés had been used as tools in the struggle between the military and political hierarchies. As soon as von Lehndorff had spoken out too loudly, accusing his own division commander of passivity and connivance, the army had decommissioned him and sent him home.

He took a swig of schnapps and climbed back into the saddle. In the shade of the trees, the clatter of hooves mingled with bird calls and humming insects. When he emerged from the woods, the baron had to shield his face with his hand the sun was so high. He began to climb up the hill in front of him. In the distance, he could see the blue-gray waters of the Vistula and the now-abandoned frontier post on the old Polish border. The entire Pomeranian province had been incorporated into the Reich. Goebbels' propaganda had insisted that these were historically Germanic territories. Kulmhof—Chełmno, for the Poles—had been founded by Teutonic knights in the thirteenth century. What Goebbels' newspapers did not say was that for seven hundred years, the area had been inhabited predominantly by Slavic-speaking populations. But this mistake was being quickly remedied by expelling the Poles to the General Government—what was left of Poland after annexations by Germany—and by importing droves of *Volksdeutschen* and settlers directly from the Reich. The whole thing was a giant chess game. In the years of the Baron's youth, it had been called *Weltpolitik*. But now the game no longer interested him.

He reached the top of the hill. A group of vehicles was advancing along the road leading to the castle. Three trucks and, at the head of the column, a Kübelwagen. The baron fished into his leather saddlebag and pulled out a pair of binoculars. In the open car, next to the driver, there was an officer in a black uniform.

14

Moscow, July 1, 1982

The order had come out of the blue. Prepare to leave in twelve hours. After leaving her to languish behind a desk for years, the bosses had suddenly remembered her. She had rushed to the document archive to get the photographs. While the technicians were fabricating a West German passport, she had stopped at the First Central Directorate, which supervised overseas actions, to receive her orders. She had wondered if it was all a mistake. A real mission. They had selected her for her language skills. "Are you sure you can pass for German?" an officer she had never met before had asked her coldly. Natalya Yakovchenko was not sure of many things, but she had no doubt whatsoever about her competence in her mother tongue. "Of course, comrade major." Natalya had been born in East Berlin and had spent the first ten years of her life in the German Democratic Republic. The major had kept a poker-face, but Colonel Žirkov had smiled at her. Natalya clicked her suitcase closed, placed it by the door, and sat on the faux-leather sofa to wait.

She knew that language had not been the only factor in being given the assignment. The KGB had plenty of female agents fluent in German. Žirkov, wo had recently returned from a long period abroad, was an old friend of her father's. It had been a stroke of luck: finally, an opportunity to get back to a career that had been sidelined. A career for which she had been prepared since childhood. Nikolai Yakovchenko, who had started out in Stalin's secret police force, and then successfully navigated the in-fights among factions after the dictator's demise, would have loved a son to follow in his footsteps. He had had to settle for Natalya. She had thrown herself wholeheartedly into the endeavor. And he had supported her. Nikolai's connections had got her into the prestigious training school at the First Central Directorate, which only took three hundred students a year from all over the Soviet Union. Most were the offspring of the apparatchiks. Natalya had graduated with honors and her first experience in the field, on a mission in Sweden, had been excellent. Then, a heart attack had unexpectedly deprived her of her father. Deep down, although she had never confessed it to herself, she had been glad. She would finally be able to make her own way, climb the ladder without any help, prove herself. But, instead, she had been relegated to the archives. She soon realized that no one climbed ladders without a leg-up. In the absence of a parent, there was only one other way for Natalya. She was not bad looking—a little on the plump side perhaps— but she had a nice body and a pretty face. The head of the tenth department with jurisdiction over Francophone Africa had been a possible candidate. They had gone out to dinner a couple of times, but when the moment came, she had backed out. She had stayed in the archives. Now thirty-five, husband-less and childless, imprisoned in a career that others had chosen for her, Natalya Yakovchenko was happy to have one last chance. She would make sure not to waste it.

The ringing of the intercom gave her a jolt. She checked once again that she had turned off the gas and went out. As soon the driver spotted her in the doorway, he leaped out to get her suitcase, loaded it into the trunk of a large, shiny, black car, and opened the door for her. Natalya's gray eyes followed the man's gestures warily. She had never received such privileged treatment. She climbed into the car. In the back seat was Colonel Žirkov.

"Thank you," Natalya said.

"It wasn't easy to push for you, but I managed in the end."

The car drove off.

"Zamorin's candidate was incompetent. How can they

expect us to provide security for the Soviet Union if they send us people like that?"

The colonel sighed deeply. In the dimness of the interior, Natalya could feel the old man's weary gaze on her. He had been fighting against the enemies of socialism for more than forty years. He and Nikolai had met in Spain in 1938.

"I am sure you will do a good job. And when you come back, we'll make sure there will be a promotion. They've kept you in the shadows too long. But now Uncle Roman is back."

Natalya gave him a knowing smile. She knew the old man acted out of sincere affection towards her and the memory of her father, but his ostentation of good intentions still annoyed her. Once again, her qualities would be outweighed by the importance of her sponsor. But by now she had learned her lesson. A promotion was a promotion, after all.

The car reached the military airport. They went through the usual checks and came to a stop next to a small hangar, where an Antonov An-24 was parked.

"Good luck," Žirkov said.

They shook hands warmly.

Natalya took her suitcase from the driver and began to climb up the steps. When she got to the top, the pilot stared at her impassively. Natalya turned to give a final nod of acknowledgment, stepped inside, put her suitcase in the overhead compartment, and settled into her seat. There was only one other passenger on the other side of the aisle, a man in plainclothes looking pensive.

"Wheels up in five minutes," the pilot announced as he disappeared into the cockpit.

As the engines increased to full throttle and the wheels of the aircraft lifted off the ground, Natalya thought about what attended her. Conscious that her emotions were dictated by petit-bourgeois romanticism, she could not help being thrilled.

15

East Prussia, October 23, 1941

T he Baron and his wife had spent the previous day overseeing the clearing of the rooms in the castle that were to be occupied by the SS. With his customary efficiency and tact, Albert had played the role of liaison officer. The von Lehndorffs intended to avoid direct dealings with the occupants as much as possible. Under the watchful eye of the major, the servants had emptied cupboards, moved furniture, tapestries, and fittings, and helped the new masters take possession of the castle. Fortunately, Major Lichtblau had turned out to be relatively civilized, for a Nazi. Moreover, he wore the red, black, and white ribbon of the second-class Iron Cross on the second button of his jacket. It was not that the baron was impressed, since he had won a first-class medal, as well as the highest Prussian honor, *Pour le Mérite*, instituted by Frederick the Great. But at the very least it meant that Lichtblau was not a shirker.

Now that preparations for the castle's confiscation were over, Wilhelm von Lehndorff busied himself creating an intense schedule of activities to be carried out from dawn to dusk, keeping himself busy at all times so as not to have to think about the wretched condition he found himself in. It was an old military technique. In a situation of prolonged difficulty, such as a retreat or a battle of attrition, adherence to discipline is the only thing that stops the troops from falling apart. In 1916 on the Somme, they had been stuck in the shelters for a whole week under the terrifying bombing of the British artillery, but he had shown up every morning, shaved and dressed in impeccable uniform, and inspected them with the scrupulousness of a sergeant major of the guard reviewing his platoon before a parade. Before lunch, after the business of property management had been taken care of, together with possible interviews with the peasants, fencing exercises had been planned.

Wilhelm von Lehndorff entered the weapons' room. He was wearing a new outfit, which he had had shipped from a store in Verona, Italy. They had his measurements so he could periodically order what he needed. The parquet floor squeaked under his footsteps. The hall, illuminated by large floor-to-ceiling windows, was decked out with weapons, helmets, and flags that the von Lehndorffs had wrested from the enemies of the Prussian state over centuries of military campaigns. There were Polish cavalry spears and Lithuanian infantry pikes, Swedish muzzle-loading muskets and British repeating rifles, crude Croatian Pandur busbies and elegant Austrian kepìs. The most valuable piece in the collection was the standard of a Napoleonic cuirassier regiment that a great-great-grandfather of his had captured after the battle of Leipzig at the cost of a slash to the forehead, which in turn had led to his death by septicemia a few days later. A portrait of Colonel Oskar von Lehndorff, in the black uniform of the 2nd Hussars with a skull on his cap, hung beneath the pennant that had cost him his life, which was reduced to a faded, moth-eaten rag. It was now almost impossible to make out the red, blue and white of the Republican flag and the gold of the imperial eagles, which had once shimmered in the sun and propelled French soldiers into battle. The baron stared at the portrait of his heroic ancestor in that forbidding castle which the SS had now confiscated. He studied the man's grim expression, his gaze lost in dreams of power and glory, and suddenly felt burdened by his family's past. Centuries of fighting and methodically perfecting the art of carnage. He did a few rounds of running and some warm-up exercises, after which he went to the rack, where a dozen foils, épées, and sabers were arranged. He pulled on his glove and selected a Solingen steel blade épée. Fencing was different. Fencing represented an ancient allegiance to an ideal of hand-to-hand combat, before the vile age of gunpowder, barbed wire and gas. He took up the first position, saluted an imaginary opponent in the French manner, and went en-garde. In the mirror in front of him, the baron saw himself execute an elegant advance-lunge.

Von Lehndorff was sparring with the dummy, an old mask covering a leather plate on the wall. He performed a series of swift and precise hits alternating between the heart, the shoulders, and the head. At one point, the sound of the tip striking its target was accompanied by the creaking of parquet. The baron interrupted the exercise and turned around. It was Hans Lichtblau.

"This wing of the castle is reserved for me and my wife," von Lehndorff said dryly, resuming his assault on the dummy.

"I am aware of that, but I wondered if you would be so generous as to allow me a few bouts. It would be a real honor to spar with you."

The baron paused. Lichtblau was carrying a large canvas bag with the Berlin SS fencing club emblem embroidered on it. Von Lehndorff weighed the proposal. He did not like the idea of granting the major's request, but he was nevertheless tempted. A fencing challenge should always be met, regardless of the opponent's technical qualities or political views. Besides, humiliating an SS officer on the piste might not require a feat of endurance, but it would at least be personally satisfying.

"Épée?" the baron asked.

"Is that your weapon of choice?" Lichtblau asked.

"The foil is for women, the saber for savages," the baron answered.

"The saber is Obergruppenführer Heydrich's favorite."

Von Lehndorff gave the major a half smile and started to lecture him.

"No wonder. The foil is a quibbling, profoundly Latin weapon. It is not by chance that the Italians excel in this discipline. The épée is reflexive. It possesses a Cartesian logic far removed from the Wagnerian frenzy of National Socialism. The saber—fast, brutal, instinctive—is the weapon that best suits the fanaticism of your political movement." The baron had intentionally used the terms "brutal" and "fanaticism," adjectives the Nazis considered positive, and Lichtblau had not resented his lexical choices. "However," von Lehndorff continued, "if we put things in historical perspective, we would find that saber-rattling fits poorly with the ideas of Adolf Hitler's disciples." The major listened attentively to the baron's monologue. "As you may know, the saber was invented by the Hungarians, who are the masters. Its curved shape is a legacy of the scimitar of the Turkish knights, against whom the Magyar armies fought for centuries. In essence, the saber is an Asian tool. It should therefore be banned by a party that aims to defend Western civilization from the Mongol threat."

Lichtblau stared silently at the baron for a few seconds, and burst into a loud laugh. "I prefer the épée, too."

"You can change in there," von Lehndorff said, pointing to the small dressing room at the back of the room.

They took a few bouts to warm-up then played a bout, which the baron won with ease. Lichtblau was not bad. He could even be a threat, especially when closer than en-garde, but he had little patience, a quality which is essential in a fencer. In the second bout, Lichtblau fared better, was more concentrated, more wait-and-see, and made good use of his *quarte* parry, from which the baron found it a little hard to extricate himself, though he still won five to three. They took a break, during which they drank a glass of Moselle wine brought in by Albert.

"I wouldn't like to be inappropriate," Lichtblau began awkwardly, "but doesn't it bother you . . . ?" He waved vaguely in the direction of the baron's black eyepatch.

Von Lehndorff did not flinch.

"Sight is a secondary sense in fencing," he explained.

"The master I had as a boy told me to look opponents in

the eye because you can guess their intentions from the way they move."

"Personally, since I was blinded in one eye, I have become a better striker. Especially with the épée, seeing doesn't help much. The target is there. You need to feel the blade as if it were an extension of your arm. You don't need eyes to move your wrist. The French call it *le sentiment du fer*, a feel for the iron. Try it." Lichtblau looked at him unconvinced. "Go for it," von Lehndorff insisted.

The major donned his mask, placed himself en-garde, and screwed his eyes shut. At first, he felt disoriented. He thrashed into the void. The baron didn't respond, merely holding himself en-garde, like an instructor in class. He would make a move and wait for the pupil's reaction, which, however, was slow to come.

"Relax," the baron advised.

Lichtblau made an effort to loosen his arm and lighten his grip on the handle. The baron executed a *tierze* bind, and the major responded with a *derobement*. He sensed his opponent's sword slide slowly along the blade, gaining distance. Suddenly von Lehndorff accelerated. Instinctively, Lichtblau performed a beat and lunged, touching the baron's forearm.

"You got me."

Lichtblau opened his eyes again. "It was a fluke," he said.

"Maybe," the baron replied shrewdly.

They did a few more bouts. During a break, Lichtblau asked the baron what he thought of electrification. Electrified foils had already been used in the Berlin Olympics. Lichtblau was amazed that the old champion was in favor. As a rule, virtuosos, especially older ones, were against the new technology that put the response of a machine before the judgment of the referee. The main objection was that this emphasized the utilitarian dimension of fencing, where the aim became lighting a bulb rather than executing an esthetic move. The baron, however, defended the impartiality of an electric circuit. Referees were often influenced, perhaps unwittingly, by the athletes' reputations. They tended to favor fencers and teams of greater prestige. If a beam of electrons determined who scored a point, the playing field would be more level.

"I don't think it will be very successful in Germany," the baron concluded, putting his mask back on. "Fair play is certainly not a hallmark of Mr. Heydrich's style."

16

Tatra Mountains, Czechoslovakia, July 2, 1982

The village was tiny, with no school or health clinic. Only a handful of buildings scattered along the road. Dr. Anton Epstein, had been called out the previous evening from the small mining town some twenty kilometers further down the valley where he worked, to attend a delivery. He had been picked up after dinner by the husband on a rickety motorcycle: a tall, lanky, sad-looking young man whose hands had already been deformed and face hollowed out by hard labor underground. He had tackled the hairpin bends that snaked up the mountain with the impatience of his age and the anxiety of a soon-to-be father of his first child. Clinging to the saddle, Anton had wondered if it might have been better to come in his car. He had never liked driving, especially at night, and in recent years his eyesight had deteriorated. He had told himself that if he was meant to die on that pothole-ridden road with a terrifying drop, he might as well have a driver help him on his way. On a couple of occasions, they had risked flying off the cliff and had avoided a head-on collision with a truck by the skin of their teeth, but they had made it to their destination in one piece. When he had examined the woman, the doctor realized that the man's anxiety had not been misplaced. The baby had not turned, as an elderly midwife had already observed. Offended by the family's decision to call a doctor, she had gone off before he arrived. The labor had been long. To avoid a breech delivery, Anton had had to turn the unborn baby, using a maneuver he had performed before, but always with the assistance of a midwife. He had succeeded on his third attempt. The baby was big, weighing almost five kilos, as the baker's scales would make clear. The woman was screaming, her face distorted by pain and fear. In the next room, where neighbors trickled in constantly to ask for news, her husband sat in a corner staring at the floor with his hands pressed over his ears. As dawn approached, the infant's cry had broken the curse that appeared to loom over the house and, by extension, over the entire community. Excitement spread among those who had waited the whole night. Shouts of jubilation, applause, shoulder pats. The midwife was the only one who refused to join the celebration.

In the uncertain light of early morning, as the exhausted mother slept and the baby looked around with still-blind eyes, stunned at having come into the world, a tired and satisfied Dr. Anton Epstein, former head of pediatrics and professor at Charles IV University in Prague, stepped out into the street to smoke a cigarette. After a couple of puffs, he was joined by the child's father and a host of male friends and relatives. The young man had become cheerful and garrulous. He embraced the doctor warmly and dragged him to a house nearby where the whole company embarked on a string of toasts with beer and *slivovitz*, during which it was determined that the baby's middle name would be Anton. His first name, Otakar, in honor of his maternal grandfather who had died in a firedamp explosion years before, had been decided long ago. The doctor could not have avoided the ritual without offending the villagers, nor would he have wanted to, despite a desperate need for sleep. The rough gratitude of these people had been one of the few satisfactions in his life for a long time.

For the return trip, since Otakar Anton's father had collapsed with his head on the table, knocked out by drink and waning tension, the doctor was entrusted to a new driver, a ginger-haired uncle with a thick ginger-gray mustache who was retired, and therefore released from the mine's grueling shifts. It was past eight by the time he dropped Anton off at his house. They exchanged one last hug, the ginger-head leaped back onto the bike, and the doctor stood there, too tired even to open the door. He watched, misty-eyed, as the former miner rode off down the street, and only when the man had turned the corner and there was nothing left of the motorbike but a cloud of black smoke, did Anton come back to his senses and plunge his hands into his jacket pockets in search of his keys.

The concierge watched him suspiciously from the hatch. She was an informant for the Ministry of the Interior. This was common knowledge and the tenants paid no more attention to it than they would a broken gutter that no one ever fixes. That morning, however, she was staring at Anton with a peculiar intensity. The significance of her special interest was evident as soon as he reached his apartment. The door was open. It had not been a break-in, as the concierge had the keys to the whole building. Anton crossed the threshold cautiously. The house was small and he soon found them. Seated around the table in the living room there was a subservient-looking man in a apparatchiki-blue suit and a woman in her mid-thirties to early forties with gray eyes she strained to make even colder. She was wearing a charcoal-gray suit and a brown acrylic blouse which concealed the shape of her body, but her face was pretty, with a thin nose and short blond hair. Although the situation ought to have made him think otherwise, Anton Epstein was upset by her presence. She was the first woman to enter his home since his wife had died. November would mark the fourth anniversary of when Anna had jumped into the artificial lake created by the dam above the village. She had always been a good swimmer but the water had been freezing cold. She had died of hypothermia within a few minutes.

The man introduced himself as a functionary in the Czechoslovak Security Services. Anton was almost delighted. In the early days, after they had been exiled to that wild place in the heart of the Carpathian Mountains, he and Anna had received fairly frequent visits from the political police. They had generally been incredibly unpleasant meetings, where they had been interrogated at length and accused of inspired crimes they would never have even imagined committing. However, it had been even worse when the officers had stopped coming. Direct persecution at least fed the illusion that they were still participants in a struggle, albeit an unequal one, while oblivion was a slippery slope where they had no choice but to slide downwards. They had been buried alive, far-removed from everything they had always considered civilized and desirable. Anna had been unable to take it.

When the official switched from Czech to Russian and told him that the gray-eyed woman was a KGB agent, however, Anton realized that this was not a routine check. His command of the language of Pushkin and Tolstoy was reasonably good, but he was concerned that he would not be able to join in the conversation. The standard vocabulary of everyday Stalinism uttered by the functionary reassured him. If that was the level, he would not miss too many semantic nuances.

"There are times when a contra-revolutionary element, even a Jew with cosmopolitan and pro-Zionist tendencies, can be useful to the cause of socialism."

Anton studied the man from the secret services, unable to imagine where he was running with this salvo.

"The Soviet Union has asked us for our fraternal help in recovering scientific material stolen by the Nazis during the war. Agent Yakovchenko has been assigned to the mission." He cast a deferential glance at his Russian colleague as if to receive confirmation that he had stated the facts correctly.

Dr. Epstein was stunned. He too looked at the woman, but her poker-face gave him no clue. He went back to staring at the man.

"Why are you telling me all this?"

"You could help."

"Me?" Epstein was increasingly incredulous.

"The person who stole the material is a former SS officer, currently working for the CIA. There are no photographs of him. At least, neither the KGB nor the services of any other socialist country, not even those of the GDR, have any. It appears from your file that you met him. His name is Hans Lichtblau."

Anton's eyes widened. That name echoed in his head like the whistle of a train in a tunnel. Hans Lichtblau. More like the howl of a dog in the night.

"Would you recognize him?" Natalya Yakovchenko asked dryly.

The doctor hesitated. "It's been a long time. People change."

"He was your jailer for more than three years. He tortured and killed your comrades. You can't have forgotten that," the woman retorted.

Anton Epstein, former head of pediatrics with a chair at the Charles IV University in Prague, lowered his head. He noticed that he was sweating. He rubbed his palms on his pants.

"Yes, I think I would recognize him," he sighed.

17

Neuhof, West Prussia, October 24, 1941

In the middle of the courtyard there rose up a large oak tree. A wooden bench circled its trunk, in the shade of its branches, where the leaves were beginning to fall. On the kitchen windowsill, an apple and cinnamon pie had been left to cool, sending a spicy aroma wafting through the air. The window was adorned with a pair of lace curtains, as white as the spotless and perfectly-kept courtyard walls. On the bench, a little girl was playing with her doll. She wore a gray woolen skirt and a light blue sweater, over which two blond braids tied with red and white polka-dotted bows fell. On that unusually warm autumn afternoon, the sun made the little girl's head shimmer as if she were wearing a golden bonnet. A few yards away, her brother, who was a couple of years older than her, was kneeling in the bare grass setting out a platoon of tin soldiers ready to attack a tin tank lurking behind the chopping block. The little boy was wearing a green felt jacket and the black shorts of the *Deutsches Jungvolk* uniform. He had the same wheat-colored hair as his sister. Dr. Goebbels himself, with his team of writers, artists, and film directors, could not have produced a more effective postcard to visualize the idea of *Drang nach Osten*, the ancestral urge of the German people to expand into the lands of Eastern Europe.

A woman looked out of the window. She looked good for her thirty years, with her hair a slightly darker blond than her children's, gathered at the nape of her neck in an elaborate bun.

"Come in for a snack," she called. She took the pie from the windowsill and disappeared inside.

The children ran into the house instantly. The doll sat on

the bench peering at the miniature infantrymen facing off the Panzer.

As the children tucked into a slice of the pie, with a generous dollop of cream on top, and drank a glass of milk, Martha Kernig went out with the laundry basket, put it on the bench, and set about hanging out the washing on a line that ran from one of the branches to an iron ring planted in the wall. They had arrived from Riga early the previous year. The Ribbentrop-Molotov pact had made the exodus of German-speaking minorities from the Soviet Union possible. Sixty thousand people had arrived from Estonia and Latvia. They had been settled in the two new districts, Wartheland and Danzig-West Prussia, which had come into being after the western provinces of Poland had been annexed to the Reich. Now that Germany and Russia were at war, and the Wehrmacht had driven the Red Army out of the Baltic countries, some of the Germans who had been born there had decided to return. Martha, on the other hand, had stayed in Neuhof. Latvia held only bad memories for her. Her husband's death and, before that, the nationalist government's confiscation of the family property, a beautiful farm with acres of land, plentiful livestock and an orchard—a little paradise of green meadows and flowering cherry trees—where Martha had spent her childhood. Germanic populations had settled along the eastern shores of the Baltic Sea in the Middle Ages during the Northern Crusades. Although they were a minority, they had ruled unchallenged until 1918. An elite of nobles and professionals—state functionaries, generals, and diplomats—had served the tsars faithfully and had been rewarded with wide margins of autonomy in local government. With the end of the Romanov monarchy, the natives had driven out the Russians and wrested their land back from the dominion of the German-speakers. The Baltic Germans had been rudely awakened from their long feudal dream. There was nothing waiting for Martha Kernig in Latvia.

In the year and a half that she had spent in Neuhof, moreover,

Martha had worked hard, and she had no intention of giving up the fruits of all her hard work. In Riga, she and her husband had run a colonial store. In her new homeland, the authorities had assigned her a shop that had previously belonged to a Polish family. It was a village emporium with a little bit of everything. The warehouse was still half-full. Martha had never asked herself where the previous owners had gone. She had not had the time. Getting the house and store in order by herself, while having to take care of her children, had been enough of an undertaking. It was not easy to achieve acceptable standards in a backward region without even the most basic principles of hygiene. But things were changing. The *Volksdeutschen* were bringing civilization to Neuhof. They were her customers. She hardly ever saw the Poles, who were holed up in their filthy, stinking hovels. The Party leadership had been explicit about this. The Poles were to be ignored. The German settlers had not been sent there to improve living conditions for the local population, but rather to fulfill their historic duty to create a master race. The Poles who were not evacuated were to become a cheap, docile labor force. A few hundred kilometers west of the Gulf of Riga, the Baltic Germans continued to nurture their ancient dream.

When she had finished with the laundry, Martha returned to the house. Elsie and Paul had devoured the snack with the appetite of children accustomed to the outdoors.

"Wash your hands and go to your room to do your homework," she said in an authoritative tone that was not lacking in sweetness. She was a widow, after all. She had to both mother and father the children.

The children attempted a raucous but brief resistance. After a couple of ill-fated objections, they resigned themselves to washing their hands in the sink and set off like good children to do their homework. Martha watched them contentedly as they climbed up the wooden staircase to the bedrooms upstairs. She tidied up the kitchen and treated herself to a short break. She pulled a pack of cigarettes out from under her apron and lit one. She smoked leaning her left shoulder on the doorframe that looked out onto the courtyard. From dawn to dusk, she was almost always on the move. Breaks were few and far between and she wanted to savor them. She inhaled deeply, admiring the majesty of the giant oak tree already tinged with autumn hues. Her farm in Latvia was nothing like this, for sure, but she had nonetheless managed to build a place that was solid, spotless, and ship-shape, for herself and her children. She stubbed out the cigarette butt on the ground in the yard and threw it in the garbage can under the sink. She gave a cursory glance around the kitchen, making sure everything was in order. Then she went to the store where she had left Hilde, the saleswoman, who was also a *Volksdeutsche* originally from Reval in Estonia. Her assistant was not particularly bright but she was hard-working and was good with the clients.

The emporium was in the same building as the apartment, on the side facing the street. Martha had decorated the window with a string of swastika flags. She had never taken much interest in politics, but the Führer had given her a home and a source of income. What is more, Paul and Elsie had been invited to join the National Socialist Party youth organization, where they played various sports and made new friends, making up for the ones they had lost when they had been forced to leave Riga. Not only was it so much more than the Latvian government—which had cheated her of her property—had ever done for her. Martha was also certain that it was more than any other government, Bolshevik, British, or Jewish, had done for its citizens.

She went into the store through the back door, which communicated with the apartment by means of a corridor. Hilde was behind the counter, her neck tucked into her shoulders. Mrs. Hoffmann was launching into one of her usual verbose and aggressive monologues whose only unshakeable purpose was to obtain a discount.

"I know perfectly well that it is not your fault. You depend on the wholesale suppliers. They are the ones making the price hikes, Jewish profiteers the lot of them. But seven marks fifty for a blouse is an exaggeration."

"We didn't get it from a wholesaler," Hilde argued unconvincingly. "These blouses are made for us by a seamstress in Warsaw."

"Even worse! You're fueling the Polish economy by doing that. I am willing to give you five marks at the most."

Hilde stammered something but was unable to finish the sentence. Martha came to her rescue and her assistant stepped aside, almost hiding behind her boss. Mrs. Hoffmann always made her uncomfortable. It was not that she had no arguments to oppose her, but they always came to her too late, when the discussion was over and the customer had already left the store.

"We are not in a *sūq*, Mrs. Hoffmann," Martha said in a tone that was meant to be jocular but at the same time firm. "We are not in the habit of haggling."

Mrs. Hoffmann flushed. "I was just telling Hilde that seven-fifty for that blouse is too much."

"It's pure silk," Martha answered as if she didn't care.

"I doubt it," Mrs. Hoffmann huffed. "If it were a hundred percent silk, seven fifty would be cheap."

"Our seamstress has a husband who used to be a quartermaster in an airfield."

Mrs. Hoffmann looked at Martha, clearly not understanding what she was getting at.

"When the Polish army surrendered, he went home with a batch of parachutes."

The customer continued to stare at her blankly.

"Parachutes are made of silk."

"Then I want to try it on again." Mrs. Hoffman picked the blouse up from the counter and disappeared behind the dressing room curtain.

Martha and Hilde exchanged complicit looks.

"The buttons are badly sewn," squeaked Hoffmann from behind the curtain. "One is practically coming off already."

"If you take the blouse, I'll go over them right away. I'll have Hilde deliver it as soon as I'm done."

Mrs. Hoffmann reappeared in front of the counter. "Put it on the bill," she said, handing the blouse over to the store owner.

"I need it by six o'clock," she added, pretending it wasn't important. "My husband and I are going to the opera this evening in Danzig."

Martha did not reply. Her hands were already in the drawer where she kept her credit book. By the time she looked up again, Mrs. Hoffmann had disappeared. The narrow escape made her give a deep sigh. Mrs. Hoffmann was impossible, but she was the burgomaster's wife, a *Reichsdeutsche*, and a good customer.

"Go get me the sewing box," she said to Hilde.

The saleswoman went straight to the backroom and came back with a dark wooden box divided into little compartments. Martha sat down by the window, chose a needle and a length of thread, slipped on her thimble, and started tightening the buttons on the blouse. Mrs. Hoffmann had been right. They would have come off after one or two attempts to do up the blouse. She must point this out to the seamstress.

The doorbell rang, and a tow-haired boy appeared on the threshold. "Is Paul here?" the child asked.

"He's doing his homework."

"I'm done!"

Martha turned toward the back of the store. Paul had come in without her noticing. He must have seen his friend coming from her bedroom window and run downstairs.

"Really?"

"Yes, Mom."

"Then go."

Paul rushed out and went to join a group organizing a ball

game in a corner of the square. Martha got back to work. Her fingers were nimble and confident.

She fixed the collar button.

The motherland burns bright and strong in our blood.

Somewhere in the house, Elsie was singing.

Martha put the second button in place. Shouts erupting from the street made her look up. One of the two teams had come close to scoring a goal. The goalkeeper had the ball in his hands and was preparing to throw it back into the center after his teammates had gone back towards the other net. At the edge of the field, two Polish children in worn-out clothes with greasy locks stuck to their foreheads were following the match.

To protect it, we will establish a new province on the border.

A harmonious mass of young, moving bodies kicked up the dust in the square. Considering the faces she recognized, Martha thought it must be a challenge between Baltics and Germans from Volinia.

The wild foreign land does not frighten us with its falsehoods and deceptions.

Paul dribbled the ball past one defender, then another, and passed the ball to a friend who was waiting unmarked a few yards from the goal. The striker's shot was unstoppable. After scoring, the boy sprinted toward Paul to celebrate. In the warm light of the sunset, the happy, sweaty kids ran side by side towards the center of the field, eager to get on with the game.

We will give her a German face with a sword and a plow. The wind is blowing toward the east.

18

Tatra Mountains, Czechoslovakia, July 2, 1982

I n an unframed canvas hanging above her desk, Anna was depicted sitting at a coffee table and smoking broodingly. The self-portrait from when she was still studying at the Academy of Fine Arts was an ingenuous attempt to imitate Otto Dix's style. The young woman was wearing a black and white checkered dress. Her legs were crossed and one arm was leaning on the back of the chair. She was gazing to one side through the fringe of raven hair that fell over her forehead, fixing an indistinct point beyond the borders of the painting. Anton had the feeling that her eyes did not want to meet his, that they avoided him on purpose because they knew he was guilty. Anton Epstein, formerly a member of the Czechoslovak Communist Party, expelled in February 1970 for his support of the deviationist line of the deposed General Secretary Alexander Dubček, had finally given in. After twelve years of exile in the Carpathians, alone, the promise of returning to Prague and regaining his faculty chair and hospital post had proved irresistible. He had tried to convince himself that the task of capturing a Nazi criminal was a noble one. Except that he would be doing it for the nation that had invaded his country, a nation that couldn't be hunting Lichtblau out of a thirst for justice. Dr. Anton Epstein was guilty of collaboration with the enemy. His wife would have been outraged. But Anna was not there to talk him out of it. Ultimately, she too had been unable to hold out. Though Anton knew that Anna's chosen escape route showed the courage and dignity that he lacked.

He opened the closet, took out a small canvas bag, and threw a few things in to tide him over for two or three days.

The rest they would buy in West Germany. If he was to pass as a citizen of Western Europe, his wardrobe left over from the five-year plan would not pass muster. They were leaving for the German Democratic Republic in the afternoon. The next day they would cross the border into the Federal Republic on East German passports. They would be posing as a doctor from Dresden and his assistant, on their way to a congress on maxillofacial surgery in Hamburg. A conference was actually being held there, and the letterhead of the invitation was authentic. The KGB must have a good network of people on the other side of the Wall willing to cooperate. Anton was not a dentist, but he was able to pass as an expert in a conversation with a border guard. He was planning to instruct Agent Yakovchenko in the basic vocabulary. The man from the Czech secret services had said there was no need to worry. There were good relations between the two Germanies and the controls would not be too thorough. The University of Hamburg coat of arms on the letterhead was sufficient protection. Once in West Germany, Anton and Agent Yakovchenko would continue their journey on different passports, casting themselves as a minor Bavarian industrialist and his secretary on a business trip.

He looked back at his wife's self-portrait. There were more canvasses in the attic, many of them abstracts, some of them finished. The only positive aspect of exile for Anna had been to be able to paint what she wanted. She worked for herself alone. She no longer had any critics or academies to please. Anton remembered how embarrassing it was for his wife to have to bend to the dictates of social realism. In people's democracies, there was no place for the formalism of bourgeois art. However painful it was, Anna had found it an acceptable sacrifice, all things considered. The new political course may have had its rough edges, but for her and her husband, and for many of their fellow citizens, it was undoubtedly a step forward for the country. Unlike the other Eastern European states, which had become communist because they had happened to end up in the

Soviet sphere of influence at the end of the war, Czechoslovakia had more or less consensually opted for an alliance with Russia. Back in 1938, in fact, the West had abandoned them to the mercy of the Germans in the vain hope of preserving the peace with Hitler. The Czechs had not forgotten the betrayal and had enthusiastically greeted the Red Army soldiers. The 1946 elections had been free and the Communists had won a relative majority. Admittedly, they had later organized a putsch and outlawed opponents, but they had continued to enjoy widespread and real support. By 1948, the Czechoslovak Communist Party had two and a half million members out of a population of eleven million: four times as many militants as the Polish Party and twice as many as the Hungarian one. The 1950s had been hard. Arrests, informers, the constant fear of sabotage and conspiracies hatched by the Americans and agents working for Marshal Tito, who had meanwhile left the Soviet camp, thus nurturing Stalin's already marked taste for purges. In all the satellite states, any elements of dubious loyalty had to be eliminated. Any suspicious activity could send you to the gallows. Anton didn't know what to make of the November 1952 Slánský trial, in particular. Rudolf Slánský, General Secretary of the Czechoslovak Communist Party, and thirteen other leaders, almost all of whom were Jewish, had been accused of being pro-Zionist and pro-Yugoslav Trotskyists. After a week's trial, with every detail reported in the papers, eleven of the defendants had been put to death in Pankrác Prison. The other three had received life sentences. One of those executed, the Deputy Minister of Foreign Trade, Rudolf Margolius, was an Auschwitz survivor. The formula "cosmopolitan Jew," used by the prosecutor, was an updated version of the Nazi idea of the "Jew without roots."

Even in those dark days, however, Anton and his wife had continued to hope that a new society was possible. They had convinced themselves that the violence, the climate of hatred and suspicion, was a consequence of the Cold War, which the Americans had encouraged in an attempt to wipe out the achievements of the world's working class. Anna had taken to drawing illustrations for propaganda posters. Rising suns on golden wheat fields. Columns of marching tractors. Muscly workers, their jaws set like Greek heroes. Little girls with blond braids and red neckerchiefs. She had even drawn Stalin in a white uniform reading a book, a poster to encourage people to go to public libraries. By the end of the next decade, the country was finally on the right track. Dubček had succeeded in combining communism with the Czechoslovak democratic tradition. By March 1968, censorship had been effectively abolished. Political and cultural publications and initiatives of all kinds had flourished. Precisely because it had given up some of its prerogatives and allowed non-Communist organizations to emerge, the Party had regained the consensus it had enjoyed in the immediate postwar period. That year, for the first time in a long time, people had gone to the May Day parade of their own free will, happy, convinced, waving their own flags and slogans. The people and the Party were progressing together and building socialism with a human face. The Soviets, who had supported Dubček to begin with, were following developments with growing alarm. The reforms were going too far. Students started demonstrating in Poland, calling for a new course in their country, too. There was a real risk that the Prague Spring would contaminate the other satellite states and bring the whole Eastern bloc crashing down. Too real to allow things to go on. On the night between August 20 and 21, 1968, Warsaw Pact troops invaded Czechoslovakia. The normalization process began gently, but little by little those who had participated in the Prague Spring ended up being removed from the positions they had held in newspapers, universities, and trade unions. Every single Party member, and there were one and a half million of them, was interrogated by agents of the Czechoslovak Secret Service working under the direction of the KGB. One-third of them were expelled. In addition to having his card torn up,

Anton had been removed from the faculty and the hospital. And Anna had had to give up her professorship at the Academy. They were exiled to the mountains so that they could meditate on their betrayal of the socialist cause.

The girl in the painting could not have envisaged an outcome as grim as this. The canvas had been painted in May 1945, just after the liberation. At the time, the future of Czechoslovakia and all of Europe felt radiant. The inhabitants of Prague offered Russian soldiers flowers. Her reference to Otto Dix, one of the great artists condemned by the Nazis as "degenerates," had been Anna's way of celebrating Hitler's defeat. Anton fished his handkerchief out of his pocket, took the portrait off the wall, and gently dusted it off. They had married a month later. He had been unable to find a ready-made suit that fit him and had had to have one made to measure. He had returned from the camps weighing fifty pounds. But he had survived, and Anna had awaited his return. The Epstein family had been exterminated. Anton was the only survivor. From then on, Anna had been his family. Anna and humanity, a new humanity that would be able to put hatred, war and its obsession with race behind it. In socialist society, there would no longer be classes or ethnicities, only men and women, finally free from exploitation and the legacy of the past.

Anton put the picture back and went to the kitchen to make himself a cup of coffee. He had been up all night, but he could not contemplate going to sleep. The news that the new dawn had brought made it difficult for him to even sit still in a chair. He paced up and down the small apartment, going back and forth to his bedroom, obsessively checking the contents of his bag to make sure he had not forgotten anything essential. The answer was always the same. He had everything he needed. He drank his coffee restlessly, threw his raincoat on, and left the house. The roads were still deserted. He walked up the main street. He left the last houses behind, turned a sharp bend, and stood in front of the dam. A thin rain was beginning to fall. The surface of the reservoir was gray, dotted with thousands of invisible pins. Anton pulled the lapels of his raincoat up and stood there, his hands digging into his pockets, looking at the dark water, a large leaden mirror reflecting nothing.

19

Soldau, East Prussia, October 25, 1941

They had been made to line up and stand still in the camp courtyard under the lashings of an icy wind. After an interminable day spent shoveling clods of earth, the wait was unbearable. And the roll call was not even halfway through. Anton felt his knees giving way and dug his nails into the palm of one hand, forcing himself to stand up straight. Soon the Kapo would call out his number. He was required to respond loudly and without hesitation. He had been in the Lager for only five days and had already become accustomed to being referred to by number rather than by name. His parents and sister had been stopped in Łódź, while he had been loaded onto another train heading north, alongside other men of working age, all shattered and starving after their long trip. His father had tried to argue with the SS guards, begging them not to separate the family. The medical officer who had examined Anton in two seconds by the track and deemed him fit to join the departing transport, had shown more courtesy and understanding than they could have hoped for. The distinguished air Professor Epstein had managed to keep up despite the hellish conditions of their journey may have contributed. Or it may have been his impeccable German. Or perhaps it was because Anton's father had introduced himself as the chief of surgery. Respect among professional colleagues was so deeply-rooted in the bourgeoisie that the radical nature of the National Socialist revolution had been unable to erase it entirely from the doctor's soul. Whatever the reason, the medical officer had been patient and explained that the Reich needed manpower. Polish peasants had been transferred by the Government and the number of German settlers who had arrived to take their place was still insufficient. They needed workers for the harvest. In Soldau—he had reassured them in the professional tone of a specialist called in for a consult—the boy would fit in just fine. Healthy country life. Physical activity. He might even be able to write to them. David Epstein had not given up. He had begged him to give them permission to accompany their son if he really had to go. Anton would be more productive his if his loved ones were with him. That was when another SS officer had intervened. His comrade was being soft-hearted. He shouldn't give that Jew the opportunity to show off his dialectical skills. Loading and unloading operations could not be slowed down. He had hit Professor Epstein full in the face, splitting his lip, and then shoved him down the ramp towards the huddle of prisoners destined to remain in the ghetto. That was Anton's last image of his family. His father attempting to stem the flow of blood dripping from his mouth with his coat sleeve. His distraught mother, torn between helping her husband or trying to wrest her son from the guards who were forcibly pushing him onto the cattle car. His sister sobbing and yelling out his name.

The train had come to a halt late at night in Soldau, a Polish town on the old border with Prussia called Działdowo before it was incorporated into the Reich. The doors had been unlocked and a breath of fresh air had hit the deportees. They had taken a deep breath. For a moment, they had been happy to have arrived. For a moment. Outside, the darkness was perforated by the dazzling beams of the photo-electric lights. The guards had forced them to climb out in a hurry, punctuating their efforts with shouts and blows with their rifle butts. They had struck at random in order to heighten the prisoners' fear and deprive them of any ideas of escape or resistance. It had worked to perfection. The six hundred farm workers had marched obediently to a row of barracks where they were allowed to sleep until dawn. After days of traveling on his feet, Anton had finally been able to lie down. He had had to sleep on bare floorboards, but it had felt blissfully restful. After which, the convoluted operation of stripping them of their previous identities had begun. They had been forced to take a cold shower in a large room with open windows. A team of barbers, who were all prisoners like them, had shaven their hair off. Finally, they had been assigned a pair of striped pajamas, a pair of clogs, a mess tin, and a number, in an mix of order and chaos, barked orders from the Kapos and advice from fellow prisoners, some scornful and others fatalistic. The next day they had been split up into work teams and sent to the camps. Anton had never handled a shovel in his whole life. A young Polish Jew had given him a crash course on how to use it, first in Yiddish, then with gestures. As a thank you, Anton had given him a piece of dry bread left over from the trip. The other boy had devoured it on the spot. Now he realized he had been reckless. Gratitude was not a sentiment to be cultivated lightly in that alien universe.

Anton looked around. He was surrounded by thousands of human beings like himself. In tatters, stooped, spent. He was reminded of a book he had loved as a boy, *The Time Machine* by H. G. Wells. The protagonist travels into the future in the prodigious invention that gives the novel its title, where repulsive Morlocks, deformed albino creatures, live underground and have to work tirelessly to produce goods for the humans above ground. One evening during his first year of studying Medicine at Charles IV University in Prague, after dinner with his parents and sister, he had memorized a few more pages of his anatomy textbook, brushed his teeth, put on his pajamas, slipped under a plumped-up goose-down comforter, and turned his light off. He had woken up in the gloomy Morlock caves and had had no idea how to get out.

Somewhere in one of the front rows, a prisoner suddenly collapsed. Anton was unable to see who it was, but he guessed it was an old man who had not been able to stand the strain. Immediately a Kapo rushed to his side. He kicked the man lying in the mud and yelled at him to get up. The man whimpered but was unable to stand. The other deportees did not react. If anyone dared to help him, they would be punished harshly. Some looked away, while others stared dully at the poor wretch as if the thing on the ground was neither a human being nor an animal but only a stump, a rock, a scrap of metal. A second Kapo arrived, another green triangle, a common criminal who had been granted the right of life and death over those who had always lived within the law, by virtue of his Aryan blood. The two men set about kicking and beating the prisoner all over. Head, kidneys, groin, belly. Anton looked down to avoid the spectacle. The Kapo's yells, the victim's rasping breath, and the sound of sticks and boots striking the prisoner's body were terrifying enough. He had been at the camp for a mere five days and he still looked at things with the eyes of his former life, still had the instinct to help others. All of a sudden, the Kapo's mouths and clubs fell silent. There followed a moment of silence and then a gunshot. Anton looked up and caught sight of an SS NCO through the rows of internees in front of him clutching a pistol. The two Kapos dragged the corpse away, hampered by the thick mud in the yard. The roll call resumed. They called Anton's number. He answered.

The Lager was an old army barracks, which the SS had requisitioned in the fall of 1939 to imprison Jews and members of the Polish ruling class. An inmate who had been there since the beginning of the war had told Anton that in 1940, hundreds of officers in the armed forces, priests, journalists, professors, and civil servants had been shot. Individual executions had been performed within the camp, while mass killings had taken place in the woods just outside town. Anton had heard other even more sinister rumors. Some people said there had been many mentally ill and severely disabled German citizens brought to the Lager over the previous year. They had been shot or poisoned with gas in special trucks. Anton did not know whether to believe the stories, although everything he saw around him told him they were credible. Jews had survived pogroms for centuries by lowering their heads and waiting for the storm to pass. But this was no pogrom. Pogroms may be violent, they may be tolerated or even fueled by the institutions, but they were outbreaks of blind violence which would sooner or later die out. The Nazis had launched something entirely new: a rational and methodical long-term plan to destroy enemies of the state. It was something that did not yet have a name.

The roll call came to an end. The prisoners waited anxiously for the order to break ranks. They would finally get their gruel, devote themselves to petty trade, and enjoy the miserable semblance of rest that was their allotted time for sleep, always too short, too uncomfortable, too intermittent. But the Kapo didn't say a word. The prisoners exchanged doubtful glances. The wind whipped them pitilessly, making their teeth chatter. The Scharführer who had delivered the deathblow to the old man rushed over.

"Wait," he shouted.

The prisoners' doubts turned to anguish. Wait for what? A collective punishment? An execution? As a rule, if someone was put to death for a serious crime, such as an attempted escape, the comrades were expected to witness the hanging.

From the back of the yard, an SS officer Anton had never seen before approached slowly. He was accompanied by the camp commander. They were reviewing the prisoners and every so often they would pick one out.

"They are forming a new Kommando," the man to Anton's left whispered.

"Is it worth joining?" Anton asked.

"It depends," the man answered neutrally. He had been in the camp since the beginning of 1940 and had long since shed the burden of hope. It made no difference whether hard labor killed him in Soldau or anywhere else. Eventually they would all die.

The Unterscharführer shoved a small, clumsy-looking boy

with rounded shoulders in front of his superior. The boy's short-sighted eyes framed in round metal spectacles stared at the SS with a terrified expression.

"A student of a rabbinical school," the sergeant said.

The officer eyed the boy.

"Have you seen my credentials?" the major asked the camp commander in an icy voice.

"Of course, major. You have permission to pick up any prisoner you wish." The camp commander was clearly ill at ease.

"And *this* is what you are proposing?" the major replied, pointing to the boy with glasses. "When I decide to open a kosher delicatessen and need an apprentice, I will get in touch with him."

The commander flushed but dared not reply. The major had a letter signed by Reichsführer-SS Heinrich Himmler himself.

"Take this poor fellow back where you found him," the major ordered.

The sergeant instantly snapped to attention and sent the boy back to his position.

The major stood in front of the prisoners, his fists clenched at his sides.

"I am Dr. Hans Lichtblau," he said in a firm voice. "I run an experimental laboratory. I need farm-workers, breeders, gardeners. And I also need a secretary. Someone with good German, written and oral, who can keep accounts. Are there any volunteers?"

Anton cast a glance to his right but the man shrugged. He looked back at Lichtblau. He was paralyzed. He could not make up his mind. Work in the fields was annihilating, but this assignment was an absolute unknown.

"Any volunteers?" the major asked again.

On impulse, Anton raised his hand.

20

Haifa, July 2, 1982

They had not said a word the whole way. They had closed the bar in silence and attended the commemoration of the fallen. A military rabbi had officiated a brief religious ceremony. Then there had been a speech by a contrite-looking army colonel who had endeavored to convince them that their sons, husbands, and brothers had not died in vain. Rivka had sought out Shlomo's eyes, which were nailed to the ground. At the end of the ceremony, some soldiers on leave had offered the relatives their condolences. For Rivka, this had been the only part she considered worthwhile. The three young men had pale, gaunt faces. In their gazes, apart from the painful memories, apart from the awkwardness of intimacy with complete strangers, apart from the difficulty of finding something to say that didn't ring false, she could see the guilt, the shame that they were the ones who were there, breathing, treading on the grass that grew beside the graves. Rivka had embraced them one by one and whispered her sincere gratitude in their ears. No one had forced them to come, to waste even a few hours of their precious leave in mourning others. Their generosity had moved her and given her comfort. Shlomo, on the other hand, had turned away from them and gone to stand under one of the palm trees between the gravestones. Leaning on the low, white brick wall that ran around the cemetery, Rivka had glimpsed the ungainly shape of Sara Mandelbaum. They had greeted one another with a nod, but Rivka had immediately turned her head. The woman made her uncomfortable. She had never gotten used to her restless gaze or her lopsided gait which, combined with her petite body, gave the impression of a broken doll. When she and Shlomo walked toward the exit, Rivka was relieved to see that Sara had already gone.

They walked slowly among the rationalist-style houses of Bat Galim, the neighborhood where the first groups of Jews who had emigrated from Europe in the 1920s had settled. As they walked past the central bus station, Rivka broke the silence.

"You promised you would stop."

Shlomo stared straight ahead.

"How do you know I was offered a mission?"

"I saw the envelope in your closet."

"Are you checking up on me? Are you afraid I have a mistress, like Mr. Goldfarb?" Shlomo chuckled.

"That would be preferable. You wouldn't risk getting yourself killed if you had an affair."

"I won't get killed."

"You are fifty-seven. You are old."

"Age doesn't matter. Eli was young and they killed him."

"And to honor the memory of our son you would like to get killed, too?" Rivka blurted out.

"We are at war. We must all accept risks."

"I'm sick of war."

"Tell that to the enemy."

They stopped at the traffic light. The light turned green and they crossed.

"When my parents came to Palestine," Rivka went on, "they weren't only looking for a country where they could live safely without persecution. They thought they would be building a more just society."

"The kibbutz was a good idea," Shlomo said. "Confidence in the future, solidarity, peace, labor. A great program. But a socialist utopia doesn't help us fight terrorists."

"Look around you." Rivka blurted. "This is a paranoid nation that knows only force. This was not the language of the Jews."

"We are not Jews, we are Israelis," Shlomo answered sarcastically.

"Well, Begin and his cronies built themselves a political career on the bones of six million dead Jews. Did you hear what he said the other day?"

"No, I didn't hear," Shlomo replied dryly. He was beginning to get fed up with the conversation.

"He said that when our soldiers stormed Arafat's headquarters, it was as if they had breached Hitler's bunker. What do you say to that?"

Shlomo did not answer.

"Hitler died thirty-seven years ago!"

"It's different for those who were not in Europe."

"Yes, I know, you've told me before. People were sunbathing on the beach in Tel Aviv while European Jews were being exterminated in the Lagers. But this is 1982." Rivka paused and added with a huff, "And our son died in Lebanon in 1982, not in a Nazi death camp."

Rivka began to cry softly, without sobbing. Tears simply streamed down her cheeks. A young couple turned to look at her. Shlomo pulled his wife to him and held her tightly in the strong arms that came from peasant stock.

"Don't go," whispered Rivka. "Did you open the envelope?"

"No."

Shlomo stroked her hair.

"The target is Lichtblau," he said. "They may have found him."

Rivka stiffened. She drew a deep breath, pulled away from her husband's embrace, and wiped away her tears.

"When are you leaving?"

"Tomorrow afternoon."

"We're going home. I have to pack your suitcase."

Rivka gently took Shlomo's hand, and the two of them walked into the salty air rising from the docks.

21

Soldau, East Prussia, Oct. 25, 1941

They had been made to line up and stand still in the camp courtyard under the lashings of an icy wind. After an interminable day spent shoveling clods of earth the wait was unbearable. And the roll call was not even halfway through. Shlomo was in the second row. In front of him was his thin, feeble father. Shlomo had told him in a whisper to try and resist but there had been no response. Since his wife had died, Baruch had become even more taciturn and absent. They had spent the little money they had left to bury Miriam in the ghetto cemetery. The following week the transfer order had come. The Reich needed farm workers, lots of farm workers. Even his father, a shadow of the man he had once been, now fit the bill. City dwellers also fit the bill. A few days earlier, Shlomo had been assigned to a team with a Czechoslovakian student who had clearly never touched a spade. In order to ensure the young gentleman did not accidentally dig him in the shins or have the whole team punished for his incompetence, Shlomo had given him some pointers on how to use the tool. The student had thanked him by offering him a piece of bread. What a chump. He still didn't understand how things worked in the Lager. But Shlomo was not that smart, either. Before they had arrived in Soldau, he had been under the illusion that life would be better than it had been in Łódź. Of course, they would have to work, but he and his father were used to working hard. And if the Krauts wanted them to work, they would have to feed them properly, wouldn't they? But when he had arrived at the camp, he had soon come to realize that the Germans did not care whether their slaves lived or died. The Kapo called his number and Shlomo answered. This may be because they had an endless supply of them: a countless rag-tag crowd of Jews, Gypsies, Poles, Russians, and Ukrainians. Rumor had it that in the Battle of Kiev alone, the Nazis had captured more than half a million Red Army soldiers.

All of a sudden, Baruch collapsed. He did not let out a groan or utter a word. He just slumped face down into the thick, squelchy mud of the yard. A Kapo ran to his side, a dealer from Königsberg. He aimed a kick at the prisoner's face and yelled at him to get up. Baruch let out a yelp like a dying animal, spat out a bloody tooth, but did not move. Shlomo stared at his father, incapacitated. He knew that if he did not intervene, the Kapo would end up killing him. But he also knew that if he did, he would be killed, too. The Kapo kicked him again, this time in the stomach. Baruch moaned feebly and tried unsuccessfully to prop himself up on his arms.

"Get up!" the Kapo yelled again.

All around him, the prisoners either looked down or into the distance, far beyond the barbed wire perimeter fence. Anyone observing the scene did so with detachment.

A second Kapo, a *Volksdeutscher* and a thief, came along. The two green triangles set about kicking and beating the prisoner all over. Head, kidneys, groin, belly. His mouth full of blood, the victim gasped in the mud.

Shlomo was about to throw himself at the Kapo but the man on his right caught his arm. His grip was firm and strong. Shlomo turned towards the tall, broad-shouldered man. He was a political prisoner, a communist, a taciturn miner who had fought in Spain. He radiated resolve even in the grotesque Lager uniform. He puffed out his chest, as proud of the red triangle sewn on his chest as if Comrade Stalin himself had pinned the decoration on him. Even the Kapo respected him. He knew that he could kill him, but not bend his will.

"Stand still," he whispered to Shlomo.

"That is my father," Shlomo stammered.

"I know," the red triangle answered.

An SS sergeant appeared on the scene. The two Kapos instantly stopped beating the prisoner and snapped to attention.

"He's a Polish Jew," the thief explained.

"He refuses to stand up," the dealer added. The Unterscharführer said nothing and drew his Luger from his holster.

"Don't look," the miner commanded.

Shlomo closed his eyes.

"You can't do anything for him now but one day you will avenge him."

"When?" asked Shlomo, feeling punch-drunk, as the tears squeezed their way out from under his eyelids and left streaks down his cheeks, soiled by the day's work in the fields.

The shot echoed through the yard.

A shudder ran through Shlomo.

"When?" he asked again.

"Rest assured, your time will come," the red triangle answered.

22

Tel Aviv, July 4, 1982

The airport was crowded. European tourists landing, Israeli tourists taking off, American Jews visiting relatives. The checks were meticulous, as always. Shlomo patiently stood in line for an interview with the security officer, a girl who couldn't have been more than twenty-five, her eyes as motionless as a reptile's, with a 9mm semiautomatic on her belt. The traveler in front of Shlomo was French. When his turn came, he handed his passport to the officer with a friendly smile which she took pains not to reciprocate.

"Where have you been?" the girl asked, carefully examining the man's document.

"In Eilat," the Frenchman said.

"And where are you traveling to now?" she insisted. Her French was excellent, with virtually no accent.

"To Egypt."

The policewoman frowned. For more than two years, Israel had resumed normal diplomatic relations with Egypt, but it was nevertheless an Arab country.

"What is your reason for traveling there?"

"Diving."

"You can't dive in Israel?"

"I did, in Eilat, for a week."

"And that wasn't enough for you? Why not go home?"

The traveler was shocked. "I would like to try diving in Egypt, too," he stammered.

The girl looked at the man over his passport. "Why?" she asked with a completely deadpan expression.

The Frenchman was increasingly stunned. Not even in

Eastern European countries had he ever been treated that way. "I'm a photojournalist. I'm doing a piece on the bed of the Red Sea for *National Geographic*."

The girl studied his face for a few moments in silence and returned his passport.

"Proceed with your check-in," she ordered.

The Frenchman hurried away and the policewoman signaled Shlomo to approach.

"Reason for traveling?"

"I'm visiting friends in London," Shlomo said, handing her his ID.

The policewoman scanned the pages of the passport. She was about to give it back when she was joined by another officer who whispered something in her ear. The female officer stiffened, dismayed that she had not realized the subject was sensitive, peered at Shlomo with her iguana eyes, and handed the passport to her colleague.

"Please follow the sergeant," she said to Shlomo.

The room was hot, the air conditioner off, possibly broken. Shlomo sat across from the officer from Shin Bet, who had introduced himself as Major Ya'akovi. A surname with a nice Hebrew ring to it. Shlomo smiled inwardly. The major's grandfather must have been called Yakovich and when he had arrived in Palestine, he had gotten rid of the Slavic suffix to erase all memory of the Diaspora. A new nation required new words. Shlomo still remembered with anguish the effort he had had to make to learn Hebrew, an archaic yet very young language prepared for the new Jews who were finally returning to Eretz Yisrael after centuries of exile. Many had made their name more Hebrew sounding, starting with the father of nation after whom the airport was named, David Ben Gurion, who had been born David Grün. Shlomo, however, had not even considered giving up his surname. It was the only thing he had left of his family.

A bored-looking official entered the room, flicked through the files in a large metal cabinet and came out with a dossier under his arm. Even though he had married a *sabra*, a Jew born in Palestine, and had spent most of his life in Israel, Shlomo still felt like an immigrant. He spoke Hebrew, but his dreams—the rare times he remembered them—were always in Yiddish.

The major proffered a pack of Philip Morris. Shlomo took a cigarette, tore off the filter, and let the man light it for him. After the bad cop, now was the good cop's turn.

"Thank you," Shlomo Libowitz said.

He inhaled deeply and relaxed in his chair. He had picked up the habit in the Łódź ghetto, where cigarettes were almost impossible to find, to the extent that even chain smokers had had to resign themselves to quitting. Shlomo had started as a sign of defiance, not because he liked it. He fiddled with the handle of the suitcase on the ground beside him with his left hand. Rivka had packed mostly summer clothes but had thrown in a few heavier items. For the time being, the trail led to England. But what would follow was still a mystery. He could end up on an atoll in the South Seas or on a peak in the Bavarian Alps. The sergeant who had accompanied him had carefully inspected his suitcase, but had she found nothing. There was nothing to be found. The two extra passports, one Polish and one American, would be handed over in London. As for weapons, he would have to procure them locally when the time came.

The major had also lit a cigarette. "Aren't you tired of your private war?" he asked in a neutral tone.

Shlomo inhaled again and decided there was no point in wasting time denying anything. Major Ya'akovi looked intelligent. He must have been about Eli's age.

"It is your war, too. You are a Jew, aren't you?"

The major stared at him in silence. He blew the smoke out of his mouth.

"Your activities might have been acceptable in the fifties, but not any longer."

"Who says?"

"The government of Israel," the major replied. He paused to find the right words. He wanted to be clear but not offensive. Men like Shlomo Libowitz inspired respect in him. "There are different priorities now. We have made peace with the Germans."

"Oh, we have, have we?" Shlomo asked with a sour smile on his lips. "We have made peace with the Germans. Good. Then how come we can't make peace with the Palestinians? It's not like they put us in the gas chambers."

The young Israeli intelligence officer and the old Polish Jew eyeballed one another.

"I didn't bring you in here to discuss politics. I just need to convey a message to you," the young officer said.

"And what is the message?" the old man replied, putting his cigarette out in the ashtray on the desk.

"That you need to stop." Men like Shlomo Libowitz inspired respect in him, but they were also a terrible nuisance. For over thirty years, his group of no more than fifty people, all of them death camp survivors, had been hunting former Nazis. They were financed by a couple of wealthy and eccentric American Jews who, instead of spending their money on women or on founding a charity, sought the satisfaction of making the Krauts pay. The venture was comprehensible on a human level but ultimately sentimental, and they had caused some unpleasant diplomatic incidents. "Your motives are noble," the major went on, "but the fact remains that you go around the world killing foreign citizens."

"Something the government of Israel would never do," Shlomo quipped sarcastically.

"There is a big difference between the government of Israel and a gang of crazy old fools," Ya'akovi exclaimed.

"Begin is ten years older than me," retorted Shlomo, "and as for madness . . . "

The major crushed the remains of his cigarette in the ashtray.

He handed Shlomo his passport. "I'm warning you. If you get caught, don't count on our help. No Israeli official is going to waste five minutes of their time trying to get you or any of your friends out of a Bolivian prison."

Shlomo took his passport, slipped it into the pocket of his desert jacket, and got up

"My friends and I have been to places that would make a Bolivian prison feel like the Grand Hotel."

23

Soldau, East Prussia, Oct. 25, 1941

I'll come," Anton called out.

The other prisoners cast a glance in his direction, some eyes curious, most of them listless. The man to his left, from whom Anton had unsuccessfully sought advice on whether to volunteer for the new Kommando, gave him a sideways look, filled with condescension. If he thought he was going to save himself by acting as an accountant for some SS project, he was deluded. He would be made to count the dead until the last name he would write in the register would be his own. The man scratched the back of his neck angrily. The lice were driving him crazy. At one time he, too, had harbored hopes and plans for the future. He had been a theater critic for a prestigious newspaper, a respected man with friends, a beautiful home, an elegant wife, and several mistresses. He had lived in a world full of beauty which had suddenly dissolved, like a dream that vanishes upon waking. With great determination, the man had forced that dream out of his mind. For him, the only possible reality was the Lager. Yet every day Shlomo came across people who persisted in their dreams, people who organized, talked about escape, planned boycotts, stubbornly insisted on keeping their faith. A multitude of Catholic priests and rabbis, communists and Social Democrats, Bund militants and Zionists. The Zionists felt like the most deluded of all. They thought the answer was to go and live in the desert. Couldn't they see that they were already in the desert?

Major Lichtblau yanked his neck towards the prisoner who had spoken. "Come forward," he said.

Anton stepped out of the ranks, stood to attention in front

of the officer, doffed his cap, and recited his matriculation number.

"Where are you from?" asked Lichtblau.

"Prague."

"What did you do before the war?"

"I studied medicine."

"What was your name?"

"Anton Epstein."

Lichtblau looked him over carefully. He looked healthy, almost athletic, and his German was impeccable. An assimilated Jew of bourgeois extraction, by far the most dangerous. A boy who could pass for an Aryan and impregnate some poor man's daughter, giving him half-breed grandchildren without even knowing it. But Dr. Lichtblau needed a reliable secretary. There would be time to stop young Epstein from corrupting the Nordic blood.

"All right," Lichtblau said. "Go over there with the others," he added, pointing to a clutch of half a dozen prisoners gathered in the middle of the yard. "I need two or three more," he added, addressing the camp commander.

Shlomo stared at the big crimson stain that stood out against the gray ground. A little farther on, he could see the first furrows in the mud made by his father's clogs as the two Kapos had dragged his body away. The tracks zig-zagged towards the barracks. They were probably already stripping him. His uniform and shoes would be handed over to another prisoner. The corpse would be dumped in a mass grave somewhere in the woods.

The miner standing next to him who had served in the Spanish Civil War watched him nervously. Experience had taught him to judge men. The boy was good-natured, but impulsive. The Party would know how to make a disciplined militant out of him, but there was no time. Any day now, the hothead might try to kill one of the two Kapos, or perhaps even the Unterscharführer who had finished off his father, and that would spell his end.

"Volunteer," he whispered to Shlomo.

Shlomo lifted his gaze from the ground and stared at his neighbor with vacant eyes. "What?"

"Volunteer," the miner replied. "They are looking for country people. This is a good opportunity for you. It can't be worse than here." With his calloused hands, he wiped Shlomo's tear-streaked cheeks as best he could.

Shlomo let him do it. He was grateful. For a moment, the contact with the man's big fingers reminded him of his childhood and his grandfather's rough caresses. "Why don't you come too?" Shlomo asked in a hushed voice.

"I am not a farm worker. Besides, I have things to do here."

Shlomo knew that the miner was a member of the camp's communist cell. He did not share his ideology but he admired their determination as fighters. If they decided to rise up against the Nazis, he would join them.

"Anyone?" the red triangle urged the prisoners.

Shlomo raised his hand.

Lichtblau scrutinized the boy. He had a strong constitution, even though he was underweight. "What can you do?" he asked.

"I'm a farmer."

The SS major nodded and gestured to him to join the other Kommando members.

The living room of the camp commandant's apartment was more comfortable than he could ever have expected. There was a stand-up piano with a metronome and open sheet music on the music stand. A large ceramic stove gave off a pleasant warmth. Two Frau armchairs and a leather sofa were arranged around a coffee table with gently curved Jugendstil legs. On one wall hung an oil painting depicting an alpine landscape. A few family photographs in heavy silver frames were nicely lined up on a mahogany dresser whose floral inlays echoed the curves of the coffee table. A rug with a geometrical maze design lay on the somewhat worn parquet floor.

Major Lichtblau sat in one of the armchairs, facing the commander and his wife, who occupied the sofa. He took a sip of brandy.

"It's very cozy here," he said, looking around in admiration.

The commander's wife was flattered and explained that she had worked hard to make the dingy quarters hospitable. She had brought all the furniture from Germany because nothing in Soldau was suitable. Her husband nodded along proudly. While reviewing the prisoners, Lichtblau had thought the camp commander was a mediocre individual, but now he realized he had one quality, at least. The short, plump little man had managed to marry a capable, relatively pleasant woman, with whom he had had three children. Lichtblau had caught a glimpse of the children playing with a German shepherd in the front yard. In this, the dull functionary had outsmarted him. *Sturmbannführer* Hans Lichtblau was still a bachelor at the age of thirty-two. If he wanted a career in the SS, he should marry quickly and produce a couple of future soldiers for the Reich.

"Have one of these. They're delicious," said the woman, handing the major a plate laden with small savory croissants, some stuffed with salmon, butter, and dill, others with smoked ham and horseradish sauce. "Our maid makes them."

Lichtblau accepted the offer. "Delicious," he agreed after the first bite.

The couple smiled smugly.

"Did you bring her from Germany, too?" the major asked.

"No. She's a girl from the camp," replied the wife. "A Jehovah's Witness," her husband clarified.

"She's very efficient; spic and span," the wife spoke again. "A far cry from the Polish girls. To begin with, I changed three maids in two weeks. Then we were lucky to find Klara."

"And you wouldn't happen to have another Jehovah's Witness, would you?" Lichtblau asked with a half-smile.

The selection had been successful. One secretary and ten manual workers. He didn't need anything else for the laboratory and greenhouses. But if he managed to add a few domestics, he wouldn't have to rely on the baron's servants. He couldn't trust any of them, especially the butler. The man had been with the old aristocrat for too long. He was one of those people who didn't want to accept that things had changed dramatically in Germany.

"I don't think so, unfortunately," the camp commander seemed disappointed to say. "However, I can check in the women's section to see if I can find someone that suits you."

"What are you looking for, exactly?" his wife asked solicitously. Before their little refreshment, her husband had whispered in her ear that the Sturmbannführer was carrying credentials signed by Himmler himself.

"A cook and a cleaning woman who could do the washing would be enough," Lichtblau said.

"I assure you that I will do whatever I can to find elements that are up to standard," the commander's wife replied. "Even if I have to explain the basics to some Lithuanian servant girl."

"My wife was a schoolteacher before we got married. Teaching is in her blood," the camp commander chuckled.

The couple exchanged a complicit glance.

Lichtblau couldn't help but feel a vague envy for their domestic bliss. At the same time, however, it was deeply foreign to him. Sturmbannführer Dr. Hans Lichtblau was devoted to science. That was how he would serve the Führer.

24

Hamburg, July 5, 1982

What had struck her most, even more than the opulence of the goods that were almost obscenely displayed in the string of store windows lining the sidewalks, were the colors. The country she came from was black and white compared to this. As she strolled through the streets and squares of that foreign city, Natalya's Muscovite eyes had been filled with extraordinary bursts of color. The billboards. The store signs. The automobiles. People's clothes. Even the street signs. But when they had gone into the department store, Natalya Yakovchenko had been struck dumb, like a little girl who had popped into Santa Claus's toy factory. It was not a matter of quantity. GUM stores were big. In fact, they were definitely bigger than this. But the variety and quality of the goods available in the west were completely unknown to citizens of the Soviet Union, even to those who, like Natalya, enjoyed certain privileges as apparatchiki. It was one thing to snap up a pair of blue jeans imported from France. It was quite another to be able to choose from twenty different brands.

Natalya turned to Anton and saw that he was watching her. He had probably sensed her enthusiasm and was probably laughing at her. The KGB agent tried to pull herself together. The Czech, on the other hand, looked perfectly at ease. Natalya had read his dossier and knew that Epstein came from a bourgeois family. All that capitalist ostentation must have reminded him of his childhood.

"I'm going to the men's department," Anton said.

Natalya nodded. "Don't overdo it," she warned him. They were allowed to buy new clothes, but their expense account was not unlimited. These were the typical things that would be contested when you got back if they wanted to check up on you.

She picked out a few skirts, blouses, and jackets with extraordinarily wide shoulders, and slipped into a dressing room. She tried on the clothes. Locked in there without anyone seeing her, she quivered with joy. She knew full well that it was just a childish infatuation with western decadence, but the fabrics were so soft, the cuts so elegantly exotic, and the choice so vast that she could not contain herself. The second time she came out of the dressing room, a nice looking young, freckle-faced, red-headed saleswoman offered to help her choose. The customer clearly wanted an entire makeover of her wardrobe and she needed all the help she could get. Natalya let her do her job.

Within an hour she had selected everything she needed, except shoes. That was another matter. There was an entire floor devoted to footwear. Sandals, loafers, boots, Oxfords, Natalya was almost dizzy but she had learned how to move with a certain ease. She pointed determinedly toward a label with an inviting Italian name.

Agent Natalya Yakovchenko was wearing an aqua-green cotton dress with a yellow and white pattern, pulled in a little at the waist and reaching just above her knee. The freckled girl had told her that the dress looked good on her. And it did. It discreetly emphasized her curves. Natalya strode up and down the rectangular carpet of the Italian-brand store, dubiously checking in the mirror the pumps she had just slipped into. Next to the stool were two boxes containing the models she had already chosen: a pair of fuchsia ballet flats and black leather boots. She didn't really need the shoes she was trying on. And they were totally unsuitable for running. Even a decrepit old Nazi could catch up with her if she walked around in those things. But she liked them. She had seen them on many women's feet on the street.

"They look a little wide to me," Natalya said.

"If you want, we can try a size down," the saleswoman proposed.

Natalya took a few more steps. "Maybe." Part of her hoped they were out of the next size down.

The saleswoman disappeared into the back room.

Officer Yakovchenko looked up and noticed that Anton Epstein was standing in the doorway. He was wearing a to-bacco-colored linen suit that fit him like a glove. The white shirt and blue Kashmir-patterned tie he had on matched the handkerchief tucked in his breast pocket. He was impeccable. Dapper. And he looked younger than the sixty-one years the dossier said his age was.

They stared at one other, both amazed at the palingenetic effect produced by the new clothes.

The saleswoman returned. "Here you go," she said, handing the package to the customer.

Natalya sat on the stool. And as she slipped off her shoes, she felt Anton's eyes on her. She turned her head sharply. The professor looked away.

She had not minded it, actually. Anton Epstein was old enough to be her father, as well as being a deviationist, but in his own way he was an interesting man. That morning at the hotel breakfast, she had taken out a cigarette and he had hur-ried to light it for her. He had made the move without any os-tentation, as if it were perfectly natural. They were bourgeois rituals to which Natalya had not been accustomed. They could be pleasant, as long as they were not exaggerated.

Size thirty-eight fit perfectly. She was on the verge of tak-ing them, but in the end a sense of duty prevailed. She took the shoes off again. "I need to think about these," she told the saleswoman. "Give me the bill for the others."

Natalya looked at her watch. It was almost noon. They had already wasted too much time. The flight to London was leav-ing at four o'clock.

25

Neuhof, West Prussia, Oct. 26, 1941

After the selection, the eleven members of the new Kommando—christened Gardenia by a particularly facetious Kapo, a con man from Vienna sent to Soldau for swindling old ladies with false treasury bonds—had been sent back to their respective barracks. They had spent the night in the Lager, and shortly after dawn, as the other prisoners were lined up for roll call, they were loaded onto a truck and transported to their next place of detention.

As the members of the Gardenia Kommando climbed into the gray Opel Blitz with the SS insignia, the miner who had fought in Spain hoped he had acted in the boy's best interests. He knew for sure that he had stopped him from doing something really stupid. Anyway, if the doctor needed specialized staff, presumably he would make sure they stayed alive. But the red triangle prisoner could not be sure of this. He had been in the camp for a year, and he had learned from experience that the Nazis' actions were often completely illogical.

Before departure, the men in the new Kommando had been stripped of all their possessions, except for their striped pajamas and clogs. They had been forced to leave behind their billycans, cutlery, and the few other everyday items that they had managed over time either to manufacture or procure by barter or theft. Several had complained, but the Kapos had been adamant. You leave the Lager as naked as when you came out of your mother's belly, the Viennese swindler had sneered. Besides, there was no need to worry. They were going to work in a castle. Over there, they would be eating with silver forks on gold-leaved porcelain plates, he had continued, eliciting chuckles from his mates: a pimp from Dresden and a multiple murderer from Thuringia, who had killed a family of four just to steal a few marks, and who was doing quite well for himself in Soldau, beating Reds, Jews, and queers all day long.

The only ones who had not made a fuss were Shlomo and Anton because they hadn't been at the camp for long and had not yet accumulated any pathetic little treasures. The day before, when they had been taken into the Kommando, Anton had greeted the shtetl boy warmly.

"Don't you remember? The other day you taught me how to use a spade," Anton had prodded, happy to see at least one familiar face in the group.

Shlomo had replied with a simple shrug, which had bewildered Anton at the time. Then someone had whispered to him that the man who had been killed during roll call was his father.

For Shlomo, leaving the place where his father had been beaten to death had been a relief. He was grateful to the red triangle, and he wished him good luck. As soon as he had climbed into the Opel Blitz, he had curled up on the floor, pulled his cap down over his eyes, and tried to get some sleep. He had no idea what awaited him. Best not waste the chance to get some rest. The others followed suit. Lulled by the rolling of the truck, all the members of the Gardenia Kommando had fallen asleep, leaning against each other. They woke up when the truck came to a halt and the late morning light was filtering through the tarp.

One of them dared to peel back a flap to take a peek outside.

"It's a village," he whispered.

Major Lichtblau opened the door of the *Kübelwagen*, stuck one leg out, and stretched in his seat. His back was killing him. The room at the Soldau inn where he had spent the night was appalling, the mattress was just a sack stuffed with uncarded wool. Not to mention the foul-smelling Turkish toilet encrusted with yellow and brown stains which, to add insult to injury, he had had to share with a traveling salesman in his early fifties from Freiburg. The man knew the area well and had assured him it was the best hotel in town. He was a little too talkative, perhaps, but not too obnoxious. A Great War fighter, Party member since 1928, he had one son in the Luftwaffe and another in the army, both on the Eastern Front. He had pulled photographs out of his wallet. Great-looking boys. At the end of the meal, after a couple of rounds of vodka, the salesman had convinced him to go to a nightclub. At first Lichtblau had been reluctant. The hotels and restaurants in Soldau were already so filthy, God forbid the brothels. Surprisingly, the whores had turned out to be the cleanest thing around. But instead of spending the night there, he had gone back to the inn and tossed and turned on that rustic mattress until dawn. He had risen exhausted and woken up his guards, who went straight to the camp to pick up the Kommando. It was not far from Soldau to the castle but they would have to make a detour. Lichtblau planned to go to Neuhof to recruit a glazier for his greenhouses. He had gotten hold of a carpenter in the camp, but there was no one who could work with glass and he didn't trust the Poles. The camp commander had informed him that there were good German craftsmen in Neuhof. "Not real Germans," he had specified, "*Volksdeutschen*." The major had avoided pointing out to his kind host that he was not a "real" German either. Having been born outside the borders of the Reich, Lichtblau was technically a *Volksdeutscher,* too.

The driver had parked in what appeared to be the main square of the village. There was a church, a town hall, a post office, and a general store. The *Sturmbannführer* yawned and got out of the car. The truck was stationary behind the car. And behind the truck, there was a second *Kübelwagen* with guards on board. The major strode toward the store. It was already open. He pushed open the door and the bell above the door-frame tinkled cheerfully.

"Good morning," he said, addressing the girl behind the counter, a lanky blonde with a rather dull expression.

"Good morning," Hilde replied.

"Would you happen to know whether there is a glazier here in town?"

The girl stared at him, frozen.

"A glazier? I don't . . . know," she stammered. "You'd better ask the mistress." And she signaled for him to follow her. The salesgirl led him into the back. They went into the apartment adjoining the emporium through a freshly repainted wooden door. The house smelled of laundry soap and blackberry pie. They arrived in the kitchen, and the girl opened the door that gave onto the courtyard. Beyond the threshold stood a large oak tree framed by yellow-brown leaves. Next to the tree, a woman was splitting wood.

Lichtblau imagined she was about his age. Pronounced Nordic features. Wide, firm breasts. Pleasantly wide hips. When she saw him, she lowered her axe and with a sharp blow sunk the blade into the chopping block. The disheveled hair, the axe, the stance of a pioneer race. Hans felt like he was looking at a heroine of the Wild West that had populated the games and dreams of his childhood. There, in a courtyard in the heart of old Europe, a few miles from the Vistula, one of those peasant warriors who had contributed to conquering the New World and shaping the destiny of a nation had materialized before his eyes. Women who gave birth on wagons traveling across prairies, felled trees, built houses, and fought Native Americans alongside their men. Like the Americans in the nineteenth century, the Germans had a frontier that was moving to the east. A border that was being pushed forward relentlessly by rifle and plow, a bloodline that separated civilization from the wilderness, inhabited by primitive and ferocious people who needed subjugating.

Martha wiped the sweat from her forehead with the back of her hand, straightened her hair with a few quick gestures, and went to greet the stranger. As she went into the kitchen, she saw immediately that he was handsome. The black uniform suited him perfectly and the scar across his right eyebrow, together with the cap worn arrogantly askew, was thrillingly daring. Martha had been a widow for five years and had never been with any man but her husband. To begin with, out of respect for the memory of poor Rolf and later, simply because she had never had the time or the opportunity. She was too busy raising her children and taking care of the house and the store to flirt. And anyway, who was she to flirt with? The young men had almost all been conscripted. Only the old men and those unfit for service were left in the village and she wasn't about to settle for any of them. But perhaps things were about to change.

Hans gave a hint of a Nazi salute with a gentle twist of the wrist. He did not want to look like one of those fools drunk with ideology. After all, he was an officer introducing himself to a lady.

"Major Hans Lichtblau, at your service," he said, snapping his heels.

"Martha Kernig, most honored," she replied, with a flirtatious curtsey.

Hans doffed his cap and tucked it under his left arm. There were tiny wrinkles in the corners of the woman's eyes, giving her honest, radiant face a veil of sadness and making it more interesting. In her gaze, Hans saw the strength and loyalty of a generation of settlers as well as the signs of daily toil, and perhaps the shadow of grief.

"What can I do for you, major?"

"A glazier. Your salesgirl told me to ask you," Lichtblau replied, indicating Hilde, who was standing behind him and straining to understand what was going on. She was a provincial girl with little experience of the world, especially as far as relationships between men and women were concerned, and yet she had the impression that the two of them were not talking about glass at all.

"Of course," said Martha, cheerfully. "Mr. Meier. If you don't mind waiting a moment, I'll gladly accompany you."

She took off her apron, threw it on a chair, and vanished upstairs. "Offer the major something to drink," she shouted to the girl on her way up.

"Would you like some coffee?" Hilde asked awkwardly.

"Don't worry, thank you."

Hans looked around. Under the table, he noticed a toy tank, a pretty good replica of a Panzer III. Mrs. Kernig had children. And she was wearing a wedding ring. And yet Hans had seen no trace of a male presence in the house. There were only women's coats and hats on the hooks in the hallway. Perhaps her husband was at the front. Hans felt churlish. To even think of bedding the wife of a soldier who was fighting for his country was unchivalrous.

Martha reappeared in the kitchen. She had combed her hair and changed into a blue and white-checked dress which suited her Baltic blue eyes and snow-white skin. Hans noticed that she was now wearing an amber gemstone set in a silver band on her ring finger. He wondered if he had been mistaken. Perhaps the stone had been turned inward and he had assumed her ring was a wedding band. But what kind of woman splits wood with a piece of jewelry on her finger?

"Shall we go?" Martha said amiably. "You mind the store," she added, addressing Hilde.

The girl nodded without uttering a word. She may be a poor provincial girl with little or no experience of the world, but she had noticed that the mistress had taken off her wedding ring. It was the first time she had seen her do so since the day she met her.

The glazier was only a few blocks from the emporium. Hans would have found him even without Martha's help. The craftsman was an old man with a thick white beard yellowed by tobacco around his lips, which clenched a carved Meerschaum pipe. He had been born on the island of Öselz, off the Estonian coast. He was very keen on the major's proposal. It was a large order for his humble workshop. Mr. Meier offered to accompany the Sturmbannführer to the castle straight away so that he could take measurements and start planning. If Herr Major would kindly return on Wednesday, he would submit his drawings to him then. The major replied that he would return to Neuhof with great pleasure. As he spoke, he shifted his gaze to Martha. For a moment, he feared he had been brash, but the woman held his gaze and did not look at all resentful. In fact, on their way back to the store, she said that if it did not interfere with his duties, he could stop by her house on Wednesday for a bite. She and Hilde would give him a taste of some of their Baltic specialties.

"With great pleasure," the major replied, kissing her on the hand with impeccable politeness.

Hans Lichtblau was in high spirits. The pain in his back had disappeared. Life was smiling on him. He had a prestigious assignment and the appropriate means to complete it. Once the greenhouses were built, the project would finally enter its operational phase. And he had even got himself a date.

"Wake up, corporal, wake up!" he shouted in a jocular fashion at the driver, who was catnapping at the wheel of the *Kübelwagen*. The man instantly pulled himself together and turned the key in the ignition. The engine responded. Lichtblau got into the car and the small convoy got moving.

They picked up Mr. Meier, who was waiting for them on his doorstep with a leather briefcase in his hand that contained everything he needed to survey the land and jot down the measurements of the greenhouses he was to build. The old man climbed into the back of Lichtblau's car. His eyes gleamed with this unexpected good fortune.

In the cargo compartment of the truck, Shlomo and most of the other members of the Gardenia Kommando had gone back to sleep. Anton and a gardener from Warsaw were watching the landscape through the cracks in the oilskin. A peasant from the countryside around Białystok triumphantly pulled a cigarette and a match from a fold in his pajamas, masterfully concealed from Kapo inspection, and started smoking with gusto.

As they left the village, they passed a column of Polish civilians walking on the side of the road, escorted by three bored-looking *Ordnungspolizei* guards. Some of them were pulling carts piled high with household goods, on top of which sat bewildered-looking children. Everyone, including the elderly and two pregnant women, was carrying bundles and suitcases. Lichtblau surmised that they were Neuhof residents who were being transferred to the General Government. They walked in the dust with their heads down like conquered Sioux being marched to the reservation.

26

Guanacaste Province, northern Costa Rica, July 6, 1982

The Douglas C-47 sitting on the runway—a strip of land between the beach and the bush—was almost forty years old but still perfectly capable of flying. While the twin-engine aircraft was being refueled, the pilot dozed under a palm tree in the cool breeze blowing in from the sea. He was a Corsican who had served in the French Air Force parachuting ammunition crates over Dien Bien Phu under Vietnamese anti-aircraft fire. He had taken off from Colombia at dawn. The small, rough-and-ready airport had been set up by the Contras, the guerrillas fighting the Sandinistas, who had risen to power in Nicaragua three years earlier by overthrowing a dictatorship that was even older than the C-47. The founder of the dynasty, Anastasio Somoza García, had become president in 1936 with the support of the United States. He had been succeeded by his eldest son and then by his youngest. Opposition had been gradually growing in the country. When it looked like they were doomed, the Somoza family had been abandoned by their powerful Northern allies. President Carter had decided that human rights violations by the National Guard might tarnish the image of the White House. By November 1980, however, the Democratic Party had lost the elections. Carter's successor, Ronald Reagan, had adopted a new communications strategy. The Somozistas, who had fled Nicaragua and were attempting to reorganize across the border, were not a bunch of murderers and torturers. They were free-dom fighters. The CIA had begun supplying them with instruc-tors and weapons, attempting to discourage rivalries among the different groups and create a functioning military structure. But guerrilla warfare is a costly activity. There was plenty of money flowing in from Washington and from the Vatican, thanks to Monsignor Marcinkus, but it was never enough. The Contras had accordingly gone into business with the Cali cartel, the biggest drug producers in the Americas. The C-47 was carrying a load of freebase for the Los Angeles market. The product was brand new: a crude variant of cocaine that could be smoked. Cheap stuff that could do your head in. Stuff that was good for the Blacks down in South Central, who had soon begun to call it 'crack' because of the crackling sound the crystals make when heated. The CIA and President Reagan turned a blind eye. The Contras were a bulwark against the spread of communism and the Blacks in South Central, when they remembered to do so, invariably voted for the Democrats.

The Corsican pilot got up, stretched, and brushed off the sand that had gotten under his shirt while he had been resting. He searched for his co-pilot, an American from San Diego obsessed with getting a tan. He saw him lying on the beach, shirtless, Ray-Bans covering his eyes. He yelled that it was time to go. The co-pilot got up without answering, dazed by the sun. He ran his hand through his hair, took his sunglasses off, and went to rinse his face in the sink behind the tool shed.

The pilot picked up the cup of coffee they had offered him upon landing and took the last sip, now cold. There was also a knife and fork and a tin plate that had contained a generous portion of *huevos motuleños*. Scrambled eggs, black beans, cheese, and hot sauce on a bed of tortillas. It was not haute cuisine but he had eaten it all with pleasure. He lit up a *Gitanes Maïs*. Compared to Indochina and Algeria, this was a pretty cushy job. They carried drugs to California and came back to Costa Rica with an assortment of hand grenades, rifles, machine guns, and plastic explosives. This was the fifth trip and there had never been a hitch. He congratulated himself on retiring from *l'Armée de l'air* and embarking on a freelance career. He stubbed his cigarette out in the sand and in no hurry at all strolled over towards the plane.

"*Tous bien*," the Quebec mechanic told him. With his assistant, a Nicaraguan with a head-waiter's mustache, they made up the airport's entire ground staff. The *Québécois* was always keen to speak with the pilot in what he considered their common language, without appreciating that the Corsican did not harbor the same enthusiasm for French.

The pilot thanked the mechanic with a nod and climbed aboard. A few minutes later, the co-pilot joined him in the cabin. The C-47's engines fired up, spitting clouds of white smoke into the air, and the propellers began to turn.

Lounging on two deck chairs in front of a bungalow a few feet from the sea, Sheldon Morris and Nelson Parker watched the transport plane glide down the runway without much interest. They were wearing garish Hawaiian shirts and smoking cheap local cigars. From the trees behind them they could hear the occasional echo of shots fired in the camouflaged jungle firing range. A group of guerrillas was practicing under the direction of a former Green Beret that Morris and Parker had hired in a hurry, alongside other former members of the US Special Forces, after the Argentine military advisers initially responsible for training the Contras had been recalled after the outbreak of the Falklands War. A second team was on patrol. The Sandinistas occasionally made forays across the border.

"Who did it? The Cubans?" Parker asked, with the typical anxiety of a rookie addressing a veteran. He had only been with the Agency a few months and deeply admired his older colleague, who had an operative since the late 1950s.

"I don't think that's their style," Morris replied dryly.

"The Jews?"

"No, they know how to get these things done. I'd say it was the Colombians."

"But didn't they have an agreement?"

"Sure, but he went against it. He increased production and invaded the market."

"So, it was the Narcos who got the newspapers involved?" Parker insisted.

"For sure. They couldn't eliminate him, but they did manage to blow his cover. Maybe they won't even need to try again. There could easily be a sniffer dog chasing him down."

"And what do we do?"

"Nothing."

"Do we dump him?"

"No, because we never took him on board. The Agency will deny in no uncertain terms ever having had any dealings with Huberman."

Parker's cigar had gone out. The younger man pulled out a lighter and lit it for him again.

"For the moment, though, he's managed to disappear without a trace," he said.

"He must be holed up in his famous hideout."

"Have you ever seen it?"

Morris shook his head.

"Wallace has been there. He told me that Huberman lives in an ancient Spanish fortress and has a whole tribe of Indians serving him."

"But . . . "

The C-47 rolled all the way down the runway and lifted off the ground just in time to avoid crashing into the trees.

"What's he like?"

"Cold, methodical," Morris replied. "Although you wouldn't know it on the surface. He looks like a hippie." The CIA agent laughed raspingly, like the chain-smoker he was.

"In what way?"

"In the sense that he has a ponytail that goes practically down to his ass and he wears those San Francisco hippy shirts."

"And the Agency kept someone like that on their books?" Parker asked, appalled.

Morris arched his eyebrows. "I saw him interrogating prisoners in Chile in 1973. He's a wizard." He inhaled the *purito*, swilled the smoke around in his mouth, and blew it out. "There was this guy. A communist leader, a tough one. Pinochet's goons had been roughing him up for two days but got nothing, not a word. So, we sent for Huberman. He showed up carrying a traveling salesman's briefcase looking like a Summer of Love veteran. After a couple of hours, though, the commie had given him a list of all his contacts in town."

"And how did he do that?"

"Trade secret," Morris replied mysteriously. He let out another grating laugh. "I don't know. He had pills. He gave the prisoner one, and the guy started singing. Huberman said that it was a drug he had developed himself. But that it doesn't always work. It depends on the person. And you have to know how to ask the questions." He went back to smoking his cigar. "An interesting character," he concluded. Morris knew that Huberman had been recruited soon after Germany had surrendered, before the CIA even existed. The old Kraut must have seen quite a bit in his time.

The C-47 was slowly rising in altitude. There were more of these transport airplanes produced during World War II than any other model. The make had been cited by General Eisenhower, no less, as being among the technical achievements that had made the Allied victory possible, alongside the bazooka, the jeep, and the atomic bomb. By the end of the war, the C-47 had made up the backbone of the American airlift to bring supplies to West Berlin during the Russian blockade. By the time the Vietnam war had come around, that twin-engine propeller-driven aircraft designed in 1935 had been equipped with weapons and employed in ground-attack missions. And many civilian airlines around the world still were still using them. Throughout its long career, the Douglas C-47 had been through an amazing series of reincarnations. Much like Victor Huberman, or whatever his real name was, Morris mused.

27

East Prussia, December 13, 1941

The two greenhouses gleamed in the pale late-autumn sunlight like little glass dwellings left behind by woodland sprites. Inside the transparent hangars, Shlomo and the other members of the Gardenia Kommando were busy preparing the ground for planting while Anton sat at a small table and logged the quantities and species of plants delivered that morning, which some of the crew were already taking out of their pots. From the castle drive, Major Lichtblau gazed contentedly at the delicate glass structures that matched the moss-clad neoclassical statues that dotted the park around the von Lehndorff property so well. Mr. Meier had done a good job. It had taken him a little longer than expected, but the results had been excellent. Not to mention that having the greenhouses built had provided Hans with an excuse for regular visits to Neuhof. Things had gone faster and further than expected with Martha. On their first date, when he had shown up at her house with a bouquet of flowers and a bottle of Bordeaux from the baron's cellar, Hans had imagined a family lunch but was pleasantly surprised to find they would be having a tête-à-tête. Martha had sent her children away to play with friends and her salesgirl to Warsaw to pick up a batch of blouses. She had given him time to have a glass of wine and taste the bortsch in order to keep up appearances. After which, she had made the first move. Martha had to open the store in the afternoon. If it stayed closed too long, it might attract attention or even give rise to rumors. She had acted accordingly, without wasting time with outdated courtship rituals. A practical spirit, which Hans shared wholeheartedly. In keeping with the exceptional era in which they lived.

In the following weeks, the Sturmbannführer had paid numerous visits to the attractive widow. She had soon stopped worrying about the neighbors' gossip. Hans was an SS officer, after all. Who could doubt their relationship was anything but honest? Not least because what had begun as a wartime dalliance was quickly turning into a deeper bond. On the surface, the two had nothing in common. She was the owner of a small village store who had never strayed far from the shores of the Baltic and had been brought up in a modest family with simple tastes. Hans, on the other hand, had lived in big cities such as Chicago and Berlin, had been to university, and lived in a material and intellectual world whose outer limits she could never divine. To all intents and purposes, they were an unlikely couple. But there was one thing that united them. Both were descended from emigrants, and were trying, with great difficulty, to make their way in a homeland they had been introduced to as adults. Hans and Martha were ethnic Germans who had left the country of their birth and eagerly seized the opportunity the Führer had offered them. Lichtblau found himself thinking about the baron. A couple of days earlier, they had had another fencing match. There was no doubt the man was charismatic. A war hero, a fencing champion, intelligent, in his own way witty. Why had he chosen to side with the enemies of the Reich? The answer, in Hans's view was that he was from the previous generation and old money. National Socialism was a young movement of people from the lower classes. The von Lehndorffs had lived in Prussia since the Middle Ages, the history of their lineage was inextricably linked to that of the German state, and yet, two *Volksdeutschen* such as Hans and Martha had more of a claim to a place in the new Germany than the baron did.

"Herr Major," a voice behind him called.

Lichtblau turned around. It was Sergeant Dietrich.

"The bishop is here."

"Tell him I'm coming," Lichtblau replied dryly.

"Yes, sir."

The Unterscharführer turned on his heels and walked back toward the castle.

Lichtblau sighed, pulled out his cigarette case, and lit a Muratti with his father's gold lighter, one of the few family possessions that had survived the Great Depression. Bishop Keller. Shit. For days the old geezer had been asking him for an interview. Lichtblau had stalled but, in the end, he had been forced to agree to a meeting. Aktion T4, the plan to exterminate the incurably ill, had created a hornet's nest in religious circles. Lichtblau did not know the details, as these matters were highly confidential even within the SS, but he had a good idea of how things had unfolded. The operation had begun in the fall of 1939, in the utmost secrecy. At some point, however, the news had begun to circulate. Catholic and Protestant priests, as well as segments of their congregations, had mobilized against what they considered a serious violation of divine precepts. They were narrow-minded people, still clinging to the commandments that thousands of years earlier their god had bestowed on a Jew. The bigots may have believed the SS was committing murder, but they had actually been acts of mercy, liberating the poor devils from a wretched existence. Not to mention the fact that the country was at war and it was imperative to increase the number of beds in the hospitals for the wounded from the front. But the die-hards had persisted in their campaign and by the summer of 1941, it had been decided to shut down the program in order to prevent the issue from being used by enemy propaganda. Their victory had revitalized religious leaders. The bishop probably had some ethical grievance or other to air. Perhaps he had heard rumors about the experiments. Access to the wing of the castle where the laboratory was located had been strictly forbidden to all unauthorized personnel, and the prisoners were housed in two huts at the bottom of the garden behind a high barbed-wire fence, with two watchtowers and Alsatian guard dogs. Nevertheless, something may have leaked. The baron's servants could move around freely.

And he supposed von Lehndorff himself might have taken it upon himself to pry into matters that did not concern him. If so, Lichtblau would indict him and have him sent to Dachau, even if he was a war hero and fencing champion.

He took one last pull on his cigarette, threw away the butt, and walked back up the drive, hoping that National Socialism would soon wipe out the last traces of Judeo-Christian morality and finally men of science would be able to focus on their mission.

Half of the greenhouse was occupied by lush plants with broad white leaves and bright red veins. They were sensuous, exotic things. Everything, from the leaden sky weighing down on the glass roof to the dark gray stones of the keep, suggested that those plants were from another world, from the Hanging Gardens of Babylon, or the Palace of Kubla Khan.

"What are they?" Anton asked Moshe Goldwasser, who before the war had been one of Warsaw's most sought-after gardeners.

"I don't know. This is the first time I've ever seen them," he replied.

"According to the delivery note, their scientific name is *Caladium seguinum*."

Moshe took off his cap and ran a hand over his shaved skull. "Never heard of them," he said.

"What are the Nazis doing with it?" Anton asked again.

"I have no idea. Maybe a giant bouquet for the Führer." They laughed and then went back to gazing at the waxy white leaves, seduced by that evocative vision of distant bountiful lands.

"What about getting on?" someone grunted outside the greenhouse.

Moshe stopped looking at the plants. He caught sight of Shlomo Libowitz's ungainly, rustic shape outside.

"We have a truckload of manure to unload," Shlomo said.

Mr. Goldwasser, whose hands had tended the rose gardens

and hedges of counts, bankers, and a minister of the Interior, donned his cap and went to join his companion.

Monsignor Alois Keller's face was wrinkled all over, dark furrows formed over the years and deepened by the anxiety that had been growing within him recently. He couldn't stop thinking about it. He was plagued with anxiety about what had become of his country and about the final verdict that would weigh on all Germans eventually. There would be God's judgment, of course, but also that of a tribunal here on earth if Germany were to emerge from the war defeated. At the moment, it felt like an unlikely outcome, but the previous war had also opened with a series of spectacular victories. The current war was not only appalling in itself, but it also represented an opportunity for the Nazi regime to achieve its long-term goals. Goals which had been pursued by stealth and never explicitly stated, but which were perfectly visible if one cared to look. First there had been that monstrous euthanasia program and now, as the Eastern Front was opening, the torturers had shifted their attention to other victims. There were only snippets of information coming in but something horrific was happening in the East. In August, a massacre had been carried out near a Ukrainian town called Kamenets-Podolski. The firing squads were not made up of monsters. Normal people, fathers of families, law-abiding citizens had pulled the trigger. This was a state under whose law the commandment "thou shalt not kill" was being erased from people's hearts. Monsignor Keller had heard an account from the son of acquaintances, a lieutenant of the *Ordnungspolizei* on leave, who had come to him in an attempt to ease the burden of his conscience. The officer had been enlisted in the *Einsatzgruppen*; special units created to secure the rear as the Wehrmacht advanced. For the Nazis, "securing" meant rounding up and killing Jews, political commissars, partisans, and any civilians who posed a threat to German troops, however vague and hypothetical the threat might be. In Kamenets-Podolski, the massacre of 23,600 Jews had gone on for three days. The officer, his eyes swollen with tears, had confided that his men had mowed down entire families, from infants to old men unable to stand on their own feet. Many of the soldiers had only been able to carry out their orders after a good ration of aquavit. There was not only blood flowing around the pits the bodies fell into. There were also copious quantities of alcohol. Keller had found it hard to believe the lieutenant's story, but eventually he was convinced that he was neither lying nor exaggerating. There were probably many slaughters of the kind taking place throughout the Soviet Union. But why was the Holy See, which was certainly in possession of more detailed information, not intervening publicly to condemn National Socialism? Many inside and outside the Church were waiting for a clear message from the Pope. But so far, they had waited in vain.

Keller looked at his watch. The Sturmbannführer was running late. He cast a glance at his secretary, Witold Grabski, a young man fresh out of the seminary, sitting next to him.

"Be patient, Monsignor," Grabski whispered.

The bishop snorted. He had been far too patient. What's more, he knew that this visit was completely useless. He was here to demand an explanation from someone who would not provide him with any, and who might even report him to the Gestapo. Many Polish clergymen had vanished into the Lagers, including two bishops murdered in Soldau. Being German was not in itself a protection. But Keller was not worried about saving his body. He was more concerned about the salvation of his soul. In order to achieve this, it was his duty to at least attempt, as best he could, to oppose the dark shadow that had descended on Europe.

The major entered the room. The greetings were hurried. Lichtblau immediately sensed the bishop's hostility. A friend of the Jews. A hypocrite. The laws "for the defense of German blood and honorability" enacted in 1935, which had secured Germany from Jewish influence, were simply a modern version of the antisemitic regulations enshrined in canon law, rules that the Church had drafted as soon as Christianity had become the official religion of the Roman Empire. The priests had done something right, at least. But their faith was for the inferior races. it was a creed suited to slaves. Keller's young assistant, on the other hand, seemed more reasonable to him. He did not have the bishop's outright condemnation in his eyes.

"Monsignor, to what do I owe this visit?" Lichtblau asked roughly.

Keller took a deep breath. He felt like the child in that Dutch story who puts his finger in the hole in the dyke. But the hero of the story saves his village from flooding, while the bishop felt the icy water coming up to his neck.

"A woman from our congregation," the bishop began, "spoke to the parish priest here about something very distressing. And the priest reported it to me."

"Are you telling me that the priest violated the secrecy of the confessional?" Lichtblau interrupted with a malevolent smile.

"The woman talked to her priest in a normal conversation at the rectory," Keller retorted testily.

"And what ails the lady?" Lichtblau's tone was jocular, but he was actually beginning to feel uneasy. Priests, especially Catholic ones, would be sure to give him a hard time if a maid at the castle had discovered the nature of his experiments with *Caladium seguinum*. Forced sterilization was not something they would take lightly.

"The lady talked about seeing heads, three human heads, inside glass jars."

Lichtblau laughed out loud. This was a far less serious matter, but the fact remained that the baron's servants posed a problem.

"Of course, the heads. No reason to worry," the major said in a conciliatory tone.

"Really? You intend to open a museum in the castle where human specimens will be displayed and there is no reason to worry?" The bishop was dumbfounded and exasperated. His knuckles gripping the arms of the chair were white. The veins in his neck were swollen, his voice shrill. Grabski put a hand on his arm in an attempt to calm him.

"I can assure you," the Sturmbannführer said, "that no museum will be opened within the boundaries of your diocese, neither in this palace nor anywhere else in East Prussia."

The bishop appeared to regain control.

"The museum will be based in Alsace, more than a thousand kilometers from your worshippers," Lichtblau added.

A few days earlier, Professor August Hirt, director of the Anatomy Department at the University of Strasbourg and a colleague from the Ahnenerbe, had stopped at the castle on his way back from a research trip to Russia. The Ahnenerbe was working on setting up a museum of the Jewish race. A highlight of the exhibit would be a collection of skulls that Hirt was assembling. After dinner, his distinguished colleague had brought out the specimens he had collected during the expedition—three Asian heads preserved in formalin—and gone into great detail illustrating the physiognomic characteristics of the Jewish-Bolshevik. Mrs. Mertz, one of the maids, had come in to clear the table and at the sight of the heads lined up on the table, had started screeching like a harpy. Amused by the woman's reaction, Lichtblau and Hirt had joked that the castle would soon be turned into a museum and that she would be expected to dust the skeletons and skulls. Their innocent prank had had unexpected and disproportionate consequences, however. Lichtblau vowed to call the commander of the Soldau camp that very day and take him up on the offer of domestic staff. The baron's servants were to be kept away.

"It was just a joke," Lichtblau concluded. "Admittedly in bad taste, but nothing more."

The bishop stared at him, appalled. The museum project

actually existed. They were not going to set it up there in Prussia but it was going ahead anyway. They were planning to put human bodies on display, presumably the bodies of people who had been murdered, as if they were stuffed animals, trophies from the monumental hunting party that Hitler and his acolytes were engaged in. Alois Keller closed his eyes. He found he couldn't breathe.

Shlomo and Moshe had almost finished unloading the truck. The bags of manure were lined up tidily along the castle wall. Other members of the Kommando had started carrying them over to the greenhouses. The two prisoners pulled the last sack down and stopped to rest for a moment. Shlomo wiped the sweat off his face with the sleeve of his jacket. Compared to the Lager, even compared to the ghetto in Łódź, this felt like a vacation. The slop was better than in Soldau and the work was not much harder than it had been back home. The red triangle had done him a favor, for sure. He hoped he was still alive and organizing the uprising.

All of a sudden, a figure in black appeared from behind the corner tower. At first Shlomo did not realize what he was looking at. The man was young, tall, and smug looking. He was wearing a cassock but strode like a cavalry officer, the Gascon stride of a lancer lieutenant.

As they were leaving the drawing room where the Sturmbannführer had received them, the bishop had felt ill. A minor episode, nothing to worry about. But the monsignor had been forced to lie down on a couch. Grabski had gone out in search of the driver, who must have been somewhere in the garden smoking. Old as he was, Keller was well-built and Grabski would not have been able to carry him to the car without help.

The bishop's secretary turned the corner and was faced with two emaciated, skull-shaven creatures in striped pajamas. The younger one wore a yellow star of David on his chest, while the other wore a yellow triangle superimposed over a pink one. Grabski knew what it meant. Besides being a Jew, the prisoner was also a sodomite. No wonder he had been arrested. The priest told himself that the ways of the Lord were indeed infinite. Something good may come out of the war, after all. The Nazis were moving ahead with their clean-up. But he could not say this to the bishop. Monsignor Keller was a pious man, an erudite scholar of St. Thomas Aquinas, but in matters of politics he was naïve. Despite all his doctrines, he still couldn't grasp one very simple fact. If the Church had prospered for two thousand years, it was because it had learned to act on this earth with the unscrupulousness of a Caesar. Shlomo and Moshe looked at the priest. The priest stared at them for a moment with a blend of astonishment and annoyance, retraced his steps, and disappeared behind the keep.

28

Honduras, Cordillera del Sur, July 7, 1982

A steady rain beat against the windowpanes. Beyond the walls, the wind stirred the dark silhouettes of the trees surrounding the fortress, built by the Spanish in the seventeenth century to keep watch over the indigenous tribes and defend the region from pirate attacks sponsored by the English. The sky was a dull, uniform gray, making it impossible to tell whether it was morning or evening. Victor Huberman rolled onto his back and rubbed his face as if he were trying to wake up. He had been lying in bed for more than a week. The time had come to get back into action. He ran his index finger over the scar that cut across his right eyebrow, reminding him of a different life in a different era.

Someone came into the room jingling silver anklets. Bare feet poked out from under a long saffron dress in a soft, almost translucent fabric.

"Are you awake?" she whispered gently.

Huberman switched on his bedside lamp and pulled himself into a sitting position.

She rushed to plump up his pillow against the headboard, so that he could sit comfortably.

"Thank you," Huberman said.

"I'll go get your medicine," she answered.

Victor watched her gracefully slip out of the room. She was still as beautiful as the day he had met her at a reception at the White House for Lyndon Johnson's victory in the fall of 1964. At the time, Melissa Blumenthal was twenty-eight years old. She came from a Texas oil dynasty and was married to a US senator with whom she had a beautiful daughter. The gossip was that she was preparing to be first lady. But the world of barbecues at the family ranch and bridge evenings with senators' wives, who all adopted the same hairstyle and the same platitudes to berate others, was too narrow for her. Melissa was smart and curious and Victor Huberman had intrigued her no end: he was nothing like any of the people she usually hung out with. While everyone around them was debating fluctuations in the price of crude oil, how many votes Johnson had been elected with, and who was whose lover, Victor and Melissa had launched themselves into a heated discussion about Buddhist meditation techniques. Less than a month later, causing great scandal among her family and in Washington high society, she had abandoned her husband and daughter to go live in Greenwich Village with that strange fellow who was much older than her and who earned his living in a mysterious fashion. Since then, they had shared everything, including the proceeds from his newly-established drug ring. Melissa, with her jet-set connections, had proved invaluable. The former debutante and graduate of Vassar College had access to customers who were able to pay any amount for quality merchandise. And Victor's merchandise was of the highest quality.

Melissa came back carrying a tray laid with a white linen napkin, a purple pill, and a small tumbler containing a clear liquid with an olive sunk in it. She sat on the bed next to Huberman and handed him the tray. He popped the pill into his mouth and took the tumbler, frosted with ice as a Martini glass should be.

"It's the wrong kind of glass," Victor said, smiling ironically.

"Nonsense," she huffed, tucking a blond lock that had fallen over her eyes behind her ears. "This is how they serve it at Harry's Bar."

Huberman brought the tumbler to his lips. He swallowed the pill and closed his eyes, savoring the cocktail. Very dry. Pure gin, with a vague hint of extra-dry vermouth to give the ice cubes some flavor. Perfect. He was about to take another sip but Melissa took the glass out of his hands.

"The rest is for me."

Victor scowled like a spoilt child.

"Dr. Wasserman says you need to take care of yourself."

"He always exaggerates," was Huberman's reply. Nevertheless, he acknowledged the old surgeon knew what he was talking about. Wasserman had been a medical officer in the Afrikakorps. He had seen his fair share of shrapnel wounds. Huberman had been lucky: the shard had missed his spine by a few inches.

"Shall I put on some music?" Melissa asked.

Victor nodded.

She took a sip of the Martini, placed the glass on the floor, and went to choose a record.

As the first notes of Herbie Hancock's *Takin' Off* floated through the room, Huberman stretched. The pill was starting to kick in.

"I'll go and make dinner," Melissa said. She picked up the tumbler and walked out.

The opening track, "Watermelon Man," was the best known on the album. Huberman recalled reading an interview with Hancock where he said he had been inspired by the sound of the cartwheels of the watermelon peddlers, who in his childhood years would beat time on the cobblestones of the alleys in South Side, Chicago's great Black ghetto. Dexter Gordon's tenor sax and Freddie Hubbard's trumpet danced elegantly on the carpet rolled out by Hancock's piano. Butch Warren on bass, Billy Higgins on the drums. The sensuality of negro music was undeniable. Huberman closed his eyes again, longing for another sip of Martini. Who knows what the weather was like in Chicago? Steamy, most likely.

The rain had grown stronger and was beating furiously against the shutters. But Victor Huberman didn't mind. He was lost in the off-beats of "Empty Pockets." The title of the song suited his situation, he felt. Now that his cover had been blown, the Agency would finally abandon him to his fate. And if cocaine remained his only source of funding, he needed to arrange for Melissa to travel to the United States again as soon as possible. He got out of bed, went to the bathroom, took off his pajama top, and began to wash. He didn't like the idea of exposing Melissa to the risk of an attack by the Colombians. He decided that this time he would go with her. And he would take a couple of his best men with him. The war on the Reds could wait a few weeks. He had been fighting for forty years, after all. He went back into his room, took off his pajama bottoms, and began to dress. Night had fallen and the ramparts of the fortress could barely be distinguished in the dark, rainy night.

29

Berlin, January 20, 1942

The invitation said, "Debate followed by light refreshment." *Sturmbannführer* Dr. Rudolf Lange hoped that was the case. He had left Riga two days earlier and there had been no dining car on the train. He had survived on what little he had managed to find at the intermediate stations. And when he had finally disembarked at Berlin's Ostbahnhof after eleven o'clock, he had had just enough time to get into the car provided by the Reich Central Security Office and drive to the meeting, scheduled for noon. He had not even had a cup of coffee. The timetable had indicated an arrival time the previous evening but transport in the East was terrible. Not only was the Soviet rail network primitive, but it also had a different gauge than the European standard. Engineering units had either had to replace the tracks or change the trains. It was an endless job and a serious hinderance to military operations. And then the cold weather had arrived. Switches were blocked by ice and lines were interrupted or clogged by convoys unable to reach the front. The Russian winter had held the Wehrmacht back just when victory appeared to be within reach. How different the snow was in Wannsee. No frozen limbs, no logistical problems, just a beautiful white coat, like candy floss, that made the streets of the elegant suburban neighborhood even more picturesque. Approaching house number 56/58, the driver gently applied the brake, swerved, and the Opel Olympia glided through the gate. As the car drove down the tree-lined driveway leading to the villa, the tires splattered the gravel under the vehicle in a spike of hail. You could just make out the lake lapping at the end of the garden.

Obersturmbannführer Adolf Eichmann, head of Section IV-B-4 of the Reich Central Security Office in charge of Jewish affairs, was nervous. His boss had given him the role of master of ceremonies. It was an honor. Winning the trust of a man like Heydrich was no easy feat. But serving as his right-hand man in a meeting with such an uncertain outcome was also risky. He couldn't afford to make any mistakes. He went around the room again, checking that a copy of the dossier he had prepared the month before was lying on the long mahogany table in front of each chair. The conference was supposed to have been held on December 9, but the Japanese attack on Pearl Harbor had forced them to postpone. Heydrich had implied that the Führer had made the decision to settle the Jewish question definitively at the end of the summer. The declaration of war on the United States had made implementing the project even more urgent. For the time being, the Reich had no way to fight America directly, but it could strike down its agents in Europe. President Roosevelt was surrounded by Jews, like Treasury Secretary Henry Morgenthau. The Führer had spelt this out clearly in a January 1939 speech. If international Jewish finance unleashed a new war, its punishment would be the destruction of European Judaism. Eichmann was certain that Heydrich was also nervous. Of course, he was not letting on. Not for nothing had the Führer called him "the man with a heart of steel," perhaps the most flattering compliment one could ever expect from Adolf Hitler. But beneath the detached mask of the fighter, Eichmann sensed Heydrich's concern. Not that there was any chance there would be any objection to the extermination of European Jews in principle. All thirteen conference attenders were ideologically a hundred percent on the same page. However, the upper rungs of the state apparatus, and many in the National Socialist Party itself, were opposed to the idea of Germany giving up a valuable source of labor. Moreover, it was one thing to get rid of the *Ostjuden*, parasitic oriental scum no one in the world would miss. It was another matter altogether to liquidate German Jews, especially if they had fought in the Great War. Finally, even if everyone agreed that it was necessary to deport all the Jews on the continent, it was by no means a foregone conclusion that civilian officials would let the SS lead the operation without complaining about it. From the point of view of a British or American statesman, the administration of the Third Reich, characterized by fierce competition among its various divisions, was quite irrational. Hitler had not convened a council of ministers since 1938. Real decisions were made in meetings like this one, attended not by department heads but by their immediate subordinates, secretaries of state and undersecretaries. They were not politicians but senior bureaucrats. And that was where the greatest danger lurked. The butler appeared at the door announcing that Sturmbannführer Dr. Rudolf Lange had arrived. Eichmann took one last look around the hall and hurried off to greet his guest.

The venue was perfect, providing both luxury and discretion. The villa, set in a park that made it invisible from the street, stood on the Großer Wannsee, the larger of the two inlets that the Havel River forms south of Berlin. The original owners, nouveaux-riches who had made their fortune in the toothpaste trade, had been ruined by World War I and the property had been sold to another industrialist. When that owner had also gone bankrupt, the mansion had been taken over by a foundation linked to the Reich security services and used as guest quarters for SS officers. "The villa offers excellent cuisine for lunch and dinner," the brochure promised, "a wine cellar with the best German and European wines, cigarettes, a billiard room, a winter garden, and every modern comfort." What Heydrich liked best was the terrace on the Wannsee. The lakeside landscape had inspired the architects to adopt the style of Lake Garda villas. The entrance was dominated by two magnificent columns of Italian marble. Once the war was over,

Heydrich and his wife intended to make the villa their private residence. The head of the Reich's Central Security Office adjusted the knot in his tie and smiled in the mirror. This was his big break, even bigger than his appointment as deputy protector of Bohemia and Moravia. He was coming out from under Himmler's shadow. At the conference, he would be the only one on the stage. At the same time, however, the team competition would continue: Heydrich and his boss against the other party officials of the Third Reich, striving to expand the power of the SS.

While waiting for the proceedings to begin, guests were seated in the Chinese drawing room, where they could admire a valuable collection of Oriental vases and miniatures while they were offered an aperitif. Waiters in white jackets circulated with silver trays laden with canapés and champagne glasses. Ministerial director Friedrich Wilhelm Kritzinger sipped his 1940 Ruinart next to a statue of Buddha. His seraphic face presented a contrast with the tense atmosphere in the room. There was no agenda accompanying Obergruppenführer Heydrich's summons, which had generated speculation of all kinds. Kritzinger was the most senior official in the room. Although he did not know all the guests, he could guess where each of them belonged based on the huddle they formed and the way they addressed the others. At the foot of the wide staircase that led to the upper floor was a group of delegates from the ministries, respectively: Interior, Justice, Industry and Trade, and Foreign Affairs. A little further on, in the center of the room, were the two representatives of the Ostministerium who, from a certain point of view, belonged to the other group but, at the same time, together with the envoy of the Government General with whom they were chatting, they were the spokesmen of the institutions responsible for civil administration in the eastern territories. The third clutch of conferenciers consisted of SS and Party officials responsible for racial issues. Highest in rank, immediately below Heydrich, was Müller, head of the Gestapo. Then came Lieutenant Colonel Eichmann. The latter looked up toward the steps and his face seemed to light up. Kritzinger followed the direction of his gaze. On the balcony overlooking the Chinese drawing room, Reinhard Heydrich had appeared.

The *Obergruppenführer* descended the grand staircase with such solemnity that Kritzinger felt like he was watching a lead actress step onto the stage. The official's timing had been carefully studied: Heydrich had waited for everyone to arrive and gathered them into a room where his sudden appearance would make an impression. He took the steps slowly, narrowing his eyes to examine the spectators as he descended. The audience erupted into an enthusiastic, "Heil Hitler!"

Heydrich observed them one by one. They were the elite of the Third Reich administration. Half were under forty years old, as was he. Only two were over fifty: Meyer, from the Ministry for the Eastern Occupied Territories, and Kritzinger, from the Reich Chancellery. Two-thirds were college graduates, mostly in law, and several had PhDs. Some of them had a truly outstanding record. Rudolf Lange, for example: PhD from the University of Jena, chief of staff of Einsatzgruppe A, and head of security forces in the general district of Latvia. A genuine intellectual and a combatant, a man as comfortable in the library as on the battlefield. A new kind of battle, particularly hard on the soldier, where the enemy may be an unarmed woman holding a baby. Or, Secretary of State Wilhelm Stuckart: thirty-nine years old, with degrees in economics and law at the universities of Munich and Frankfurt; the best brain in the State Department, in many ways more important than Minister Frick himself. Stuckart was one of the authors of the 1935 Nuremberg Laws, which had stemmed the Jewish cancer that threatened to devour Germany. The laws defending "German blood and honorability" had achieved a great deal, but they were only the first step. They were acceptable for peacetime. The war offered National Socialism a historic opportunity, the chance to rid the continent of Jews for good. Failing to seize that opportunity meant bequeathing the problem to future generations. Europe could not afford it. Heydrich hoped that civilian officials would understand this, especially Stuckart and Kritzinger. The former would probably try to defend the legislation he had contributed to, which the conference was supposed to bury. The latter had an impeccable career on his side, but he was an old man and his ideas were out of date.

"Is the champagne to your liking, gentlemen?" Heydrich asked, hinting at a smile.

Some of them were smoking. Others had brought a half-full champagne flute with them. They all stared at the head of the Reich Central Security Office, sitting at the center of the long rectangular table waiting for Eichmann to close the door. The servants had been warned to keep their distance once the conference began, but Heydrich would not utter a single syllable without being certain that he would be heard only by those he had summoned.

Eichmann closed the door and took his seat next to Heydrich. Behind them, a stenographer in SS uniform was hunched over his machine on a small field table, his fingertips on the keys at the ready.

"As you know," Heydrich began, "I have been designated by Marshal Göring as the person in charge of the final solution to the Jewish problem in Europe." This had been said at the beginning of the invitation letter. Göring was the most powerful man in Germany, immediately after the Führer. Heydrich had made no reference to him, either in writing or in speaking, but it was clear to all that Hitler was behind the Reichsmarschall's request. "This meeting was convened to clarify the basic issues, the technical and organizational aspects, of the solution. Our aim is to coordinate the actions of all the institutions involved in the process." Heydrich paused. Apart from the clacking of the stenographers, there was absolute silence in the room.

"The responsibility for the final solution to the Jewish problem, regardless of geographical boundaries, lies with Reichsführer-SS and German police chief Heinrich Himmler." Heydrich stared at the civilian officials one by one. No one made a sound. The Obergruppenführer abandoned the rigid posture that he had held until that moment, with his elbows planted on the table, and leaned back in his chair. Beside him, Adolf Eichmann was taking notes. For the moment, everything seemed to be running smoothly.

"Until last fall," Heydrich resumed, "our policies focused essentially on emigration. The goal was to use legal methods to clear German living space of the presence of Jews." He turned to Eichmann, who responded promptly.

The lieutenant colonel put on his glasses, opened the folder he kept under the papers he was writing on, and pulled out a typewritten page covered with figures.

"From when we came to power to October 31, 1941," Eichmann said, "some 537,000 Jews were induced to leave the territory of the Reich. Of these, 360,000 had been resident in Germany, 147,000 in Austria, and 30,000 in the Protectorate of Bohemia and Moravia. The emigration was financed by the Jews themselves, by means of a tax proportional to the wealth of each, so that the wealthier segments of the community paid for the journey of the poorer ones."

Eichmann adjusted his glasses on his nose. Heydrich signaled that he continue.

"In the meantime, owing to of the difficulties of emigrating in wartime, and in consideration of the new possibilities that have opened up in the East, the Reichsführer-SS has halted emigration." The head of the Reich Central Security Office paused for a moment. "Emigration abroad," he resumed, "with the preliminary endorsement of the Führer, has now been replaced with a new policy: the evacuation of Jews to the east.

These actions, however, are to be considered transitional solutions which will enable us to gain practical experience of the highest importance in view of the future final solution to the Jewish problem."

The conferenciers reacted in the most disparate manner to those words. Some nodded with conviction. Others stared at the ceiling, absorbed in their own thoughts. Still others exchanged quizzical glances. But the mere suggestion of the Führer was enough to silence any possible objection.

Lange wondered how many had really grasped what Heydrich's was saying. It was in a coded language in order to avoid the truth being leaked beyond the confines of a circle of initiates. But perhaps it was also a way for the initiates themselves to hide reality behind those sterilized words. "Action" meant killing. Everyone at the table must have known this. "Evacuation" had the same meaning. "Evacuate to the east" meant exterminate. Between November and December, Lange himself had participated in the "evacuation" of 25,000 Jews in the Rumbula forest near Riga. Almost all were natives, except for about a thousand who had been deported from Berlin in the days before. It had been problematic. Shooting in the back of the head a distinguished-looking gentleman who looked like your high school physics teacher could create qualms even in comrades of proven faith. Reichskommissar Hinrich Lohse, a Party member since 1923, head of the civil administration in the three Baltic states and White Rutenia, had on several occasions tried to prevent Lange and his colleagues in Einsatzgruppe A from liquidating German Jews. Convening the conference had been an excellent idea. There could no longer be any uncertainty or friction.

"The final solution to the Jewish problem," Eichmann was saying, "regards about eleven million European Jews, divided among the various countries as shown in the table in the dossier." Rustling their papers, the participants pulled the correct sheet out of the folder. The Obersturmbannführer's tone was flat: a business executive outlining sales trends at a board meeting. The list covered the entire continent, including neutral nations and those at war with the Reich. It ranged from 3,000 Jews in Portugal to five and a half million in the Soviet Union. The exception was tiny Estonia, which was already *judenfrei*. Einsatzgruppe A, which had jurisdiction over the former Baltic republics, was doing a good job. "In the case of foreign countries that are not under our direct control," Eichmann specified, "the figures are indicative, and presumably destined to increase, since in those nations Jews are included in the census only on the basis of religion and no racial criteria has, as yet, been adopted to distinguish them."

"But this serious problem," Heydrich intervened with a smile, "will soon be taken care of by our armed forces." The joke was met with a few chuckles. "For the moment," Heydrich continued, "we already have our hands full with the Jews in the territories we administer."

"The Warsaw and Krakow ghettos are already terribly overcrowded," Secretary of State Dr. Josef Bühler, delegate of the Government General, blurted out. "If this final solution consists in dumping all the Jews of Europe in Poland, as you've been doing for months, I regret to inform you that the system is on the verge of collapse. If this goes any further, there will be outbreaks of typhus."

Heydrich stared Bühler down. Eichmann fiddled with his fountain pen. "They will only be settled in the ghettos on a temporary basis," the Obergruppenführer responded. "We plan to rake through the whole continent, beginning with the Reich, including the Protectorate of Bohemia and Moravia. The evacuated Jews will be taken to transit ghettos . . . " Bühler opened his mouth to say something but Heydrich stopped him with a firm wave of his hand. " . . . and from the transit ghettos they will be taken further east where, under proper direction and in the most appropriate ways, they will provide a labor force. Organized into large work units and separated by sex. Able-bodied male Jews will devote themselves to road building, which will no doubt lead to a substantial decrease in numbers by natural causes." Heydrich looked around. At his side, Eichmann had resumed taking notes. He had instructed him to take the minutes of the meeting, which would then be delivered to each of the participants. No one had countered or objected. Perfect. The head of the Reich Central Security Office resumed speaking. "Finally, to the survivors, who certainly will be the strongest among them, will be given the appropriate treatment. Otherwise, as the product of natural selection, if any were to be left alive they could form the germ cell of a new Jewish strain, as history has taught us."

Kritzinger flipped through the pages of the dossier looking perplexed. He was not sure he had understood the meaning of the Obergruppenführer's words.

"Work units?"

The question had come out of his mouth almost unintentionally.

Heydrich looked him steadily in the eye.

"Exactly."

"But if the very data you provided us with say that more than seventy percent of Soviet Jews are from merchant classes and the intelligentsia: clerks, doctors, intellectuals," Kritzinger waved the page citing the figures in question, like a lawyer presenting evidence during a trial, "what possible use can these people be in road construction?"

"Exactly," Heydrich replied frostily.

Kritzinger put the sheet of paper down.

"Do we intend to shoot four million people?" Stuckart interjected. "Do we have enough bullets?" he added with a nervous laugh.

"We will have," Secretary of State Erich Neumann from the

Ministry of Industry and Trade answered. "Provided the Jews currently working in the munitions factories are spared. Until replacements are available, we cannot do without them."

Rudolf Lange looked around in irritation. Apart from him and Eberhard Schöngarth, head of the security forces in Kraków, no one in that room knew what it meant to kill. Yes, one or two of them had fought in the other war. Stuckart had been in the Freikorps. Shooting an enemy who might shoot back is a completely different matter. This lot were a bunch of desk warriors who would never see the effects of the decisions they were about to make. The problem was not the bullets. Human beings were the problem. Lange would have liked to say something, to explain that conducting shootings for days on end was no easy feat. But he was at the bottom of the food chain at that table.

Heydrich caught the rebelliousness in the Einsatzgruppe A chief of staff's look. "Please, Dr. Lange, enlighten us on your experience," he said affably. "That's why I invited you here today."

The Obergruppenführer's use of his title was his way of making him feel important, over-riding the fact that he was the lowest in rank.

"Large-scale actions present multiple logistical problems," Lange began. "Burying 25,000 dead is no small feat. There can be excessive nervous strain on our men." That was why, whenever he could, Lange tried to use teams of Latvian auxiliaries, who seemed happy enough to do the Germans' dirty work. An image flashed through his mind of a rosy-cheeked little boy cheerfully playing an accordion from atop a pile of corpses. "Liquidating Jews is a thankless task that no one can do lightheartedly. Several of my men, good comrades, were unable to go through with it in the long run."

Heydrich nodded gravely. "Unfortunately, conditions in the

Soviet Union are harsh. It is a huge territory with totally in-adequate road and railway infrastructure. Over there, the only way forward is to proceed on the spot. That is what the four Einsatzgruppen deployed in the vanguard of the war front are doing, represented here by Dr. Lange, whom we thank for his self-sacrifice to the cause."

Lange gave a shy nod, like a schoolboy ashamed to be praised by the teacher in front of the class.

"Poland, on the other hand," Heydrich resumed, "is smaller and has a reasonably reliable transportation network. We will be able to go ahead there applying innovative methods, which will be more effective and humane."

All eyes were on the Obergruppenführer.

"It is not the time or place to address the technical solutions to the problem. The aim here is simply to synchronize the vari-ous mechanisms and agree on a plan of action for rounding up the Jews of Europe. We have to determine *who* will be evacu-ated." Heydrich looked first at Stuckart. He was sure he would intervene in defense of half-breeds who under the Nuremberg Laws were not classified as Jews. Then he looked at Neumann, who was justly concerned about industrial efficiency. Heydrich understood the needs of war production and was willing to make exceptions. As long as they were limited, circumstantial, and temporary. "And we have to determine *when* they will be evacuated." At this point he turned to Bühler, as if to reassure him that the inhabitants of the Governor General's ghettos were at the top of the list. "As for *how*, suffice it to say that adequate infrastructures are already being set up." Heydrich paused and met Müller's gaze for a moment. The Gestapo chief had a face like a sphinx but he was one of the few people in that room who knew all the details. In the Kulmhof Lager, gas trucks had been in use since December. Aktion T4, the plan which had rid the Reich of the burden of seventy thousand in-valids and mentally-retarded individuals, had been a valuable experience. In the course of the program, in addition to bullets and injections of Luminal, special vehicles had been used. The exhaust pipes had been fed into the cargo compartment where the subjects to be eliminated were loaded. In Bełżec, in the Lublin district, they were building a camp with fixed stations that could process thousands of items per day much more effectively and discreetly than execution platoons. More stations would soon be set up in four Lagers distributed between Silesia and the General Government. Places with obscure names no one had ever heard of, which would slowly sink into oblivion along with the Jews: Treblinka, Sobibór, Majdanek, Auschwitz. As the Führer had said, with his usual lucidity, who still talks about the massacre of the Armenians today?

"These facilities," Heydrich resumed, "will obviate the problems highlighted by Dr. Lange."

Eichmann's gaze was fixed on Heydrich, as was everyone else's, but there was a strange light in his eyes: unconditional admiration for the leader. And pride in being one of his most trusted collaborators. Eichmann knew that so-called men of action, such as Schöngarth and Lange, harbored only scorn for pen-pushers like him. Yet, in many ways, the solution to the Jewish problem was no more than a giant exercise in mathematics and geography. And like any bureaucratic organization, once it was set in motion, inertia would keep the machine moving and there would be no need for flair or intelligence. Train schedules, batches to be delivered, materials to be disposed of, profits, losses. Nevertheless, there was more to it than the mere calculations of an accountant. What Schöngarth and Lange did not see was the extraordinary imagination behind the plan. The Nuremberg Laws, drafted by that stuck-up Stuckart, were nothing more than a re-elaboration of anti-Jewish legislation dating back to the Middle Ages. Even in terms of propaganda, the Party had simply recycled old ideas, which had been used and re-used from Luther's day to the nineteenth century. But what they were propelling into action now was radically new.

To transport several million individuals across Europe, kill them quickly and secretly, make the bodies disappear, and redeploy their assets was a gargantuan undertaking. Nothing comparable had ever been accomplished. The system had been invented from scratch. Obersturmbannführer Adolf Eichmann did not feel like a bureaucrat at all. He felt like a creator, an artist. This was National Socialism, after all. The most complete expression of German aesthetic genius.

"Gas, gentlemen. Gas is the best tool." Heydrich had spelt the words out clearly. There was no chance that anyone in the room had not heard him. "Zyklon B, a pesticide. We tested it on Russian prisoners at the end of the summer in the Auschwitz camp. It works very well."

Absolute silence fell in the room. The clacking of the stenographer's keys had also stopped. When the head of the Reich's Central Security Office had started talking about *how* the final solution was to be achieved, Eichmann had signaled the secretary to stop.

Ministerial Director Friedrich Wilhelm Kritzinger stared blankly straight ahead. There was something perverse about the way Heydrich had revealed the secret. It was not even a real secret anymore. The fact that, since the opening of the Eastern Front in June 1941, Germany had begun exterminating Jews was well-known in that room. Perhaps some of the delegates did not know some of the details, specific examples, or technical arrangements, but the general picture had been clear to everyone there. Rather than inform them, Heydrich had wanted to compromise them, to make them accomplices. Kritzinger wondered what his father, a Lutheran pastor, would think if he were there. But these were exceptional times. Events could not be judged through the filter of conventional morality. Jews were a problem. He and the other fourteen men sitting at the table were being called upon to solve it. The proposed solution was radical, inhumane even, but Germany was at war. It was engaged in a relentless struggle against enemies determined to annihilate it. Was it not right to respond? Besides, orders are orders. An official, even a high-ranking one such as a ministerial director or a secretary of state, should never question the directives he receives. Otherwise, there would be chaos. Barbarism. If worst came to worst, he could resign. Kritzinger pondered whether leaving the administration might be the right thing to do and put the data sheet on the work activities of Soviet Jews back into his dossier.

Heydrich's proposal to take a break and have an early lunch was met with general applause. Getting out of that dark wood-paneled room impregnated with smoke and words, if only for half an hour, would do everyone a great deal of good. They ate and drank, watching the snowflakes fluttering silently outside the window. The buffet was excellent and brandy was served at the end, which helped make the continuation of the discussion livelier and more polyphonic.

"So," Heydrich exclaimed, intent on maintaining the fast-moving pace he had established at that morning's session. The aim of the conference was to apprise the delegates of the overall plan and invite them to accept it. Nothing further. "Jews over the age of sixty-five will not be evacuated but transferred to ghettos for the elderly such as Theresienstadt in the Protectorate of Bohemia and Moravia. Jews who received serious injuries fighting in the Great War or were awarded the first-class Iron Cross will be sent to the same ghettos. This solution will enable us to deal efficiently with the extensive list of exceptions that will almost certainly be presented from all quarters for those Jews who distinguished themselves in the other war." Many of those present assented. "Major evacuation operations," Heydrich continued, "will depend largely on developments in the military situation. As for measures relating to the final solution both in the occupied territories or those under our sphere of influence, I think the best thing is for the Foreign Ministry experts to make arrangements with the officials of the Reich Central Security Office in the various countries."

Eichmann provided the relevant data on the generally high level of cooperation of the various governments allied with the Reich: Slovakia, Croatia, Romania, Italy.

Secretary of State Martin Luther spoke sadly about the difficulties of implementing anti-Jewish policy in Scandinavia. Since these communities were very small, it was decided that the deportation of Danish and Norwegian Jews could take place at a later date. On a more positive note, Luther foresaw few difficulties in southeastern Europe.

Kritzinger grew increasingly uncomfortable as Martin Luther spoke. The Secretary of State clearly wanted to please Heydrich. At the beginning of the conference, Kritzinger had hoped that a bloc of civilian functionaries would unite in opposition to the dominance of the SS. But this had been an illusion. Heydrich had won the match before kickoff. The secretaries of state had no intention of fighting. His last hope that ministerial prerogatives would be preserved had been his bright young colleague, Stuckart. Kritzinger had counted on the fact that the author of the Nuremberg Laws would try to rein in the head of the Reich's Central Security Office as soon as the discussion touched on the issue of the *Mischlinge*. If Stuckart, armed with his knowledge and prestige, had challenged Heydrich on the legal status of the half-breeds, Kritzinger would have intervened in his support.

Heydrich would have liked to consider *Mischlinge* of the first degree, those with two Jewish grandparents, the same as *Volljuden* who were 100 percent Jewish, and evacuate them all. He knew, however, that this was not politically viable. The Führer was sensitive to German public opinion, which would have frowned upon a change in the Nuremberg Laws. Not to mention that many *Mischlinge* were currently fighting at the front. But Stuckart's resistance had been mild and his proposal to overcome the impasse—to sterilize all half-breeds, thus solving the problem of cross-breeding at its root—had provided the SS with an acceptable solution. As Gruppenführer Otto Hofmann from the Central Office for Race and Settlements observed, the solution was more than acceptable for the *Mischlinge* themselves who, when faced with the choice of whether to be sterilized or evacuated, would certainly prefer the former. Even Müller smiled at this.

The debate continued, going into increasing detail. In addition to first-degree *Mischlinge*, there were second-degree *Mischlinge* who had only one grandfather of Jewish origin. In principle, these were to be classified as having German blood. There were exceptions, however. Distinctly Semitic physical traits, for example. Anyone who looked Jewish was Jewish. As well as suspicious behavior in political or security terms. Those who behaved like Jews were Jews. In such cases, the second-degree *Mischlinge* would be treated as fully-fledged Jews and evacuated to the East. And then there was the delicate matter of mixed marriages: between *Mischlinge* of the first and second degree, or between *Mischlinge* and Aryans, with or without offspring. These would be decided on a case-by-case basis whereby either the Jewish spouse would be evacuated or, in view of the consequences this might have on German relatives, transferred to a ghetto for the elderly.

The subject of half-breeds and mixed couples was the trickiest part of the entire conference. Kritzinger did not say a single word on the subject.

In his closing lines, Secretary of State Bühler stressed the need to give priority to the General Government. "More than anywhere else," he explained, "Jews constitute a grave danger here both as carriers of disease and as agitators, resulting in a permanent state of turbulence in the economic structure of the country. What is more, out of the two and a half million Jews who would be affected by the measure, the majority are unfit for work."

Heydrich nodded and was sincerely pleased and a little astonished when Bühler concluded, "The Central Security Office of the Reich will be responsible for solving the Jewish question within the confines of the General Government. Its efforts will receive the full support of Government authorities. My only request is this: the Jewish question should be solved in this territory as soon as possible."

The whole debate had lasted less than a couple of hours. As soon as the conference was over, the guests had stopped to chat for a while and then left, alone or in small groups.

Stuckart and Kritzinger had gone out onto the terrace to look over the placid waters of the Wannsee. Little puffs of breath hovered in the crisp air. Stuckart pulled out his cigarette case and offered one to Kritzinger, who shook his head.

The ministry director was on the verge of saying something but decided not to. He rubbed his hands together. He had left his gloves at home.

"Beautiful, isn't it?" Stuckart commented, looking at the lake.

"Very" Kritzinger agreed.

The guests had departed. They were either on their way back to their comfortable Berlin offices or leaving for the eastern lands where duty called. Heydrich, Eichmann, and Müller were the only ones left at the villa. The master of ceremonies officiated the last ritual of the day. Eichmann led his superiors into a room lined with bookcases and took a bottle of Rémy Martin out of a cabinet. A log fire crackled merrily behind a metal flame guard. The three men took their seats. Heydrich poured himself a generous measure of liquor and was offered a cigar by Müller. The Obergruppenführer had not touched any alcohol or tobacco during the conference. In fact, Eichmann had very rarely seen him drinking or smoking. This must have been a very special occasion. Heydrich had been subjected to enormous pressure. But the result was excellent, beyond his wildest predictions. The head of the Reich Central Security Office sat back and stretched his muscular, tapered legs out in front of him, taking a sip of cognac.

"At this point," he said, "the Jewish question is nothing more than a transportation issue."

PART TWO

Operation Berserker

30

Warthegau, February 24, 1942

I t was still cold, but spring was already in the air. In the forest, patches of snow were beginning to thaw into a muddy slush. A terse southerly wind had been blowing all night and instead of the usual low, leaden horizon, dawn had brought forth a bright blue sky. The baron tugged at the reins and dismounted. He had treated himself to an unusually long ride and the bay needed a rest. He took his tobacco pouch and pipe out of his jacket pocket and began to press the shredded leaves into the bowl with his thumb. He was in an excellent mood. The previous evening, he and Carlotta had decided to eat in front of the fireplace in the small living room rather than in the dining room, which was too big and austere. Kate had made a succulent roast pork with cranberry sauce and one of Carlotta's favorite desserts, *far Breton*, a French recipe that the cook had learned many years before to please the young baroness's palate that was eager for foreign food. Kate had been the only servant apart from Albert who had been saved from the Sturmbannführer's purge of the castle servants. Bishop Keller's visit, provoked by Mrs. Mertz's gossip, had sent Lichtblau into a rage. The baron had only managed to retain his butler and cook because he had vouched for them personally, swearing on his honor as an officer and an athlete that they would never report what took place within the palace walls. All the others had been removed and replaced with internees from the Soldau concentration camp. Albert and Kate had been extremely skeptical of the newcomers' dubious credentials as servants in some nouveau-riche family or waiters in third-rate hotels but, in the end, the pair had agreed to attempt to instruct their unlikely subordinates. The one exception was an Austrian Jehovah's Witness, a nurse by profession, whose precision and cleanliness Kate had immediately appreciated, but she had been commandeered by Lichtblau as a housekeeper for his section of the castle.

The von Lehndorffs had first tasted *far Breton* on a trip to Paris, in a bistro on the Place Saint-Michel, behind the Le Coudurier armory where Wilhelm had been training with one of the city's most prestigious fencing masters. It had been a long time ago, when they had been young and happy, before the Great War and everything that had ensued in Germany and in their marriage. But that evening, after Albert had served coffee, Carlotta and Wilhelm had suddenly found themselves making love on the couch, as passionately as young lovers. They had gone on to uncork a bottle of champagne and resume their activities more sedately in Carlotta's bedroom. She had complimented her husband: for a man of fifty, he still had enviable vigor. Her comment had all the seriousness of a winemaker discussing the qualities of one grape variety over another. Wilhelm was aware that her expertise in the matter should irritate him. Partly because he still loved her—only now did he fully realize it—and partly because she had appealed to his male vanity. However, he had taken it as a compliment and left it at that. They had finished their champagne and fallen asleep snuggled close to one another. "The last time we spent the night together," she had said in the morning, her eyes twinkling, "Brüning was still in the Chancellery."

"The day may come when Hitler will no longer be Chancellor," Wilhelm had thought. Someone needed to shake themselves out of the spell that provincial magician had cast over the entire nation. The officers and soldiers should remember that their honor comes before the oath they had sworn to the Führer.

Carlotta had stroked her husband's face, guessing why he had suddenly looked so serious. "Sooner or later, he, too, will go. Nothing lasts forever," she had said, planting a kiss on his lips. "But let's go and have breakfast now. I'm hungry."

The baron stuck the match deeper into to the bowl of the pipe and sucked on the stem. The bay grazed on the anemic shoots of a little plant sprouting out of the snow. Von Lehndorff knew the road to Kulmhof lay somewhere ahead. It couldn't be much further. He took a few more puffs, picked up the reins, and set off, his pipe clenched between his teeth. The horse picked up its pace obediently.

He reached the edge of the woods. The road was a dirty, half-melted strip of snow with two muddy tire tracks in the middle. Beyond, more dark, silent forest.

He was about to ride on when he heard the hum of an engine. A few moments later, a large, squat, gray truck appeared. It was proceeding extremely slowly. It looked like a truck belonging to a moving company. Except that there were two men in SS uniforms in the driver's cab. The truck drove past the baron and came to a halt a few yards away. Nobody seemed to have seen him. One detail caught von Lehndorff's attention. The truck's exhaust pipe was not free. A rubber hose had been attached to it, which then vanished somewhere under the truck.

Suddenly, ghosts started to flit in the shadows of the large fir trees on the other side of the road. The baron had no idea what else to call them. They were dressed in rags, their faces were gaunt, and worn out, their eyes dull. Two individuals in the same striped tatters, with green triangular badges on their chests instead of the yellow Star of David, were barking orders and waving clubs in the air. The baron followed his instincts and hid behind a tree trunk

The ghouls threw the truck doors wide open. Von Lehndorff was quite far away but the stench reached him anyway. A blend of vomit and excrement. The cargo compartment of the truck was chock-full of corpses. From where he stood, the baron could not say exactly how many there were, but there must have been at least forty. The bodies were stuck together, covered in foul slime, their faces purple, their tongues swollen between their teeth. Some were still struggling. The ghosts began to pull them out of the truck and drag them into the trees from where they had sprung. They worked in pairs. One would take a corpse by the feet and the other by the hands. But to carry the children, one of them was sufficient. They heaved them onto their shoulders, or carried them in their arms, like loving fathers. The efficiency with which they performed their duty revealed that this was not their first time.

"This is it," the baron said to himself. The Nazis had moved on to extermination on an industrial scale. Locking people in a synagogue and setting them on fire was far too conspicuous. This was a more effective and discreet method.

"What are you doing here?"

The baron started. Absorbed as he had been in the contemplation of that hellish scene, he had not realized that one of the two SS drivers, a young, nervous-looking lieutenant, had spotted him and approached him. Von Lehndorff stared at him opaquely.

"Get out of here at once if you know what's good for you," the driver snarled.

"I am Baron Wilhelm von Lehndorff," he countered, collecting himself. "My estate is on the other side of the woods. I was out riding."

The Obersturmführer seemed intimidated by the noble title.

"Then please move along," he said in a more conciliatory tone of voice.

Von Lehndorff mumbled something unintelligible, mounted his horse, and rode off at a slow trot. Before the bend in the road, he turned around. The operation was almost over. He could see the truck and two ghosts who were intent on cleaning out the cargo compartment as best they could. Their companions were evidently burying the bodies in a mass grave in the thick of the woods. The forest was immense. It could accommodate a vast cemetery.

Von Lehndorff reached Kulmhof in half an hour. The foul smell was still in his nostrils. The stench of death stuck with him. In the other war, as the bodies of friend and foe alike rotted in no man's land, he had breathed it in for months. Sometimes, the corpses ended up becoming part of the trenches. But what the baron had seen in the woods was different. It was not war. It was something worse. Or perhaps it was the terminal stage of a process that had started in 1914, a terrible era of iron and blood that had come to belie the promise of peace, prosperity, and *far Breton*, which had been made at the beginning of the century to Wilhelm von Lehndorff and other Europeans of his generation. "Socialism or barbarism," the Spartacists had yelled in 1918. Back then, von Lehndorff had hated them with every fiber of his being. Now, however, he was willing to concede that Rosa Luxemburg—that little red Cassandra— had guessed what the future held in store for them. Socialism may not have been the right answer, but here barbarism had already been achieved.

He entrusted his horse to a milkman's boy who was grooming a nag pulling a cart, and walked over to the brewery the boy had pointed out. His legs were shaking and he was struggling to put one foot in front of another. He made the effort to pull himself together.

The room was spacious. There was a long counter with a big mirror behind it and a portrait of the Austrian corporal hanging over it. There were half a dozen customers, scattered between the bar and the small tables. In one corner, a woman who had the air of being the proprietress was examining some fabric samples. Sitting beside her was a blond woman, perhaps a seamstress commissioned to sew new curtains, or a friend who had come to give advice.

The baron went up to the counter and ordered a Schnaps. He knocked it back it in one go. He felt a little better. He ordered a second one. He downed that one, too. He had to warn them. He had to tell those people what he had seen, what was happening on the outskirts of their pretty little town, filled with small businesses and lace curtains.

"The truck . . . ," the baron muttered almost to himself.

"I beg your pardon?" the brewer from behind the counter asked.

"The truck, the gray one, with the hose attached underneath."

They looked one another in the eye for a moment, but then the brewer quickly looked away and started drying glasses with a tea towel. Von Lehndorff got the message. The man knew, or at least he had been able to guess. Everyone in there could guess what was going on in the woods. That distinguished gentleman in a vest the color of a goose's beak, the pharmacist, the school principal, perhaps even the burgomaster sitting on his own by the window knew. The two peasants propping up the counter and chatting as they drank out of tall pewter mugs knew. The blond lady commenting with the proprietress on the quality of the white fabric with thin blue stripes knew. Everyone knew. The baron paid and made his way out.

He walked slowly. The snow had turned into gray slush on the sidewalk. Soon, there would be a thaw even in Russia, and the Wehrmacht, pinned by the winter to the gates of Moscow and Leningrad, would resume its offensive. Baron Wilhelm von Lehndorff hoped that the Russians would be able to drive them back and defeat them, as they had done with the Grande Armée in the previous century. It was a thought that troubled him to the core, because it went against everything he had always believed in. There was no hope for Germany.

31

London, July 8, 1982

Business lunches and dinners had always bored him to tears. And that meeting at the Savoy with new Australian partners was no exception. On such occasions, Harry Dobbs would put on a mask which he had tried and tested over the years, and which allowed him to pretend he was interested in the conversation while letting his mind wander. One of his favorite activities was studying people at nearby tables and trying to imagine their lives from the few available clues: their attire, body language, and scraps of conversation. That night, he had been lucky. Fate had placed an extraordinarily interesting couple next to him. She was Chinese and very thin, her hair pulled tight over the nape of her neck into a small bun, her face so shriveled it brought to mind an Amazonian shrunken head. She could have been fifty or eighty: it was impossible to tell. She wore a long, black dress with long sleeves and a row of buttons over her left shoulder. She was wearing large pearl earrings. Another pearl stood out on the hairpin tucked into her bun.

"The value of our shares in Asian markets has almost doubled."

The statement required a convincing smile of assent. Harry Dobbs' facial muscles obeyed.

Asian markets were a constant feature of his work lunches. Making money from the stock market was fine. That was what he paid his consultants for, after all. But talking about it for more than five minutes was intolerable. All the more so at dinner. Why ruin a meal at the Savoy by discussing things that could safely stay inside a boardroom? What he appreciated about his work was the creative aspect. He had enjoyed founding the company right after the war. And he liked comparing notes with researchers, dreaming up new products. But he had no patience whatsoever for financial details. That was why he had sent his son first to the London School of Economics and then to Harvard, so that he could take care of all those numbers. George seemed to really like that stuff. To use the language of the women's magazines his wife liked reading, there had never been much dialogue between the two of them. They had complementary skills and passions, though, and the company was grinding out profits.

"The acquisition of the majority stake in MVC opened up South America. Not just Brazil but the whole continent."

George Dobbs cast a glance at his father, inviting him to participate more actively in the conversation. He was CEO but the old man was still president and, as such, he was expected to dip his oar in every now and again. Harry made an effort to say something coherent. The two executives from Sydney seemed satisfied, which meant Dobbs could go back to studying his neighbors. The man was European, in his early sixties, and huge. He was wearing a beautifully tailored white tuxedo with a red carnation tucked into his breast pocket. There were two lobsters on the plate in front of him. He cracked the carapace with consummate efficiency, extracting the flesh, which he distributed equally between his plate and hers. While her slim figure might suggest otherwise, the Chinese woman ate with a good appetite. As soon as a morsel landed on her plate, she put it straight into her mouth. Dobbs imagined that these were regulars. Perhaps they were celebrating something: a wedding anniversary or a business partnership.

"With the new government, people have finally started working again in this country. Things couldn't go on any longer as they were."

They had moved on to politics. Harry Dobbs was more interested in this subject. As an enthusiastic supporter of Margaret Thatcher, he joined in the conversation. They agreed in condemning the Labor Party, the unions, and the leftist intellectuals as ludicrously out of date. Without ever having done a day's work in their lives, these people thought they could tell entrepreneurs how to run their businesses. At the same time, however, Dobbs continued to keep an eye on his neighbors. They were speaking in French. The film in his mind was perfect: she was a former brothel keeper in Saigon, he a wealthy landowner and one of their best customers. They had stayed in Indo-China after French colonial rule came to an end, romantic figments of a faded imperial past. But the arrival of the Communists in 1975 had forced them to flee. He imagined them with a suitcase full of diamonds and Swiss francs, having gotten hold of two tickets on the last flight for Paris, as the vanguards of the North Vietnamese army entered the suburbs of the city. *Vive la France éternelle.*

The ordeal was over. Liquor was being served. After two rounds of scotch and brandy, the Australians had finally announced they were going back to the hotel. His neighbors were also at the hard liquor stage of the meal. As soon as she had finished her dessert, she had dozed off and was now sleeping peacefully, her chin reclining on her chest. He had had a bottle of cognac brought in, which he seemed intent on finishing, along with a large cigar. A swarm of waiters buzzed around the table and the man was handing out ten-pound tips. They must have left Indochina with at least two suitcases of diamonds and Swiss francs.

The Dobbs and the Australians got up from the table and headed for the cloakroom. George whispered a few words of approval to his father. By his standards, he had been quite talkative that evening.

They left the restaurant, shook hands, and made an appointment for the following month at the company's annual convention. Harry Dobbs got behind the wheel of his dark blue Bentley Mulsanne. As he pulled out of the parking lot, another car—a Mini Minor with the name of a car rental agency on its side—slipped out of the shadows and drove up behind him.

32

Allenstein, East Prussia, March 4, 1942

Witold Grabski reread the typewritten page for the third time. It was a carbon copy printed on almost transparent tissue paper: a detailed description of all the meetings he had had with Anja and the other young ladies at the *maison* over the past six months. The information was complete: day, time, cost, duration, and details of his performance. If it had not concerned him so closely, he would have admired the precision with which the job had been done. The Gestapo agents had discovered every detail of the bishop's secretary's clandestine life. They had informed him that they also had extensive photographic documentation. In support of the claim, a man in a black leather raincoat had shown him a specimen from the collection. "That's you," he had said sarcastically, pointing to the photo, "but this doesn't look to me like a holy water sprinkler. And that woman is most certainly not repenting her sins." Grabski had remained silent. He knew, or could imagine, what they wanted.

Bishop Keller had been deported to Dachau a few weeks earlier. This had not surprised Grabski one bit. The old man had been looking for trouble. And for what? To help the Jews. He had tried hard to convince him to let the matter go. It was not their job to interfere. But Keller was stubborn and one night they had come for him. Grabski did not miss him. The new bishop was far more reasonable. But the Nazis were still suspicious. They wanted someone to keep an eye on him and, if necessary, report back. And who better than Witold Grabski? They had started putting together his dossier back in Keller's time and now they had pulled it out. He got up from his desk and opened the wood stove. He watched the sheet of paper burn in an instant and secured the door.

The detailed account had made him lust for a woman. The damage was already done. And it wasn't worth talking to Anja about it as it was obvious that they were blackmailing her, too. The Reich was full of informants, voluntary or otherwise. The Gestapo was everywhere, especially there in the eastern provinces, where the Germanization process was being closely watched. If he didn't want to be deported to the General Government like many of the city's Poles, he should watch out. If the expulsions continued at that pace, they would soon find themselves without any worshippers. Nor were they the worst off. In Wartheland, Catholicism had practically been outlawed. But one way or another, the Church would survive. It had done so for 2,000 years, after all. "Political regimes come and go," Grabski said to himself. "The Holy Roman Church is here to stay." He went to his bedroom and dressed in his Prince of Wales suit with a matching blue woolen tie. He put on his coat and hat, and went out. As he walked through the deserted streets, Father Grabski hoped that Anja would be available that evening.

33

London, July 9, 1982

Dobbs Ltd. headquarters were housed in a futuristic, glass building near the financial heart of the city. Natalya and Anton had been waiting since early that morning, sitting in a tearoom across the street, or jostling through the busy crowds on the sidewalk. So far with no success. After lunch they phoned from a booth. The secretary answered and said the president was not in his office. She offered to make an appointment if they wanted. The president was always happy to meet with doctors, pharmacists, or anyone else who used the company's products.

They went to Dobbs' home in Knightsbridge. A beautiful Regency-style mansion, overlooking a square with a garden in the middle. At a quarter to six, Harry Dobbs stepped out of the house. He may have been going to the pub, like many of his countrymen at that hour. Whatever his destination was, he did not get there. After walking a block, he was about to cross the street when Officer Yakovchenko stopped him.

"Mr. Harry Dobbs?" she asked flirtatiously. One of the instructors at the First Central Directorate school, a Hungarian who had been in the Red Orchestra—the spy network that operated in Nazi-occupied Europe—had taught her that flirting was a useful skill. The human male is a simple creature. A pretty face, fluttering eyelashes and an adoring stare are usually enough to lower his guard.

This time, however, the trick did not seem to be working.

"Yes?" Dobbs answered guardedly from behind large sunglasses before attempting to dodge her.

Natalya grabbed him by the arm. With her other hand she

pulled a small-caliber pistol from her purse and pointed it at him.

"Come with me."

Dobbs tried to order his thoughts. The woman was much younger than he was, had a strong grip, and was armed. He didn't stand a chance. Besides, the street was empty. Around the corner, however, there was a subway station.

As Dobbs weighed the odds of being able to get away, Epstein drove up in a green Ford Escort. Natalya opened the passenger door, pushed the Englishman inside and sat beside him.

"Prisoner again, lieutenant?" Anton asked, smiling in the rearview mirror.

Dobbs stared at him, completely stunned.

The Ford Escort sped away. As he weaved through the crazy traffic with everyone on the wrong side of the road, the former chief of pediatrics with a professorship at Charles IV University in Prague realized he was almost enjoying himself. He put his foot down on the accelerator and went through a yellow light

"Stay below the limit," Officer Yakovchenko commanded from the back seat.

They had rented an anonymous two-story house in a residential area. They had spent the previous evening in the living room with its floral armchairs, fake fireplace, and brown carpet. Anton and Natalya had eaten fish and chips and watched television. Neither of them would ever have admitted it—he out of contempt for the supreme symbol of cultural homologation, she out of ideology—but both were genuinely impressed by the opulence of western programs. They had stayed up late into the night, jumping from one channel to another. TV shows. Game shows. Even the weather forecasts were fascinating compared to the ones on state television in the eastern bloc. Now Harry Dobbs was sitting in one of the floral chairs, his hands tied up with a rope. His sunglasses had been removed. His left eye was purple.

"I've already told that other guy everything," Dobbs whimpered.

Anton and Natalya exchanged an inquiring glance.

"Who?" they asked in chorus.

"The other . . . " He wanted to say "Jew," but had restrained himself. "He was there . . . at the castle. I don't remember his name. He was one of the farm workers."

Epstein's mouth twisted in a sneer.

"Farm workers. Nice definition. Slaves. That's what we were."

"Yes," Dobbs agreed mellifluously. "We all were."

"No, you were a prisoner of war."

"What difference does it make?"

"The difference between life and death. The Nazis respected the Geneva Convention in your case. You were able to receive Red Cross packages, you had your uniform, your rank."

Anton went up to Dobbs, lifted his chin, and glared at him.

"I worked for them because if I didn't, they would have thrown me into the gas chambers. You did, because you wanted to." It was true. Obvious, even. And yet, Anton knew that he would never be able to rid himself of the shame of his enslavement. Which increased his anger.

Dobbs was silent.

"And there was even a handsome payoff in it for you."

"What are you talking about?" Dobbs blurted.

"I saw you that day, before the Russians came. You had a backpack full of stuff on you when you came out of the lab."

"Then why didn't you try to stop me?" Dobbs retorted defiantly.

"I had more important things to consider," Epstein said. His voice almost died in his throat.

Thirty-seven years had gone by, but every detail was still vivid. After the Germans had left, Anton had entered the lab where Lichtblau carried out his experiments and found them. Eight small bodies lying naked on the floor. The white tiles on the walls. The test tubes and apparatus on the counter. The smell of disinfectant. Together with Shlomo and another inmate, a Hassidic Jew from Galicia, they had buried the children in the garden under a large oak tree. Once they had covered the makeshift graves, the Galician had recited the kaddish. Anton never heard it again. There was no one left in Prague when he had returned. All the Jews he knew before the war, friends or relatives, had either died or emigrated to Palestine or the United States. No Jewish community, no Jewish funerals. The Party was not displeased with the fact, but Comrade Epstein would only understand that later. *Cosmopolitan, pro-Zionist, pro-Yugoslav Jew.*

"There was a war," Dobbs replied. "It was hard for everybody. You Jews think you are the only ones who suffered. Always feeling sorry for yourselves."

Anton's fist flew almost without him realizing it. Dobbs fell out of the chair and hit his head on the floor. Anton was waving his right hand in the air, gasping with pain. He was reminded of something he used to tell young mothers who were anxious their little ones might get hurt. "The frontal bone is practically indestructible." So was the cheekbone. He chuckled as he blew on his sore knuckles. But he immediately clenched his other fist and delivered a second blow. He could have gone on until he killed him. Part of him was not even shocked at the realization.

Natalya looked on, puzzled. Rather than interrogating the man, he was extracting revenge, which was perhaps understandable on a human level but completely futile from the point of view of the mission. She took command, separated the two men, grabbed Dobbs by the lapel, and sat him back in the chair. In addition to a black eye, he now had a swollen cheek. Natalya stared at that mask.

"Now tell me what you told the other guy."

"There was a priest."

"What priest?"

"A priest who helped Nazis escape."

34

East Prussia, May 18, 1942

M any things were exactly as you would expect. The Führer's portrait on the wall. A photograph of Major Lichtblau with his troops at the front. The framed doctoral diploma hanging above the fireplace. The latest issue of *Das Schwarze Korps*, the SS magazine on the arm of a chair. But there were a few incongruous details, too, starting with the modernist elegance of the Bauhaus lamp, displayed in all its glory on the desk: a reminder that, before the Third Reich, Germany had been home to the most advanced forms of European aesthetic experimentation. "Degenerate art," the Nazis called it. Lieutenant Harry Dobbs, from the defunct British Expeditionary Force, had immediately had the feeling it would be an interesting encounter.

An SS corporal had accompanied him into a room and told him to wait. Sturmbannführer Lichtblau would be there at any moment. While waiting, Dobbs had taken the liberty to look around a little. In the small, dark-wood bookcase there was an assortment of scientific books in English and German. Chemistry and Botany. Dobbs had studied some of those texts in college. He had been more surprised when he checked out the shelf under the gramophone. There was a stack of 78s. There was no Wagner, Bach, or even Mozart but rather a collection of American musicians, one of whom was black. George Gershwin, Tommy Dorsey, Benny Goodman, Duke Ellington, Glenn Miller. And there was even worse: a record of *The Threepenny Opera*, no less, composed by the Jew, Kurt Weill, together with that communist playwright.

Footsteps echoed in the hallway. Dobbs placed himself bang

in front of the door. As soon as Lichtblau entered, the prisoner snapped to attention and gave a military salute.

"At ease, lieutenant, at ease," Lichtblau said in a friendly tone as he sat at his desk and pulled Dobbs' file out of a drawer.

"Oxford. Magna cum laude. Congratulations. Who was your professor?"

Dobbs muttered a name. He was stunned. The man's English was flawless and without an accent. If anything, he had a light American inflection. Lichtblau was a scientist for the SS who listened to music banned by Reich authorities and spoke like an American. Perhaps, if he had looked harder, he would have found Sigmund Freud's books somewhere.

"May I offer you a cognac?" Lichtblau asked. He got up, went to the bar trolley and poured two generous measures of Vieille Réserve.

"War booty," the German said with a smile. Lichtblau had a friend at the Gestapo who would occasionally sell him something valuable retrieved from the piles of possessions which flowed into Germany, seized every day from Jews all over Europe. A gold lighter. A piquet shirt. A pair of mother-of-pearl cufflinks. That bottle had come from the home of a banker in Amsterdam.

Dobbs took the glass the SS officer handed to him. Drinking with the enemy. Colonel Nichols would certainly disapprove. Dobbs had been in the camp for almost two years and he couldn't stand the old fanatic any longer, with all his roll-calls, uniform checks, and obsessive adherence to regulations. Nichols was doing everything he could to keep a team spirit going with the prisoners. But to what end? The war was lost. Or at least, it had reached a stalemate. The RAF and the Navy fleet had stopped the Krauts from landing in England, but there was no way they could ever set foot on the continent again, even with American help. The superiority of the German Army was overwhelming. Dobbs had seen it with his own eyes. The Wehrmacht had crushed them in France in a matter of weeks.

In the meantime, he might as well have a cognac and wait for someone with some practical sense to initiate peace talks.

He lifted the glass to his lips and took a sip. He felt giddy almost immediately. He was no longer used to it. He had not touched alcohol since he had been taken prisoner, along with the rest of his battalion, in Calais on May 26, 1940. But the flavor brought him back to happier days before the war. He knocked back another sip and struggled to stay on his feet.

Besides, was victory really desirable? A victory allied with the Russians? Wouldn't it be preferable to seek a compromise with Hitler, keep the Empire in one piece, and let the Germans wipe the Bolsheviks off the face of the earth? When he expressed those views with his fellow prisoners, shouts and insults rang through the barracks. Nichols was deluded. He thought that one of His Majesty's regiments would appear on the horizon one fine day, marching to the sound of drums and bagpipes, and chase the enemy away without a fight. That all they needed to do was fly the glorious banners of Blenheim and Waterloo. Poor bastard.

"If you accept my offer," Lichtblau was saying, "you'll get extra rations, and I may even be able to get you quarters at the castle. It would be easier if you lived here rather than at the camp."

Food didn't matter much to him. The slop wasn't too bad and Red Cross parcels arrived fairly regularly. Still, having the chance to escape constant criticism from Nichols and his cronies was an enticing prospect. Lichtblau probably knew that perfectly well. The guards were well aware of the disagreements between Dobbs and the other prisoners.

"And what would my task be?" the Englishman asked, striving for a detached tone.

"To be my assistant in experiments and data processing."

The two men stared at each other in silence.

"You are an officer," Lichtblau added. "According to the Geneva Convention, I cannot force you to work."

Yes, the Kraut knew everything. He knew that Dobbs could no longer stand living in that shack, being ridiculed and provoked all the time, and he was taking pleasure in baiting him.

Dobbs arched his eyebrows with a philosophical air, as if to signify that life was more complicated than the dry articles of a code of international law.

"When do I start?" he asked.

35

London, July 10, 1982

One steak is enough to make you forget years of hunger. Anton Epstein couldn't remember where he had read that phrase, but it fit him perfectly. He had left Czechoslovakia less than a week before, and Real Socialism already felt like nothing more than a bad dream. He was sitting at the counter of one of the bars in Terminal 2 at Heathrow Airport, intent on sipping a Manhattan with the nonchalance of the man of the world he felt he could aspire to be. He was wearing his tobacco-colored linen suit with a pair of brown and white dovetailed Church's on his feet, which smelled of leather. Hand-stitched. Made in England. He had bought them in a store on Oxford Street when he had managed to escape Officer Yakovchenko's scrutiny for half an hour. He had also wanted to stop at Savile Row, the legendary street of London tailors, where his father had once had a superb grisaille suit made. But it would have taken too long. Perhaps another time. He popped a cashew in his mouth and closed his eyes, allowing the extraordinary chatter in all the languages of the world to fill his ears. *Cosmopolitan Jew.*

Sitting on the stool next to Epstein, Officer Yakovchenko was on edge. The deviationist was going too far. He had grown increasingly bolder since they had set first set off. At passport control, he had started blathering with the British policemen, spouting a string of absurd details about their business trip. Natalya had no idea what the officers had thought, nor did she want to know, since they probably imagined she was his mistress. Mostly, though, it did not feel like a good idea to attract the attention of the authorities with antics of the kind. Be that as it may, they had given the passports back without question. For a citizen of the Soviet Union, and particularly for a member of the Secret Service, this was unheard of. It was amazing how a social system as loose as this one could function. The British Airways flight to Rome was delayed, and they had stopped at the bar. And there, too, the deviationist had made a spectacle of himself, discussing cocktails with the barman like a decadent playboy. She had ordered a tonic water and sat glowering at him in silence, but it had done no good. The strangest thing was that the bartender seemed to enjoy his company. Natalya convinced herself that they paid him to be nice to customers and laugh at their jokes. This was capitalism. If you don't laugh, you're fired.

"I'll be right back," Agent Yakovchenko announced dryly, setting off to the restroom.

The conversation with the bartender inevitably moved on to the World Cup. England, the bartender admitted, had deserved to be eliminated, even though they had not lost any matches. "In any case," he added, "it was our first qualification in twelve years." Anton knew nothing about football. He had never seen a single game. Yet the character he was playing was supposed to be a fan. He improvised and limited himself to nodding at the bartender's comments. "Lots of people blame Greenwood but it's the team that's not been on form. He is a good coach. West Ham's results prove that." The two agreed that the Germany-England match had been mediocre and the bartender wished the German customer good luck in the final.

"Are you sleeping with the *shiksa*?"

Of all the world languages around him, that had been the only one missing. A language that he had not heard in forty years. Anton turned toward the man who had spoken, but he already knew who he would see at the other end of the counter. He had known as soon as Dobbs had spilled the beans. The *other guy* could only have been Shlomo Libowitz. And there he was. Older, fatter, and now bald, but there he was, with his big peasant hands and that cagey expression.

"So, are you sleeping with the *shiksa*? Yes, or No?"

Anton laughed inside. *Shiksa*. The great erotic dream of the circumcised male. How long had it been since he had heard that word? His grandmother always used it when she talked about Uncle Herschel. Whenever someone mentioned her youngest son, Grandma's eyes would moisten and the old woman would start sighing and cursing her daughter-in-law through her teeth. "They had the baby baptized," she would say. A scandal. He was only eight years old but Anton had guessed why Uncle Herschel had married that *shiksa* from Frankfurt. Aunt Lotti had eyes the color of a bright-blue summer sky and long blond hair, and when she smiled it gave you goose bumps. "Jesus Christ! One of my grandchildren is going to believe in Jesus Christ!"

"I've never touched her," Anton said.

"I figured as much," Shlomo replied. "You intellectuals are only good with talk."

The bartender stared at the two men, trying to figure out what language they were speaking, but a group of soldiers arrived and he had to serve the new customers.

Shlomo abandoned his seat and went to sit on the stool vacated by Natalya next to Anton.

"What have you been doing all these years?" Anton asked.

"I've been waiting for the Messiah."

Anton laughed and took a sip of his Manhattan. He wondered whether they should give each other a hug. It was what his instincts told him, but Shlomo did not seem to agree.

On the other side of the diagonal counter, the bartender was pumping the beer tap. The five NCOs from the Royal Marines were thirsty. They had downed their first pint in a few minutes and orders for the second round were already being shouted out. Shlomo observed them closely. They were young. The oldest could not have been more than thirty years old. One of them was trying to tell a little story but another kept on interrupting him, amid outbursts of hilarity. Perhaps they were on their way to the Falklands. They looked happy, an aura of invincibility about them. Shlomo wondered whether Eli and his fellow soldiers had been like that, too.

"See you in Rome," he said, getting off his stool.

"The flight is delayed," Anton answered. He did not want Shlomo to leave. He had so much to tell him that he had not been able to say a single thing.

"The *shiksa* is coming back."

Anton turned and saw Natalya cutting through the crowd with a confident stride. When he turned back to Shlomo, he had already vanished.

"Who were you talking to?" Natalya growled.

"An old schoolmate."

"Enough with this behavior."

"Don't you ever relax, Officer Yakovchenko?"

"When we have identified the target and recovered what he has stolen, I will relax."

"What if there is nothing to recover? Have you thought about that? It happened a long time ago."

"It is likely that he has carried on with his research. There must be something."

Leaning on a column in Terminal 2, Shlomo watched Anton Epstein and his *shiksa*. The Czech was dressed like a dandy. He looked like a *goy*. He wondered why he was working for the Russians. Perhaps he was still a communist, although, judging by her expression as she spoke to him, it did not look like they got along too well. Perhaps the KGB had coerced him in some way. Or Anton Epstein had made a habit of working for the enemy.

The loudspeaker announced the British Airways flight to Rome. Shlomo waited for them to make their way to the gate and stepped into line behind them.

36

East Prussia, May 20, 1942

"S ome military scholars believe that the best strategic environment for war is the desert," Lichtblau said as he donned his lab coat. "No cities with museums and monuments to preserve. No civilians to evacuate. No natural impediments, except for the heat of course. A desert is an empty space, a blank sheet on which the geometries of the art of war can be drawn in absolute freedom."

Harry Dobbs, at a respectful distance from Dr. Lichtblau, struggled to imagine what the man was getting at. Sitting at his desk at the back of the large, white-tiled room, Anton Epstein had already guessed. It was not the first time he had been subjected to one of those monologues.

"It is the same in this laboratory," the Sturmbannführer continued. "Thanks to the exceptional conditions created by the present conflict, it is possible to conduct our scientific experiments without the usual impediments of morality and religion." He eyeballed Dobbs, who had still not understood. At which point, he turned to Anton.

"Go and call No. 18," he ordered.

Leaning with his back against the trunk of one of the trees in the garden, Shlomo was taking the last greedy puffs from a cigarette. He was holding the butt with a needle so that he could smoke the thing to the bitter end. It was not the usual leftover cigarette end. It was a luxurious Lucky Strike from the International Red Cross. The day before, a British prisoner had given him a whole packet in exchange for three meters of wire. He flicked a shred of tobacco off his tongue, sucked at the butt one last time, pulled the needle out, and threw away the small lump of wet, shredded paper that remained between his fingers.

"Shlomo!"

He raised his head. Epstein came down the driveway taking small, nervous steps. He had grown up in such cushy conditions that he was not prepared for the war and its consequences.

"Shlomo!"

He threaded the needle through the sleeve of his jacket leaving the tip on the outside.

"What?" he asked brusquely.

"He wants Stiller. Right away."

Shlomo said nothing. He just stared at the fellow prisoner.

"Come on, move it," Anton urged him.

The two of them, and the rest of the Kommando Gardenia, were not doing too badly at the castle. Some of them might even survive. The opposite was true for the others: the ones Lichtblau had brought in from Soldau together with the new servants.

"Stiller is an old man. He survived last week. He won't make it this time," Shlomo said.

"And what can I do about it? He said No. 18. That's Stiller."

Usually the two communicated in Yiddish, which Anton had mastered quite well by that point. But he had uttered the last sentence in his native tongue, adopting the dry, threatening tone of the superior race. He was immediately ashamed.

"It's easy for you," Shlomo retorted. "You stand in there with your fucking abacus. But I'm the one who has to fetch them."

"It's anything but easy in there, and you know it."

Shlomo knew, but he was unable to resign himself to the situation.

"Would you rather I take Sara?" Anton said.

Shlomo did not answer.

"Or maybe you want to go?" Anton pressed.

There it was: the bottom line, every time. *They* lived because *others* died. Shlomo was not noble, courageous, nor foolish enough to choose to die for another, or together with another. He had not been able to, even when it was his father's turn. Shlomo Libowitz wanted to live. He reminded himself what the red triangle prisoner had said to him that day during roll call, desperate to believe it. *You cannot do anything for him now but one day you will avenge him.*

Without uttering a word, he walked toward the barracks where the prisoners were housed.

Shlomo slid the big bolt back and went inside. Sara ran up and gave him a hug. When she had arrived at the castle on her own, after her family had been displaced by numerous deportations, she had chosen him as her guardian. With the instincts of a child, she had sensed that there was a wise and caring older brother behind the tough exterior and she had trusted him blindly. Shlomo, in turn, had done what he could to protect her, bringing her food and small gifts. Sara had run to hug him but none of the other occupants of the shack had moved. From the bunks and benches where they awaited their fate, they stared mutely at Shlomo with a mixture of hostility and fear. That ordinary-looking boy, identical to so many other boys they had come across in the shtetls of Poland and Russia, was a harbinger of death.

"Stiller," Shlomo called out in a thin voice.

A vacuum was created instantly around the old man. The prisoners closest to him stepped aside so that he could pass, but mostly so that he wouldn't brush against them. As if, by mere contact, Stiller could drag them down into the maelstrom with him. They held their breath without so much as a nod as they watched him walk out. Stiller said nothing either.

Shlomo pushed Sara away with a caress and whispered in her ear that he would try to come and see her before nightfall. He offered the old man his arm. Stiller could hardly walk. There was a thick bandage on his right thigh, under the striped pajama pants.

"Come, Professor," said the boy.

When they were outside, Stiller stopped and closed his eyes, letting the pallid Polish spring sunshine warm his face.

"I've been a man of science all my life, but I didn't think I'd end my days serving the cause as a lab rat," the old man chuckled.

Professor Stiller's humor was completely alien to Shlomo, but he forced himself to laugh so as not to deprive the condemned man of that last little satisfaction. Anton had explained to him that Berliners took pride in their caustic and subtle irony. They considered it *modern*. They were the ones who invented the jokes about Hitler that circulated secretly in the Reich. Shlomo thought that if they had opposed the Nazis when it was still possible to do so, instead of telling jokes, perhaps things would have turned out differently.

Harry Dobbs was on his first day on the job and he wanted to make a good impression, partly because his transfer to the castle had not yet been finalized. He was beginning to realize, however, that being Dr. Lichtblau's assistant would be more complicated than he had imagined. The prisoner had accompanied an old man inside and told him to lie on the operating table. Lichtblau's intentions were quite clear, but Dobbs could not quite believe it.

"Jew Epstein, take notes."

Lichtblau said it naturally, without any particular emphasis on the qualifier before the surname. It was a formula. The alternative would have been to call him by his serial number. Anton would have found that more humiliating. The former student at the Faculty of Medicine at Charles IV University in Prague took a brown leather notebook out of the drawer, unscrewed the cap of the fountain pen, and prepared to write.

"Subject No. 18, gunshot wound to the left leg." Stiller lay motionless on the operating table, his eyes screwed shut. Lichtblau opened two buttons on his scrubs, fished for his gun holster, and pulled out his service pistol.

"You are a follower of Dr. Freud, aren't you?" he asked the old man. Stiller nodded, gritting his teeth in preparation for the pain he knew was coming.

"Fair enough," said the Sturmbannführer. "Interpreting dreams has been a Jewish science since Joseph and the prophet Daniel." He took the safety off the P38. "We are not interested in the unconscious. We are interested in blood." He pointed the weapon at the old man's leg.

Anton looked down. Dobbs, on the other hand, could not take his eyes off the gun.

The shot exploded violently in the room.

The old man let out a helpless cry and reached for his thigh, trying to stem the flow.

"Lieutenant, Preparation B."

Dobbs couldn't move. He may not have understood the order.

"Preparation B, the one we worked on this morning!"

The Englishman seemed to recover, went to the counter, and picked up a syringe. His hands were shaking. He pushed the needle into the bottle containing the bluish liquid and pulled back the plunger to fill it. But as soon as he tried to pass it to Lichtblau, the syringe slipped from his fingers, fell to the floor, and broke.

The Sturmbannführer's gaze was icy.

"You are a prisoner of war, Mr. Dobbs. I imagine you must have seen a little blood before you surrendered."

"Yes, sir."

Dobbs bent down and began picking up the pieces of shattered glass on the floor.

"Forget it. Go and get me another one."

Stiller's mouth was wide open. In an attempt to cling to life, his jaw emitted a rhythmic, mechanical clatter which did not appear to be produced by a human being.

Lichtblau approached the old man, took his right hand, and felt his pulse. His heartbeat was speeding up.

"Administration of the painkiller can wait. Conditions are harsh on the battlefield. It may take a long time for a wounded person to receive assistance. But wasting a syringe is a real shame. I thought you British had better self-control," he added sardonically,

Dobbs handed him a second syringe, ready for use.

Lichtblau took the syringe, pointed it upwards, tapped twice with the nail of his index finger, and after a drop had come out, bent over patient No. 18 to administer the injection. Anton pulled up Stiller's sleeve so that the Sturmbannführer's Aryan fingers would not come into contact with an inmate's uniform.

"Clean up."

Anton picked up the shards and wiped the stain on the floor. The Englishman stood to one side, far enough away not to be in the way, but close enough to intervene if required. Dobbs did not know what to think. Lichtblau's methods were ethically dubious, for sure, but one had to give him credit for his determination as a scientist.

The idea of war as a blank sheet of paper for scientists to fill with whatever they wanted was strangely seductive.

The SS officer checked Stiller's pulse again. It had gone back to normal.

"Go get Wasserman," he ordered.

"Right away, Herr Major."

Dobbs followed Epstein with his eyes. Anton instinctively averted his eyes, as he did with Lichtblau and all the other Germans. He left the room and closed the door behind him.

Dobbs took a step toward the Sturmbannführer.

"My apologies, Dr. Lichtblau," he said. "It won't happen again."

The SS officer shrugged as if to say that the incident was to be considered closed.

"That was really interesting," Dobbs added.

"I don't like doing these things," Lichtblau replied. He had assumed a confidential tone. "No civilized individual would like it. But it is necessary for the sake of the Nordic races: mine and yours."

Anton hurried down the corridor looking for the surgeon. He knew Wasserman would extract the bullet and suture the wound without anesthesia, simulating the worst possible conditions in a combat situation, but for poor Stiller it was still better than continuing to bleed out. The Nazis talked about "militant science." It was not science. It was a parody of science. Just as National Socialism was a parody of politics. He wondered whether and how it would end. Germany could lose the war, although it did not seem likely. And in any case, would he and the other prisoners live long enough to welcome the liberators? He arrived at the door of Wasserman's study, checked that his uniform was in order, and knocked. For the moment, Lichtblau was keeping them alive, but the day Anton and the other members of the Gardenia Kommando were no longer useful to him, they would all end up on the operating table.

37

Los Angeles, July 10, 1982

This place was not a city. It was a conurbation of cities connected by freeways: West Covina, Long Beach, Glendale, Pasadena, El Monte, Inglewood, Pomona, as far as Burbank and San Fernando. A stretch of two-story houses between the desert and the ocean, a giant carpet of concrete, wood, stone, and asphalt. An area so huge that no one would ever walk there. The wide sidewalks were empty except for the odd bum or old man with an expired driver's license. Everyone else was in a car. They drove to go and buy cigarettes or a bottle of milk at the corner store here. Victor Huberman had spent his formative years in two cold cities in the North—one on each side of the Atlantic—where the ubiquitous strumming of the elevated trains accompanied his days. He did not trust a city where the sun was always shining and there was no subway. The traffic light turned green. Huberman drove onto Pico Boulevard, went straight onto Fairfax Avenue, and turned right. Unlike him, Melissa loved Los Angeles. She loved their Venice home: an ochre and white bungalow overlooking the sea. She loved the neighborhood, a bohemian enclave wedged between Santa Monica and Marina Del Rey, populated by artists, skateboarders, and expat Europeans. The quarter was so eccentric that people even walked there. Every morning, Melissa would take a long walk along the beach. She loved the vast swathes with no center, which she would cross in her Ford Thunderbird convertible like a child riding up and down on a bicycle, enjoying the sheer pleasure of being on the move. She would get behind the wheel and drive halfway across town to see the view from the terrace of the Griffith Observatory, or to dine at Musso & Frank's on Hollywood Boulevard. She loved the Mediterranean way the residents were laid-back and the architectural quirks of the old down-town movie theaters. There was a bit of everything: Egyptian, Mayan, Chinese, and Assyro-Babilonian facades. Victor had dismissed them as a mess. Melissa had shown him the Bradbury Building, at the intersection of Broadway and 3rd Street, a building created in the late nineteenth century by a visionary architect who had conjured up a large central courtyard on several floors lined with stairs, wood and decorated iron balustrades, and flooded with natural light that rained down from immense skylights. Remarkable, for sure. Union Station was not bad either, with its polychrome marbles, terracotta floors, and sumptuous leather armchairs in the waiting room. But they were exceptions, islands in a sea of anodyne, if not grotesque, buildings, such as the countless revivals of European fashions of centuries past: English Revival. Tudor Revival. French Eclectic. Spanish Colonial Revival.

Victor Huberman had been born in Chicago, and Los Angeles offered nothing comparable to the vertical masterpieces that filled your eyes going up Michigan Avenue. There was nothing in Los Angeles that could hold a candle to the ineffable 1920s beauty of the Carbide and Carbon Building, whose champagne-bottle-shaped golden tip perfectly embodied the golden age that had preceded the Great Crisis. Nor was there anything that could even approach the austere perfection of Mies van der Rohe's skyscrapers: black blocks that the last director of the Bauhaus had scattered across the skyline of the proud Midwestern capital. Huberman turned onto Saturn Street and instinctively slowed down. The street was badly lit, and it was impossible to read the numbers. In the distance, he could hear a yelling-match taking place. Further away, the siren of a police car echoed. There was no curfew like in Watts but in any case, he had better be cautious. Huberman parked, got out of his car, closed the door, and walked to what he assumed was No. 25: a Norman cottage with dormer windows and a sloping roof. Ideal for a city where it never snowed.

William "Monterey" Jackson came to open in his usual outfit: flip-flops, Bermuda shorts, and a Hawaiian shirt. That night, however, his shirt was a kind of reinterpretation of the Hawaiian theme in a dark key. First of all, it was black and white, negating the very essence of a Hawaiian shirt. And then a line of bomber planes dropping napalm hovered above the rows of palm trees. Huberman smiled.

"Take a seat," Monterey said with a half bow and a playfully emphatic gesture of invitation.

"Nice new house," Huberman lied as he looked around. It was his first time there. It was filled with the same junk as his old apartment. The only difference was that it looked a little less dirty. The move must have taken place recently.

Monterey shuffled over to the couch and slumped down into it. On the stereo, there was a bootleg Thelonious Monk recording. Huberman took a seat next to him. Opposite them was a low table covered with magazines and newspapers. Monterey opened one of the drawers, pulled out some papers and a bag of marijuana, and started rolling.

He owed his nickname to the first steps of his brief career in the music industry, when he was on the staff of the legendary Monterey Pop Festival in June 1967. That was before he decided that selling narcotics was a more lucrative and less strenuous business than taking down a stage at two in the morning. Victor and Monterey had met at a Ravi Shankar concert, where LSD tablets were going around like candy on Halloween night. Acid circulated in abundance at the time, but in the case of the sitar virtuoso's performances, it was essential because without psychedelic support his strumming was unbearably boring. Huberman had frequented counterculture environments since the early Sixties. He had started on the East Coast between

New York and Boston, then moved to California. They had been years of rapid change. The average American had been frightened by them. Victor Huberman, on the other hand, was so aware of the world and its ways that the Summer of Love had not worried him particularly. Berlin in 1932 was more or less the same shitshow as San Francisco in 1967.

Monterey had finished. As always, the result was impeccable. The toke was elegantly tapered. The man was a true virtuoso. His creations were more than joints; they were origami models. Huberman had once seen him devote a good half hour to folding a fat tulip and filling it with hashish. He had almost regretted lighting the delicate paper sculpture. Monterey lit the toke, gave two long pulls, and handed it to him.

Victor inhaled deeply too. He let the smoke descend into his lungs and then blew it out.

"It's good," he said, wrapped in a little cloud.

Monterey arched his eyebrows as if to say, "Of course."

Huberman took another drag. "Local production?" he asked.

The pusher nodded. "Silver Haze."

There was a long silence. They passed the joint back and forth. The room was filled with smoke. Somewhere out there, the yelling went on.

"How's business?" Huberman asked, as detached as if the question did not concern him.

"Great. The freebase you sent is going fast. They're lining up in South Central."

Huberman nodded with satisfaction.

"There are a few problems with the Colombians, though," Monterey added. "They're starting to get nervous. The other night they took out one of our guys who was dealing in their area."

"Who was it?"

"A new guy. You don't know him."

"The business is full of unknowns," Huberman commented.

"That's what I've been telling myself," Monterey answered seraphically.

Huberman gave one last drag and stubbed out the roll-up in the ashtray on the coffee table.

"I brought you more freebase and some premium coke for your show-business friends," he said, indicating the duffel bag he had left by the door.

"Great," Monterey replied. "I'll go get the cash." He got up from the couch and disappeared into the bedroom.

Victor flicked through a magazine he had picked at random from a pile on the coffee table. It was an issue of Time that was at least three weeks old. There were several articles about the war in Lebanon, one entirely devoted to the Israeli prime minister. There was a picture of Begin visiting the front, another of him speaking at a rally, and a third, taken when he was young. In the first two, he looked grim but in the other picture he looked relaxed and almost comical. The big nose, the glasses, the black mustache. Huberman thought he looked just like Groucho Marx. All he needed was a cigar.

"Jews," he muttered to himself.

38

East Prussia, June 8, 1942

T
he brass insignia on his jacket lapel were polished. The badge depicted a grenade with tongues of fire and the motto *Ubique*. The Latin adverb—which the Engineers had adopted since 1832, courtesy of William IV—indicated that the Royal Engineers Corps had taken part in every war the nation had ever fought in. Despite his regiment's supposed ubiquity, Colonel Nichols had not stepped outside the limited perimeter of the remote prison camp somewhere on the Vistula for almost two years. The contradiction was jarring, and Nichols never failed to see its irony. He smiled, tried to smooth out the creases in his uniform with his hands, put it on, donned his cap, and waited for Corporal McKenzie from the 51st Infantry Division to report to the barracks. At 6:45 A.M. sharp, as he did every morning, McKenzie knocked on the door.

"Good morning, Colonel," he said loudly, lifting his right hand to his forehead, palm facing out, in accordance with the custom of the British armed forces.

"Good morning, Corporal."

Nichols had been taken prisoner in the spring of 1940, while he and his men had been trying to blow up a bridge. He had been the ranking officer and therefore command in the camp had fallen to him. Not that he found this particularly gratifying, beyond the fact that he could avail himself of the services of an orderly. McKenzie was the only non-commissioned officer among the more than four hundred internees. This was an *Oflag*, an officers-only camp. In compliance with the Geneva Convention, McKenzie had been transferred there specifically to provide for Nichols's needs. There had been a few escape attempts to begin with, none of which had been successful. Two of the escapees had been executed, while three others had been brought back and locked in solitary confinement for weeks. After those failures, Nichols had made sure any new plans were shelved. Some of the younger men, especially among the commando members, had objected: after all, prisoners of war were duty-bound to attempt escape. Nichols, however, had succeeded in imposing his will. The camp was at the very heart of the Reich, too far from Allied lines or neutral countries. Escape was impossible, a foolish waste of human life. On the other hand, the colonel had worked hard to keep his men's spirit intact so that they would not be cowed by captivity. They were and would remain His Majesty's officers. He thus insisted on punctilious adherence to regulations and forbade any socializing with the enemy: a thankless endeavor that required constant attention to detail. There were times when Nichols wished the Krauts would capture a general, although, as a rule, generals ended up in more luxurious prisons than theirs. His only chance would be to be replaced by a colonel who had served longer than him. But even that was unlikely. Nichols had joined the army before the Great War. Usually, men of his age would have fought safely in the rearguard. The problem was that in the Norway campaign, the rear was only a few kilometers from the line of fire. And anyway, Nichols was not that kind of officer. He had been captured because he had gone to oversee the mine-laying in person. The Germans had surprised them almost immediately. Evidently, they had been much closer to the front than central command thought. Or perhaps they had been deliberately sacrificed in a desperate attempt to slow down enemy forces as they marched towards the port of Åndalsnes, where the British expeditionary force was re-embarking.

Nichols stepped out, where his small team awaited him. Captain Jordan, Welsh Guards. Captain Fitzsimons, Australian and New Zealand Army Corps. Lieutenant Buckles, 1st Army

Tank Brigade. As soon as they set eyes on the colonel, the three officers snapped to attention and saluted him.

"At ease, gentlemen, at ease," Nichols said, saluting them in return. "Any news?"

"A Mercedes with SS insignia drove by at dawn on its way to the castle," Lieutenant Buckles volunteered. "Maybe it was coming back from the funeral," he added with a spiteful smile.

The four men exchanged a look of satisfaction. The Butcher of Prague was dead at last. On May 27, Reinhard Heydrich had been the victim of an assassination attempt. Two members of the Czech Resistance, who had trained in England, had opened fire on his car, seriously wounding him. After several failed operations, Heydrich had passed away. A solemn state funeral had been held on June 7 in the presence of Hitler and all the high-ranking SS officials. Nichols and his staff had heard the news on the radio the night before. The rudimentary set, built by a telegraphist major and concealed under the floorboards in the colonel's barracks, was an essential tool for Nichols. It was both a direct link to the homeland and a valuable source of information. The BBC had described the ceremony as "a gangster's funeral, in the pompous style of Chicago's Italo-American Mafia bosses."

"Spread the word," Nichols ordered. "The news must reach the other camps." In addition to the *Oflag*, there was also a *Stalag* nearby for British and French troops and a Lager where Russians of all ranks were jam-packed and where the Geneva Convention was worthless. Under the pretext that the Soviet Union had not signed the Convention, the Nazis abandoned prisoners from the Eastern Front to starvation and disease. Nichols had seen the Russian forced labor details being marched along the road outside the *Oflag* fence. Skeletal and filthy, they would do anything for a piece of bread. It was rumored that there had even been cases of cannibalism. Nichols was not particularly fond of the Bolsheviks, but he recognized that they were fighting with determination. At that junction, in fact, the greatest burdens of the war had fallen squarely on their shoulders. And the inhuman treatment being inflicted on them was yet more proof that there was no possibility of compromise with the Germans. It was the second time they had set fire to Europe in just over twenty years. They needed to be wiped off the map.

"Let's get started," Nichols said. The four men set off for their morning inspection, tailed at a respectful distance by Corporal McKenzie. Every day, before roll call, Nichols made a tour of the camp. The message was that prisoners answered to him before the Germans.

They set off down the avenues of the *Oflag*, stopping occasionally to say hello and exchange a few words. Two *chasseurs alpins* were sharing a cigar in front of the French barrack. Sitting on a wooden crate, a tank driver was sipping tea. He was wearing corduroy pants and a brightly-colored scarf that had nothing to do with his uniform, but he was a Desert Rat from the 7th Armored Division and they were very proud of their college-student eccentricities. The market was already open in the roll-call yard. A wide variety of goods were being exchanged: food, soap, books and magazines, small tools, and tobacco in all its forms. Even pornographic photographs were being traded, and none-too covertly. Personally, the colonel thought it unworthy of an officer, but he realized that it helped morale and looked the other way.

Nichols had just said goodbye to Major van de Kaap, of the 1st South African Infantry Division, when a second lieutenant of the Royal Fusiliers ran up to him.

"Dobbs," he said in a shrill voice. He pointed to the road that flanked the camp on the other side of the barbed wire.

Everyone looked where the second lieutenant was pointing.

Beyond the barbed wire, two men were riding bicycles. One was wearing an SS uniform: a private, or perhaps a corporal. The other was a British infantry officer. They pedaled side by side, conversing.

Nichols walked over to the fence and the others followed. No one spoke. In silent contempt, they gawped at the man who had been their fellow prisoner. He ignored them and cycled past as if nothing were out of the ordinary. The German said something, Dobbs laughed, and the pair pedaled away on their rusty bikes.

The colonel smoothed his gray mustache. "Let's continue," he said. The small group turned around and went back to their business. The men imprisoned in the *Oflag* had fought in Norway, France, North Africa and had been defeated at every turn. The Nazis had occupied Paris and were now the masters of continental Europe. Their divisions were on the offensive on every front, from Egypt to Leningrad. Yet, the Empire was resisting. The Krauts had not set foot on the British Isles. The RAF had beaten them in the skies. The Royal Navy, comprising a mass of gin-swilling perverts, continued to hold its own against the enemy. And now the Americans had arrived. Sooner or later the wind would change. It had to change. And then Dobbs, and others like him, would end up before a military tribunal.

Nichols turned to cast one last glance at the now-distant outline of the two cyclists.

"A gangster's funeral," he muttered to himself.

39

Rome, July 11, 1982

Under the red, white, and green flags flying from the balconies, the excitement on the streets was palpable. It was as if the whole city was holding its collective breath in anticipation of the event that evening: the World Cup soccer final. Anton imagined it was the same all over the country. Millions of Italians were waiting to watch the game against West Germany. It was a stroke of luck for their mission. It provided the perfect opportunity to get into Monsignor Grabski's home. The prelate lived outside the Vatican borders, in a building near Piazza Farnese. The only person guarding the place was the doorman who, like the vast majority of his compatriots, would surely desert his station as soon as the live broadcast from the Santiago Bernabéu stadium began. They could have clubbed Grabski to death in the hallway and no one would have got up from their couch. There had been minimal time to plan the action, but the opportunity was too good to miss and the margins of risk limited. All they needed to do was get into the house. Grabski had helped Nazis escape from Europe. He had every interest in keeping the story under wraps. He would sing.

Once they had checked the place out, Anton and Natalya had wandered around the neighborhood like an ordinary tourist couple. Once they realized that speaking in German was attracting attention, and on one occasion derision, they had switched to Russian. Or, rather, Anton had switched to Russian because Agent Yakovchenko, as was her wont, hardly said a word. However, when they had sat down outside a café in Campo de' Fiori, and he had pulled a chair out for her, Natalya had smiled without any shame. The beauty of that ancient city had overwhelmed her. In London and Hamburg, the Western world had shocked her with its naked display of merchandise, but here there was something more subtle. The idea that life could be sweet, studded with small pleasures such as sitting in a café in a beautiful square at sunset and sipping a cocktail (something Epstein had suggested, proving once again that he knew his stuff when it came to the customs of bourgeois civilization). Natalya sat comfortably, her legs crossed, one elbow resting on the coffee table, and let herself be lulled by the tinkling of the ice cubes. She felt she could stay there forever.

Anton gazed into her eyes and nodded. The old man seemed to have sensed her thoughts. He was sharp; there was no doubt. Anyway, Natalya said to herself, he wasn't that old. Agent Yakovchenko flushed with shame at the thought. She had a mission to accomplish; she must act professionally. She uncrossed her legs and looked at her watch. Kick-off would be soon.

Negroni. As he scanned the menu, the name had sounded familiar but Anton couldn't remember why. Then the image had become clear in his mind. An amaranth-colored liquid, ice, a slice of orange. He remembered it vividly, although he had never actually drunk it. His parents used to order it during their summer vacations at the Venice Lido. Shortly before noon, Dr. David Epstein and his wife would go up to their room and change for lunch, while he and Greta stayed a little longer on the beach under the English nanny's watchful eye, until she took them to the cabin to get changed. They would dry themselves off in white bathrobes that smelled of lavender and had the hotel name on them, embroidered in blue. When they arrived, the parents would already be seated. They would usually be chatting and sipping that reddish drink. Sometimes, his father would whisper something in his mother's ear and she would burst out laughing. Many of Anton's peers would be reprimanded harshly for showing up at the table after the adults, but he and his sister had enjoyed a liberal upbringing.

Anton would rush into the large hall and zigzag between patrons and waiters. Behind him, Greta would complain about having to wait for him, while Miss Piggott would beg him to no avail to compose himself rather than run around like a savage. His mother would greet him with a kiss and tell him to put his napkin on his lap, while his father inquired with sincere interest how much he had read of Winnetou's adventures or some other Karl May hero that day. David and Rachel Epstein had believed in kindness and progress. Anton had no idea where they were buried, assuming there had been a burial. In a horrific mass grave, perhaps. Or reduced to ashes in the wind. On the spur of the moment, Anton had ordered two Negronis. Officer Yakovchenko, for once, had indulged him.

Natalya was wearing the teal dress she had bought in Germany. Anton thought it suited her very well. He admitted to himself that he was behaving pathetically, given that he was twenty years older than her. But Natalya's crossed legs, the arch of snow-white flesh, her bare ankle, had awakened a desire in him that had been dormant for too long.

The waiter brought the drinks, accompanied by a bowl of olives, one of chips, and an ashtray.

Anton raised his glass in the air.

"To our success."

Natalya raised her glass to his.

The taste was slightly bitter. He could feel the alcohol rush, although the reddish color and the ice made it look like a children's drink. The Negroni went down easily, momentarily chasing away the heat of summer. There was nothing like it in Czechoslovakia. Presumably, not even in Russia. Over there, you drank strong, tasteless stuff. You drank to dull the senses, to forget, to punish yourself. It was solitary drinking, even when in company. In Italy, on the other hand, you drank to refresh yourself, to enjoy food more, to be with others. It was a pleasure, not a resentful, impotent gesture.

Anton stared into Natalya's gray eyes and read his own

thoughts there. He nodded, as if to convey that the café, the square, the sunset, were all real. It looked as though Agent Yakovchenko was about to say something not about the mission. He waited. But she looked at her watch and stood up.

"We have to go," she concluded.

Epstein concealed his disappointment.

"I'll go and pay," he replied. He got up and told himself that he had been ingenuous. What a gullible old fool he was.

As he stepped into the bar, the commentator was announcing who would be playing. A dozen customers and all the waiters thronged under the large color television set on a shelf. *Zoff, Collovati, Scirea, Gentile, Cabrini, Oriali, Bergomi, Tardelli, Conti, Graziani, Rossi.*

Anton signaled for the bill. The waiters looked at one another. One called out a woman's name, perhaps the cashier, and pointed over the counter toward the door leading to the back, but no one appeared. Finally, an older waiter came over, went to the cash register, and tapped the keys quickly without taking his eyes off the screen. For a moment, the ringing of the register covered the voice of the correspondent from Madrid.

One linesman, the speaker was saying, was Israeli and the other was Czech.

40

Government General, November 27, 1942

I n a metal dish affixed to the wall above the sink was a piece of brown soap speckled with grains of pumice stone. Obersturmführer Rudolf Brandt, Himmler's personal assistant, had explained that the Reichsführer-SS loathed nicotine stains and the stench of cigarettes. If an officer who smoked was summoned before Himmler, he was required to wash his hands thoroughly before meeting him. The mechanical instructions sounded like a museum guide giving a tour for the umpteenth time. Lichtblau didn't need them as the boss's idiosyncrasies were well known. Moreover, Lichtblau had already met the Reichsführer-SS, though Brandt may not have remembered it because it had been the year before. In fact, he had refrained from smoking since the previous evening. He had nonetheless paid a visit to the toilet indicated to him by Brandt and vigorously rubbed his hands with the bar of soap. That morning after breakfast, he had brushed his teeth with special care and even rinsed his mouth with mouthwash. The train started to move. The buildings that made up the small station began to parade by through the window, blurred by the heavy rain. A freight car platform. A locomotive depot. A signal box. Lichtblau breathed into the palm of his hand and sniffed. He was embarrassed to feel like a schoolboy trying to cover up his smoking at recess. Moreover, Himmler had made him director of the project in October 1941, and in thirteen months he had not yet produced any significant results. It would not be a good idea to further compromise an already compromised situation. Lichtblau dried himself with one of the linen towels stacked under the washbasin, glanced at himself in the mirror, fixed his hair quickly and precisely, put his cap back on, and went out.

Brandt was waiting for him halfway down the sleeping-car aisle. Himmler's private train had come to Małkinia, where the major had parked his vehicle, to pick up Lichtblau. The orders he had received did not specify where they would be going. He was told simply to report to the station in that village on the Warsaw-Białystok line. The convoy, Brandt had told him, was coming from an inspection tour in the Ukraine. Everyone knew that Himmler liked making field trips to check up on his troops and he was often on the road, both inside and outside the Reich's borders. When Brandt had mentioned a possible visit to the castle, Lichtblau had been more worried than surprised. Their meeting was going to be difficult enough. The sight of a well-equipped laboratory that had produced almost nothing would be far worse. His experiments with analgesics had had disappointing results, as had his research on drugs, where he was working in parallel with the Dachau team. The goal was to produce a substance that would prove useful during interrogations, a kind of truth serum. He had tried hashish, cocaine, opium, and mescaline, but none of these had been effective. The error lay in the very premise of the experiment since taking drugs made the subject structurally unreliable. His colleagues in Dachau had come to the same conclusion, but this had been a meager consolation. Even the material seized from the Soviets, on which Lichtblau had pinned so much hope, had turned out to be useless. The Russian scientists' notes had been missing and the laboratory samples were not sufficient to work out what the guiding principles of their experiments had been.

They crossed the bridge over the Bug. The train started to pick up speed.

"Wait here," Brandt said.

At a bend, Lichtblau caught sight of the last carriage in the convoy: an armored car with two anti-aircraft guns. A flock of ducks flew across the cloudy sky in a giant V formation.

Lichtblau wiped the condensation on the window with the sleeve of his jacket to get a better view. The rain was getting heavier, about to turn into snow. Winter was coming. In Russia, the Wehrmacht would grind to a halt again. The war bulletins were as enthusiastic as ever but the rumors were very different. The 6th Army had been surrounded in Stalingrad. In North Africa, Rommel's troops were on the defensive. Defeated at El Alamein earlier in the month, they had had to pull back as far as Tunisia. The war would go on for longer than many, even the best-informed, had originally thought.

The door at the back of the carriage opened.

"The Reichsführer is waiting for you," Brandt said from the doorway. Lichtblau joined him.

They made their way along another sleeping car and the dining car where six or seven men were seated—some in SS uniforms, others in civilian clothes—drinking cognac and talking, who lowered their voices as soon as they saw Brandt and Lichtblau.

They reached the car that housed the study of the supreme chief of the SS and German police, Reich Commissioner for the Consolidation of German Nationhood, and founder of the Ahnenerbe. Brandt knocked. When Himmler answered, the secretary opened the door and stepped aside so that Lichtblau could go in.

Himmler was sitting by the window facing away from the door. His head stuck out from the back of a small green armchair. His hair had been freshy cut, revealing a high forehead. The back of his neck had been shaved revealing his slightly stuck-out ears. Lichtblau could not help thinking that he looked outlandish. The Reichsführer-SS turned and signaled for him to approach.

"Have a seat," he said, pointing to the chair opposite his. Between them, there was a small table strewn with typed and handwritten papers, as well as a map of Eastern Europe. Lichtblau saw that the areas where the *Volksdeutschen* had settled—or would be settling as soon as when the military situation allowed it—had been indicated in red and blue ink. The position of Reich Commissioner for the Consolidation of German Nationhood—the original title, Commissioner of Settlements, was insufficiently grandiose and Himmler had changed it accordingly—meant that he was responsible for re-settling various groups of ethnic Germans within their new borders. Heinrich Himmler was far more than the Reich's guard dog. He was also one of the main architects of the grand plan to reconfigure European territories that had been set in motion by the National Socialist revolution.

"So," Himmler exclaimed, coldly, "you have made good progress since we last met."

Lichtblau was baffled. He couldn't make out whether Himmler was commenting on his failure sarcastically or whether he was being serious. What progress? The Reichsführer-SS might have been a narrow-minded bureaucrat, as many people said through their teeth, but he was extremely scrupulous and he had studied agriculture. There was no way Lichtblau could fool him. He decided to confess.

"The experiments with *Caladium seguinum* have not achieved the desired results," he said with some embarrassment.

"The mass-sterilization project is no longer relevant," Himmler retorted dryly. "That is precisely why I have summoned you here," he added in a gentler, almost complicit tone. "I want to show you the new direction our war has taken. I am sure it will be of use to you in your future research." Himmler liked to play the role of patron of the sciences. At their previous meeting, when he had been given the assignment, he had delivered a long monologue on the subject, urging Lichtblau to direct his research towards what he considered most interesting, and not to be afraid to take unconventional paths if he was convinced that they would bear fruit for the German nation. That was why Himmler had founded the Ahnenerbe in 1935. It now comprised more than two dozen institutes working in the

humanities as well as in the natural sciences with output ranging from historical, archeological, and linguistic studies on the
origins of Germanic civilization—the initial core of the society's
interests, as its name indicated, was "ancestral heritage"—to
meteorology and geology. "*Taraxacum kok-saghyz,*" Himmler
said with an enthusiastic smile.

Major Lichtblau took a few seconds to realize what he
was talking about: a kind of Dandelion leaf discovered in
Kazakhstan in 1932. The Russians were trying to make rubber
out of it. Lichtblau had added it to one of his last reports in order to stretch it out and attempt to hide the lack of results, but
he hadn't imagined it would work.

"I have already ordered extensive cultivation in the Ukraine
and White Ruthenia. It will prove decisive for the war effort."

Himmler looked ecstatic. German industry desperately
needed rubber, which it used to import from Southeast Asia
before the war. The SS chief was eager to present himself to the
Führer as the man who had guaranteed the Reich a supply of an
essential raw material for the war effort.

Lichtblau nodded with conviction, attempting to conceal his
surprise.

"I knew I had set my sights on the right person," Himmler
added. Ahnenerbe botanists had fought fiercely for his position. The Sturmbannführer was aware that he had been lucky
to have been awarded the honor. And evidently, Lady Luck
was still on his side. *Taraxacum kok-saghyz*. Lichtblau wanted
to laugh out loud.

Eventually, the rain turned to snow and the landscape was
soon powdered white. Then, suddenly, the clouds opened and
the sun began to melt the light dusting of snow between the
tracks and on the fields surrounding them.

"Hörbiger was right," Himmler muttered, looking out the
window. His lips had twisted into a childish smirk.

Lichtblau hastened to confirm that he agreed completely.
Hanns Hörbiger and his followers claimed that the universe

was dominated by the struggle between fire and ice and that the conflict would bring about periodic catastrophes on Earth, the most recent being the disappearance of Atlantis. With shamelessly mendacious resolve, Dr. Hans Lichtblau agreed that this theory, which Himmler had followed enthusiastically and which for a time had even won over the Führer, had been dismissed too hastily by the scientific community. In 1938, as a result of the discredit thrown on Hörbiger's speculations, Himmler had ordered that the Ahnenerbe no longer deal with the "cosmic ice theory," or at least that no publicity be given to it. It seemed that the Reichsführer-SS had accepted the setback.

"Liquidated too hastily, there's no doubt," the major repeated.

Himmler turned to Lichtblau and stared at him gratefully.

"It is so obvious," he said.

He was about to add something else, but Brandt arrived to inform Himmler that Hauptsturmführer Thomalla had asked to liaise with him before they arrived.

"We will continue later," Himmler said.

Lichtblau saluted, turned on his heels, and walked away towards the dining car. He had a desperate urge to smoke.

He had ordered a small glass of cognac. The Reichsführer-SS not only detested cigarettes but also disapproved of excessive alcohol consumption. Lichtblau sipped it slowly, trying to make it last. Heinrich Himmler was the exact opposite of his former right-hand man, the late Reinhard Heydrich, both physically and temperamentally. While Heydrich had been the embodiment of the ideal of a Nordic warrior, Himmler was anti-heroic and looked decidedly puny. A man of few words, Heydrich was always direct and clear in his communications. Himmler, on the other hand, suffered from verbal diarrhea and spun endless yarns, weaving obscure theories with pseudoscience. Lichtblau, however, like Heydrich, owed a great deal to the founder of the Ahnenerbe, even though he was unable to distinguish genuine research from chicanery. Long before putting him in charge of the project, Himmler had been responsible for a decisive turning point in his life. In a 1935 speech, he had insisted on the need to consolidate the biological core of the Reich by bringing the German-speaking communities who lived outside the national borders "back" to the homeland. Among others, he had cited the millions of German-speakers who had settled in the United States. American newspapers had reported the news with scathing irony but for Hans Lichtblau the speech had been an epiphany. The new Reich founded by Adolf Hitler was the answer to all his problems. Three months later, the young *Volksdeutscher* had purchased a second-class ticket for a one-way trip on the ocean liner Bremen. A homeland he had never seen awaited him and was happy to embrace him as a citizen.

Hans Lichtblau had grown up on the North Side, the area of Chicago where the Germans who had crossed the ocean en masse in the nineteenth century lived. Theirs had been a success story; an undistilled American dream. After landing at Ellis Island in 1893, his father had started out in Newark, New Jersey, then moved to Chicago. On the bottom rung of the ladder, he had gotten a job in the Union Stock Yards, the giant slaughterhouse district that contributed to the fortune of that fast-growing metropolis. The city was the industrial meat-packing capital of the world. Every day, thousands of animals—cows, sheep, and pigs—arrived by train from the agricultural states of the West and were slaughtered, butchered, and canned by a multitude of immigrants who were paid a pittance. Workers were able to reduce an animal to the sum of its parts in minutes owing to a scientific organization of labor that would later become Henry Ford's model for the assembly line. His father had sweated all day alongside Poles, Irishmen, and Ukrainians, immersed in the stench of blood and entrails. By the early 1910s, however, with the support of his wife—an indomitable and parsimonious woman also of German descent—he had managed to set up his own sausage factory that sold its products in the whole of Illinois. Mr. Lichtblau was not ashamed of his humble origins. In fact, he was proud of them. Every now and again he would take Hans and his two older brothers to visit the Union Stock Yards so that the boys, who had lived a comfortable life, could breathe in that fetid air and realize what life had been like for him.

Back then, the German community was well-respected in the United States. They were praised for their industriousness, precision and culture. This was unsurprising given that, of the diverse panoply of the American melting pot, a German—especially one of the Lutheran persuasion—was as close as one could get to the master race of white Anglo-Saxon Protestants. Then, Gavrilo Princip had assassinated Franz Ferdinand, the Archduke of Austria, on June 28, 1914, in Sarajevo, and everything in Hans Lichtblau's world had suddenly changed. German-Americans opposed the idea that their adopted country would side with France and England. They were good Americans but they were also attached to their mother country. In this respect, they were akin to the Irish, who did not want to fight alongside the oppressors of their former homeland. Germans, however, found themselves in a more complicated situation. They spoke the language of what the newspapers called "the Huns." Many even had portraits of the Kaiser hanging in their homes. When President Wilson had declared war on Germany in April 1917, the position of the Germans of America had become unsustainable. Some—not many, but enough to fuel the climate of paranoia—had turned to sabotage. Many Germans, moreover, had become active in the Socialist Party, which opposed the war. Suddenly, German-Americans no longer enjoyed the status of model citizens. They had become spies in the pay of the enemy, dangerous subversives. Although he was only six years old at the time, Hans had a vividly searing recollection of his father being beaten up by a mob of "hyphen-less" Americans. The child had witnessed the chilling scene from the bay window in the living room of their beautiful Fullerton Avenue home. The maid had covered his eyes with her hand and moved him to his room as soon as she had realized where he was. But he had seen enough.

Within a few months, the schools and German-language newspapers had been closed. The dozens of Midwestern towns previously called Berlin had been renamed Lincoln. In Chicago, the Bismarck had become the Randolph Hotel. German-Americans had been forced to abandon their language and culture and become Anglo-Saxons. In some ways, it was an honor. Hans Lichtblau's parents, defending the American dream to the last, were resigned. They had removed the Kaiser's portrait from the living room and had stopped speaking German, at least outside the home. By the twenties, the Lichtblau's were one hundred-percent American. The dream was safe. Trade was brisk. The stock market was growing. Hans was studying Botany at the prestigious University of Chicago, founded by John D. Rockefeller. His elder brother worked with his father in the company and was preparing to take his place, while the younger one was an engineer in San Francisco. But on October 24, 1929, the spell was broken again, this time permanently. His elder brother, who had invested almost all his family savings in the stock market, downed a bottle of whiskey—proving his American bona fides—and jumped from the fifth floor of a hotel on La Salle Street. Within a year, the factory had closed. Hans had been forced to stop studying. From San Francisco, Karl—who became Carl in 1919—sent money every now and again, but he too was in troubled waters, with a young child and a second one on the way. After years of sacrifice and hard work, Hans's parents had gone back to living in two cramped, poorly-heated rooms. They had died of grief and shame within weeks of one another. Hans was living hand-to-mouth. Himmler's appeal had been like a stay of execution for a dead man walking.

The Reichsführer-SS train had pulled into a station. The sign on the platform said "Treblinka." The name meant nothing to

Lichtblau. A convoy of cattle trucks came in from a branch line that vanished into the forest. Some of the carriages had their doors open and appeared to be empty. The convoy was picking up speed. As soon as it had gone by, Himmler's private train took the same track. It proceeded through the trees for a few minutes. Then the locomotive braked.

There were about ten of them on the platform. Himmler, Brandt, Lichtblau, and the men from the dining car. These latter were staring at the Sturmbannführer with distrust.

"Dr. Lichtblau, from the Ahnenerbe," Himmler said, introducing him to the others. He paused theatrically and added, "He is here on an educational trip."

One of the men chuckled.

Lichtblau looked around. They were standing in a muddy clearing. A few objects were strewn around, seemingly misplaced by careless travelers. A bundle. A woman's shoe. An umbrella. There was a small station. A ticket office, a luggage deposit, a café, and numerous signs, "To Białystok," "To Warsaw," "To Siedlce." There was something odd about it, though. More than a station, it looked like an imitation of a station. The details were missing. There was no clock, no mailbox, no timetable hanging on the wall. Most conspicuously, there were no people. No stationmaster, no conductor, no porters. A little further on, the platform came to an end with a buffer. How could anyone go to the places indicated in the signs?

There was a slightly sweet, sickening smell in the air. Something began to take shape at the back of Lichtblau's mind. Himmler was watching his reaction with interest. Lichtblau shifted his gaze beyond the station. There were six-meter-high fences intertwined so thickly with pine branches that it was impossible to see what lay behind them. There were deep anti-tank ditches, defensive *chevaux de frise*, and watchtowers equipped with machine guns. Lichtblau's mind strove to deny the evidence provided by those clues. If this was a station, it was a place one departs from. Who cared if the platform ended and there was no conductor? There were signs indicating that one could travel to Białystok, Warsaw, or Siedlce.

An SS officer, a captain, walked towards them from the fence. He greeted Himmler and some of the others. He, too, cast a suspicious glance at Lichtblau. One of the men in civilian clothing exchanged a few words with him, but Lichtblau could not hear what was being said.

"They just closed the doors," the captain said.

The group moved on, leaving the little station behind.

They went through the outer fence and past the *chevaux de frise*. Inside, there were rows of pitiful, hastily-constructed huts. Clearly, they had not been built to last. A few prisoners in striped pajamas moved between the huts, stooped intently under what they were carrying into one of the buildings. Lichtblau went to look inside. There were no windows. The hangar was piled high. There was the most diverse array of objects, sorted by type. Shaving brushes. Jam jars. Combs. Coats. Strollers. Belts. Books. Ties. Musical instruments. In one corner, two prisoners were washing their hands with eau de Cologne. One was cupping his hands while the other poured the scented liquid out of the glass bottle. Then they reversed roles.

"Water is rationed in the camp," the captain who had come to receive them said. Lichtblau had not even noticed that he had approached. "Only the guards can wash with water," he explained. Lichtblau stared at him in shock but said nothing and followed him. The visit continued.

They arrived in front of a big, grim-looking stone building. It could have been a church. A few flowerpots made the entrance less austere.

"With the ten that we have added, we have gained 320 square meters," Lichtblau heard someone say. He did not turn to see who it was.

"There used to be four?"

"Three, and small ones at that, barely 16 square meters

each." Farther on, a large bulldozer was digging under a yellow dust-storm.

"How long does the process take?"

"Twenty to twenty-five minutes."

Lichtblau tried hard not to pay attention to the banging and screams coming from inside the stone building.

Next to the building ran narrow-gauge tracks. Lichtblau took a few steps in that direction but immediately turned to look for Himmler, who gestured to him, like a mother encouraging her child to venture into the garden or onto the beach: there was nothing to fear. Lichtblau followed the tracks. On the side of the building there were several doors. In front of each door, there were self-balancing trolleys in rows on the track. Next to each trolley, was a pair of prisoners, waiting. Lichtblau walked on. The tracks led to a network of large pits. A bulldozer was digging relentlessly. Lichtblau looked into the nearest pit. It was filled with decaying organic matter. Flesh, bones, skin. In that mass, there were wide-open eyes, wild faces, hands clenched in grotesque poses. Lichtblau again strove to ignore the details. He was not to think of them as people. It was like the Chicago meat-packing district. There was a job to be done and it was being done. The procedure was similar. The arrival by train. The teams of workers, each with a specific task. The rails. The machines. The stench. It was a disassembly line, just like one churning out hot-dogs. A factory, in short. But what was it producing? Lichtblau made an effort to come up with a plausible answer. Hygiene. The factory was producing racial hygiene. It was a terrible task but it had to be done, for the good of Europe and the world. *They* had been the cause of the 1929 crisis. A response was necessary in order to annihilate that dark invisible empire.

He had turned back, walking slowly so as not to betray the fact that his legs were shaking. Himmler had rewarded him with his gaze, saying nothing. Lichtblau had gotten as far as one of the huts and stopped to catch his breath, leaning against the wall with one hand. Now he really needed a smoke. A gunshot echoed. The Sturmbannführer turned the corner. In front of the hut with "Infirmary" written on the façade was a long bench and, a little further on, a deep pit, already half full. Miserable creatures of all ages and appearances were lined up on the bench. Cripples, amputees, people so old that it was clear from the way they were sitting that they could no longer walk. A Ukrainian auxiliary with a Luger stopped in front of each of them, put the gun to their head, and pulled the trigger. Calmly and methodically, he shot one after another. They didn't utter a sound and simply sagged in on themselves. Helping himself with a rake, the Ukraine pushed them into the pit. The others waited, saying nothing. They stared into the void or kept their eyes closed, praying under their breath. The children cried softly. Compared to the industrial process Lichtblau had witnessed moments earlier, this procedure looked unbelievably archaic. Here, the clamor of machine civilization had fallen silent and death had regained its most intimate dimension. The Ukrainian saw the Sturmbannführer in his nice shiny boots and warned him in elementary German not to get them dirty. Lichtblau realized that he was only a few inches away from a pool of thick, dark blood. He stepped back, or rather, staggered. The Ukrainian chuckled and went back to work. He slaughtered an old woman, a man with gout, and a young boy with polio.

Not far from the pit, two prisoners were digging a smaller hole. When they had finished, a third prisoner arrived with a wheelbarrow full of papers. Identity papers. Letters. Postcards. Drawings. Childish doodles. Diaries. Notebooks. School books. Wedding announcements. The prisoner tipped everything into the hole. One of them emptied a canister of gasoline over it. The other lit a match and threw it in. A column of smoke rose from the fire, which annihilated that mountain of messages, memories, and hopes in no time at all. A few flimsy sheets of tissue paper hovered above them in the heat, swirling as light as butterflies. But tongues of flame soon licked at them and swallowed them whole.

Around the pit, a few scattered items had escaped destruction. A bus ticket. The floor plan of an apartment. A telegram. A holiday snap. Lichtblau picked up a college exam register. It looked just like the one he had had in Berlin. The hard cover with the coat of arms printed on it. The student's details alongside a photograph. A list of exams with grades and the professors' signatures. This person's name was Stefan Dorn. He had studied Philosophy in Warsaw. As far as Lichtblau could tell from the list written in Polish, the student had taken advanced Logic. It may have been the subject he had planned to major in. The disquiet the booklet was causing him was about to turn to horror. Lichtblau closed it and threw it into the flames.

"I hope your educational trip was fruitful."

The major looked up. Standing in front of him was the Reichsführer-SS.

"Of course," Lichtblau stammered.

They were alone. The Ukrainian had finished his target practice and gone back to his hut. The three prisoners on paper-disposal duty had slipped away as soon as Himmler had come close.

The SS leader stared at him with an intensity that had been entirely absent in the conversation on the train. Now Lichtblau knew. Not that he hadn't known before but now he had *seen* it. He had been made one of the custodians of the secret. Would he know how to act accordingly, Himmler appeared to be asking. The Sturmbannführer nodded.

"We cannot let pity rule us," Himmler continued, his eyes flashing with geopolitical ambitions. "All of this is terrible, of course. It is the most arduous task one can ask of a soldier. And yet, it is necessary."

Lichtblau nodded again.

The silence was palpable, broken only by the distant roar of the mechanical digger. Lichtblau waited for something more: a word or a nod. But the Reichsführer-SS had nothing to add.

In the distance, the whistle of a locomotive could be heard.

"Let's move," Himmler said, in a tone that meant back to business. "Another convoy has arrived. We must clear the track."

41

Rome, July 11, 1982

Wherever there is a carcass, there the vultures will gather."

The quote had seemed appropriate to him, but the man he was speaking to did not seem to appreciate the irony.

"Matthew 24:28," Monsignor Grabski specified.

Shlomo Libowitz shrugged.

"Well, I suppose you have not read the New Testament" the cardinal said.

The conversation was languishing. The old Jew had sneaked into the house. It can't have been the first time he had done it. He had opened the door without a squeak and surprised him in the living room watching TV. Grabski would not have called himself a fan, but he had wanted to watch the final. Just as Italy missed a penalty shot, amidst yells of dismay, the man had jumped him and threatened to kill him if he called for help. He was certainly capable: his hands were huge and he looked like a killer. Grabski sat quietly on the sofa. At first, he had feared it would be about the Banca Ambrosiana affair, but as soon as he realized why the man was there, he had had to stop himself from laughing out loud.

"But you must know the Old Testament. What you call the Tanakh," Grabski resumed.

Shlomo shrugged again.

"God is not at the top of my concerns," he said. "He never has been, even before the war. In my family, the only one who cared was my mother. It didn't do her much good. She died of typhus in the ghetto in Łódź. Everyone died, whether they had faith or not."

"There is more to the Old Testament than faith, you know.

It is the Jews' version of *De bello Gallico*: an account of the Israelites' military campaigns to conquer the Promised Land. Campaigns conducted with the help of the most powerful of allies, which Psalm 46 calls "the Lord of hosts." The scriptures make it abundantly clear that Palestine was already inhabited and that God could only promise it to the Jews if he took it away from them. The Old Testament God knows no mercy. After He brought down the walls of Jericho, Jewish warriors slaughtered every animal in the city with their swords. He is a greedy God, too. After conquering Midian, he wanted Moses to give him a share of the war booty." Grabski paused to catch his breath, but before he could open his mouth to talk about the book in the Bible most imbued with martial spirit that exalts war in defense of the homeland—*1 Maccabees*—Shlomo grabbed him by the lapels of his shirt and lifted him clear off the couch.

"Theology class is over," he growled.

It occurred to the cardinal that the rabbinic tradition did not consider the two books of Maccabees sacred. Protestant editions of the Bible, which followed the Jewish canon, put Maccabees, Tobias, Judith, and a few other books he could not remember, in a separate section known as the apocrypha. But trying to engage in a discussion of any depth with an animal like him was futile.

"I've already told you everything I know," Grabski said, without a hint of fear. "Go back to the stinking *shtetl* you came from."

Shlomo pulled the cardinal towards him and head-butted him in the face. When he felt the bone crack against his forehead, he dropped him.

The clergyman lay limp on the carpet. Specks of blood mingled with the patterns. He screwed his eyes shut and clamped his nose with both hands, but he did not let out so much as a groan. Witold Grabski had never feared physical pain. It is transient. Only the suffering of the soul is eternal.

Shlomo went to the kitchen, picked up a dishcloth, returned to the living room, and threw it to the priest.

"Clean yourself up and tell me your story all over again."

Grabski obeyed. He wiped the blood away as best he could and sat back down on the couch.

"I put Lichtblau on the list in the fall of 1944," he began.

"Why him? He was small fry. There must have been a lot of them begging."

"I received directions from above. I suppose he had connections."

For a moment, Grabski feared that he had unwittingly revealed something. This was the only bit he had to lie about. But the answer seemed to be accepted and it was followed by another question.

"When was it exactly?"

"November, early December at the latest."

"Are you sure?"

"Yes. I distinctly remember closing the list on the day of the Immaculate Conception."

"That's enough with the catechism, or I'll give you another head butt."

"December 8," Grabski hastened to explain.

"Go ahead."

"That's all there is to it. I put his name down and then I never saw him again. He was supposed to go to a convent in Bolzano, then Rome, and then Argentina. But he never made it to Italy."

"How do you know?"

"Months later, I talked to the prior of the convent. The Russians must have taken him, or the Americans. Or maybe he escaped to Sweden, who knows? Germany was a mess at the end of the war."

The former deportee let out a hoarse moan. "I remember," he said.

The two men stared at each other in silence.

"Why were you helping them?" Shlomo asked.

"They needed help."

"Does that sound like a good reason?"

"We helped the Jews, earlier."

"How can you put victims and executioners on the same level?"

"There are no victims and no executioners; only sinners."

Grabski looked relaxed despite his purple nose. It was as if he actually believed what he was saying. Shlomo punched him in the jaw. Grabski collapsed on the couch.

"You priests were on the side of the Nazis from the very beginning. Especially in Poland."

The cardinal pulled himself up and started rubbing his cheek.

"The Church doesn't take sides."

Shlomo could not take his eyes off the cardinal. The man's hands were shaking. Part of him hoped the old anti-Semite would react in some way, at least make a wise crack, so that he could tear him apart.

"Hitler grew up in a Catholic family," Shlomo said. "He never formally abandoned the Church, and it never occurred to the Church to excommunicate him."

"Ours is a merciful God, not like the Old Testament God," Grabski was on the verge of retorting. But he kept his counsel. He could bear a little mortification of the flesh, but this monster could well send him to the House of God before his time.

His nose was still bleeding. Grabski tried to stem the flow with the dish cloth.

"Is that any way to treat a cardinal?" a voice behind them asked.

Shlomo and Grabski both turned around. Anton Epstein and his *shiksa* were at the door.

"You two are always late," Shlomo said.

"We just send you ahead to do the dirty work," Anton replied. He looked down at Grabski and examined him with a professional eye. "Mostly because you do it so well." He looked up at the man who had once been a fellow prisoner. "What were you talking about?"

42

East Prussia, December 24, 1942

Major Lichtblau had had a fir tree felled in the forest and set up in the lobby. He had personally taken care of the decorations. By that point, he was playing the master of the house in every respect. He had also organized a Christmas soiree for SS personnel and their families visiting for the holidays. Mr. and Mrs. von Lehndorff had also been invited, but the baron had declined. He refused to be treated as a guest in his own home. Moreover, von Lehndorff was not a fan of the kind of sickly-sweet petit-bourgeois rituals that Lichtblau seemed intent on offering in his particularly ostentatious celebration. There was even a film screening planned for the party. That morning, a Waffen-SS truck had unloaded a 16mm projector, along with a cameraman in full dress uniform. To the baron, cinema had always seemed a rather elementary, coarse form of entertainment. Flickering, insubstantial shadows, unlike the protagonists of literature or theater. A system for creating illusions that may be fine for children, or for the kind of pornographic images projected in brothels. Carlotta claimed some films were worth seeing. That they could even be called "art." His wife might be right, but there was no way the little party organized by Sturmbannführer Lichtblau would present him with a convincing showcase for the aesthetic qualities of cinema.

From the first-floor landing, his elbows propped on the banisters, the baron smoked his Meerschaum pipe and gazed at the Christmas tree below him. It was so tall that if he had stretched his foot out, he would have been able to touch the silver star perched on the top. On its branches were blown-glass balls, some transparent and others painted in bright colors. There were little white bells, felt angels and Santas, dried orange slices, red bows, and cinnamon sticks whose pungent aroma wafted up into von Lehndorff's nostrils, mingling with the smell of tobacco.

One of the new servants appeared in the hall and placed some presents at the foot of the tree. The major had been thorough. He had probably invited his mistress, too, with the two children. Von Lehndorff had caught sight of them on several occasions. The first time she had come to the castle, Lichtblau had made a point of introducing them officially. The woman, visibly in awe, had curtseyed awkwardly, like a peasant.

Von Lehndorff removed his pipe from his mouth and his lips curled into a smile. Major Lichtblau was a man of simple tastes: movies and country girls.

"Have you put the gifts out?"

Lichtblau's voice was sharp and firm.

"Yes, Herr Major," the servant replied.

The heels of the Sturmbannführer's boots echoed through the marble lobby.

"Then go and help the others set the table."

The servant obeyed instantly.

Lichtblau raised his head and met the baron's gaze.

"Will you and your wife really not join us?"

The question had been framed politely, but von Lehndorff felt that Lichtblau was mocking him.

"Kate is making something for us," he replied, stepping away from the banisters and making his way back to his rooms.

"Well, Merry Christmas," Lichtblau called out. This time, the mocking was explicit.

The baron did not reply and went into his study. As he closed the door behind him, he heard Lichtblau barking more orders to the servants.

Von Lehndorff emptied his pipe into the big, green, glass ashtray on the desk, turned on the radio, and settled into his armchair. The news from Stalingrad was either very bad or very good, depending on your point of view. Even Nazi propaganda could not hide the gravity of the situation. Goebbels spoke of the battle taking place on the banks of the Volga as a modern version of Thermopylae, with General Paulus in the role of Leonidas. Only that the fallen heroes would number 250,000 rather than 300. Von Lehndorff hoped that one day Adolf Hitler and his acolytes would pay for the massacre.

The first thing they had done was watch the movie: an adventure story based on a novel by Karl May. Lichtblau thought it was pretty mediocre, a bad copy of a Hollywood movie, but the children had liked it and that was all that mattered. The party was mostly for them. When the screening was over, the grown-ups had had a glass of champagne in the living room and were finally seated at table. The dinner had been delicious, especially the roast goose stuffed with chestnuts. Lichtblau reminded himself that he should write to the camp commandant in Soldau to wish him and his wife a Happy New Year and to thank them again for the Jehovah's Witness maid they had sent him, who was a godsend.

Martha was wearing a black velvet dress that she had bought for the occasion in a store in Danzig that Mrs. Hoffmann had recommended. Against her milky neckline, the coral necklace Hans had given her the month before looked terrific. Martha adored the necklace and the man who had given it to her. No one had ever treated her so well. Poor Rolf had not been a bad husband, but he had been a small-town shopkeeper, nothing like Hans. He had not proposed to her yet, but it would happen in time. Martha understood that Hans's work was very important for his career and for the Reich. Having her and the children around all the time would be a hindrance. At the very least, they had to wait until the end of the war. Martha hoped it would not be long coming.

The guests got up and the servants began to clear the table

immediately. The men, led by Professor Schenk, who had already pulled a cigar from his leather case, headed straight to the smoking room. Meanwhile, the ladies tried to control the excited children, who kept asking when they would be allowed to open their presents.

"Don't take too long in there," Martha said sweetly.

"Just long enough for a drink," Hans replied. He thought that the coral necklace looked very good on her. He had bought it from his Gestapo friend. And it was nothing compared to the string of pearls he would give her that evening. The friend had shown up at the castle with a whole range of them: two trunks full of stuff, with which he was making the rounds of his most loyal customers for Christmas. Hans was at the top of his list. In addition to the pearls, he had bought gifts for Elsie and Paul, and a silk tie for himself.

The new dress looked good on her, too.

"You look beautiful," Hans whispered to Martha, stroking her neck in passing while no one was looking.

In a corner of the drawing room, on a *völkisch*-style chest that was an eyesore in the understated elegance of the other furnishings, Schenk had placed the National Socialist version of a Christmas tree. The trunk of an ash sapling, stripped of its biggest branches and planted in the hub of a wagon wheel. Hanging from the trunk was a wreath woven out of evergreens with candles and various decorations made by the professor's children and wife. Apples, gold and silver painted nuts, figurines made out of sweet dough. As a member of the SS and the Ahnenerbe, Lichtblau was more or less familiar with the symbolism, but Schenk had given him a veritable lecture on the proper way to celebrate "Holy German Night," an ancient festivity linked to seasonal cycles that the Christians had replaced. The tree alluded to Yggdrasil, the cosmic ash tree that in Norse mythology held up the nine worlds that comprised the universe. The wheel symbolized the sun. The decorations, too, had specific connotations. Apples and nuts represented hibernating life, which would awaken with the arrival of spring. Sweet-dough figurines portrayed characters from the Norse pantheon: Odin, his bride Frigg, and the eight-legged steed Sleipnir. The chest the trunk had been placed on was also part of the ritual. In accordance with the precepts explored by Obergruppenführer Fritz Weitzel in his handbook *The Conduct of Festivals Throughout the Year and the Life of the SS Family*, Schenk had insisted that the tree should be placed on a chest dedicated to Yule, the last month of the year, and had commissioned one from a craftsman in Neuhof. He had had runes and other traditional motifs carved into it, such as the ear of wheat, the rooster, and Yule's wild boar. Hans found the chest appallingly ugly. Once the holidays were over, he counted on moving it up into the attic along with the Christmas decorations until Yule came around once more. Schenk had also tried to convince him not to have a Christian Christmas tree. Lichtblau, however, had not been swayed. He had promised Martha's children the best Christmas of their lives and that is what they would have, complete with a tree with angels, glass balls and a star, even though his fellow SS, Weitzel, had warned that they were a sign of a Semitic cult's perversion of ancient Germanic ceremonies. Hans simply could not understand how Schenk—a man of science with extensive experience of the world, a veteran who had fought in Norway and the Balkans—could take such rubbish seriously. Believing in Odin was as absurd as believing in Jesus Christ.

Lichtblau took a sip of cognac and approached Wasserman, who was speaking softly to Captain Kiesel, commander of the castle's small garrison.

"Hoth's attack has failed," the officer was saying in a grave tone. "There is no way to break the encirclement."

"But why didn't the 6th Army make more effort to move closer to Hoth's troops?" Wasserman asked.

"How? On foot? They don't have a drop of gasoline left."

The shadow of Stalingrad had loomed over them that evening from the start, although no one had dared refer to it explicitly. There was a real risk that it would be the Reich's first strategic defeat. The El Alamein fiasco was on a secondary front. The Volga, on the other hand, was the main theater of operations.

"The command will organize a new offensive," Lichtblau intervened.

Kiesel shrugged. "Maybe. If they can get enough reinforcements in time."

"They could get them from France," Wasserman said.

"France is far away, and transportation to Russia is a disaster. Last winter I was there myself. Sometimes it's hard to move a platoon from one village to another, let alone get an armored division to the front. In my opinion they are doomed."

Schenk and Lichtblau were silent. The professor smoked as he watched the snow falling outside the window. Hans would have liked to say something but he felt that Kiesel was right. Martha's appearance released them from their gloomy predictions.

"We can't hold them back any longer," Martha said, bursting into joyful laughter.

Behind her, through the door, a throng of children were clamoring to open their gifts.

Elsie and Paul were ecstatic. The little girl had received a three-story dollhouse with furniture, furnishings, and windows and dormers that could be opened. Hans, on the other hand, had been presented with a large Märklin box containing a steam locomotive, four freight cars, tracks, two switches, and a transformer. It was the best Christmas Elsie and Paul had ever had. Without needing their mother to prod them into saying thank you, they had thrown their arms around Major Lichtblau's neck and kissed him on both cheeks.

Martha clutched a dark blue case with a string of pearls

inside. She was speechless. She stared at Hans and was on the verge of kissing him right there in public and in front of the children but held back. Elsie and Paul had long sensed how things were between them and they did not seem to begrudge her for it. In fact, they were growing fonder of Hans every day. He was kind and attentive to them, the father they needed. Martha unhooked her coral necklace and put the new one on. Holding her breath, as if she were playing a childish game, she ran a finger over the pearls, one by one. No one had ever treated her so well.

In the outside pocket of his jacket, Lichtblau felt the weight of the silver cigarette case Martha had given him. She had had a dedication engraved inside. He gazed at her. She was radiant with the string of pearls around her neck. She was beautiful and strong. Hans told himself that perhaps he should make up his mind to marry her. He was amused to reflect that Comrade Weitzel would certainly support the idea.

With the help of the other children and Dr. Wasserman, who seemed by far the most excited of them all, Paul set about assembling the electric train track. The chaos was absolute, what with contradictory orders, conflicting skill sets, and technical inexperience. But eventually the track was laid. Paul picked up the transformer and a hushed silence fell in the room. All eyes were on the model locomotive with its convoy of carriages. Paul turned the red knob and the train started moving amid clapping and shrill cries of excitement.

Hans wondered what Paul would think had he known that the trainset was originally intended for another child. A child who may well have vanished: buried—along with his family, friends, and neighbors—in a large pit dug by a bulldozer that worked non-stop. For a moment, Major Lichtblau felt his legs buckle under him. His Gestapo friend had told him that the Märklin box had already been packed when it was seized from a wealthy house in Lille. Paul might be horrified. He was still too young. However, at twelve Paul would be able to appreciate that stealing from a thief is not a crime. For centuries, Jews had been accumulating wealth without breaking a bead of sweat on their foreheads by virtue of their financial intrigues. The model train had been purchased with money earned through skullduggery. Paul would understand. Anyway, like everyone his age, he had taken an oath to the nation and to Adolf Hitler.

I swear to do my duty in the Jungvolk, in love and loyalty to the Führer and our flag, so help me God.

The model train chugged around the track. Paul followed it, spellbound. The boy lay on the floor, watching from the vantage point of an imaginary little person next to the ballast and, right there in front of him, was the pure magic of miniature linkages.

He was a bright boy. He would understand.

43

Rome, July 11, 1982

The street was deserted and the silence was only broken by the occasional blast of sound blaring from an open window. It felt as if the whole city had suddenly been abandoned and nobody had bothered to turn off their TVs. Every house was tuned to the same channel so that it was easy to follow what was going on as you walked down the street.

Cross by Cabrini. Header by Bernd Förster. Back to Oriali. And again, Oriali on the ground.

Shlomo, Anton, and Natalya were walking down a narrow cobblestone street without having to dodge cars or motorbikes as there was no traffic whatsoever.

Rummenigge, foul on Oriali. Free kick. Gentile's cross.

All of a sudden, a roar broke through the still-warm evening air.

Rossi! Paolo Rossi has scored a goal in the 12th minute of the second half.

Several people came out onto their balconies to shout for joy, wave flags, and blow stadium horns.

"The Krauts are getting thrashed," Shlomo said smugly.

They were the first words they had spoken since they had left Grabski's building.

"Shall we go and get something to eat?" Anton suggested cheerfully.

"This isn't a vacation, you know," Natalya said. "Let's go back to the hotel." She set off at a stride in the direction of Piazza Farnese.

Shlomo rolled his eyes at Anton, who raised his eyebrows in return.

"We'll meet again," Epstein said.

"Of course. Next year in Jerusalem," Shlomo replied. Despite his mocking tone, Anton was moved to hear the phrase that was usually sung at the end of the Passover Seder from a fellow Jew with whom he had shared the experience of the camp. "We are staying at the Caravaggio Hotel," he whispered.

"Get moving," Officer Yakovchenko commanded. "I have no instructions for a joint operation with the Mossad," she hissed as soon as Epstein was by her side.

"Shlomo does not work for the Mossad."

"I don't care who he works for. We will avoid any contact with him."

"We are looking for the same man for different reasons. Why can't we hunt him together?"

Natalya Yakovchenko stared in shock at the deviationist. Exile was not enough for someone like him. He should have been shot. *Cosmopolitan Zionist pro-Yugoslavia Jew.* To think that she had even fantasized about him a little that afternoon. She didn't quite know what to think about the other man. He may not be Mossad but he was potentially a competitor. She had no intention of sharing any information with him.

Standing at the corner of the street where until a few minutes earlier he had been walking with Anton and the *shiksa*, Shlomo lit a cigarette. The couple had turned into a street lined with stores and vanished. He imagined she was scolding Epstein for being gullible. Anton had not changed. He was still the tongue-tied young student he had met forty years before. But he was a tongue-tied young student from *his* tribe, and Shlomo would sacrifice a hundred *goyim* without hesitation to save his life. Besides, Agent Yakovchenko was too nervous. It must be her first important mission. You could see right away that she lacked the confidence of a veteran like him. Shlomo remembered his early jobs. It was a miracle that he hadn't gotten himself killed. Neither he nor the majority of his comrades had ever been trained specifically. Sure, they had fought. Some in Italy with the Jewish Brigade of the British 8th Army; others in the 1948 war against the Arab states. But only two of them had any experience in clandestine guerilla warfare: one as a member of the Jewish Combat Organization behind the Warsaw Ghetto uprising; the other in the Irgun, the Zionist right-wing group that had orchestrated an effective but bloody terrorist campaign against British troops administering Palestine. These two men had been their school. They had learned from them how to move discreetly through a city, how to tail someone or lose a tail, how to procure the weapons they needed, and how to kill quietly.

In the wild, anarchic days that followed the liberation, Shlomo had acted either alone or with sporadic accomplices. A band of four of them had once ransacked a German farm. As they searched everywhere for food and clothing, a portrait of the Führer had turned up in the woodshed. Although the two farmers swore that they were against the Nazis, they had executed them and then set fire to the house. Another time, Shlomo had stabbed an SS officer who had stopped at the same barn as him to get some sleep. The occupation authorities had given them free rein. The Allies evidently believed that survivors were entitled to some compensation. But then the policy had changed. The country they had been called on to administer had been completely wrecked. It had no infrastructure, almost no housing, and there were millions of people—concentration camp survivors, prisoners of war, foreign laborers, German civilians from the eastern provinces who had fled upon the arrival of the Red Army—wandering the streets. Law and order had been imposed with Nazi-like alacrity. A curfew had been instituted and anyone caught stealing risked the noose. But at that point, Shlomo's priorities had changed, too. What mattered to him was getting to Palestine. Building a state for the Jews.

After the successful war against the Arabs, once Israel had

earned its standing among other nations, Shlomo Libowitz had thought back to the words the red triangle had whispered to him during roll call at the Soldau concentration camp. *You can't do anything for him now but one day you will get your revenge.* But there was more. The Nazis were rearing their heads again. Without any fanfare, they were returning to positions of power. The Cold War was underway and the US could not accept Germany being banned forever. Getting the German economy back on its feet was as essential to the stability of Western Europe as the armed forces of the newly formed Federal Republic were to its defense. The Americans had selected General Reinhard Gehlen to organize their new ally's intelligence services. Having been the head of the Third Reich's military intelligence on the Russian front, he had enlisted many former comrades. Of course, Gehlen was shrewd and well aware of his country's debt to the Jews. He did what he could to help Israel. But it was a glaring contradiction, and it was not the only one. In 1952, Ben Gurion had accepted war reparations from the presentable face of Germany in the person of Chancellor Adenauer. Herut, the party born out of the ashes of Irgun and led by Menachem Begin, had scornfully rejected the offer. But it was a minority and marginal force, at home as well as abroad. When Begin had visited the United States in late 1948, prominent members of the Jewish intelligentsia, including Albert Einstein and Hannah Arendt, had publicly accused him of being a crypto-fascist. Ben Gurion's Labor government, on the other hand, with healthy social-democratic pragmatism, had taken the money. Shlomo knew it had been the right choice. Israel was poor and surrounded by enemies, an alliance with the United States had not yet been forged (the first massive shipment of American arms would only arrive in the early 1960s during John Kennedy's presidency). They needed the money. But Baruch Libowitz's son had found it hard to accept anyway. The compensation had not been only for the Israeli state. It had also been offered to any individual who could prove that they had been deported to the camps. The Germans were offering five marks for every day spent in a Lager. It had taken Shlomo three weeks to pluck up the courage to go to the bank and deposit the check.

With Adenauer's money, Shlomo and Rivka had taken over the bar in the Haifa market. That bar was his livelihood, but he had bought it with his father and mother's life as well as that of six million other men, women, and children. Reparations had been just the beginning. They had been a premise for normalizing relations between Israel and what Ben Gurion called "the other Germany." Shlomo Libowitz had known that Ben Gurion was right. He had voted for him. But he had not yet embraced the idea of normality. Hundreds of people would pass by the café every day. Shlomo would talk to everyone. Often about politics. Some of the customers had been in the camps or in the Resistance. And among them, there had been some like-minded people. At first it had been just talk. But, little by little, the plans had become more concrete. Two actions had been organized. In Austria, a Lager commander was found hanged in his home. The police closed the investigation ruling the death a suicide. In Italy, a Fascist mayor who had handed over entire families to the Germans had ended up at the bottom of a crevasse while picking mushrooms in a forest. The body was found by a forest ranger, months after the fatal accident. Then backers had turned up. Two American industrialists who had lost friends and relatives. A French banker whose parents had been gassed in Auschwitz. The Group—the name they gave themselves, without any acronyms or flights of fancy—had been active inside and outside Israel. A handful of operatives, a documentation and research center, a network of informants and sympathizers in Europe and the Americas. The first action in which Shlomo had taken part was in November 1953. The target was former Secretary of State Wilhelm Stuckart, the man who had been responsible for drafting the laws "for the defense of German blood and honor." They had faked a traffic accident. Some newspapers had speculated that it had been an assassination attempt, but it had never gone any further. Rivka had not been keen on it, but she was a *sabra*, born and raised in Palestine. No one had ever locked her in a Lager, ghetto, or gas chamber. But she had not opposed it. Galvanized by his early success, Shlomo had continued. Irregularly, but nonetheless he had gone on. The actions were few and far between because the Group was relatively small and consisted of people with normal lives, jobs, and families. Moreover, the research was getting more complex as memories faded. He had continued, though. And had only pulled out when Rivka could take no more and gave him a stark choice: either Nazi hunter or father and husband. Shlomo had chosen. They had been happy. Then Eli had died. And Lichtblau had resurfaced.

Shlomo threw the unfiltered Lucky Strike butt on the road and stubbed it out with his shoe. He wanted to talk to Rivka, but it was against the rules. The phones could be tapped. Shin Bet was aware of what they were up to. They did not approve, but neither did they stop them as long as they kept a low profile. But perhaps even that tacit agreement had been done away with. The officer at Tel Aviv airport had made that clear.

He walked towards the street lined with stores that Anton and the *shiksa* had walked down. He went down into a subway station. By the time he came back up to road level, a few blocks from his hotel, the match was over. People were starting to take to the streets. Cars crammed with people leaning out of the windows, yelling, and waving flags, wove past him. A monstrous cacophony of horns filled the air. He crossed a square with a park. In the middle was a kiosk selling soft drinks and watermelons. There were about twenty people sitting at the small tables, talking loudly, laughing, and eating slices of watermelon, which the owner was relentlessly cutting. As Shlomo walked past, the man handed a slice to him.

"It's on the house."

"I'm not Italian," Shlomo explained.

"*De donde?*" the barman asked, imagining he was perhaps Spanish.

"Israel."

The man's face broke into a knowing smile. He must have been about Shlomo's age. "Then you really must celebrate with us," he said.

Shlomo smiled back and sat on one of the plastic chairs to eat his slice of watermelon. It was refreshing and sweet, and Shlomo thought again of Rivka and their bar in the Haifa market.

44

East Prussia, July 12, 1943

The rear plate of the BMW R75 was almost illegible; the fork, wheel spokes, and sidecar plastered in mud. The Waffen-SS corporal turned off the engine and took off his goggles, revealing a tired, drawn face. In the sidecar, the other order-bearer was asleep, his chin resting on his chest. They had taken turns driving, only stopping to piss and get gas, all the way from Berlin. The orders had been clear. Without waking his partner, the corporal dismounted, stood to attention in front of the sergeant commanding the castle guards, and handed him an envelope addressed to Major Hans Lichtblau.

As the two were sent to the cook to be refreshed with sausage, black bread, and schnapps, Sergeant Dietrich took the envelope straight to his commander. It was from Reichsführer-SS Heinrich Himmler in person.

Lichtblau sat at his desk in the study and opened the envelope. In the letter, Himmler informed him that an SD agent stationed in Switzerland had gotten hold of samples of a substance synthesized by a certain Dr. Albert Hofmann in the laboratories of Sandoz, a pharmaceutical company in Basel. The substance had been christened *Lysergsäurediäthylamid*, or LSD. Himmler had tried it himself. At this point the letter started to ramble. The Reichsführer-SS spoke of a powerful inner revelation and quoted passages from the Tibetan Book of the Dead. Hans shook his head. He had no time for Himmler's mystical obsessions. He was a man of the twentieth century. Neither magicians nor soothsayers could guarantee Germany's victory. The nation needed technicians with their feet firmly planted on

254 · GIAIME ALONGE

the ground, like Albert Speer or the late Reinhard Heydrich. Himmler ended his missive recommending that Lichtblau experiment with the substance as soon as possible. "I am sure that your research will benefit from it."

Major Lichtblau opened the small package that had arrived with the letter. It contained two small orange squares, half the size of a postage stamp. He picked one up and examined it closely, with little conviction. Himmler had said he should melt it on his tongue. The man may have been an ignorant and superstitious former chicken farmer, but he was nonetheless Reichsführer-SS. Besides, his own research had ground to a halt. He placed the colored square on his tongue and closed his eyes. Nothing happened. He got up and took a few steps around the room. Still nothing. Lichtblau smiled. Himmler had been wasting valuable resources with the secrets of the Templars, runes, and the lost city of Atlantis for years. While Himmler had been organizing archeological expeditions in search of the holy grail, the British had been working on fine-tuning the radar.

The hall clock struck nine. Hans Lichtblau poured himself some Jim Beam and sat down in the armchair by the fireplace. It was pretty mediocre bourbon. His Gestapo friend had run out of booze and the local black market had nothing better on offer. Nonetheless, the first sip of Jim Beam tasted extraordinarily good to him. He had never realized the flavor was so intense. And the chair felt extremely comfortable. The upholstery seemed to adapt perfectly to every protrusion of his body. The room began to spin faster and faster until the major was drawn into a vortex and he was unable to distinguish anything around him. All he could see were flashes of light and spots of color dancing in a milky maelstrom. He felt himself being lifted off the ground. He looked down and saw that he was hovering just above the castle. He saw the two soldiers who had delivered Himmler's package climbing onto the motorbike and revving up. In the distance, the prison camp floodlights lit up the night with intermittent flashes. He made as if to swim and floated further up. By that point, the castle was a dark patch in a bend of the Vistula, whose waters gleamed in the moonlight. To the east, two races were fighting over who would rule in future. A great battle was raging at the Kursk salient. He wanted to fly over, comfort his fellow soldiers, and announce that victory was nigh. But a headwind was pushing him north. He had no arms, no legs, no face: only wings with soft hazel-colored feathers and a short, sickle-shaped beak. He flew north over the sea. As the sun rose above the waves, he spotted a rocky, desolate shoreline with no harbor or any other sign of human settlement. He flew into the heart of that unknown region over immense expanses of fir trees until he came upon a snow-covered mountain on the summit of which stood a colossal tree. Its roots clung onto the mountain face and its branches stretched as far as the eye could see, merging with the sky and the clouds. He let out a cry and landed at the foot of the tree to rest.

He was no longer a hawk and again in possession of his arms and legs. He was completely naked but he did not feel cold. He felt a deep, warm breath behind him. He turned around. There was a bear looking at him mildly. "You are here, finally." The bear had not spoken. At least, it hadn't opened its mouth. Hans Lichtblau nodded and sat down in the snow. He blinked. The animal had disappeared. In its place were eight men. Except for bearskin over their shoulders, they were naked, too. They were beautiful. Blond, proud, wild. They were from a remote time, before history, before Judeo-Christian morality weakened their spirits, before machine civilization had withered their muscles. They passed around a light leather bag and fished out what looked like dried mushrooms. They chewed slowly with their eyes closed. They offered some to him. The mushrooms were bitter and as hot as gushing lava once he swallowed. The warriors all stood up at the same time. They handed him a bear-fur coat and a spear and, together, they set off through the deep snow. They ran through the trees all day, tailing their prey, never stopping, and Lichtblau didn't feel tired. As the sun set behind them and the light grew dimmer, they saw a deer with majestic horns grazing on the bark of a tree. All of a sudden, the deer looked up. It must have picked up human scent. It started to bound off but the hunters were quicker. A spear caught him in the thigh. The deer was felled, staining the snow dark red. One of the men finished it off, slashing its throat with a knife, and they took turns drinking the animal's warm blood. He drank with them. He observed those sons of a primeval age. Their sculpted limbs, their gaze clouded by the intoxication of the hunt, their lips stained purple. And at last, he understood.

Sturmbannführer Hans Lichtblau lay face down on the carpet. The clock was striking the hour. He thought he counted six chimes but he wasn't sure. He wouldn't have been able to say whether it was six o'clock in the morning or in the evening anyway. He struggled to get up and staggered to the window. It was dawn. His body was shaken by tremors, he had a headache and was terribly thirsty. He looked around. He managed to get to the drinks cabinet and filled a glass with soda water. He downed it in one gulp. He ran a hand over his sweat-soaked face, straining to remember, to put together all the pieces of that extraordinary mosaic.

When Sergeant Dietrich knocked on the door of his quarters at a quarter to eight, as he did every morning, Major Lichtblau was standing there, his uniform in disarray, his hair disheveled, and his face very pale. Lichtblau said he was feeling unwell. It was nothing serious, but he needed to rest and would be in perfect form in a day's time. He dismissed Dietrich and went to lie down. He stared at the ceiling and thought back to the previous night's experience. Himmler's words now made sense. And some of the materials seized from the Russians, including the bird-headed shaman mask, also began to make sense. In addition to the samples from the greenhouses, they had also taken the library from the experimental station. Unfortunately, NKVD agents had lost, or destroyed on the spot, the researchers' notes.

Without them, Lichtblau had only been able to guess what the Soviet scientists had been working on. When he first came to the castle, he had examined everything that had been taken. There were books in German and English, standard botany textbooks he already knew. As for the hundred or so books in Russian, he had had the titles and a few chapters here and there translated by a Red Army prisoner, an officer who also spoke German. The man had been recalcitrant to begin with, but the promise of decent meals for the duration of the job had changed his mind. In any case, nothing interesting had been revealed. The library also contained an ethnographic section: mostly research on shamanism among the peoples of Siberia and Central Asia. This strand of research must have been related to the abundant quantities of dried *Amanita muscaria* that had been found in the experimental station. Siberian shamans used *Amanita muscaria*, a hallucinogenic mushroom that lives symbiotically with birch trees, to fall into trances and communicate with spirits. Lichtblau had tried using it in small doses as part of his research on analgesics. The results had been disappointing. Morphine was far superior. The screams of Romany gypsies echoing through the ground-floor halls for days had proved this beyond doubt. But now things had taken on a new dimension. The major washed his face, quickly tidied himself up, and rushed to the laboratory tingling with excitement.

The books taken from the Russians had been piled up in the scrubs room. Lichtblau fished out the volumes that interested him, sat cross-legged on the floor, and sank into reading. *Der Schamanisimus bei den sibirischen Völkern*, published in Stuttgart in 1925, explained that *Amanita muscaria* was consumed not only by shamans but also by reindeer hunters as a stimulant to endure fatigue. The very origins of shamanism dated back to the hunting rituals of the Stone Age. The shaman helped hunters find game, provided weather forecasts, and made propitiatory journeys to the Great Mother of the Beasts. In essence, the tribes of Siberia used plant hallucinogens to escape the laws of physics and access other planes of existence. In this respect, their culture, however primitive, was in tune with the great currents of Asian mysticism, where asceticism was often accompanied by extraordinary powers. Western travelers claimed that Tibetan lamas were able to increase their body heat in order to dry their wet clothes while they were wearing them, and to walk hundreds of kilometers without stopping. Lichtblau looked up. A year and a half down the drain. *Amanita muscaria* was not for the wounded. It was to develop super-fighters, and in far larger doses than he had experimented with.

There was a book in French. Georges Dumézil, *Mythes et dieux des Germains*, Paris 1939. Pages 73 and 74 were all underlined, the margins filled with notes and asterisks. Hans's French was elementary but one of the illustrations was familiar to him. He had seen it on a slide during an Ahnenerbe seminar a few years earlier. A bas-relief found in a Viking settlement depicting a man wearing a bearskin and brandishing a sword. Lichtblau could guess what pages 73 and 74 were about. That is, the *Berserkir*, the "beast warriors" of Norse tradition whose legendary bravery bordered on insanity. Roman historians had also mentioned how they evoked both fear and amazement. *Furor Teutonicus*, they called it. Hans had found the lecture decidedly thin on evidence and had never thought about it again. Dr. Hofmann's drug had brought it back to his mind. Or perhaps he had known those stories all along: since before he had entered the Ahnenerbe, since before he had learned to read. Maybe Jung had been right: humans did indeed possess an ancestral memory that linked them to past generations, back through the chain of time. Lichtblau had always thought that psychoanalysis, even when practiced by an Aryan like Jung, was a ludicrous pseudo-science. Yet what he had seen, what he had *felt* a few hours earlier, persuaded him that there might be a kernel of truth in the theories. Maybe there was something below the brutal surface of the world. And maybe that was the path they should all have followed. Since long before they had seized power, the National Socialist movement had always been divided between mystics and technocrats, between those who believed in spirits and those who believed in statistics. The Führer, and the demands of war, forced them to work together but once they won the war, and once Adolf Hitler was too old to hold the helm, the two factions would clash. The stability of the Reich would be at great risk. The twin souls of the Party would have to be reconciled. Hans Lichtblau, with his research, could contribute to the reconciliation.

He strode out of the laboratory and went to his study. He sat at his desk, took pen and paper, and wrote to Himmler. He thanked him profoundly for the LSD samples. The result had been extraordinary. Hofmann's drug had redesigned the framework of his entire research. The main goal now was to produce a substance that would sustain German soldiers physically and psychologically, enabling them to fight for days without eating or sleeping, and more generally to bear the brunt of whatever tasks they might be called upon to perform. The "educational trip," the major commented, had been fruitful. Lichtblau also proposed a name for the project. A name he hoped the Reichsführer-SS would appreciate: Operation Berserker.

45

Rome, July 15, 1982

They were feeling around in the dark. They had left London convinced that Grabski would put them on the right track but they had gleaned nothing. Agent Yakovchenko had gone to the embassy to request an interview with the KGB. She had been told to wait. Anton had refused to shut himself in the hotel and wait for feedback from her Soviet comrades, if and when they felt like it. He had bought himself a guidebook and set out on some sightseeing. Natalya had not objected. She was so nervous that she preferred not to have a deviant like him around. Anton had visited he Colosseum and the Imperial Forum. He had had lunch in a trattoria in Trastevere. He had strolled down the Via Veneto. He had sat down to rest on the Spanish steps. When he had gone back to the hotel at dinnertime, he had found Agent Yakovchenko in a better mood. The KGB were activating an informant in the Italian Secret Service. They would get in touch soon. Two days went by with Natalya locked in her room, smoking near the phone, like a girl waiting for a call from a boyfriend in a long-distance relationship. Anton continued with his sightseeing. He loved the Vatican Museum but found the Trevi Fountain a bit disappointing. It looked bigger in the film. The informant called on the third day. He spoke excellent German. An appointment was made outside the English Cemetery at Porta San Paolo. Anton wondered why they had made such an original suggestion: a non-Catholic cemetery in the world capital of Catholicism. He supposed it would be relatively empty, especially of Italians.

When Anton and Natalya arrived, the informant was already

there. He was sitting on a bench outside reading a newspaper. After a quick round of introductions, they went in. Perhaps he wanted it to look as though they were tourists, although in truth there was no one to deceive except the doorman in his kiosk doing crossword puzzles, and a few cats napping in the shade of the tombstones. Or perhaps it was because he truly loved the place and wanted to share it with others. Whatever the reason, instead of immediately relaying the information in his possession about the Lichtblau case, the Italian set about telling the history of the cemetery, zigzagging through gravestones, memorial plaques, and monuments, mentioning the names of the most famous dead. Anton was thrilled. Agent Yakovchenko a little less so, but said nothing.

They began with the centerpiece: John Keats and Percy Shelley. The setting was perfect for two romantic poets. There were time-worn marble headstones, words engraved in the most diverse languages, nature mingling with art. Not only was the cemetery dotted with trees, but here and there the graves were almost hidden by creepers and bushes. It really looked like they were in a Caspar Friedrich painting.

"What's that?" Anton asked, pointing to the pyramid towering above the Roman wall which surrounded the cemetery.

"The pyramid of Caius Cestius, completed in 12 BC The walls are from the third century. When they were built, under Emperor Aurelian, they decided to incorporate the pyramid into the perimeter, effectively turning it into a rampart."

"Was Caius Cestius an emperor? "Agent Yakovchenko rolled her eyes. She did not want to be rude to the Italian, but those two were going too far.

The informant laughed. "No, he wasn't an emperor. Nor was he a leader. He was just a rich boor who wanted a tomb in the Egyptian style. Kind of like people today have their villas built with towers and battlements."

Anton looked at the pyramid again. It really was an entirely incongruous construction. His mother would have dismissed

Mr. Caius Cestius with one word—*parvenu*—which was the worst possible insult.

The tour continued and Agent Yakovchenko could take it no more. But just as she was about to explode, the informant twisted the knife. Anton found it very Italian. Alongside English and American literati and diplomats from around the world, the mortal remains of one of the great protagonists in the history of European communism were buried in that cemetery. The tombstone was a bare slab with an urn at its feet. The inscription read simply "Gramsci. Ales, 1891. Rome, 1937" The three stood in silence for a few moments. Anton was struck by the extreme simplicity of the grave. It was a far cry from the titanism of Lenin's mausoleum, but there was no equivalent in Western parties either. Maurice Thorez had been laid to rest at the most famous cemetery in Paris, the Père-Lachaise—along with dozens of other leaders of the labor movement and the Resistance—next to the wall where the Communards had been shot. It had been a gathering place for French leftist demonstrations since the late nineteenth century. Gramsci, on the other hand, was in a kind of limbo, a little corner of England transplanted to Italy. Of course, he had been buried during the Fascist dictatorship. At the time, a discreet choice of this kind must have been necessary. And yet, no one had thought of moving him or building him a larger tomb after the war. He had been left there, under that unadorned stone, a non-Catholic, a foreigner in his homeland.

Officer Yakovchenko decided that this silent homage to the great man had gone on long enough. "So?" she said, addressing the Italian, desperately trying to conceal the impatience in her voice.

The informant walked away, as if he did not want to disturb Gramsci's repose.

"Hans Lichtblau was captured in Bolzano on May 12, 1945," he began. "That's why we have a file on him. He was caught by a partisan unit which turned him over to the Allies."

"And then?"

"And then he followed the career trajectory of so many like him. A little jail time and then a nice contract with the US Department of Defense. He was one of the many Nazi scientists hired under Operation Paperclip."

"Yanks," Natalya muttered scornfully.

Anton wanted to say that if it hadn't been the Americans hiring Nazi scientists, it would have been the Russians. By all accounts, they had managed to grab a few. Of course, most scientists had opted for Uncle Sam. The Krauts preferred Miami to Moscow. Comrade Epstein couldn't blame them. Yet, in spite of everything, he missed the enthusiasm and confidence of the past, when he and Anna had embraced communism as a way to eschew the evils of humanity's exploitation of itself.

"Where did he go?" Natalya asked.

"It doesn't say in the file. But it is reasonable to assume that he was transferred to America. The US was usually reluctant to give entry visas to Hitler's closest collaborators. They would put them to work in American military laboratories on German soil. But this was not Lichtblau's case. What is more, he was American born. It would have been easy enough to get him into the country."

"Well, if everything went so smoothly, why did he end up in Latin America like Eichmann and the other fugitives? "

The Italian shrugged. "Who knows? If he was still working for the Americans, they might have sent him."

Natalya struggled to conceal her mounting annoyance that the informant was not providing her with any information. Three days wait for a few assumptions? She would have been better off touring the streets of Rome.

"Anything else?" she prompted, in a last-ditch attempt to get something out of the man.

"I have a photograph."

Natalya gawped. Why had it taken him so long to get to the point? One would almost think he was being paid by the hour. The informant produced an envelope and handed it to the Soviet agent.

"It is a photocopy of the Swiss passport that Lichtblau was traveling on. The partisans confiscated it."

Natalya opened it. Folded inside the copy of the passport was another photocopy of a much more recent identity document. "And what is this?"

"It was in the file. It is a report from the Carabinieri at the Ostia station. I put it in for the sake of thoroughness, but it is clearly a coincidence. Three years ago, an American citizen named Victor Huberman was stopped for drug possession at a poetry festival in Castel Porziano, just outside Rome. He was caught with a briefcase full of marijuana and mescaline at the end of a reading by Allen Ginsberg. He was released the next day, I guess after the consulate intervened."

Natalya stared at the informant, trying to figure out whether he had made up the story on a whim to spice up his report. But she found no clues in his dark, smiling eyes. She slipped the envelope into her bag and started walking towards the exit.

46

Eastern Prussia, November 21, 1944

J ew Epstein!"
  Sturmbannführer Hans Lichtblau's voice rang through the laboratory rooms as he looked for him. Anton closed the register, got up from his desk, and hurried out of the office.

"Jew Epstein, what are you doing? Are you preparing candles for Hanukkah?"

Anton lengthened his stride. When Lichtblau was being funny, it usually meant that he was nervous.

"Jew Epstein, where are you?"

"I'm here, Herr Major."

Anton walked into the lab and snapped to attention.

"Round up the prisoners. All of them."

"Including the Kommando?"

"Yes, them too. But not the girl who arrived last week from Soldau."

Nina, a fifteen-year-old Polish girl. Anton had no idea whether being excluded was good or bad news for her. In any case, there was nothing he could do about it so it was pointless to wonder.

"I want them lined up outside."

Lichtblau went to the coat rack and grabbed his black leather raincoat. Lieutenant Dobbs, diligently helped him put it on. "You, obviously, are exempt," he added, addressing Epstein. "I still need you." He walked up to Anton and eyeballed him. "The last of the Mohicans."

Dobbs broke into a sincere-sounding laugh that pleased Lichtblau.

Anton lowered his gaze.

"Yes, sir," he said, and walked out of the room.

Anton walked quickly down the driveway circling the castle. The gravel crunched under his wooden clogs.

From the window, Baron von Lehndorff watched him. Anton slowed down for a second. The July attack had changed his mind about the old Junker. Before then, he had thought he was under house arrest owing to a mistake on the part of the Gestapo, the work of some overzealous or fanatical official. A Prussian nobleman, a career officer to boot, could not actually be anti-fascist. But the Rastenburg bomb proved that was not the case. When an excited English prisoner had told him that a Wehrmacht colonel had almost succeeded in blowing up Hitler, he had not been able to believe it. He thought it must have been one of the many baseless rumors that were going around all the time. But there had been several confirmations, not least from Lichtblau himself. The Weimar Republic had the most influential Social Democratic Party in Europe as well as a combative and well-organized Communist Party. Neither party had been able to stop the Nazis from rising to power, nor had they attempted to overthrow them. But a clutch of aristocrats and ranking officers had tried in their place. Good for them. Anton acknowledged von Lehndorff briefly with a nod and hurried on.

Lichtblau held a crimson-colored pill in his fingers. He looked at it with immense satisfaction. He had been working on it for more than a year. There had been failures and moments of despair, but in October he had finally achieved a result that he considered fully satisfactory. He had taken the formula to Viktor Capesius, the head of the pharmaceutical laboratory in Auschwitz. He had stayed in the Lager for a week so that he could follow every step of the production process. And now the big day had finally arrived.

"Dobbs," he ordered. "Bring the bottle and follow me."

Anton pulled the bolt to and opened the door of the hut.

"Everyone out," he said.

The prisoners stared at him, appalled.

Sara studied him with her big black eyes.

"What are we supposed to do?" she asked.

"I don't know. He wants you lined up in front of the castle." Anton sounded desperate.

The prisoners started to file out in an orderly fashion. Anton stood at the door. As Nina walked past, he grabbed her by the arm. He felt nothing as he touched her. She was a beautiful girl. Before the war, he would have found her attractive. But he hadn't thought about anything like that for a long time

"Not you," Anton said.

"Why not? "

Anton shook his head. He wanted to tell her that most of the things that happened in that place were beyond comprehension. He wanted to comfort her. But he was unable to comfort himself. He simply repeated mechanically, "Not you."

There were about twenty of them: members of the Gardenia Kommando and other prisoners; male and female, young and old. They were lined up in two rows. Sturmbannführer Lichtblau stood in front of them, with Epstein and Dobbs behind him.

"Prisoners," Lichtblau said.

There was a deathly silence.

"You are lucky. You have the opportunity to take part in a scientific experiment of the utmost importance."

Anton's knees began to tremble. He struggled to control himself. They had reached the end of the line, the moment he had always dreaded. The moment when Lichtblau would no longer need them.

"You will be given a pill. It is a miracle drug, at least I hope it is. And you should hope so, too. If the pill works, you will have a chance to survive."

Lichtblau drew his gun from its holster and removed the safety.

"See that hill?"

The prisoners turned to see where the major was pointing: beyond the woods, far away, there was a bare knoll.

"Those of you who reach the top of that hill will save their lives."

A murmur ran through the group of prisoners.

"I'll give you a twenty-minute head start. Then I will come and fetch you, and I will bring Captain Kiesel, his men, and their best friends along."

A hundred or so meters away, the full garrison was deployed in front of one of the castle towers. Eight privates, a corporal, and a sergeant, plus Kiesel. Rifles on their shoulders and German shepherds on leashes.

Anton wondered what he should do. Perhaps the time had come to act, to rebel, as long as there was someone to do it with. Better to die fighting than go to the slaughter like lambs. But he did nothing. And when Lichtblau ordered him to do so, he picked up a large bucket of water and a ladle and gave the prisoners, who had lined up in front of him and Dobbs, a drink. The Englishman handed out the pills and Anton told them to swallow them.

When Shlomo's turn came around, he looked him up and down belligerently before ingesting the pill. "You city folk have all the luck, eh? "

Anton began to stammer an answer, but the line had already moved on.

Sturmbannführer Hans Lichtblau checked his watch.

"You have twenty minutes from now."

The prisoners cast dismayed glances at one another. An icy wind lashed their emaciated bodies, protected only by their threadbare pajamas. Shlomo looked over at the hill. It would have been hard enough even under normal conditions, let alone after nearly four years first in the ghetto and then in the Lager.

"Move!" Lichtblau yelled. He pointed his gun at a random prisoner and pulled the trigger. When Shlomo saw Mr. Bloch's brains spray everywhere, he grabbed Sara's hand and started running. The others followed suit. They ran down the driveway leading off the property. Strangely, the little girl managed to keep up. Shlomo could hear the rest of the group behind him panting.

They ran past the mill, the barn, the farm workers' houses, and into the woods. Shlomo turned around. They were all there, even the older ones. Maybe the pill was really working. He didn't even feel too tired. Sara smiled at him. They started running through the woods.

From the castle, Kiesel kept his eyes trained on the prisoners through his binoculars as one by one they disappeared from view into the woods.

"Shouldn't we go?" he asked nervously.

"I said twenty minutes," Lichtblau replied amused, "and twenty minutes it will be. Where is your fair play, captain?"

"What if they run away?" Kiesel rejoined.

"Where do you think they can go? Don't worry, they will run to the hill because it is their best chance to be saved."

The captain approached Lichtblau. "Why are you doing this?" he asked, speaking in a low voice.

"I need to check. If any of them make it, despite the malnutrition, the dogs, and the bullets that are soon going to be whistling past them, it means the pill is working. "

Lichtblau checked his watch.

"Sergeant Dietrich," he barked. "Go get the truck."

Shlomo and Sara had stopped to rest for a moment. They were sitting at the foot of a tree, leaning on the trunk. Goldwasser and Mrs. Berman were a little further back. The rest of the group must have spread out behind them.

Shlomo got up and yanked Sara back to her feet.

"Can you manage?" he asked softly. The little girl nodded.

They set off again, the other two fast on their heels. As they came out of the woods, they saw the hill in front of them. Sara gave a whoop of joy. They made their way up the slope with Goldwasser and Berman still behind them. Farther back, to the right, Shlomo could see three more prisoners: the gypsy and the two Dutchmen. They, too, were tackling the sharp incline. "Keep going!" Shlomo urged, accompanying his words with a sweeping gesture of his arm. All of a sudden, a German shepherd leaped out from behind a bush and bit one of the Dutchmen. After a moment's hesitation, the gypsy and the other Dutchman threw themselves at the dog in an attempt to free their fellow prisoner. The men's screams and the dog's yelps were pierced by another sound. A Mauser going off. The gypsy crashed to the ground.

Shlomo swiftly picked up Sara, who was very light, and redoubled his efforts. His progress up the hill was fast, faster than he would have thought possible. A bullet whizzed past his ear.

They did not have far to go, they were almost at the top. Shlomo ran even faster.

"Look out!" Sara shouted.

A dog was at their heels, baring its sharp teeth and preparing to bite. Shlomo acted quickly. He was amazed at himself but felt in control of the situation. He jumped to one side just as the German shepherd was about to leap. The dog crashed into a rock. Shlomo let go of Sara, grabbed a large rock, and pounced on the animal. With two blows, he had smashed its jaw. Sara had run a few steps ahead and was waiting for him.

"Come on!" she implored.

Shlomo set off at a pace. He grabbed the girl's hand and, in a flash, they reached the top. He fell to the ground and held Sara close. He was out of breath but he had made it. He closed his eyes. He could die now. He didn't care. He had proved to those sons of bitches that he could do it.

Sounds of footsteps. Sharp orders. Howls. In the distance, moans and more orders. Gunshots. "Anyone missing?"

"No one. Two tried to escape through the woods, but we caught them."

"Did you execute them?"

"Yes, sir. "

Shlomo waited for the shot but it didn't come. He opened his eyes again. Looming over him was Sturmbannführer Hans Lichtblau's smiling face.

"Bravo, Jew Libowitz. Charles Darwin would be proud of you."

47

Rome, July 15, 1982

The night before, on returning to the hotel, the receptionist had handed him a note. Mr. Greengrass had been looking for him. He would be arriving the following day on the 5:25 P.M. Pan Am flight. Shlomo had thanked him and gone up to his room.

They used that name as a homage to Barney Greengrass, the "Sturgeon King", the Upper West Side diner where the Group's emissaries had first met their American backers. The pact had been sealed with bagels, smoked salmon, raw onion, and cream cheese. Thirty years had gone by, but the payments still arrived punctually in the account the Group had opened at the Cypriot branch of the Banque du Liban et d'Outre-Mer.

That morning, Shlomo got up early and the first thing he did was go and check on Epstein and his *shiksa*. This was more out of curiosity than any real operational requirement. He saw that they had not left yet. Presumably, they were still running around in circles. Shlomo had been one step ahead of them ever since the hunt had begun. And if what he had been waiting for arrived from America, he would be ahead of the game. Though he hated to admit it, deep down he would be a little sorry not to get another chance to meet Anton.

The Boeing 707 landed on time. At the Arrivals Hall, Shlomo was waiting in the front row outside the exit. He spotted Larry Zevi's freckly face right away in the steady stream of passengers. They had not seen each other for a long time, but they hugged with their usual warmth.

"How much stuff did you bring?" Shlomo asked, nodding

at his friend's suitcase. It looked too big for what he imagined would be a very short stay.

"I thought I'd take a little vacation while I was at it. The kids have grown up now and Meggy is on a construction site in Arizona."

They left the terminal and stood in line for a cab.

Larry was a corporate lawyer. An upright citizen, like many others. Flag flying on the porch, barbecue on the Fourth of July, Yankee Stadium with his sons. But his family history was less average. His parents were Italian Jews who had fled Europe just before the massacres started. At the end of 1939, they had escaped to France, where they applied for visas from any country willing to grant them one. In May they had embarked for the United States. By June 14, the Wehrmacht had been parading down the Champs-Élysées. Aldo and Micol had saved their lives but many of their friends and relatives hadn't been as lucky. He had enlisted in the American army and taken part in the liberation of the Dachau Lager. Returning home, he had earned a law degree through the government veterans' aid program and then started his practice in Elizabeth, New Jersey. A few years later he had joined the Group's network of supporters. Aldo Zevi had died young, of stomach cancer that killed him in six months. His son had taken his place in the Group's North American section. Larry loved traveling. When there was a delivery to be made, they called him.

"Where are we eating tonight?" Larry asked as he got into the cab.

"In the ghetto. Where else?"

When dinner was over, they stopped for one last drink at the hotel bar. Later, Shlomo accompanied Larry to his room, where the American had taken the valuable item out of the double bottom of his dark leather briefcase. Shlomo had been looking forward to opening the envelope, but it seemed a bit of a shame to leave straight away. Larry understood, let out a sonorous yawn, and said he was very tired from the trip. Shlomo wished him good night and scurried back to his room. He sat down on the bed and ripped open the envelope. His hands were shaking, as if Lichtblau were standing in front of him. The US Department of Justice had finally launched an investigation into former Nazis residing in the United States. During Operation Paperclip, several politicians and even some generals had been against the idea of recruiting dozens of German scientists, some of whom had even been tried at Nuremberg. But the Cold War had been underway. The Third Reich's missile program had been twenty years ahead of the American one. It did not pay to be choosy. Now, however, the situation was different, and someone had decided that the time had come clean up their act a little. They had just started. They had not yet gone public, but the Group had a good friend who was on the Attorney General's staff. They were asking questions about the chemist Otto Ambros, the former head of the IG Farben plants at the Monowitz Lager, a close collaborator and former schoolmate of Himmler's. How had a man convicted of war crimes become an adviser to the US government? There were also three pages on Victor Huberman, born Hans Lichtblau, describing the Sturmbannführer's career since the war and, more importantly, where he was likely to be at present.

The phone rang.

Shlomo was sitting on the bed. He put the papers down and picked up the receiver.

"There's a call for you, Mr. Libowitz."

A few seconds later, Sara Mandelbaum's croaky voice came out of the receiver.

Shlomo was disappointed. He had hoped it would be Rivka, even though his wife did not even know what country he was in.

"Did you get the package?" Sara enquired.

No matter how hard the woman tried to appear detached, her voice communicated anxiety. The mission was as important to her as it was to Shlomo. Perhaps even more so. Sara had never had a family. She lived for her job as a math teacher and for revenge. Sometimes Shlomo regretted enrolling her in the Group. He had met her again by chance in the early 1960s. Rivka had convinced him to close the bar for a couple of days and go to Tel Aviv to attend a performance of *La Traviata*. She was very keen on the idea. There was no opera house in Haifa. So, they had taken a vacation. One evening, while strolling along the waterfront, he and Sara had bumped into one another and recognized each other instantly. Shlomo had struggled to hold back his tears. In the following days, they had spoken again on the phone. When the school year had ended, Sara had visited them in Haifa. And Shlomo had told her about what he was doing.

"Did you get the package?" Sara asked again.

Shlomo grunted an answer in the affirmative.

"Is everything there?"

"Everything I need. There is one small problem but I plan to solve it. "

A long silence ensued.

Shlomo was about to hang up, but Sara broke the silence.

"Shlomo."

"Yes?"

"Kill him."

"I will."

48

Allenstein, East Prussia, Dec. 5, 1944

The diocese was housed in a sumptuous baroque red-brick building, but Father Grabski's office was a small, bare cell. The window, however, had a spectacular view of the fourteenth-century castle overlooking the old town. Lichtblau thought the place spoke volumes about Witold Grabski. On the surface, he was genuinely modest, but deep down he harbored unbound ambition. The Sturmbannführer had looked into the priest's history. Grabski was from Polish peasant stock. The hands clasped on the desk were certainly delicate and manicured, but the pronounced, almost ape-like arch of his brow betrayed his humble origins. Centuries of hunger, poverty, and wretched labor. Aside from emigrating, a career in the church had probably been his best ticket out. Someone must have noticed the peasant boy's intelligence; his astuteness and determination had done the rest. Lichtblau could envisage a bright future for the young priest. If he survived the war, that is. With the Soviet offensive just around the corner, that was the same for everyone.

Grabski was not quite sure what to expect. The major had asked to meet, but he hadn't said why. There hadn't been any other complaints, or even gossip, concerning the activities taking place on von Lehndorff's property. Grabski knew this for sure. Bishop Keller's arrest had shut many mouths.

"So, Major, what do you want to talk to me about?" Grabski asked.

Lichtblau leaned back and took out a photograph, which he placed on the leather pad that covered most of the desk. Grabski stretched his neck out to take a look.

In the photograph there was a girl of fourteen, or maybe fifteen. Grabski had never been able to tell people's ages accurately. She was naked from the waist up. Her face was beautiful, a perfect oval, with long black hair gathered at the nape of her neck, as if she were about to tie it into a bun: a pose requested by the photographer, no doubt. In fact, the gesture was awkward. There was something artificial about it. The girl's eyes betrayed her embarrassment. And yet, this did not spoil the overall effect. On the contrary, it made the portrait more authentic, and thus more disturbing. The girl's lifted arms accentuated her already magnificent breasts. Two firm, barely-ripe apples with pert, rosy nipples pointing upwards in a direct challenge to gravity and men's desire. Grabski made himself look up.

The Nazi was smirking suggestively.

The bishop's secretary took a deep breath and carefully weighed each word.

"I have already received a visit from your colleagues. We have reached an agreement," he said dryly. Unable to conceal a certain anxiety, he added, "In any case, I have never seen this girl."

Lichtblau burst out laughing.

"You've got the wrong end of the stick. I didn't come to blackmail you. I know the Gestapo has been doing that. I am here to propose an exchange." He gestured at the photograph.

Almost against his will, Grabski's eyes lingered over the girl. The young, voluptuous body was a promise of endless damnation and delight.

"She is still a virgin," Lichtblau added. He'd ordered a gynecological examination performed by Dr. Wasserman. "I'm only telling you this because I know that for you Catholics it's an important detail," the major commented, still smiling.

Grabski tuned out completely. He was mesmerized. She wasn't any old whore. She was a woodland nymph. She was the Venus of Milo. She was the Virgin Mary in a Renaissance painting of the Annunciation.

The priest looked up, bewildered.

"I picked her up in a Lager," Lichtblau explained. "I washed and fed her. She is ready for you. You can do anything you want with her." He said it again, stressing the syllables this time. "A-ny-thing."

The priest paled and then came out in red blotches, which spread over his glabrous face. Lichtblau felt he had him in his clutches and went in for the death blow. "You can come to the castle to meet her. Or, if you have somewhere to keep her, you can have her."

He hoped Grabski would be able to arrange it somehow. Wasserman had guessed what the young Polish girl had been selected for, but Lichtblau was certain he would keep his counsel. But he could not count on Kiesel and the others doing the same. Besides, hosting a priest's love-nest could prove embarrassing for the von Lehndorffs, especially the baroness. And for Martha, too—the thought came to him spontaneously—though it had been several months since she had come to the castle. She had always said she didn't mind, but the fact that he hadn't made up his mind to marry her had taken its toll. Hans knew there was a man in Neuhof who was courting her: a one-armed, retired NCO. For many women, a one-armed husband was preferable to a lover equipped with all his limbs.

Grabski's head was spinning. The proposal was indecent. Women who had chosen the path of sin for money was one thing. Taking advantage of a young victim of unfavorable circumstances was quite different. But was she really a victim? If she had been arrested, she must have done something, surely? Behind that angelic face, a devious subversive, murderer, or terrorist may well be lurking. What's more, if he accepted the offer, the girl would escape the Lager, and that would be an advantage for her. Witold Grabski knew that he was clutching at straws, but he continued to lull himself with specious arguments. Part of his mind was already scheming. He might be able to lodge her with Anja. Or put her in the attic. No one would hear them up there. He should reinforce the door, though. Right now, you could knock it down with a finger. No, Anja's house was the best solution. Just for a few days and then he would let her go. If she was not a fool, the girl would cooperate. He looked at the photograph again. When would he get an opportunity like this again? It would be worth it, even if he were to burn in eternity alongside all the other sinners.

"And what would you want from me in exchange?" Grabski asked in a whisper.

"To be included in the list you are compiling."

Of course. Why hadn't he thought of it? Mechanically, Grabski got up from his desk, lifted off its hook on the wall a portrait of one of the prince-bishops that had once ruled the region—at that moment he would not have been able to say which—and opened the safe. He took out a manilla folder and sat back down.

There were a dozen names on the list. High-ranking members of the National Socialist Party and the state apparatus. Grabski picked up the pen next to the glass inkwell, but when he dipped the nib into the bottle, he realized it was empty. He was about to open the drawer when Lichtblau handed him a black lacquer fountain pen, inlaid with silver.

The prelate turned it over in his fingers. "Very nice," he said.

"It's a limited-edition Dupont," Lichtblau explained proudly. He had bought it from his friend in the Gestapo, along with a Swiss passport.

Grabski put the list back in the folder.

"I will be able to give you precise instructions in a few days' time," he said.

Lichtblau nodded. He hoped it would not be necessary. The military situation may be less disastrous than it appeared. Secret weapon may indeed turn the tide. Something was happening, for sure. V-2s were blitzing London and British flak had been unable to stop them. Komets and Messerschmitt 262s had been ripping the sky open at a speed that had previously been unimaginable for propeller-driven aircraft, inflicting serious losses on Allied bomber squadrons. And his research could also play a role. But Hans knew these were details. The overall picture was bleak. If the Reich crumbled, Major Lichtblau had no intention of being caught by surprise. He was an American citizen, after all.

49

Los Angeles, July 15, 1982

The mansion sprawled over the hillside amidst thick patches of scrub, which made it invisible from the street. The garden boasted a large, round pool. It was the first thing you encountered as you walked up the driveway from the parking lot to the main building: a concrete and glass strip that ended in a terrace jutting out on steel pylons. Below, as far as the eye could see, stretched the green mass of the Santa Monica Mountains. For once, Victor Huberman did not feel compelled to criticize Los Angeles architecture. This revisitation of the Prairie School style was elegant and the setting was simply stunning. But the positive aspects of the evening ended there. The buffet was absurdly insubstantial, as it so often was in wealthy homes. That was how they had made their money: by saving on dips. Communists called it primitive accumulation.

The guests were a motley assortment of characters from the entertainment industry. Producers. Directors. Singers. Screenwriters, easily recognizable because they sat apart from the others, looking as if they had been dragged there against their will and were hating every minute of it. Actors and actresses, distributed along the many shades of the spectrum, ranging from young promise to old glory. And a coterie of agents, mistresses, pimps, gigolos, con-men, yoga masters, and advisers of various disciplines, backgrounds, and specialties. The chatter, laughter, and disco music was producing a hellish din. And the bartender was unprofessional, to say the least. A young body-builder, who would have been more at home doing push-ups at Muscle Beach, was mixing stupid cocktails with umbrellas and chunks of fruit strewn around haphazardly. Huberman had asked him if he knew how to make a Stinger. That boy gawped without managing to utter a word. Huberman had fallen back on something basic. "A bourbon on the rocks." He had grabbed the glass and sought out a place as far away from the crowd as possible. He hated those people and their parties. But since Monterey was no longer with them, they had no choice. Luckily, Melissa was in charge of everything: congratulating the hostess on a very successful party, making brilliant conversation, and conducting business negotiations.

Huberman took a seat on a white sofa next to a large stone fireplace with the skull of a cow on the mantlepiece. Some interior design geek must have charged a fortune for that piece of kitsch, perhaps throwing in a reference to Georgia O'Keeffe to reassure the clients that they were spending their money well. Huberman brought his glass to his lips and silently toasted the memory of his friend. He and Monterey had worked together for thirteen years. He was thirsty for revenge, but he knew that turning against the Colombians was madness. He could only hope to rake in a good haul and go back with enough supplies to carry on with the operation.

The din in the hall increased as the white powder was handed from one guest to another. Retailing was exhausting but the market was responding well. Huberman got up to fetch more bourbon and, as he walked through the crowd, he came across the perpetually smiling face of Timothy Leary. As usual, Leary was surrounded by an adoring audience. He was discussing the difference between visionary ecstasy, usually practiced alone, and magical-ritual ecstasy, which was inevitably group-oriented. When Leary caught sight of Huberman, he immediately left the circle. "*Hermano*, it's been so long . . . ," he said, hugging him warmly.

Huberman had met Leary in 1963, at Millbrook, in upstate New York, where the former *enfant prodige* of US academic psychology who had been kicked out of Harvard for administering LSD to some freshmen had settled to pursue his research into hallucinogens and inner freedom. Together with a group of followers, he had gone to live in the elegant mansion of three scions of the Mellon dynasty, who had been swept away by the charisma of the man who was becoming the most influential figure in psychedelic culture. President Nixon would later call him the most dangerous man in America. Back in 1946, when the US Army Chemical Corps had offered him a job, Huberman had offered his new masters the results of his research. They had been enthusiastic to begin with, but when they realized that the stimulant was addictive, they lost interest. Huberman considered the US military narrow-minded. The former SS major didn't consider addiction an impediment. In any case, they had re-employed him to conduct research on mind conditioning. He was back to pursuing a truth serum. In the early 1950s, the CIA pinned high hopes on LSD, not just for interrogation purposes. They thought lysergic acid could shape people's personalities and even turn them into killers on command. They conducted experiments on human guinea pigs who were mostly poorly informed or completely unaware. Sometimes, however, Agency operatives took the acid. In jargon, they were known as "enlightened agents." Huberman was one of their gurus. He had devised a plan to dissolve large quantities of LSD into the water system of a large Soviet city. He had joined Dr. Wilson Greene in his psychochemical warfare project. Drugging enemy soldiers rather than shooting them. Then counterculture discovered acid. Leary and Ginsberg were convinced they were on the cutting edge, when they were more than a decade behind. Although the research was on the same topic, their perspectives were very different. The CIA saw LSD as a tool for taking control, while the hippies saw it as a means of liberation. The Agency had sent Huberman to Millbrook to keep an eye on the alternatives. He had introduced himself as a European intellectual expat and offered to give a seminar of sorts. Eliade's studies on shamanism. Artaud and peyote. Ernst Jünger's reflections on LSD. Huberman had met him once. His true-life

account of the trip he had shared with Jünger and Albert
Hofmann in the summer of 1959 in Zurich had been a stroke
of genius. The audience, including Leary, had been won over.
In the following years, Huberman had been a regular guest at
Millbrook until the circus of the lysergic revolution had moved
to San Francisco. They were nothing more than a clutch of per-
petually-stoned dreamers, more dangerous to themselves than
to national security. Leary was an interesting character, though.
His mystical monologues about the Tibetan Book of the Dead
had reminded Huberman of Himmler. And when Leary told
him that Jung was the only Western thinker worthy of note,
while he felt that Freud had allowed himself to be sidetracked
by what he called "the overheated atmosphere of his Jewish
family," Huberman had begun to think that the affinities were
not entirely coincidental.

"I'm working on something new and very powerful," Leary
said with his usual blind and infectious enthusiasm, the same
enthusiasm that had led him to stand in the 1969 election for
governor of California. Some people had actually thought he
could pull it off. John Lennon had written a campaign jingle for
him. "I'm doing a show with Gordon Liddy."

"The Gordon Liddy who put the bugs in at Watergate?"
Huberman asked, surprised but not astonished.

"That's him. It's a whole new formula for a show: a two-way
debate on the hottest topics of the moment. You'll see, it'll be
a hit."

Huberman was about to reply, but just then a young girl
dressed in a white tunic came out of the crowd and clung to
Leary's arm, begging him in a doll's voice to finish what he had
been saying before. "It's so rare to find someone who is truly
progressive," the girl chirruped. Leary stared at Huberman
mutely and shrugged. He had a duty to his audience. Old Victor
would certainly understand.

"*Adios, hermano*," Huberman said, looking amused and
waving goodbye to Leary as the girl dragged him away. "We

debut next week," Leary managed to yell. "I'll get you two tickets. I value your opinion."

The evening was in full swing. Olivia Newton-John was yelling out of the stereo speakers. Guests were dancing, diving into the pool, kissing in corners. Some had already collapsed and were sleeping in an armchair or lying on the floor. Others were walking around the parking lot trying to remember where they had left their car. Huberman was done in. He had hardly gotten any sleep since Monterey had died. It was his third party in four days, but it had been worth it. They had managed to offload the whole shipment. He reached into the inside pocket of his jacket and pulled out a small silver box from which he fished out a pale purple pill. Melissa handed him a half-filled glass.

"What is it?" Huberman asked, stifling a yawn.

"Gin and tonic."

Huberman downed the whole glass and gave it back to Melissa together with the box. She took a pill, too. They let a few seconds go by in silence. The noise around them gradually tuned into individual sounds that they were able to distinguish. A shrill laugh. A glass breaking. A door slamming. A needle scratching at a vinyl record. This made the din easier to bear and somehow imbued it with meaning. Huberman offered Melissa his arm and they made their way together to the exit.

José was sitting in the driver's seat. He was dozing, his neck on the headrest. Next to him, Carlos was smoking a Marlboro. His arm was out the window, and his fingers were drumming on the bodywork to the rhythm of the song coming from the house.

Let's get physical, physical.

Carlos saw *el jefe* and *la señora* coming down the driveway. He threw away his cigarette and elbowed his colleague. As he stepped out of the limousine to open the rear door, the first volley flew by, missing him by a hairsbreadth. The bodyguard threw himself to the ground and reached for his gun. The windshield shattered. Hiding behind the car, Carlos pointed his weapon in the dark and fired blindly.

At the first shots, Victor and Melissa had jumped behind a bush. If the Colombians had waited a few seconds longer and surprised them out in the open in the middle of the parking lot, they could have been killed. But the shooters had been impatient and had opened fire too early. Typical behavior in inferior races. Huberman grabbed the Walther P38 from the leather holster on his back. Melissa had already retrieved the revolver from her purse.

She knelt on the ground on one knee, tightened her hold on of the Colt with her left hand as her ex-husband had taught her, and aimed for a large agave plant from where the shots seemed to be coming.

José was inert on the seat, splattered with blood and covered in shards of glass. Crouched behind the black limousine, Carlos was reloading the Beretta. He was about to get up but suddenly felt a terrible pain in his shoulder. He managed to spin around. About ten meters away was a man brandishing an M16 assault rifle. The weapon must have jammed because he was fumbling with it. Carlos aimed and pulled the trigger. The man fell to the ground.

Two gunmen were running toward him, firing wildly. The sound was impressive, but the results mediocre. Victor squinted and took aim calmly. Of the eight bullets in the magazine, five hit their target, including two to the head and one to the abdomen.

The chubby little man with a baggy shirt open over his chest was squatting against the car door. With such an indescribably ugly color, it was a classic car for a pimp. He was holding his head in his arms, in a bracing position. When Melissa Blumenthal leaned over to look at his face, he burst into tears.

"Is the car yours?" she asked.

The man nodded.

Melissa held out her left hand (she was still holding the revolver in her right hand), her fingers splayed and her palm up.

The man said nothing. In fact, he seemed almost relieved. He handed over the keys right away.

Carlos had managed to reach the Uzi under the seat in the limousine and was keeping the gunmen at the parking lot entrance busy. The music up at the house had been turned off and the screams were getting louder by the minute.

Huberman crawled over to his bodyguard.

"José?" he asked.

Carlos shook his head, leaned over the side of the limousine that was riddled with bullet holes, and let loose a volley. Huberman followed suit.

Behind them, an engine roared. They turned and saw a lemon-yellow Alfa Romeo.

Shots continued to rain down on them from the gate, albeit with lesser intensity.

"Get in!" Melissa yelled, opening the passenger door.

In the distance, a police siren was wailing.

Huberman told Carlos to go first, emptied a whole cartridge on what was left of the Colombian commando, and climbed in after the bodyguard.

The Honduran had had to fold his giant body into the cramped space of the back seat of the coupé. One hand was compressing his wound and he was gritting his teeth, trying not to scream. As soon as Huberman had sat down next to the *señora*, Carlos handed him the Uzi.

Hands firmly on the steering wheel, Melissa pressed the accelerator and the Alfa sped off toward the exit.

Victor leveled the machine gun out the window. Brandishing a 600-round-a-minute weapon gave him an exciting sensation of power. As the tires burned out of the parking lot, their headlights lit up two stocky, dark-skinned bodies. Big flat noses with abnormal nostrils. Black hair stuck to their foreheads. Pure Amerindian phenotype. The man who had once called himself Hans Lichtblau did not hesitate. He stretched his arm out of the car, in the opposite direction from the curve the car was driving around in order to keep the targets in his sights. The scream rose up from deep within him without him even realizing it. It was wild and liberating and it mingled with the ricochet of bullets that swept through the night.

"*Untermenschen!*"

50

Eastern Prussia, January 18, 1945

The snow was falling thickly outside the stained-glass windows, making the weapons room in the von Lehndorff's ancient castle look even gloomier than usual. The baron and Sturmbannführer Lichtblau had been fencing for almost an hour. The major had managed to win two assaults. He had won the first through sheer fury. All of his hits had been at infighting distance and the overall effect had been as unseemly and vicious as a sailor's brawl. Von Lehndorff had despised his style but acknowledged defeat. In the second match, however, in addition to the strength of a wild boar, Lichtblau had proved he had some technique. In particular, he had surprised the baron by protecting his target area. The baron had lunged at his opponent's chest, but the major had suddenly crouched and set off the *point d'arrêt* on his arm.

"You have improved," the baron said coldly. He had not sparred with Lichtblau since he had witnessed the truck with the rubber hose attached to the exhaust three years earlier. The major had suggested it several times, but he had always refused and eventually the major had gotten the message. Von Lehndorff wiped his forehead with a white linen handkerchief and took a sip of Bernkasteler Doctor. This time, he had decided to accept. "One last match," Lichtblau had said. The day before, three large empty trucks with SS license plates had arrived at the castle. The major and his associates were clearly preparing to flee. The baron had not been able to refuse. In fact, he had greeted the challenge with a certain enthusiasm. He wanted to humiliate the Nazi. But he had lost two assaults because his burning desire for revenge had made him less effective.

"I've been training with Captain Kiesel," the Sturmbann-führer explained as he, too, took a sip of wine. "Of course, it's not the same as playing against you." He looked around and added, "I'm going to miss this weapons room very much.

"Didn't Gauleiter Koch say that evacuation plans are unpatriotic?" von Lehndorff asked, feigning nonchalance.

"Gauleiter Koch is commandeering a train to take the families of the Königsberg Party bigwigs to the west," Lichtblau replied sharply. "And as for me, I have received direct orders from the Reichsführer-SS."

The two men stared at one another in silence.

"What about a saber assault?" the baron proposed.

"Didn't you say that sabers are for savages?" the major asked in amazement.

"Savage times await us. We must prepare ourselves," von Lehndorff replied dryly as he went to the rack to choose a blade.

"You're right," Lichtblau retorted. "We saw what the Slavic hordes are capable of at Nemmersdorf." He approached the baron and examined the weapons. Von Lehndorff was already making some cuts in the air to try them out.

"Finally, people like you will stop saying it's all propaganda. The attack from the steppe is real. If we fail to defend the borders of the Reich, western civilization will be wiped out."

The baron put his saber down.

"You woke the monster of Bolshevism. And the crimes that took place in Nemmersdorf are a response to the equally horrendous crimes committed in Poland and Russia by our troops."

"Are you saying that you consider Jews and communists on the same plane as German women and children?" the major retorted.

Again, the two men stared at one another in silence. Von Lehndorff donned his mask and stepped onto the platform. Lichtblau followed him.

They played five angry, brutal bouts. The Sturmbannführer won three. He was fast and accurate, and his quinte parry was impossible to break through. Striking from above, the baron failed to pass even once.

"You are definitely better suited to the saber. You should choose it as your main weapon," the baron commented as he took his leave.

"I may well take your advice," Lichtblau replied, holding out his hand. "It has been a pleasure to make your acquaintance."

The old Junker stared at the Nazi with his hand in midair, without twitching a muscle. "I'm afraid I cannot say the same," he replied.

Lichtblau pulled his hand back awkwardly. "As you wish," he said resentfully. "In any case, I advise you to get out of here. If the front gives way, the Russians will be here in a few days."

The "if" was wishful thinking. Everyone in East Prussia, including Lichtblau, knew full well that the front would give way. The Wehrmacht was in complete disarray. It had exhausted its supplies of fuel, ammunition, soldiers, everything.

"I don't think your Gestapo friends would be happy if I left the castle," the baron replied.

"In your place, I would rather face my Gestapo friends than your Bolshevik friends. They're not going to care that you have a reputation as an anti-fascist. They'll line you up against the wall like all the other aristocratic enemies of the people."

The baron did not reply.

Lichtblau put his saber back on the rack, wiped his face with a small white towel, tucked the mask under his arm, and strode out of the room.

The baron was practicing saber in front of the mirror. Advance-lunge, retreat-en garde. Advance-lunge, retreat-en garde. Those three defeats stung him, not just because defeat always stings, and because they were inflicted by a Nazi, but also because above all they were due to his age. Of course, the blind impatience with which he had sought victory had not helped, but that was not the only factor. While the slow pace and cerebral, chess-like nature of the épée still allowed him to prevail over younger opponents, the swiftness and childlike simplicity of the saber made his fifty-four years impossible to make up for. He positioned himself en garde and began taking the duck-like steps required by the saber, slowly at first, then faster, until he took a lunge that was supposed to be lightning fast but that von Lehndorff knew would not catch Sturmbannführer Lichtblau by surprise. He paused while he was in the lunge then returned en garde, only to hurl his saber on the floor in a fit of rage. He was instantly ashamed of the gesture, which represented a total negation of the spirit of fencing.

As he was bending down to pick up the saber, von Lehndorff realized that Albert was watching him from a respectful distance.

"I'm sorry to disturb you, Herr Baron."

Von Lehndorff walked over to the old servant.

"What is it, Albert?"

"If you allow me, I'd like to show you something. It's the farm workers."

They walked through the woods for a good ten minutes. When they reached a clearing, Albert pointed to a spot under the branches of a large tree with a gnarled trunk. Von Lehndorff could not see anything. The butler bent down and brushed away the leaves. A rudimentary trapdoor made of birch branches appeared. They lifted it up. Underneath was a hole a couple of meters deep and three or four meters wide. They must have broken their backs digging it as the winter was particularly harsh and the ground as hard as stone. Von Lehndorff looked at Albert waiting for an explanation.

"They want to hide in there," the butler said. His tone was both apprehensive and contemptuous. "They even put supplies in."

The baron peered into the hole. In one corner, he could see a mud-stained jute sack. How many supplies could it possibly hold? A few potatoes. A piece of lard. A few loaves of bread. There were a dozen farm workers living on the property, without counting the children. What did they imagine? That the Russians would come for a few hours and then go away again?

"The Bolsheviks will find them," Albert insisted. "They will rape the women and then kill them along with the men, like they did in Nemmersdorf."

The baron could not take his eyes off the pit. That hole in the frozen ground was the vanishing point of hundreds of years of German history. Luther and Goethe and the Ninth Symphony and the glory of Sedan would end up in a dirty hole full of worms, a mass grave designed for the living that would most likely be stuffed with corpses. Cramming themselves down there to escape the fury of the invading army was a solution from the time of the Thirty Years' War. The seventeenth century, where Hitler had dragged them back to. And they would inevitably be going back even further in time, to when Prutenian warriors painted their faces before going into battle and smashed their enemies' skulls with obsidian axes.

"Go get the farmer," von Lehndorff said without looking up from the pit.

51

Rome, July 16, 1982

In the parade, the men held the spoils of war high over their heads. Some of the figures had laurel wreaths on their heads and were beaming with pleasure. Anton Epstein and Shlomo Libowitz stared at the section of the frieze where a group was carrying an unwieldy *menorah* on their shoulders. The destruction of the Second Temple. The beginning of the Diaspora. The two men sipped lemon slushies in paper cups through bright green straws, blending in perfectly with the other tourists gazing in admiration at the bas-reliefs. It was cool under the marble vault of the Triumphal Arch but a little farther along, at the end of the Via Sacra, the imposing mass of the Flavian Amphitheater was gleaming in the scorching sun. Shlomo, in sandals and a white shirt, was perfectly at ease. For over thirty years now, he had no longer been a part of the Diaspora. Anton, on the other hand, was suffering in the heat of a Mediterranean summer. He was wearing a wide-brimmed straw hat, a passable imitation of a Panama he had bought at the Porta Portese flea-market. He had even taken his jacket off. But it didn't make much difference. His pale Central-European skin was finding it hard to cope.

Shlomo cast a sideways look at the man who had been a prisoner in the Lager with him. He watched as he let the last drops of slush drip onto his tongue in an attempt to prolong that short-lived sensation of coolness. He laughed inside his head, just a little.

"Let's go," he said, setting off towards the subway stop.

Anton hesitated for a moment before relinquishing the shade of the ancient ruins. He glanced one last time at the monument and followed Shlomo, leaving behind the memories of

Emperor Titus's magnificent victories and the tears of the lost kingdom of Judea.

When she saw Shlomo sitting placidly on the couch in the hotel lobby with a fake smile plastered on his wrinkled old face, Officer Yakovchenko had to rely on the last shred of her self-control to avoid throwing a fit in full view of the receptionist and the hotel guests coming and going. Epstein was truly a lost cause. *A pro-Zionist, pro-Yugoslavian cosmopolitan Jew.*

"What the hell were you thinking?" she growled at him in a low voice

She yanked Anton's arm and started pushing him towards the elevators as if she were teasing him.

"Shlomo has a proposition for us," the cosmopolitan Jew said.

"I've already told you that we don't negotiate with Mossad," Natalya answered as she continued to shove him.

"He knows where Lichtblau is."

Agent Yakovchenko stopped in her tracks.

"Then why doesn't he go and get him?"

"He'd like us to go together."

Natalya was dumbstruck. She did not know what to think. Nor did she notice that Shlomo had stood up and was approaching her.

"Come with me, Comrade Yakovchenko."

The fake smile had been replaced by a serious, professional expression. That of a businessman hellbent on bringing a difficult negotiation to a successful conclusion. "Let's sit down and talk."

They sat on the uncomfortable Swedish couches that were too small for anyone who was not a child or a dwarf.

"Lichtblau is in Honduras," Shlomo Libowitz said. "He's fighting the Sandinistas."

"And what do you need me for?" agent Yakovchenko asked sharply.

"It's a war zone. It will not be easy to get in. Plus, Lichtblau always has his bodyguards with him."

Natalya understood.

"Then it's better to go through Managua," she said. "And maybe show up at the rendezvous together with a Nicaraguan army battalion."

Shlomo lay back on the couch, in as much as it was possible to relax on the thing, and clasped his hands behind his balding head.

"You're a smart girl, Comrade Yakovchenko."

"Do you need me as your guarantor?"

"That's right. You get me to Nicaragua and get me an armed escort. I take you to Lichtblau. You can take all the loot. All I care about is killing the bastard."

Epstein looked at Natalya with the eyes of a child pleading with his mother to buy him an ice cream. The woman wanted to slap him in the face.

"Moscow will not approve," she said.

"You could always try and ask," Libowitz answered shrewdly.

52

Eastern Prussia, January 21, 1945

Hans Lichtblau admired himself in the mirror, gazing with satisfaction at the new insignia on the left collar of his uniform. Next to the four Sturmbannführer stars there was now a vertical chevron. Martha had stitched it on for him. He had gone to meet her at Neuhof with the excuse of that little sewing job, which any of the castle maids could have done. The children had not been home. In fact, they were no longer children. Elsie was with a group of schoolmates making bandages for the field hospital just outside the village where the wounded from the front were pouring in. Paul, who had turned fourteen and had therefore joined the Hitler Jugend, had been drafted into a unit of the Volkssturm along with other boys his age and a bunch of old men and invalids discharged from the Wehrmacht. In theory, military service was only compulsory from the age of fifteen, but there were children as young as ten manning some of the anti-aircraft batteries. Martha did not even know where her son was. In his last letter, he had said that he was in Allenstein, but more than a week had gone by. She was terrified that the Russians would arrive, but she did not want to leave without her son. She had asked Hans if he would intervene. He knew Himmler, after all. Instructions from him would surely be enough to free Paul from the militia. Hans had said he would take care of it in order to comfort her, but the matter was beyond his reach. Getting out of the armed forces was almost impossible. Itinerant martial courts were tracking the rearguard at the frontline and looking for deserters, who were executed on the spot. Martha had cried, wiped away her tears, and sewed on his insignia. They had laughed as they used to do, and made love. After that, the woman had informed him that she was getting married to her one-armed sergeant, who was also in the Volkssturm. He was due in Neuhof in a few days' time on a marriage license. "If I get killed, at least you will be entitled to a pension," he had told her in his wartime marriage proposal. "With you it was different," Martha had remarked. Hans had wanted to say something appropriate in return but all he managed to do was wish her good luck. He had put his jacket back on and returned to the castle.

In mid-December, SS headquarters had received the first batch of pills from the pharmaceutical laboratory in Auschwitz, where they had been packaged under Lichtblau's supervision. They had administered them to the enlisted men in an infantry battalion fighting on the Ardennes front. The results had been extremely promising. The men had fought at a hundred percent efficiency for three days and nights and had hardly needed a rest. At dawn on the fourth day, they had been wiped out by a unit of American troops with more soldiers and weapons than them, but the defeat did not invalidate the quality of the product. After the New Year, Lichtblau had received a letter brimming with praise from Himmler, who had promoted him to Obersturmbannführer and ordered him to move the laboratory to Berlin. They could not risk the fruit of years of research falling into the hands of the Bolsheviks. The Reichsführer-SS had also advised him to travel to Königsberg and then make the rest of the journey by sea. The roads were under constant air attack, while the Soviet Baltic fleet was largely inactive. The SS had already asked the Navy to provide a ship. Hans, however, had delayed his departure. He wanted to go on working at the castle as long as possible. He imagined that there would be no way to continue his research in Berlin. The city was a pile of rubble. The end of the war was months away, maybe even weeks. He had an escape route at the ready, but he didn't want to use it yet. He owed Heinrich

Himmler a great deal and he intended to honor his debt. He would report for duty.

The Obersturmbannführer ran a finger over his insignia, first the left and then the right. Hearing from Martha that she would be marrying another man had not been pleasant, but she had made the right decision. There was no room for a woman in the life he was planning. He put on his fur-lined coat, gloves, and cap and went down to the laboratory. He walked through the deserted halls, checking to make sure he had not forgotten anything essential. On the floor of the operating room were the eight guinea pigs Wasserman had eliminated with a lethal injection. Eight Jewish children, lined up on the floor. Their faces were relaxed, their eyelids closed. There had been no screaming. Wasserman had done a good job, as usual.

He bumped into Lieutenant Dobbs in the archive. He was helping Schenk burn documents in the stove. The room was billowing with smoke.

"Let's go Schenk, there is no more time. You can hear the Russian cannons."

The Englishman held out his hand.

"Good luck, Major," Dobbs said. The man seemed genuinely moved.

"Lieutenant Colonel," Lichtblau corrected him in a jocular tone, pointing to the silver insignia.

He walked to the yard followed by Schenk. The others were already there, along with the vehicles: three Opel Blitzes into which material had been loaded, a Kübelwagen, and a sidecar. Against a wall, there was a messy pile of bodies. All the servants who had been brought in from the Soldau Lager. The white plaster was covered with an abstract composition of bullet holes and blood spatter. In the mass, Lichtblau glimpsed the face of the Austrian Jehovah's Witness, her mouth open, frozen in a last, hopeless cry. He had considered sparing her to begin with. Then reason had prevailed. As for Mr. and Mrs. von Lehndorff and their two servants, the Russians would have to take care of them. Lichtblau looked up at a window in the baron's quarters. The Junker was there with his wife. They were standing close to each other and staring down at him. Lichtblau saw condemnation in their eyes. He ignored them.

"All aboard!" he ordered, tossing into the Kübelwagen the voluminous black leather folder containing his notes: the pulsing heart of Operation Berserker.

Members of the guardhouse and laboratory staff began to take their places in the vehicles. Sergeant Dietrich approached Lichtblau. "We still have to get rid of the Sonderkommando survivors," he whispered.

"You haven't done it?" the Obersturmbannführer replied testily. At that very moment, a Sturmovik flew over the castle. The red stars on its wings gleamed against the gray sky. The pilot flew low, but did not open fire. Maybe he had run out of ammunition or had no time to waste on such an insignificant target. He could report their position, though. Lichtblau knew that shooting at them was futile. The largest caliber they had was a machine gun and that airplane had an armored fuselage that was virtually impenetrable with light weapons. It could even withstand flak fire. They had to get on. The prisoner hut was at the end of the park. At a good pace, it took at least a quarter of an hour to walk there.

"We are leaving," Lichtblau told the sergeant. "You will catch up with us on the motorcycle."

"Yes, sir," the Unterscharführer replied.

Lichtblau climbed into the Kübelwagen. At the wheel was a corporal whose name he could not remember. Wasserman and Schenk were in the back seat.

"Let's go!" Lichtblau yelled.

As the column began to move, Sergeant Dietrich checked the magazine of his machine gun and drove off toward the park.

On the other side of the woods, he could hear the drumming of Red Army artillery getting closer.

53

Department of Olancho, southern Honduras,
July 17, 1982

The second pilot came to wake him up at the last minute, when the runway was already below them. He and Melissa had fallen asleep immediately after boarding, despite the fact that the old C-47 offered no creature comforts. They had lain down on a mattress stuffed between crates of weapons and ammunition and had drifted into a deep sleep, shutting out the vibrations and the roar of the engines. Victor Huberman felt better. He stretched and followed the second pilot into the cockpit. He was also starving. In the crazy week he had spent in Los Angeles, not only had there been no time to sleep, but he had not had a moment to enjoy a decent meal. He thought back to Timothy Leary and his show with Gordon Liddy. It was as if he had chosen a member of Stalin's secret police as his sidekick. Maybe Timothy had opened the doors of perception a little too wide. Or maybe it was just the spirit of the times. An ex-hippy and a former hippy-hunter might well perform a successful vaudeville act together. The logic of show business dominated everything. Even the president of the United States was from show business, though he had only ever played a bit part. Washington was clutching at the scraps left by Hollywood.

"We're landing," the pilot announced.

Huberman nodded and went back into the cargo compartment. The jungle leg was not long, but it was always tiring. Clothes stuck to you with the humidity. Insects, in every bizarre shape or form, were everywhere. The steep path through the forest, which the trucks struggled to climb. The ancient roots and deep potholes that strained the vehicle's suspension and the passengers' backs. Before leaving, Huberman had taken one of his pills, but he was still suffering.

Finally, a stone statue appeared through the leaves, heralding the end of the journey. A little man with clasped hands and a hieratic face, sitting under a huge mushroom. That statue was what had first brought him here. In 1958, Hofmann had isolated the active ingredients of *Psilocybe cubensis*, a mushroom that the Aztecs called Teonanácatl, "flesh of the gods." Two years later, in Mexico, Leary had ingested seven all at once. The feathered serpent, the hanging gardens of Babylon, and the sacred Nile had appeared to him. Leary had been thirty-nine years old and the experience had changed his life and work dramatically. He had returned to Harvard and had set up a research program on what they started calling psychedelic substances. However, Huberman had already conducted a study of plant hallucinogens and the magic mushroom cult in pre-Columbian civilizations two years earlier, with funding from the RAND Corporation. He had gotten as far as a remote valley in the mountains between Honduras and Nicaragua, where he had found pure-blooded Indians, in whose culture mushrooms still played an important role, despite the fact that the Church had done everything in its power to erase these pagan practices. The *Psilocybe zapotecorum* was already a big mushroom—the stalk could be as long as twenty centimeters and the umbrella more than ten in diameter—but around a marshy pond not far from the statue he found some even more gigantic exemplars growing. Huberman had never seen any that big, either in Mexico or Guatemala. The body of the mushroom ranged from dark purple to dark-brown, while the stems were red, green, or blue. Artaud commented that peyote was not for the white man because the peyote rite created an interaction with spirits and, in the view of the Indigenous Indians, the white man had been abandoned by them. But Artaud had been a subversive who died in a lunatic asylum. Huberman managed to convince the shaman to let him participate in the ceremony. The mushroom had not been just exotic looking. It had also been also extremely powerful. The trip had lasted three days.

Twenty-five years later, Huberman had remembered that remote corner of Central of America after the CIA had gone to war with the Sandinistas. It was perfect. The border with Nicaragua was not too far away. And there was an old Spanish fortress near the village where they could set up their head-quarters. Huberman had recruited the whole tribe: the men as guides or soldiers and the women in logistics and coca cultiva-tion. He had contributed to re-awakening the warrior virtues of the tribe and had ended the adverse influence of Christianity by putting a bullet in the priest's forehead. The old shaman had been pleased. Now he knew why he had once trusted that stranger and revealed some of his secrets to him. It had not been just for the money. Huberman was a messiah who had come from afar to bring them new prosperity while helping them re-store the original order. Huberman had amazed the tribe with the power of his magic. He had brought electricity, terraced the land, and introduced chemical fertilizers and pesticides. He had given them a hospital with a real doctor and trained them in modern warfare. Victor Huberman had been king of a realm in the middle of the jungle.

As the trucks pulled into the clearing the children thronged jubilantly around them. The vehicles proceeded slowly toward the fortress as the kids ran alongside them yelling. As usual, Melissa threw candies and packs of chewing gum out of the window. She always bought them specially, whenever she went to the United States. A group of women were pounding mush-rooms in stone mortars in front of a hut. A little further on, the shaman greeted Huberman with a gesture. Huberman waved and leaped off the truck.

He looked around for Guillermo Rocas, his army commander.

A short, skinny man with a muscular physique came for-ward. In his early thirties, he was wearing a pair of threadbare US Army camouflage pants with black squiggles on a dark green background. He was wearing nothing else except a few necklaces decorating his chest, which had long scars running down it that were barely visible on his brown skin.

"Welcome," he said. The tone was deferential, but not servile. A steward addressing his master. They were a proud race. They were grateful to Huberman for what he had done for them, but they were well aware of how much they did for him.

"I have brought new weapons," Huberman said.

"Including the rifles and grenade launchers?"

"Yes, those too."

The commander looked satisfied.

"When do we attack?" he asked.

54

Eastern Prussia, January 21, 1945

S ergeant Dietrich pulled the bolt and opened the door of the smaller hut that had housed the Gardenia Kommando. He craned his neck and looked inside. Three prisoners were lying on their bunks. At the far end of the room, the last embers were flickering in the wood stove.

"Out!" Dietrich ordered.

The surviving members of the Kommando did not move and did not say a word

"As you wish," the Unterscharführer muttered between his teeth, pointing his MP40 at the man closest to him. He wasn't sure who it was, because they were all huddled in their blankets and he could only see their eyes, but it looked like the Czech who had served as Major Lichtblau's secretary.

"That's enough."

The sergeant turned around and saw Baron Wilhelm von Lehndorff wielding an ancient Mauser, model 1912.

"That's enough," the baron repeated. "The war is lost. Killing these three changes nothing."

For a moment, the Unterscharführer appeared not to understand. He looked dumbly at the baron, who was on the verge of repeating himself a third time. The SS sergeant lifted the muzzle of his machine gun.

The baron pulled the trigger.

He shot him in the throat.

The sergeant dropped his weapon and clamped his hands on the wound. He pushed down as hard as he could, but it was impossible to stem the spurt of blood gushing from it. He fell to the ground. He tried to speak but only blood came out.

Dietrich was rapidly losing color as he writhed in an ever-widening pool of dark red blood.

Von Lehndorff stepped over Dietrich's body and walked into the hut. The prisoners were still lying in their bunks. No one had spoken a word. They stared in shock.

"They've gone," the baron said.

An old gas-powered truck was parked in front of the castle. A crowd of farm workers from the von Lehndorff estate thronged around it. They each carried one piece of luggage, including the children. One woman was clutching an infant to her breast. The baroness had bought the truck from a mechanic in Allenstein. She had paid for it with a diamond ring that she had never liked very much, the gift of a wealthy suitor with no taste

"Is everyone here?" Carlotta asked the farmer.

"Everyone, except Albert and the baron."

"Start climbing in!" Carlotta called out to the crowd. "You sit up front, with Kate and me," she added, addressing the farmer.

The peasants began to take their places under the wax tarp that covered the truck. Carlotta watched them clamber into the truck and felt foolish. The role of the redeemed whore didn't suit her. She was turning into the heroine of a cheap melodrama. Still, someone had to take responsibility for getting these people out.

Just outside the main entrance of the castle, Albert followed the operations, as impassive as ever. Carlotta walked over to where he was standing.

"Are you sure you don't want to come?"

The butler shook his head and gave an embarrassed smile, as if apologizing for some shortcoming on his part.

"Perhaps you could still try to convince the lord baron," he suggested, pointing to something behind Carlotta's back.

She turned and saw her husband striding toward them.

"What happened? We heard a shot," she asked in alarm.

"Nothing serious," said the baron. "But the Russians could be here any minute. You must go."

He stroked her face.

Carlotta pulled him into an embrace and could not hold back her tears.

"Come with us," she whispered. "I will sell my other jewels. We can go back to Paris. Maybe our friends are still alive. Maybe they are still our friends. I'll get a job, any job, and you'll teach fencing."

Baron Wilhelm von Lehndorff stared into his wife's eyes, eyes that had avoided his for many years but that, against all expectations over these few challenging years, had begun to seek his gaze again. Carlotta's project tempted him. Paris. The fencing salle, Le Coudurier. The smell of the leather platforms. Master Dubois would be in his seventies by now. Perhaps he needed an assistant. He saw himself drinking pastis with students after class. It might be hard to begin. The French would be suspicious, but they would accept them in the end. The city had always welcomed exiles. They could rent an apartment on the Boulevard Saint-Michele and eat *far breton* in the bistro on the square. A new country, a new language, a career. He looked up at the castle. The building seemed to be watching him. The windows and gables were like so many eyes through which his ancient lineage observed him, pulling him into a dark vortex of honor, discipline, and death. Baron Wilhelm von Lehndorff could go nowhere. He gave Carlotta a tight squeeze, kissed her, and spread his arms wide.

"Leave," he said.

The baroness did not attempt to argue. Of all the failures in her life, this was the most painful and the most predictable. She had known all along that it would be impossible to convince Wilhelm. She turned away in silence and walked back to the truck. Everyone was already inside. Sitting in the front passenger seat, Kate wiped her tears with a handkerchief. Next to her, the farmer sucked on an unlit pipe, his gaze lost in the void. Carlotta pulled herself up and sat behind the wheel. She turned the key in the ignition and the engine started quietly. Driving the truck was not that difficult. She had practiced for a couple of afternoons with the mechanic who had sold it to her. There had been no one else on the estate who knew how to drive. Carlotta steered to make a U-turn.

Albert and the baron watched in silence. They only went back in when the truck had spluttered down the entire driveway and vanished behind a row of trees.

Far away, in the silence that loomed over the von Lehndorff mansion, he could clearly hear the dark monologue coming from the front. The baron was sitting at the table in the smoking room. He had thrown the disgusting Nazi *völkisch* chest out of the window—he wasn't sure why exactly—then he had opened a bottle of wine and started playing Babette. The rest of the furniture would probably be going the same way. Within a couple of days, that room and the whole castle would be turned into billets for soldiers. Drunk *muzhik* would vomit on the carpets and take potshots with the Wedgwood service that Carlotta had bought in London. Before they left, they would set the whole place on fire. His family history would come to an end there and then, and perhaps it was a good thing. The world could do without the von Lehndorffs and Prussia. The baron took a card from the pile. Jack of diamonds. He placed it on the queen of the same suit. The image of bodies crammed into the van with the hose attached to the tailpipe, swollen tongues hanging out of their mouths, flashed through his mind. The world could do without Germany. The Red Army was about to give the Germans a master class in a subject the Germans thought they were the experts in. Nemmersdorf had simply been the beginning. Four of spades. He looked in vain for somewhere to put it. After what the Nazis had done in the East, it would be naïve or hypocritical to be surprised by the Russians' conduct.

They would kill and rape and annihilate everything in their path, from the Vistula to Berlin. Ten of clubs.

Albert came into the room quietly.

"Is there anything else you need from me, Herr Baron?"

Von Lehndorff, absorbed in his game of solitaire, absent-mindedly said there was nothing. He added the ten of clubs to the three of diamonds.

"In that case, I would like to take my leave."

The baron looked up from his cards and stared at Albert. The butler was standing in front of him looking stiff in his livery. Von Lehndorff understood. He should have guessed. Albert would die as discreetly as he had lived. The baron got up, walked around the table, and held out his hand to his butler. Albert could not refrain from feeling a certain excitement as his fingers touched the baron's. This was the first time in his life that he had shaken the hand of a Junker.

"There will always be lords and servants," Albert commented, "but they won't be like us. The rules that have governed our world, whether they be right or wrong, represented something that brought order out of chaos and that has lasted for a long time." The butler paused. He had never spoken like that to anyone, least of all to the lord baron. Von Lehndorff looked attentively at him. He nodded slightly and thrust forward his chin, as if he were inviting his butler to carry on, which Albert did. "The future does not belong to us. The baroness and all the others can go elsewhere, but you and I are destined to stay here."

The baron agreed.

"Goodbye," Albert said.

"Goodbye."

The baron's old uniform from the Great War still fit him. He had struggled a bit to fasten the buttons on his jacket, but he had finally succeeded. Von Lehndorff pinned the first-class Iron Cross on his chest, knotted the *Pour le Mérite* around his neck, and donned the steel helmet with which he had fought at the Somme. At the time, the battle had felt like hell on earth, the final labyrinth where European consciousness had lost its way. Instead, it had been just the beginning. Albert's words had touched him, but the baron knew there was something essential missing, however profound and heartfelt his speech had been. Albert, like all those Germans who had grown up under Kaiser Wilhelm, was inclined to regard National Socialism as a mysterious natural calamity, a bizarre product of chance that was extraneous to their history. In violation of his innermost instincts that would have led him to draw the same conclusions as Albert, in his moments of greatest despair—which were also those of greatest lucidity—Wilhelm von Lehndorff had had to admit that Adolf Hitler and his supporters were not monsters without a past. They were, rather, the product of a shared history that included the House of von Lehndorff. Frederick II of Prussia, the victorious Battle of Sedan, neo-romanticism, the Volk myth, the courage and self-sacrifice that his generation had demonstrated in the trenches of the Western Front, had all contributed to the advent of Hitler.

The stable was almost empty. Most of the horses had been sold or slaughtered. Only the bay and Stella, Carlotta's filly, were left. The baron stroked Stella's beautiful black coat. He gave her a lump of sugar, groomed her, and filled her trough. He hoped a good Cossack would find her and know how to take care of her. Maybe Stella would see Berlin.

The baron took Lightning outside, mounted, glanced back one last time at the castle, and set off in the direction of the woods. He rode without looking back. Lightning's hooves reverberated on the packed snow. He threaded his way through the trees. When he reached the point in the forest where the pine trunks were curved, he stopped to give the bay a rest. Maybe the old peasants had been right. Maybe these trees really were a sign that the ancient gods wanted to take back what had been taken from them.

As he rode out of the forest, there was a sound that was not the blowing of the wind. At first, he could hardly hear it, but it gradually it became more distinct. A rhythmic noise coming closer. A clanging of metal. Prutenian warriors banging their swords on their shields before throwing themselves in battle. The horse neighed nervously. Von Lehndorff sat up straight in the saddle, trying to catch a glimpse of the enemy. There were lords and there were servants. He was the lord of these lands. He drew his sword in order to defend what had belonged to his family for centuries.

Lieutenant Borodin was tired and cold. He stuck his head out of the turret of the T-34 and the wind stung his unshaved cheeks. They had hardly stopped since the launch of the attack nine days earlier. Sometimes he felt as if they hadn't stopped since Stalingrad. They had crossed the vast steppe, one kilometer after another, surrounded by the stench of diesel fuel and gunpowder. And at last, they had arrived at the gates of Germany. Prussia was flat, with few natural obstacles. And the harsh winter had frozen over the rivers and lakes. They were ideal conditions for an armored offensive.

"Who the fuck is that?" someone asked from inside the tank, but their voice was lost in the hypnotic screeching of the tracks, steel clanging endlessly against steel.

"Who the fuck is that?!" the voice yelled again.

Borodin was wiping the condensation and snow off the lenses of his goggles. When he put them back on, he saw the man on horseback. If that was all the Krauts were sending his way, they would be in Berlin in a couple of days.

"Fire!" ordered Borodin without thinking.

A few seconds passed, during which the knight continued his absurd charge. Levering himself up in the stirrups, his knees planted firmly against the horse's flank, the man leaned his torso forward. His arm was held straight out in front of him, forming a single line with the blade. The pose was elegant, a perfect exercise in horsemanship.

A long burst from the T-34's coaxial machine gun went off. Horse and rider crashed to the ground, staining the snow red. Borodin cast him a fleeting glance as the column drove by.

"One less Nazi."

The baron lay supine, with one leg under the horse's body. His belly had been ripped open and was reduced to a pulp of flesh, blood and cloth. Lightning was neighing in despair. He, too, was mortally wounded. Von Lehndorff watched the shadows flit by as if in a dream. Six white titans with red stars on their turrets, puffing smoke. They went by fast, in a white whirlwind. Then came silence. The only sound was the horse wheezing. The baron slipped his wrist out of the cloth ring of the dragoon, threw down his sword, and with some difficulty opened his holster. He pulled out his pistol and tried to sit up. He felt his strength failing him. He spat out a thick, glutinous lump, and forced himself to sit up straight. Propping himself up with his left arm, Von Lehndorff managed to place the barrel over Lightning's ear. The horse whinnied weakly.

The shot echoed in the stillness of the plain. A cawing raven answered from afar.

The baron fell back into the snow. He no longer felt any pain.

Above him, the sky was growing dark.

55

Rome, July 18, 1982

W hen the Mossad agent pretending not to be a Mossad agent had mentioned a "Jewish restaurant," Natalya was expecting, without any enthusiasm, a dinner of *gefiltefish*. Instead, she had been assailed with all sorts of exotic flavors. The artichokes were delicious: the outer leaves crispy, almost burnt, and the heart soft and sweet. "In Italy," Shlomo had explained in his Yiddish-inflected German Jewish food, "Jewish food is Mediterranean."

Anton signaled to the waiter that they had finished the wine and a second flask of Frascati appeared on the table. Natalya found the straw basket so picturesque. She let Epstein serve her.

Despite her fears, Moscow had approved the project. KGB headquarters in Managua had already been informed. They would make contact with the Sandinistas, who would see to the logistics.

"To our hunt," Libowitz said, raising his glass.

Anton and Natalya joined him in a toast.

She was confused by the fact that she did not find the company of the two men at all unpleasant. Libowitz was a constant source of jokes and anecdotes that vied with one another in their stupidity but still had the power to amuse her. The one about the old rabbi on his deathbed while his wife made strudel had made her laugh until she cried. Epstein's repertoire was more refined, comprising mostly stories from his family history. The cousin who pretended to be a widow even though her husband was alive and well and lived two blocks away with a seamstress. Uncle Max, a renowned urologist, who had once been called to see Prince Esterházy, one of the largest landowners in the Habsburg empire, and later told the family that the prince had three testicles. Epstein was a vivid and humorous storyteller, but there was always a hint of melancholy, especially considering what had happened to the world he was describing. At one point, Natalya had the impression that Libowitz was trying hard to make himself sympathetic, but not to overshadow Epstein, as if they were a team. Natalya wondered fleetingly what game they were playing. Without knowing why, she was flattered.

The last customers had gone. The waiters had already begun to place the upturned chairs on the tables. The owner offered them a last round of liquor, after which they paid and left.

"See you at the airport," Epstein said.

"See you tomorrow," Libowitz replied as he turned and walked towards the subway.

Anton and Natalya were left alone. She was wearing her aqua-green dress.

"That dress looks very nice on you," Anton said, immediately regretting the cliché. All evening he had been trying hard to make brilliant conversation and now all he could come up with was a banality.

"Thank you," Natalya replied, looking away.

As they walked back, they didn't say much. He feared he would stumble into another commonplace. Without Shlomo to back him up, he felt much less secure. She, on the other hand, was lost in her own thoughts. The situation was in danger of taking an unprofessional turn.

They reached the hotel, collected their keys from the reception, and went up to their floor. Their rooms were next to one another.

Anton lingered at Natalya's door.

"Well, good night," he said hesitantly. It was time to act. Part of him longed to kiss those cool lips, but another part was paralyzed. He was a schoolboy in the body of a sixty-year-old man.

"Good night," Natalya said.

Her mouth creased into a smile, which Anton decided to interpret as an invitation.

He came a little closer and she let him kiss her.

Natalya Yakovchenko woke up with a start. Tossing in her sleep, she had felt Epstein beside her. That contact had woken her up instantly. It had been a long time since she had slept with anyone. She ran a hand over her face and through her hair. She was sweating. Even with the window open, it was hot in the room. The alarm clock display told her it was 3:24. Why had she done it? And with a much older man. The answer was so obvious that it didn't really deserve the question. To add insult to injury, he was a deviationist. She laughed at herself and her prejudices.

She got up, opened the fridge, and grabbed a bottle of water. She took a long sip and put the bottle back. She was naked. She put Anton's shirt on, the only thing at hand. Their clothes were scattered around the room. She picked up her lighter and cigarettes and went over to the window. The street was deserted. The imposing facade of a church gleamed in the moonlight. Anton would know what it was called and probably which masterpieces it contained. Natalya lit a Gauloises. She inhaled the full-flavored, vaguely sweet smoke deeply. It was annoying to admit it, but Western cigarettes did taste better. And she didn't mind Epstein's decadent ways one bit. She would just have to manage the situation so that it didn't interfere with their mission.

She heard Anton getting up behind her. She did not turn around. She stood there, with her elbows resting on the window frame and her cigarette burning between her fingers. A breath of wind made the ash burn brightly for a moment.

Anton came to her side.

"Would you like one?" Natalya asked, waving the cigarette in the air.

Anton took a Gauloises out of the pack.

Natalya handed him her lighter.

"Don't make a habit of it," she said.

Anton smiled and lit the cigarette.

They smoked in silence, watching the sleeping city.

Natalya took one last drag and threw the butt away. The red dot drew an arc in the darkness before landing on the sidewalk. Natalya leaned her head against his shoulder.

"Don't make a habit of it."

"You already said that."

"Just to be clear."

Anton threw his butt down into the street, too.

"Let's try and get some sleep," Natalya said. The trip to Mexico City would be long. And then they would have to wait four hours for the connecting flight to Managua.

Natalya walked back to the bed. She still had Anton's shirt on. He shrugged it off her and dropped it on the floor. He started stroking her breasts, squeezing them softly, then he bent down to suck her nipples. Holding her hips, he gave her a gentle push until she was lying down. Natalya felt his moist tongue licking her navel and working its way lower and lower.

She closed her eyes.

"Don't make a habit of it," she said again, unsure whether she was speaking to him or to herself.

56

Eastern Prussia, January 21, 1945

The landscape was a white expanse without a single landmark. The snow covered the road so deeply that it was hard to see which way to go. The convoy made its way slowly, the Kübelwagen in the lead, followed by the three trucks.

Lichtblau heard gunshots in the distance. He looked at his watch and wondered why the sergeant was taking so long to catch up with them. They had left the castle more than half an hour before. The Obersturmbannführer turned to Wasserman.

"How much longer is Dietrich going to be?" he asked. The doctor gave no answer. The question was rhetorical and they both knew it. They weren't going to wait for him.

As if to obviate any possible qualms, two Sturmoviks suddenly appeared out of a gray cloud. They dipped, one after the other, and attacked the column. Before the Germans were fully aware of the danger, the first plane had already opened fire on them with its 23mm cannon. A maelstrom of bullets hit the truck behind the Kübelwagen. The corporal driving the truck instinctively slammed his foot on the gas pedal, which made the fuel tank explode. Blistering shrapnel flew in all directions. Fiery shards fell in the snow, extinguishing the flames. One piece ripped through the Kübelwagen's canvas top and landed in Professor Schenk's neck. He collapsed on top of Wasserman.

The first plane had already passed the convoy and was beginning to turn around. The second, was flying in its wake.

The Kübelwagen skidded off the road into a ditch a little further on.

"Get out!" Lichtblau ordered. He grabbed the leather bag, opened the door, and ran.

From under the wings of the second Sturmovik, two missiles honed in on the targets.

The trucks exploded with a terrifying blast.

Crouching behind a tree trunk, Lichtblau watched the carcasses of the three Opel Blitzes burn like midsummer bonfires. With a twang of anxiety, he started searching through all his pockets. Eventually, he found a small bottle of pills in the outside pocket of his jacket and calmed down a little. He clutched the bottle in the palm of his hand. In addition to the notes in his bag, it was all he had to show for more than three years' work.

The planes made a second pass, mowing down some of the survivors who had managed to jump out of the trucks. Then they gained altitude again and vanished back into the clouds.

Lichtblau stood up. A little further on he could see that Wasserman and the corporal had also managed to get to their feet. The doctor was attempting to wipe Schenk's blood off his bespattered coat.

They walked toward the trucks still enveloped in flames. Observing from his hidden vantage point, Lichtblau had hoped that it would be possible to salvage at least some of the material but it was clear that the fire was destroying everything.

Captain Kiesel came up to him. His face was black with smoke and his eyes were panic-stricken. Lichtblau imagined he looked the same. They stared at each other for a few moments, saying nothing. Their breath came out of their mouths in little white puffs. They walked over to the Kübelwagen. The corporal climbed in behind the wheel and tried to start the engine, which responded without any problems. When he went into reverse, the vehicle did not move.

"Let's push," Kiesel suggested.

The three men spread out around the front of the car with their hands on the hood, at the ready.

"Now!" the corporal said, his foot on the gas.

As the engine revved up and the tires spun, splashing slush all around, the vehicle didn't budge. All of a sudden, however, the Kübelwagen backfired and the truck started moving. Their success was greeted with a collective sigh of relief. Allenstein was at least thirty kilometers away.

Just as they were about to drive away, another survivor appeared. A private. He had been shot in the arm and was bleeding. Wasserman made a makeshift bandage by tearing shreds from a shirt he had in his bag. Lichtblau was about to spontaneously offer the wounded man one of his tablets, but he stopped himself just in time. They were his safe-conduct and he could not afford to waste any.

They all climbed aboard and the truck drove off into the emptiness of the frozen countryside.

Above them, the sky was getting darker.

57

Rome, July 19, 1982

The railway embankment on the way to the airport was dotted with poppies: incongruous splashes of red strewn among the gray stones in a countryside brutalized by the city. "Beautiful things come about where you least expect them," Anton said pointing at the flowers through the window.

Natalya pretended not to understand and went on reading an editorial from the *Frankfurter Allgemeine Zeitung* packed with lies about the Soviet Union.

"I know, I mustn't get into the habit," Anton said.

Natalya put the newspaper down.

"Yesterday was yesterday and today is today," she said patronizingly.

"Message received," Anton replied, turning back to flipping through *Der Spiegel*. There was a long article about Paul Marcinkus and the collapse of the Banco Ambrosiano. In the complex web of the IOR's dodgy financial dealings, it appeared that the Vatican had also been funding Solidarność and the Contras. As soon as the article became too technical, Anton gave up and turned to the horoscope.

They met Shlomo at the Alitalia counter. They checked in and went through security in different lines and met up again in front of one of the duty-free shops. Natalya cast furtive glances at the window displays.

"I'm going to buy cigarettes," she said and walked into the store.

Shlomo took Anton aside and whispered sympathetically, "How did it go last night?

"How did what go?" Anton replied coldly. He detested conversations like this and the kind of people who indulged in them. At least, that is what he had always thought.

"Look, I've noticed your attempts at seduction," Shlomo insisted. "If you don't tell an old friend, who are you going to tell?" He was about to add, "It's not like I'm going to spill the beans to your wife," but luckily, he remembered just in time that Anton had mentioned he was a widower a few days before.

Shlomo was still tempted to be witty. "Who would I tell, anyway? All our mutual friends were murdered by the Nazis."

"Well, Zev may still be alive," Anton corrected him.

"He may well be, but Zev doesn't count. Hassidic Jews don't want to hear any saucy little stories. So did you fuck the *shiksa* or not?"

"Hassidic Jews are more interested in saucy stories than atheist Zionists," Anton replied. "And for your information, the answer is yes." Anton feigned an exasperated tone, as if the information had been forcibly extracted, but in truth Anton was desperate to confess. He had always thought he was different from other men. He had never cheated on his wife, with the exception of a brief affair with a nurse—the worst possible cliché in a hospital—and he had been very careful not to tell anyone. At the fine old age of sixty-one, he finally realized that he was just like everyone else. *Telling* someone about it was almost as important as *doing* it. He wondered if it was like that for women, too.

"Bravo, Professor Epstein," Shlomo exclaimed, smiling approvingly.

Natalya reappeared with a carton of Gauloises under her arm. And a box of Chanel in her purse. An Arab customer had bought Number 5 and she had copied her. Before that, though, she had tried out a few different perfumes.

Anton sniffed ostentatiously in the air as he circled her.

"Don't make a habit of it, Comrade Yakovchenko," he said in her ear.

Natalya ignored him and walked off towards the gate.

They were very early. Shlomo let Anton and the *shiksa* go ahead, stopped at a bar, and exchanged three thousand-lira bills for telephone tokens. Those two were enjoying a romantic trip on the KGB expense account and he wasn't even allowed to call his wife? Procedure be damned. He found a public phone and tried to push the bronze coins into the slot. He had some difficulty to begin with because he hadn't realized that the two sides were not the same. On one side there were two grooves and on the other, only one. As soon as he had gotten the hang of it, however, the machine started to gobble up tokens as fast as a slot machine.

Shlomo dialed the number and let it ring.

"Hello?"

Rivka sounded tired.

"Hey."

"Hello!" Rivka was amazed. It was the first time Shlomo had phoned her when he was on a mission. She immediately thought the worst.

"What's happened?" she asked, alarmed.

"Nothing, don't worry."

"Really?"

"Really. I just wanted to hear your voice."

Rivka made an effort to relax.

"How are you?" she asked, pretending not to care. She didn't quite know what to say or what kind of questions he could answer.

"I found an old friend from the camp. A Czech. I told you about him. We were together in Soldau and then at the castle."

Rivka grew more and more concerned. With the exception of Sara Mandelbaum, Shlomo had never found any of his fellow prisoners. And now this old friend pops up as well as Lichtblau

"Are you doing the job together?" his wife asked.

"Yes."

"Are you happy with that?"

"Yes."

Rivka was getting impatient. This was so typical of Shlomo. He would make a nice gesture, a phone call you weren't expecting, after which he would express himself in monosyllables. "When are you coming back?"

"I don't know." Shlomo searched for something with a semblance of truth to tell her without providing Shin Bet agents who may be listening in with any useful information. "If all goes well, in a couple of weeks. Maybe three."

"What if it goes badly?" Rivka couldn't help herself saying.

"It will be fine."

Silence.

"I've run out of tokens. I'll call you back when I can," Shlomo added.

He looked at the last two metal tokens in the palm of his hand.

"Do what you have to do and come home," Rivka said.

"Of course."

The line went dead. Shlomo stood there motionless staring at the tokens without hanging up. Between the two grooves there was an engraving of a telephone.

Outside the phone booth a tall man with a blond crew-cut and blue eyes was frowning at him.

"Das Telefon ist öffentlich," he said.

Shlomo looked up.

"Go fuck yourself," he answered in Hebrew.

He hung up, put the tokens in his pocket, and walked out of the booth.

58

Eastern Prussia, January 21, 1945

The Gardenia Kommando no longer existed. Of the eleven men who had been selected, one had died of septicemia the previous winter and the other eight had been killed in the hunting parties Lichtblau called "scientific experiments." Only Shlomo, Anton, and a Galician Hassidic Jew were still alive. When Sergeant Dietrich opened the door of the hut, the three surviving members were in bed, numb with hunger and cold. They had not received any rations since the day before. Roll call had not been taken. They had shared the last of the potatoes and wiled away the hours sleeping under several layers of blankets. Over the weeks of the experiments, the living had appropriated the possessions of their companions as they died. The more companions died, the warmer the survivors were. The Unterscharführer had shouted at them to get out, but none of them had moved. It had not been a conscious act of disobedience. It was simply the warmth of their beds compared to the frost they knew was outside that had paralyzed them. Only when Dietrich had pointed the machine gun at him did Anton decide he should move. At that point, however, something incredible had happened. The baron had appeared and had shot the Unterscharführer.

"They've gone," the Junker had said.

Now Dietrich's body was blocking the entrance of the hut. An icy draught was whistling through the door.

They slowly stood up in unison, saying nothing. The only noise was the floorboards creaking under their unsteady footsteps. There was no sound coming from outside, either, except for the wind rustling the leaves on the trees in the garden and occasionally making the closest branches scratch against the roof of the hut.

They went outside. Three castaways on a beach gazing at the shipwreck after the disaster from which they had been saved, either by miracle, by chance, or because they were stronger, more capable, and more reckless than the others.

"Bravo, Jew Epstein. Charles Darwin would be proud of you," Anton whispered.

Lichtblau would repeat that line whenever he got the chance. Anton knew perfectly well that the Nazis did not like evolutionism. The idea that all of humanity—whites, yellows and blacks, Aryans and Slavs—shared the same ape-like ancestors negated the very existence of a dialectic between superior and inferior races. And yet, the mechanism of natural selection fit well with their worldview, provided, of course, that they were ahead.

First, they went to the hut next door, which housed the other prisoners. It was deserted. Many had died. Others had been transferred to Lagers further away from the front line. Some of the children were still at the castle, though. Anton was certain of this because he had been the one to compile the list of those who had been sent away. When he had told Shlomo that Sara Mandelbaum was on it, the Pole had glared at him.

"We don't know if it's for the better or the worse," Anton had said to encourage him. And it was true. Just as in Soldau, there was no logical correlation between events here either. In the new camp, Sara might have a better chance of survival. Or worse. Or the same. As for Nina, one morning in mid-December, Lichtblau had come for her and no one had seen her since.

The three prisoners approached the fence. The gate was open, the guard turrets empty. They stared at each other doubtfully. Anton wondered if this was yet another extreme test that Lichtblau had conjured up.

It was Shlomo who made the first move. He took one step, then another, and found himself on the other side of the fence.

Nothing happened. No gunfire, no siren, no sentry order, no German shepherd barking.

They crossed the park without meeting anyone and reached the castle. A few meters from the castle wall, lying on its side on the gravel in the courtyard, was an inlaid chest. It looked as though it had been thrown out of a window.

Suddenly, two airplanes flew at low altitude over their heads. The insignia were those of the Soviet Air Force, their wings heavy with bombs and rockets. The sight seemed to release the three men from a spell. It was true. The Germans had left. The Red Army, so long awaited, was finally on its way. They all started talking at once, without listening to one another. Even Zev, who was usually silent. As the words tumbled out of them, they entered the castle. Their voices echoing in the empty halls.

They headed for the kitchen. There were some leftovers. Some stale barley bread. Half a jar of jam. A small lump of lard. They lit the stove, heated some water for tea, and sat down to eat, without stopping talking. They chewed, talked, and laughed.

"In a few days the Russians will be in Berlin."

The image of the red flag flying over the rubble of the capital of the Reich was too good to be true.

When they had finished eating, they split up and explored the rest of the building.

They took anything that might be useful: most importantly, clothes. In the baron's study, Shlomo found a pistol. He slipped it into the pocket of his new wool jacket, along with the bullets that were in a drawer.

In one of the servants' rooms, Zev came across a corpse. The man was hanging from one of the beams with an upturned stool at his feet. He felt no compunction in checking out what the dead man was wearing. The uniform, though in good condition, did not interest him. The outfit was clearly impractical. The shoes, on the other hand, looked sturdy, though they would probably be too tight. He decided to take them off anyway. It was not an easy task. The body was already stiffening. He tried them on. Too small. Zev tied the laces together and hung them around his neck. They may fit Anton. He looked in the closet. He chose a flannel shirt, a scarf, and a pair of gloves. He closed the door behind him without making a sound.

Anton had a thick woolen navy jacket on. It was such a pleasure to be wearing something so warm and comfortable. He had found it in one of the rooms on the second floor, where the baron and his wife had lived. Along with the reefer jacket, he had taken a sweater and a pair of cord pants. To hold them up, he had had to fasten a fine leather belt with the crest of a university fraternity on the buckle on the last hole. Then he had set off to the library on the ground floor, next to the smoking room. The room was lined with dark wooden bookcases full of books, and there were two ladders on iron rails to get to the top shelves. In the three years he had spent at the castle, Anton had often cast longing glances toward that room, but he had never been allowed to go in. Now he had it the whole place to himself and he was disappointed. During his imprisonment, when his need to read had become more acute, Anton had imagined the library contained who knows what wonders, but all he found were books on military history and agronomy journals a few decades out of date. Still, there was something interesting there for him. In a dusty corner, he found a copy of *The Jungle Book*. As a child, in the long weeks he had spent in bed with measles, his mother had read the whole book to him four or five times. She had tried to suggest other books but he only wanted to hear the stories of Mowgli, Bagheera, and Rikki-Tikki-Tavi. By the end, rather than reading, his mother would be reciting the book from memory. Anton slipped the book into one of the pockets of the reefer jacket and went down to the laboratory. He knew what he might find and was frightened by it. He had witnessed killings and torture of all kinds and he could take anything. Anything but this. He was afraid, and he was grateful to that fear that made him feel human again, more brutally but

more substantially human than d'Artagnan or Ivanhoe might
have felt.

In the archive, the stove was still warm. The floor was covered in papers. Anton cast a distracted glance around and
moved on. Lichtblau's study was even more cluttered. All the
drawers were open. File cabinets had been knocked over on the
floor. Hunched over the large mahogany desk, Harry Dobbs
was packing something into a backpack. When he saw Epstein
in the doorway, he froze.

"What are you doing?" he asked.

"Collecting my severance pay," Dobbs answered and went
right back to work. From a rack with several glass test tubes
lined up on it, he took one containing a purplish substance,
wrapped it inside a few pages of newspaper, and placed it with
great care into the outer pocket of his haversack.

"Where are the children?" Anton asked.

"Try the operating theater," Dobbs answered, without taking his eyes off the material he was examining.

Anton walked down the hall. His heart was pounding. He got
to the room and reached his hand out to the doorknob. His fingers were trembling. He opened the door. There they were, lined
up, side by side. Eight small naked bodies with their eyes closed.
Anton fell to his knees. The smell of disinfectant nauseated him.
Confusingly, behind him, he heard someone come out of the lab.
He did not turn around. He continued to stare at the children. He
pulled out the book. He realized that he had picked it up for that
very reason. He looked for the page and began to read aloud.

> Then something began to hurt Mowgli inside him, as he
> had never been hurt in his life before, and he caught his breath
> and sobbed, and the tears ran down his face.
> "What is it? What is it?" he said.
> "I do not wish to leave the jungle, and I do not know what
> this is. Am I dying, Bagheera?"
> "No, Little Brother. That is only tears, such as men use,"

said Bagheera. "Now I know thou art a man, and a man's cub no longer. The jungle is shut indeed to thee henceforward. Let them fall, Mowgli. They are only tears."

So, Mowgli sat and cried as though his heart would break; and he had never cried in all his life before.

Anton closed the book, wiped the tears from his cheeks with his jacket sleeve, and stood up. Shlomo and Zev were there beside him. He had no idea how long they had been there.

"I saw Dobbs leaving," Shlomo said, trying not to look at the children. "Nichols will take care of it. They'll court-martial him."

"Nichols is dead," Anton answered blankly. "Petechial typhus."

"When?"

"Last week."

"How do you know?"

I heard Dobbs telling Lichtblau. He was happy. He said the new commander was 'more reasonable'."

Shlomo brandished the gun.

"Then we'll take care of him," he growled.

Zev and Anton stared at the Luger in surprise.

The Galician laid a hand on Shlomo's shoulder. They searched each other's eyes.

"We have to bury the children," Zev said.

Shlomo let a few moments go by and then he put the Luger away.

In any case, he had never fired a gun in his life. He didn't even know how to take the safety off. He should learn to shoot. The first thing he should do was learn how to shoot.

They went to the tool shed and grabbed some picks and spades. They discarded the idea of burying the children in the castle cemetery on the spot. It was full of crosses with German names. They chose a nice spot in the garden under the branches of a large oak tree. The ground was frozen and they struggled

330 · GIAIME ALONGE

to dig a grave. They wrapped the bodies in makeshift shrouds using linen they had found in the bedrooms, and lowered them into the pit, side by side just as they had found them. Then Zev recited the *Kaddish*. In theory, he was not allowed to do so because the rule was that at least ten adult males must be present. His rabbi would not have approved. But his rabbi had died and so had all the villagers. Zev recited it anyway.

There was a sack full of beets in the tool shed. In the chaos of the escape, they must have been left there by mistake. Zev offered to make soup.

"I'll warm up some water and start peeling," he said. "You go and get more wood. We'll need it tonight." He shouldered the sack and carried it towards the kitchen.

Anton and Shlomo found an axe and a wheelbarrow and began to search the garden. They remembered the chest. Shlomo broke it to pieces in seconds.

"What are you going to do now?" he asked Anton out of the blue as they loaded the wood into the wheelbarrow.

Anton looked at him quizzically.

"What do you mean?"

"Where will you go?"

"Home." His eyes said, "Where else?"

"My home no longer exists," Shlomo replied.

Anton stopped for a moment to reflect. He realized that he had never really thought about it. He had simply assumed that, once the war was over, life would resume where it had left off. "Well, my family may be gone, but Prague is still there. I will go back to my books. Besides, there might be a girl waiting for me."

"You're kidding yourself if you think she's still alive."

"She's not Jewish."

"A *shiksa*," Shlomo commented, with a blend of admiration and surprise.

"I'm not Jewish either," a voice inside Anton Epstein

whispered but the voice had grown faint. Anton, who had sung *Ich hatt' einen Kameraden* in school like every other German-speaking child, and who had never had his Bar Mitzvah, now felt that he was also Jewish. The Lager had been his initiation.

"And what about you?" he asked Shlomo.

"Palestine."

Anton was taken completely aback.

"Have you become a Zionist?"

"Liquidate the Diaspora, before the Diaspora liquidates you," Shlomo said. "In this whole cesspit, the Zionists are the only ones who ever understood anything."

"Zionism is just another form of nationalism," Anton retorted. "Nationalism led us to this," he added, making a broad gesture with his hands to embrace the castle, the common grave at the foot of the oak tree, and the prison camp at the end of the garden.

Shlomo shrugged.

"You may be right. You are a student and you know a lot more than I do. But what I do know is that I want to live in a country where I will never have to meet a *goy* again."

Anton looked for something convincing to say, something about a noble project of humanity, peace and internationalism, but Shlomo's words brooked no argument.

They finished loading the creaking wheelbarrow and pushed it back to the castle kitchen.

Above them, the sky was getting dark.

59

Cordillera de Amerrisque, northern Nicaragua,
July 20, 1982

They had been marching through the jungle all morning and the effect of the pill was wearing off. Guillermo Rocas, who was at the head of the column, turned back to Huberman and gesticulated that he was hungry. The German nodded.

"We'll break soon," he said.

Without pausing, Huberman untied the handkerchief knotted around his neck and used it to wipe his forehead. Not that it did much good. A few steps later, his forehead was already beaded with sweat again.

They had left the border behind them several kilometers back. They were getting close to their destination. They trekked on for another half hour and met the scouts who had been waiting for them in a clearing, chewing salted meat.

The unit stopped. There were about thirty of them, most of them armed with secondhand M16s left over from the Vietnam War. But some, like Rocas and Huberman, had the latest French FAMAS assault rifles. They were all equipped with a machete or hunting knife. And at the back of the column, there was a man with a flamethrower.

Through the trees, they could hear a stream flowing down from the mountain.

"It's not deep," the oldest of the scouts said. He was in his mid-30s, while the other was a young boy. "It's easy to pass. The village is downstream. No soldiers, just a few militia men."

Huberman shrugged off his backpack and pulled out the tan pouch where he kept his pills. He took one and handed it to Rocas.

The wind carried the voices of children playing. When they came out of the bush, there they were: a dozen or so children and an old man sitting under a tree.

With dilated pupils and bloodshot eyes, Guillermo Rocas let out a piercing war cry and broke out into a run towards the village with a feral, yelling mob hot on his heels.

Victor Huberman was right behind Rocas, clutching his rifle tight. Images and thoughts floated lazily in his mind, and then suddenly picked up speed. While the children had run away in a flash, the old man had been slow on the uptake. He hobbled away, trying to run, but the weight of his years meant he could barely walk. At one point he dropped his hat and went back to pick it up. Huberman was deeply offended by the old man's stupidity. He brought the rubber-coated butt of the FAMAS up to his shoulder, calmly took aim, and fired a short burst of bullets: more than enough for such a slow target. The old man fell to the ground and his hat hit the dust. Huberman stepped over the body and examined the hat. It was an old misshapen sombrero.

"*Untermenschen*," he muttered to himself.

The red and black flag of the Sandinista Front hanging from the rusty balcony on the second floor was the only thing that distinguished the building from all the other miserable constructions and perhaps indicated that it played an institutional role. In any case, whatever the significance, it was the only resistance the invaders had met so far. Random volleys rained down on them from the windows, frequently enough to force Guillermo Rocas and his men to stay under cover They had spread out around the house with the flag, some behind an old pickup truck, most under cover of the low wall that surrounded the park. They returned fire but had not yet tried to storm the building.

A bullet pierced Octavio Perez's heart, presumably completely by accident, and Guillermo Rocas decided he had had enough. He signaled to the group behind the pick-up for cover and stuck an anti-tank shell into the grenade launcher on his rifle. When he was sure everyone was ready, he aimed at the door of the house, just below the flag. He pulled the trigger and the doorway exploded in a spray of rubble.

"Let's go!" he yelled, leaping over the low wall.

His men followed. As they approached the house, the M16s providing cover fire were aiming at the windows.

"You're dead," Guillermo Rocas shouted as he stepped into the breach opened by the grenade.

The interior was filled with smoke. He sensed movement somewhere in front of him. He opened fire without hesitation. A moan confirmed that his hunch had been right.

"Duarte, with me," he said addressing the man who had come in after him and pointing to the staircase at the back of the room. He turned to see who else was there. "Alfonso and Segundo, you two with me. The others clean up this floor," he ordered.

They moved in silence. Rocas and the other three advanced cautiously toward the staircase, their weapons leveled. A hand grenade rolled down the steps. Guillermo Rocas grabbed it, threw it back up, and curled up on the floor cradling his head. The explosion deafened him. He waited a bit and then got up. He was covered in white dust. The staircase was still standing, but two men had fallen through a giant gash in the ceiling. One was still alive. Duarte slashed his throat with a quick, precise movement.

A few gunshots echoed somewhere in the distance and then there was silence.

When they emerged, they saw that the men who had stayed outside under Huberman's command had started slaughtering the animals and setting fire to the village.

The man with the flamethrower went methodically from one house to the next. He would kick in the door and shoot a red tongue of fire inside. Anyone who got in his way was executed on the spot. They killed a peasant woman who tried to defend her pig and an old man who attacked the flamethrower with a machete. While overseeing the operations, Huberman happened to see one of the guerrillas dragging a young girl into a house. He signaled to Rocas, and the commander acted immediately.

The girl was on the floor and the man had already pulled his pants down when his commander came up behind him.

"You know the rules," Rocas said sharply.

The man turned around, stared at Rocas, then lowered his gaze and pulled up his pants.

From the ground, the girl looked terrified.

Guillermo Rocas did not deign her with a glance. He yanked the man by the arm and pushed him toward the exit. No sexual intercourse was permitted with people in the lowlands. It was one of the few rules Huberman had set. He had explained that their blood was pure and that they should not corrupt it. The inhabitants of the lowlands were mestizos who descended from slaves. Warrior stock should not mix with the scum of humanity.

Half the village was in flames. Victor Huberman ranged through the dusty streets confidently pointing at the targets he wanted his men to strike. A small gesture of his hand was enough to trigger death and destruction. Those degenerates in the CIA had told him that his methods were too brutal. Poor bastards. They still thought they were supposed to win "hearts and minds," like in Vietnam. Hadn't they learned their lesson? Only two things worked with scum: fire and iron.

When they arrived in front of the school, a small, freshly-painted building with flower pots in the windows, the teacher was standing at the front door. He was a thin young man with raven hair down to his shoulders and a shaggy beard. Huberman wondered if it was worth wasting a bullet on a pathetic cliché like this idealistic student standing there staring at him scornfully. Huberman hit him in the face with the butt of his rifle. If he wanted to be a martyr, maybe that would satisfy him. He

pushed the teacher inside and dragged him into the only class-
room. A desk, a few rows of tables, and a portrait of Augusto
Sandino on the wall.

"This is a school, not a military target," the teacher said,
wiping the blood away from his nose. There was no trace of
fear in his voice.

Huberman gave him an icy glare.

"Precisely because it's a school, it's a military target," he said,
taking his aim. When he saw the dark mouth of the FAMAS
rifle right in front of his eyes, the martyr lost his faith and tried
to escape martyrdom. He took a clumsy, sideways leap, like a
turkey.

Huberman rotated his torso slightly, holding his sights on
the target.

The teacher's brain splattered all over the blackboard.

Untermenschen.

60

Allenstein, East Prussia, January 22, 1945

T he rations of Hitler Jugend members, sanctioned by the Volkssturm, included chocolate instead of cigarettes. It was Reichsführer-SS Himmler who had insisted that the health of German youth should be supervised. Paul and his four mates all smoked, though. If they were old enough to deal with hordes of Bolsheviks, then they were old enough for tobacco. And for that matter, they should be old enough for women, too. Of the five members of the fighter-tank team, the only one who had been with a woman was Ernst, the oldest, who was a corporal and commanded the unit. Paul and the other three, ranging from fourteen to sixteen, were still virgins. A few evenings before, under the guidance of the dashing and garrulous Ernst, they had visited the town brothel, only to find that it was closed. The doorman had said that the young ladies had moved west and that, in any case, no *maison* of any repute would admit brats like them. Paul pretended to be as disappointed as the others, but he had actually been relieved. In recent months, especially since he had joined the militia, he had felt increasing desire and curiosity for a female body. But the moment the idea had become a real possibility, he had been seized by panic. Ernst had promised that he would find them some girls. Paul looked forward to it, but at the same time he hoped that fear of the invading Red Army would make all the girls run away from Allenstein. He also hoped that his mother and sister had escaped. In his last letter, he had begged them to leave Neuhof. There had been no reply—the postal service only worked intermittently and then there was censorship—but he doubted his mother had listened to him. She had put so much into the house and store that she couldn't just abandon them to the invaders' mercy. And besides, she had assured him several times that she would never leave without him.

They finished their coffee, put out their cigarettes, and walked out of the bunker where they had spent the night. The air was bitterly cold, and the sky clear, streaked with the pink fingers of dawn. It was not ideal weather for fighting. Fog came in handy when ambushing armored units, but they had a good supply of smoke grenades. They had all had their baptism of fire. Ernst and Peter sported a silver ribbon with an outline of a Panzer in the middle on their right sleeve, indicating that they had destroyed a tank. They were a good team. Paul felt safe with them, and he wanted to win a silver ribbon, too.

"It is sweet and fitting to die for one's country!" Hasso shouted cheerfully, stamping his feet to get the damp out of his bones.

"It is sweet and fitting to die for one's country!" the four others chortled. Laughing, they climbed onto their bicycles, with the Panzerfäuste attached vertically to the handlebars, one on each side, and rode to their assigned position.

Lieutenant Borodin was crouched in the corner of the room with his back against the wall. He stared at the girl lying on a mattress stained with dark, congealed blood. She was naked and cold, with a black hole in the middle of her forehead. Borodin had shot her. He and the others had raped her and then put a bullet in her head. One less fascist whore. He kept saying the phrase to himself, but now that he had sobered up and slept a few hours, the full import of what he had done hit him.

She had said her name was Nina. They had met her the evening before, when they had billeted in that cluster of houses just outside Allenstein. Nor was she hiding. She was waiting for them brimming with confidence. In fluent Russian, she had told them that she was enrolled in the youth federation of the Polish Communist Party and that this was the reason she had ended up in a Lager. But that in November an SS officer had taken her out of the camp and given her to a priest in Allenstein. She had been sent to occupy a room in the town brothel. Nina had been vague about this part of the story, but it was clear that she had been abused by the priest. When Soviet airplanes had flown over the town, and the roar of cannons had begun to be heard, the priest and the whores had left. And the young communist girl had rushed out to greet the glorious Red Army. Borodin and his men had looked at one another in disbelief. That story was so crazy it could even be true. "If you fucked a priest who was friends with the Nazis, you can fuck us who are comrades," Karmin, the tank driver, had said. The smile had vanished from the girl's face. They had had their way with her. Somewhere in his addled brain, Borodin knew that what he was doing was wrong. But those days were going by as if they were living inside a kaleidoscopic haze, in a state of permanent stupor as a result of too little sleep and too much alcohol. As villages burned in the night, the conquerors cannoned their way through the houses. "We're advancing like lava," an artillery officer, a literary man, had told him a few days earlier. He was writing a poem about their offensive in Prussia. He had recited a few lines to him. Borodin remembered only two: "A girl becomes a woman /A woman becomes a corpse." He dropped his head and clasped his temples. He had been an honest and decent person who did not kill people before. Before, he had been studying History of Art at Leningrad University. Before, he owned a dog and talked about love to a redhead student called Sofia. He stared at the decomposing body he, Konstantin Vasilievich Borodin, had deprived of life. This was the worst thing the Nazis had done to him. Not invading his country, killing millions of his countrymen, condemning millions more to flight and terror. And that was why he would slaughter them all, one by one. He rose to his feet, pulled up his suspenders, put on his jacket, and staggered out of the room.

When he stepped out into the courtyard, the unit was in full swing. Sergeant Sorin, efficient as ever, handed him a cup of hot tea.

Borodin gave him a mumbled thank you and took a sip. The drink made him even more confused. Nina's distraught face danced in front of his eyes.

"Conscience is nothing but a Jewish invention," he said, taking a second sip. "Do you know who said that?" he asked the sergeant.

Sorin shook his head, embarrassed. Borodin was not a bad officer, but he was overeducated. Sometimes he couldn't understand him.

Borodin supplied the answer. "Adolf Hitler,"

The sergeant broke into a knowing smile.

"So," Borodin pressed, "let's go show the Krauts that we're not Jews."

"Of course, comrade lieutenant," Sorin said. "I'll go take care of the diesel fuel." And he walked away quickly.

Borodin sat on the running board of an American-made half-track, to which a Russian cannon was attached. A truck was parked next to it. Two soldiers with Asian features were loading various objects, both useful and useless, into the truck. A vacuum cleaner, wine bottles, a couple of candlesticks, a baby carriage, picture frames, umbrellas, a rocking chair, a typewriter with Latin characters. Red Army combatants, especially those from the countryside, were stunned at the wealth of German farms. Solid brick houses, asphalt roads connecting towns, even the smallest settlements. The opulence had incited their hatred even more.

"Ready to go."

Borodin looked up at the sergeant. He stood without answering and walked toward his T-34. The company set off. They overwhelmed the fragile defensive line outside the city and headed for the railway station. To their left, a squadron of SU-122s was heading toward the castle, clearly visible on the hillside in the crisp early morning light. As they advanced,

Borodin scanned the steeple of a church straight ahead of them through the periscope. A beautiful Gothic building. Fourteenth century, probably. There must be a sniper, or an artillery observer, up there.

"Sergeant, take out that belfry over there!" Borodin ordered.

The gunner and servant immediately set to work. They opened fire within seconds. After the third volley, the bell tower came crashing down.

"Let's advance like lava!" Borodin shouted excitedly.

The SS major presiding over the itinerant court-martial had a deep scar on his left cheek from a duel and the countenance of someone with no time to lose. Four men accompanied him, all armed, and all with the same dogged expression. They had stopped them up on a hill overlooking the town as they were drove north out of the city. One of the four had planted himself in the middle of the road, with a military police paddle clearly in view and a machine gun in his other hand. The corporal driving the Kübelwagen had had no choice but to pull over.

"Where are you headed?" the major asked.

"Königsberg," Lichtblau called out from the passenger seat. "I have orders from the Reichsführer-SS himself."

For a moment, the major appeared to hesitate.

"Papers," he asked sharply, but a little more politely.

Lichtblau took out his credentials and transfer order and handed them over.

"Get out of the vehicle," the major ordered.

"Everything is in order," Lichtblau reassured him.

"We'll see about that. In the meantime, get out," the major said, collecting the papers of the other four occupants of the car, who were beginning to climb out of the truck. The last to get out was the private. His arm was in a sling and he struggled to get out of the back.

Lichtblau looked at his watch. It was almost seven o'clock. A setback like this was the last thing he needed. The ship

Himmler had commandeered to get them away would not wait forever. Not to mention that the Russians could surround Königsberg at any moment, or even conquer it. Behind them, the red-brick turrets of the castle of the prince-bishops of Varmia stood out against the blue sky. The first cannonades of the day could be heard echoing beyond those walls.

The major stepped away from the Kübelwagen with one of his men to examine the documents. They talked quietly but intensely, while the other three kept an eye on Lichtblau and his men.

"It's just a formality," Wasserman said, in an attempt to reassure himself, more than anyone else.

"That's all we need," Kiesel blurted out, lighting a cigarette nervously.

Lichtblau took out his cigarette case, too, but passed it around first, starting with the three men from the itinerant court.

"There won't be any problems," the man with the paddle said in a conciliatory tone as he took a Muratti out of the case.

Lichtblau was about to agree, but at that instant one of the bell towers in the city blew up.

The eight men stared at the cloud of dust hovering over the rooves of Allenstein.

They took deep drags on their cigarettes. No one spoke.

"There won't be any problems," the man with the paddle repeated.

"Well, not too many," the major interjected as he retraced his steps. He handed the credentials back to Lichtblau and Wasserman. "You can go."

Lichtblau stared at him blankly.

"You two can go," the major repeated.

"What about Kiesel and the others?"

"They are deserters. I'll take them."

"Deserters?" Kiesel yelled indignantly. "I was decorated with the Knight's Cross with Oak Fronds in Sevastopol!"

The major ignored him. He continued to address Lichtblau. "Your transfer order mentions only the scientific personnel, namely you and Dr. Wasserman."

Lichtblau couldn't believe his ears. "But they are my escort," he stammered.

"In the documentation you produced, there is no mention of any escort."

"It's obvious."

"We are at war, nothing is obvious." The major's gaze was glacial and immovable. Lichtblau was dumbstruck.

The rumbling of battle was getting closer but no one paid attention to it. The two sides stared at one another with open hostility. The men accompanying the major had clicked the safeties off their weapons. They hadn't gone as far as pointing them at Kiesel and the two others, but they were preparing for action.

"I'm off," Kiesel said resolutely and started to walk towards the Kübelwagen.

"Don't move, captain. You're under arrest," the major barked, drawing his pistol from its holster.

"You'll have to shoot me to stop me from leaving," Kiesel said, opening the door.

The major fired three shots in quick succession. Kiesel fell to the ground without uttering a sound.

"You two can go," the major repeated. Without saying a word, Lichtblau and Wasserman climbed into the truck, paying no heed to the others, who were begging them not to leave them to their fate.

The president of the court-martial began to recite the ritual formula. "In the name of the Führer, and by the authority vested in me by the commander-in-chief of Army Group Center, Field Marshal Schörner, I find you guilty of desertion and I therefore sentence you to death by firing squad."

Lichtblau tried to drive away as quickly as he could, but the echo of the gun burst reached him anyway.

The outer defenses had given way and the Russians had penetrated the city. The real battle was just beginning with exhausting house-to-house fighting. Mines had been placed at the beginning of the avenue leading to the castle, which is where the invaders suffered their first losses. Since the Germans had blown up the buildings at the corners of the cross streets and erected barricades with the rubble, the Russians had no choice but to proceed down the avenue in compact formation. At the head of the convoy were the riflemen, whose task was to flush out any anti-tank weapons. Behind them came the armored, self-propelled SU-122 vehicles. They were excellent tank hunters. At close range, their cannon could knock out a Tiger or Panther with a single shot. But like all self-propelled vehicles, with no machine guns or rotating turrets, they were ill-suited for fighting infantrymen, especially in urban environments. The Soviet command intended to use that unit of SU-122s against the few remaining armored forces that aerial reconnaissance had spotted around the castle. But first they had to get to the end of that corridor where the Krauts were doing all the shooting.

The Russians were halfway down the avenue. One of their teams of sappers had succeeded in locating and destroying a mortar hidden in a courtyard, which had been targeting the invaders since they had first set foot in the neighborhood. A machine gun nest had also been neutralized. But a second MG42 was still firing at them from the window of what had been the best cake store in Allenstein. It was being handled by a 60-year-old veteran of the Great War, a 15-year-old member of the Hitler Jugend, and a one-armed former Luftwaffe pilot. From the upper floors of the houses, other Volkssturm fighters were hindering the enemy advance with light weapons and hand grenades. In response, the 122mm muzzles of the Soviet self-propelled vehicles sprayed bullets blindly, flattening everything in their path.

A Navy infantryman leaped out from behind a tree trunk that

had fallen on the road. His ship had been sunk by British tor-
pedo bombers just outside the harbor of Kiel and the survivors
of the shipwreck had been absorbed into the militia. The only
sign that he had once been in the Kriegsmarine were his blue
pants, because the rest of his outfit consisted of a paratroopers' jacket and a sand-colored Afrikakorps helmet stuck over a
black woolen shawl fastened on his chest with a large safety pin
that covered his head and shoulders. Behind the sailor came a
French volunteer from the Waffen-SS Charlemagne division,
wearing his unit's camouflage with a Soviet busby on his head,
complete with a red star. He took up his position at the base
of a broken statue, dropped on one knee, aimed his machine
gun, and took out the two riflemen flanking the tanks at the
head of the enemy column. The sailor was clutching a magnetic
grenade. As soon as he saw the two Russians fall, he sprinted
over to the SU-122, attached the anti-tank device to one of the
wheels, tore the fuse at the top of the handle off, and ran away.
He threw himself into a hole a moment before the blast. One
side of the self-propelled vehicle fell open. The caterpillar belt
clattered out of control and the vehicle skidded wildly until
it came to a halt crosswise in the middle of the road. As the
crew tumbled out, the Frenchman took them out one by one.
After that, he zigzagged back through the ruins, followed by
the sailor. They vanished into a doorway. The company command was on the third floor.

When they entered the room, the Kampfkommandant, a retired officer recently recalled to duty who was wearing a pastern from the years of the Weimar Republic, was looking at the
results of the action out of the window.

"Good job," he said without taking his eyes off the binoculars aimed at the self-propelled vehicle enveloped in flames.
Another vehicle was trying to push it to one side with no success.

"It's time for the squad with Panzerfäuste to go into action,"
the commander said, turning to his order-bearer, a corporal
from a mountain infantry regiment that had been annihilated

the year before in the Carpathians. The corporal had barely taken a step towards the door, when the sailor stood in his way.

"Do you really want to send these kids to their deaths?" the sailor growled at the Kampfkommandant.

"Forgive him," the Frenchman intervened, "he is the victim of an acute form of decadent humanitarian sentimentality." He burst out laughing as he replaced the magazine of his machine gun.

The Kampfkommandant eyeballed the sailor. "You are a good fighter but I'm the one giving the orders here. Thanks to the two of you, for the moment we have managed to stop the Russians. We must use the situation to our advantage. And we will do that with what we have. If you have any objections, you can put them before a court-martial."

The sailor shrugged. Those mugs in the court-martials were scary enough, but they were nothing compared to the Russians. The terror of being taken prisoner by the Bolsheviks was what kept German soldiers fighting. Apart from giving civilians time to escape from the eastern provinces. It was noble, but there was a price to pay. The sailor stepped away from the door and reached for the cigarette the Frenchman had already lit for him.

A cannonade blew up the machine gun in the bakery window. At this point the company had no more heavy weapons.

"Move!" the commander shouted to the order-bearer. The corporal sprinted downstairs and out into the street, heading for the barricade at the end of the avenue where Ernst's squad was posted. The boys greeted the instructions with a mixture of excitement and dread.

A second SU-122 had joined the other and, between the two of them, they had almost succeeded in moving the wreckage. Paul crawled through the rubble along with his comrades. Bullets whistled over his head but all he could hear was the sound of his teeth chattering furiously.

"Smoke bombs!" Ernst ordered.

Hasso, Peter, and Uwe opened their haversacks, pulled out their grenades, and lobbed them. Within moments, the Soviet vehicles were plunged into a thick fog. The boys scattered on both sides of the road behind the vehicles. What was left of the company covered them from the roofs and balconies by firing whatever they had and even throwing tiles and bricks. The boys went to find shelter from where they could shoot. Paul slipped into an anti-tank ditch along with Peter. He raised the scope of the Panzerfaust and slung the weapon over his shoulder, as he had been taught at the course. His hands were shaking. Peter seemed just as nervous, which helped Paul steel his nerves. The diesel breath of the self-propelled vehicle grew closer and closer in the fog. Paul focused. His fingers were steady on the firing lever now. He was prepared. After what felt like a very long time, the self-propelled vehicle appeared to float out of a white sea. It was reversing slowly: a perfect target. When it was right in his crosshairs, Paul squeezed the lever.

The bullet hit the engine fair and square. The blast was terrifying. The vehicle immediately caught fire. Paul could hear Peter praising him, and the others around him shouting jubilantly. He was overjoyed. He would get the silver ribbon. And to celebrate their victory, surely Ernst would find girls that night. He had no idea what kind of girl he wanted. His craving was urgent but unsubstantiated. What he did know, however, was that he would not be afraid. He could do anything now. He was so happy that he didn't notice a bullet piercing his helmet and cracking his skull. He felt breath and soft lips. He felt breasts in the palm of his hand. Then darkness.

61

Cordillera de Amerrisque, northern Nicaragua,
July 22, 1982

Smoke still rose from the ruins of the village. Even the houses the invaders had spared were smoldering as the wind had fanned the flames, which ended up devouring almost everything. They found the teacher's body hanging from a tree in front of the school, with a sign around his neck saying, "Sandinista." Peter Jennings took off his black beret, ran a hand through his sweaty hair, and told his men to cut it down. He also told them to go and look for survivors. Judging by the number of corpses lying in the rubble, some of the inhabitants must have escaped the massacre.

He lit himself a cigar, one of the good ones Colonel Reyes from Cuban Intelligence had given him. He savored the taste of the tobacco on his palate. Huberman's group had been getting more and more aggressive. They were fiercer than any of the other units working with the Contras, who had never been particularly moderate. According to information that had been made available to Reyes, Huberman had a coca plantation. On the North American market, a kilo of *blanca* was worth sixty thousand dollars. Huberman didn't need the CIA to finance his campaigns. But in Honduras there was no tradition of growing coca. Jennings had spoken to a professor in the Faculty of Agriculture at the University of Managua, who explained that it was possible to grow a plant outside its region of origin. "They have vineyards in California, after all. To do it on a large scale, however, you need considerable expertise and a lot of money." Evidently Huberman had both. His refuge was presumably near the plantation. "In Bolivia and Peru," the professor had observed, "coca grows on the slopes of the Andes." The information had not narrowed down the search much, since eighty percent of Honduras was mountainous. In addition, the professor had a further consideration: that coca can be grown in greenhouses. In short, Huberman could be anywhere.

The cigar had gone out. Jennings roamed the streets of what was left of the village, thinking as he chewed *purito*. He had arrived in Nicaragua six months earlier, along with a score of other Soviet advisers. This was his first mission outside Managua. Until now, he had been training officers and soldiers from the People's Army. At first, the Russians had been wary of the Sandinista National Liberation Front. They considered them ideologically unorthodox. Moscow would have preferred the Communist Party of Nicaragua to lead the dances. But by the end of 1981, Fidel Castro on the one hand, and favorable reports from KGB headquarters in Managua on the other, had convinced the Supreme Soviet of the Sandinistas' revolutionary rigor. Help had started to trickle in. Jennings liked that assignment. Since he had gone over to the other side of the Wall, it was the best job he had been offered. He also liked the fact that he had been sent to the North to flush out that old bastard Huberman. Jennings was a fighter. Training soldiers in a garrison courtyard ultimately bored him. He was determined to catch the old bastard. Huberman's base could not be too far from the border, otherwise he wouldn't have been able to conduct raids so easily. But it was not easy to guess where. Huberman's men showed extraordinary resistance to fatigue. It was not just that they were natives, accustomed to the climate. The Sandinistas were the same. Huberman's band was able to march for a full day in the jungle, fight through the night, and set out again at dawn. Peter Jennings had never dealt with anyone like this, either when he had been an officer in the Special Air Service or later, when he had gone into the service of the Union of Soviet Socialist Republics. He had been pounding the area for weeks, hunting for ghosts, but had not yet managed to spot a single one. All he could see was the aftermath of their attacks.

"We found them," Nestor announced proudly.

Nestor was Major Jennings's orderly. He was seventeen years old, a farmer's son who had studied with the Jesuits, and an enthusiastic supporter of the revolution. He had admired Peter Jennings unconditionally from the first day he had met him. Nestor had only the vaguest idea of why the gringo was in Nicaragua. He did not know that he had gone to Eton. He did not even know what Eton was. Nor did he know that in Northern Ireland he had killed a man he had not wanted to kill, and that he had betrayed his country, partly for money and partly for amusement. All Nestor knew was that Jennings was a gringo who could have led the comfortable life that gringos always lead, but who had come to this place with them instead, to live off cold beans and risk getting killed. Peter Jennings had come from far away to help the revolution and, if necessary, Nestor would follow him to hell.

"They ran into the forest as soon as they saw us coming. They thought we were Contras," Nestor explained.

He pointed to a group of about thirty people. Men and women, old people and children. Tired, dirty, scared. That was the war Victor Huberman was waging: a war on civilians, a war against the most basic rules of humanity.

"Are we going to get him?" Nestor asked anxiously.

Jennings stared into the boy's eyes.

"We're going to get him," he promised.

Nestor smiled contentedly, clicked his lighter, and held the flame closer to allow his commander to relight his cigar.

62

Königsberg, January 30, 1945

From the lampposts along the riverfront hung stiff bodies, some in uniform, others in civilian clothes, an identical placard around their necks: "I am a deserter." The wind rocked the swinging bodies and the heels of their shoes clacked against the iron. Passersby pretended not to notice. Only children stopped to gawp. Lichtblau strode towards the harbormaster's office, ignoring the living as well as the dead. He had been going there every day for a week now, several times a day. When he and Wasserman had finally succeeded in reaching Königsberg, they had discovered that the destroyer sent by Himmler had been sunk by a Soviet submarine. Wasserman had not been discouraged. The doctor had his own evacuation plan. Before the war, he had worked at Stockholm University and had kept up with people there. His wife was already in Sweden. The plan was for her to rent a boat and pick him up on a beach on the Sambia Peninsula, near the port of Pillau, about fifty kilometers from Königsberg. For some time now, Lichtblau had sensed that his friend and colleague had been preparing an escape route. He could not blame him. He, too, had made own contingency plan. Despite the terrible cold as Wasserman prepared to leave, Lichtblau had accompanied him to the edge of town. The water of the Vistula lagoon was sufficiently frozen over to be able to walk across it. Every morning, thousands of refugees walked to Pillau, from where ships shuttled to the western Baltic. Most went on foot, but there were also sledges driven by French and Belgian prisoners who had been in Prussia since the beginning of the war. The journey was dangerous and some of them would turn back, especially women with small children. The ice packs were mobile, there were blizzards, and the fog meant you could lose your bearings. There was always the chance of an air attack, too. But anyone who wanted to leave, had to get to Pillau. Wasserman had hired a nearby villager to accompany him on a sled with a sail. He had given him his beautiful gold watch. Before parting ways, Hans and the doctor had embraced. "Next time, we'll be on the winning side, "Wasserman had whispered before jumping into the strange vehicle and disappearing in a flurry of snow. Obersturmbannführer Hans Lichtblau was on his own.

In front of the harbormaster's office, a man dressed completely in black, except for a greasy white collar sticking out of his coat, was standing on a fish crate. He was admonishing people entering and leaving the building with all the breath he had. "So, the angel swung his sickle in the earth, gathered the grapes from the earth, and threw them into the great winepress of God's wrath."

A clerk at the harbormaster's office opened a window and leaned out.

"Cut it out, you old fool. We're trying to work here!"

The preacher fell silent, staring grimly at the clerk, but as soon as the clerk closed the window, he resuméd at once.

"And the winepress was trodden outside the city, and the blood that flowed from it rose as high as the bridles of the horses!"

Lichtblau did not believe in the Bible, but he admired the beauty of Luther's translation, the greatness of that enterprise, when God's word had become German. Silent shadows, wrapped in cold and fear, flitted around him restlessly. God seemed to have abandoned Germany. Lichtblau grabbed the brass handle, pulled the door to, and entered the captain's office.

The office was quite large, but it had not been designed to accommodate that number of people. The staff could hardly move. A crowd of petitioners thronged in front of the office doors, animated with endless negotiations, interwoven with prayers, threats, and attempts at bribery.

On the ground floor were crammed the Party officials responsible for issuing passes. All able-bodied males were to remain in Königsberg. The problem was to determine who was an able-bodied male.

"He is nearsighted and has asthma," a mother wailed pointing at her son, who was following the conversation without saying a word from under a heavy woolen cap, the lenses of his glasses all fogged up.

The official shook his head.

"He is fifteen years old. Without a waiver signed by a military doctor, he's not going anywhere."

The first floor was occupied by Navy personnel. They were coordinating Operation Hannibal, Großadmiral Dönitz's plan to evacuate as many people as possible from areas that had been isolated by the enemy offensive. Even with a pass, getting a place on one of those boats was not easy. The Kriegsmarine had confiscated anything that could stay afloat. Warships, merchant ships, ocean liners, fishing boats. But there were tens of thousands of people to evacuate. Lichtblau had a pass. His transfer order had gotten him one right away. The problem was finding a ship. He crossed the lobby. In a small side room, a number of men in various SS and SA uniforms were gathered around the radio. The Führer's speech was due to be broadcast any minute. Lichtblau had no time for politics. Stubbornly fighting for a lost cause was childish. It was fine in Walter Scott's novels, but not in reality. He walked on, climbed the stairs, and reached the office of Lieutenant Commander Looss. After a week of daily chats, they had become quite intimate, owing in part to the fact that the Obersturmbannführer had gifted the naval officer his limited-edition Dupont fountain pen, along with a silver tie clip.

"Lieutenant Colonel Lichtblau," Looss greeted him cordially

when he saw him at the door. "I was just wondering why you hadn't come to see me yet this morning."

Lichtblau took his cap off and unbuttoned his fur-lined coat. The room was small and cozy. The wood fire burned briskly in the tiled stove. For a moment, the warmth made him forget the difficulties he was in. The map of the front hanging on the wall brought him straight back to the harshness of the world. Colored pins marked the positions of German and Soviet troops. A red line snaked inexorably from Warsaw to the Baltic coast, cutting Prussia off from the rest of the Reich.

"Today I wanted to put off the moment when you told me I was out of luck for a while longer." Lichtblau said philosophically.

Lieutenant Commander Looss flashed a broad smile. "And instead . . ."

Lichtblau held his breath.

" . . . I've found you a very comfortable first-class cabin on a ship sailing in two days."

The tension that had accumulated over that week of negotiations suddenly drained out of him and Lichtblau slumped down in the chair in front of the captain's desk.

"As a rule," Looss started explaining in an ironically formal tone, "first-class cabins are reserved for wounded officers and pregnant women, but in your case, we have managed to make an exception. You will have to share it with a traveling companion, but I am sure you will be able to adapt."

Looss opened a drawer, took out an envelope on which Lichtblau's first name, last name, and rank were written, and handed it to him.

The lieutenant colonel's fingers were trembling a little. For a moment, he was afraid to open the envelope, in case there was something wrong with it. But nothing was wrong. The travel documents were perfectly in order.

He left the harbormaster's office whistling. On the way back to the hotel, he was seized with anxiety that he had not checked the papers properly. He pulled off his gloves and examined the ticket. Again. The terse wind blowing from the lagoon ruffled the corners of the sheets. In order to read, Lichtblau had to hold them with both hands. Everything was in order, but he had failed to notice one detail in Looss's office. The name of the ship. In pure disbelief, he burst into a long, loud laugh, which drew suspicious looks from passersby. Lichtblau pulled himself together, put the envelope away, and set off with excitement. He was to sail on the *Bremen*, the very same liner that had brought him from America to Germany years earlier.

PART THREE
The New World

63

Warsaw, August 22, 1945

R ubble. Wherever Rivka Berkovits looked, all she could see was heaps and heaps of rubble, with no end in sight. Standing alone in the midst of those cement and stone dunes made out of what had once been buildings, factories, and churches, were bullet-pocked walls, accidentally-spared chimney-stacks, or the ruins of people's homes, their supporting structures still intact but with no roofs. In the area that had once been designated as the ghetto, the devastation had been total. Not even one empty, ripped-apart husk. Nothing but a uniform expanse of rubble out of which the oddest objects sprouted. Washtubs, gutted sofas, stoves, water pipes, and twisted iron beds that looked like the skeletons of prehistoric creatures.

Rivka noticed a large pot-hole caused by a grenade opening in the middle of the road and slowed down. After checking in the rearview mirror that no one was behind her, she swerved, and swung the jeep around the crater. She carried on down the avenue towards City Hall. The landscape didn't change. It was as if the god of war had taken a sledgehammer and pulverized the entire city. There was nonetheless life in that desert, as there is in any desert. There were people picking their way through the ruins. Rivka wondered how they could live like that, but quickly realized that the question made no sense. She had made too quick a leap from gardens to deserts. Only a week earlier she had been in Haifa, a city where everything was working, where there were streetlights, public transportation, restaurants, schools. The contrast made her head spin. The inhabitants of Warsaw, at least the ones who had survived, had had five years to get used to it, day by day, bomb after bomb. From the invasion in 1939 to the fighting in 1944, through the ghetto uprising of 1943, the city had been torn apart bit by bit. Before retreating, the Germans had bulldozed almost everything that was still standing, including the Royal Castle—to which the Baedeker guide devoted no less than three pages—the fourteenth-century cathedral and the national archives. Almost all of the housing in the Polish capital had either been destroyed or was uninhabitable.

Approaching an intersection, Rivka had to brake. A column of Red Army trucks was coming the other way. From the side of the road, amidst the swirls of dust, a clutch of raggedy little boys gestured to her for something to eat. She arched her shoulders and made an effort to ignore them, looking straight ahead. She had already given what was supposed to be her lunch to two other boys who had approached her when she had pulled over to look at the map. They looked no older than seven or eight but with these levels of malnutrition it was impossible to guess their age. Everywhere in Europe, from Naples to Kiev, crowds of orphans survived by begging, stealing, and selling their bodies. Not that life was any easier for adults. Throughout the war, millions of men and women had been plundered, raped, and enslaved by invading armies. And although officially the hostilities had ceased in May with the surrender of the Third Reich, there was still fighting in many countries, local conflicts kindled by the World War which continued to burn independently. In Greece, a civil war was raging between monarchists and communists. In the Baltic republics, nationalist partisans opposed the Soviets. An ethnic clash had erupted along the Polish-Ukrainian border and, as usual, the civilian population was paying the greatest price with mass killings and forced relocations. The entire continent had sunk into appalling poverty and brutality, and Rivka was unable to see how it could recover, despite reassuring words from leaders on the victorious side and the efforts of UNRRA, the UN agency charged with handling the refugee emergency. She rummaged in her bag on the passenger seat, pulled out a pack of Camels, and lit one. The survival of European civilization was not her concern. The Soviet column had driven past. Rivka shifted into gear and drove off.

As agreed, Nahum was waiting for her in front of the ruins of City Hall, where a large tent flying the UNRRA flag had been erected. The khaki uniform of the British 8th Army and the pipe clenched between his teeth gave him a distinctly British air, but the Star of David on his left shoulder indicated that he was a special officer of His Majesty's army. Major Nahum Goldstein had fought in the Italian campaign as part of the Jewish Brigade, currently quartered on the Austrian border. He had managed to procure a long leave of absence for non-existent health issues and was working full time for Berihah, the facility that took in and shipped survivors from the camps to Palestine. There were members of the Resistance who had fought the Nazis in the ghettos and forests of Eastern Europe. There were soldiers from the Jewish Brigade, like Nahum. And there were people who came from Eretz Yisrael, like Rivka, who were working on behalf of the central committee of the Socialist League of Palestine. Nahum was a moderate Labor Party cardholder and when he found out what her political affiliation was, he had made a spiteful comment about what he considered the political naiveté of the League and its allies in Hashomer Hatzair, the only Zionist organizations that had spoken out in favor of a two-state Arab-Jewish nation. The night before, Nahum and Rivka had argued for hours. In exasperation, Rivka had yelled that she almost preferred those fascists in the Irgun: at least they had the courage to say openly that they wanted to drive the Arabs out by force. Ben Gurion's Labor Party, on the other hand, simply avoided the issue of the Arabs, as if they did not exist. That had been the case since the earliest days of Zionism. "A land without a people for a people without a land," had been the founder's motto. But in the streets and squares of Haifa, Rivka could see that their land was inhabited by another people. She was certain the two-state solution would prevail in the end. It was the only feasible way forward and the only solution that would respond to the principle of justice, a principle that was very dear to the Jews. Building a state where Jews could live safely was essential, of course, but it was not sufficient. It was also necessary to build a state where nobody exploited others, whatever race or religion they belonged to. Rivka pulled up at the curb and threw her bag into the back seat. Nahum jumped in.

"How did the meeting go?" she asked as she set off again, zigzagging with difficulty through the haggard, anxious crowd that had suddenly begun to throng from all sides toward City Hall. Rivka cast a glance over her shoulder. They had opened the canteen A long line had already formed outside the tent. The red and white flag of the United Nations agency flashed for a moment in the rearview mirror, then the jeep turned.

"Better than expected," Nahum replied. "The UNRRA people are beginning to get the message that the Jewish refugees should not be divided according to their nationality but settled together."

"What about the Russians? "

"The Russians are almost as anti-Semitic as the Germans. They can't wait for the Jews to leave. They will do nothing to hinder us, and neither will the Poles."

Rivka did not answer, but Nahum's remark had somehow hurt her. It had undermined her admiration for the homeland of socialism. It was the glorious Red Army that had beaten the Nazis at Stalingrad, driven them back to Berlin, and liberated the concentration camps. Still, she knew that Nahum was right. In the *Great Soviet Encyclopedia*, which she had read compulsively in the library, the fact that Karl Marx was Jewish was never mentioned.

"And you?" Nahum asked.

Rivka shook her head.

"The usual," she said. "The Irgun keeps refusing to let

younger Jews leave first. According to them, we should be taking people in their eighties, too."

Nahum emptied his pipe out of the window and started packing it again. "They are fanatics. They lead to trouble, here and back home."

Rivka agreed. The previous year, Irgun had launched a terrorist campaign against British troops in Palestine. Of course, the British should leave, but attacking them while they were still at war with Germany was absolute nonsense. By doing so, Begin had become a *de facto* ally of Hitler. Rivka did not believe in the palingenetic virtues of violence, even revolutionary violence, but in Menachem Begin's case she was willing to make an exception. The day they shot him as an enemy of the people would be a good day for the inhabitants of Eretz Yisrael, whether they were Jewish or Arab.

64

Managua, Nicaragua, July 23, 1982

The beer was warm and did nothing to offer even an illusion of refreshment, but Shlomo gulped it down greedily anyway, only for it to come back out in the form of sweat. Trickles of salt glistened on the nape of his neck through the now-gray hairs covering his back and shoulders. It was late at night, but the air was still stifling. Bare-chested, Shlomo leaned over the rusty railing of the little balcony in his hotel room, waiting for the sporadic breeze that afforded him occasional relief. He emptied the bottle and went back in to get his cigarettes. Anton and Agent Yakovchenko were not sleeping, either. He heard bed springs creaking and muffled sighs through the wall. When they had arrived at the hotel, Natalya had insisted on three single rooms but evidently the cards had been played differently. Shlomo lit up an unfiltered Lucky Strike and went back outside. He was a little envious of his friend. He had never had a *shiksa*. To tell the truth, he had never been with any woman except Rivka, except for a couple of torrid, teenage affairs from before the war. It depressed him at times, but compared to the miserable train wreck that his life might have been without her, marital fidelity had been a small price to pay. He took a drag on the cigarette. On the facade of the building across the street, in the light of the feeble streetlamps, he could just make out an imposing mural with the wrinkled face of Augusto Sandino under that wide-brimmed hat of his that made him look more like a hero from the Far West than a guerrilla leader. Shlomo took one last drag and threw the butt over the railings. Rivka would have liked Nicaragua. She would have liked the girls with rifles on their shoulders patrolling the streets. She had been one of them many years before, in a country Rivka no longer recognized. When Begin had become prime minister in 1977, she had been so distraught that for weeks she had tried to convince Shlomo to emigrate to France or Italy, or at least go and live on a kibbutz. Being surrounded by people who had voted for that fascist revolted her. Shlomo, however, had been adamant. He would never consider returning to the continent where his entire family had been exterminated. And as for secluding himself in a commune to hoe the earth and pretend that capitalism was over, the solution did not appeal to him one bit. He had been born in the countryside and knew what country life was like. The egalitarian utopia would not make it any more pleasant. He might have considered moving to the United States. When he was a boy, he and his father had often talked about it. America felt like a more practical and manageable dream than socialism. But to Rivka, the Yanks were no better than Begin voters. And then there was Eli. He was an adult and would decide for himself. Leaving Israel was not an option for him. Rivka had surrendered to the will of the majority. Then Begin had decided to invade Lebanon and Eli had been called up.

Shlomo lit another cigarette. He wondered whether the time had come to consider moving away. Perhaps it would help Rivka. In Haifa, everywhere she turned, something reminded her of her son. There was nothing to keep them in Israel now. Sell the bar and go. Still, everything conspired to keep them there, especially Shlomo himself. He couldn't imagine living anywhere else, not even in America. It may have been an attractive and achievable dream, but it was not his. It had been his father Baruch's dream.

At dawn, the rain came to relieve him of the heat and wash away the thoughts that had been sifting through his mind during that sleepless night. Thick drops fell in the darkness. Shlomo leaned his head back and closed his eyes. He stood there in the rain for a few seconds. He ran a hand over his wet face as if to confirm that his body was finally cooling off. The storm was growing stronger. Shlomo stayed on the narrow balcony for a little longer and then went back into the room. He closed the shutters, leaving the French doors open, and threw himself on the bed. He fell asleep in the gentle breeze filtering through the shutters accompanied by the incessant drumming of the rain.

When he woke up, the sky was blue. He shaved, put on the last clean shirt he had, and went down to breakfast. Anton and the *shiksa* were already in the breakfast room. Shlomo greeted them with a nod and sat down with them. The waiter brought the usual platter of scrambled eggs, rice, and string beans. They had been in Nicaragua for three days and had basically eaten nothing else except for some chicken at dinner. Shlomo took a long sip of coffee. Now *that* was really good. On the other side of the table, Anton was grinning like a child. "To everything its time," Shlomo thought with a trace of disapproval. He may not have had an exuberant sex life, but at least he had never come across as an old man drooling over a woman twenty years his junior. He looked sideways at Natalya. She was not bad looking. Nice and curvy. He went back to studying his ecstatic-looking friend. "Nice and curvy but there is a time for everything," Shlomo decided. In addition to his amorous conquests, however, Anton Epstein, had another reason to be happy that morning and he shared the news promptly.

"We've received permission to leave," he said. "The guide is coming to pick us up in the morning. We are going to join an elite battalion of the Sandinista army." He paused, looked around circumspectly as if he were about to reveal some kind of military secret, and added in a whisper, "A Soviet military adviser is commanding it."

"There are no Soviet military advisers in Nicaragua," Natalya said pointedly. Her tone was not aggressive. It had sounded more like a mother correcting a child's mistake than an official denial from a functionary. "He is a comrade internationalist, a volunteer in the Nicaraguan people's revolution," Natalya explained.

"A mercenary, you mean," Shlomo quipped sardonically.

Agent Yakovchenko stiffened.

"Think what you will, but I warn you: your cynicism and irony will not find many admirers around here. You'd best keep your comments to yourself."

Shlomo said nothing and focused on his eggs. Natalya Yakovchenko may be an attractive woman, but she was still a KGB agent. She probably had a portrait of Lavrentiy Beria embroidered on her underwear. If he could get it up with a woman like her, Professor Epstein had been in the wrong line of work all along. All those years spent poring over books, when he could have made a dazzling career as a gigolo. Shlomo chuckled to himself.

"I've fulfilled my end of the bargain," said Agent Yakovchenko. "Now it's your turn."

Shlomo looked up from his plate.

"Don't worry," he told her. "As soon as we get to the operational area, I'll tell you where Huberman's hideout is. It's in an ancient Spanish fortress."

"No less," Natalya said, feigning surprise.

"Ancient fortresses have thick walls. Your Sandinista friends had better bring something appropriate with them," Shlomo replied sharply.

He went back to his breakfast. He chewed slowly, his gaze lost in the square teeming with life that he could see through the restaurant window. Soon he would be back in the fray of battle, one last time. Shlomo did not fear death. Since the Lager, he had never feared it. But he knew Rivka could not bear to lose him, too. That was reason enough to be afraid. Shlomo Libowitz wanted to live. But he also wanted revenge. He hoped that one did not exclude the other.

65

Klagenfurt, Austria, British Occupation Zone,
Aug. 28, 1945

They had herded them into the camp all together, Germans and Poles, Ukrainians and Baltics, men, women and children, all fugitives driven out by the Red Army, all lining up for the same soup. Martha Kernig was in line, too. She kept her eyes downcast, and with a nervous gesture, kept smoothing down the wrinkled skirt she had been wearing for weeks and muttering things to herself that nobody paid any attention to. Martha was talking to Elsie. She cautioned her against the dangers of sloppiness: "You must always take care of your appearance, even in a place like this. You can make a difference with very little effort." She shook her head and continued to iron her stained skirt with the palms of her hands. Her daughter, however, could not hear her lectures on home economics. Elsie had been kicked and punched to death. Every now and again, the chilling image of her naked little girl, the features of her face deformed by the blows she had received, would come to her mind and then Martha would fall silent, holding her breath. As soon as the image faded, her monologue resumed.

Paul had begged her several times, in person and by letter, to leave Neuhof. Her new husband, who would be officially declared missing in February, had also tried to convince her in the few days they had spent together during his marriage leave. Martha, however, had not listened to either of them. She refused to go without her son. By the time she heard that Paul had been killed in action, it was too late. The enemy was closing in and there was no escape. The Volkssturm unit deployed to defend the town had been wiped out on the spot. The Russians had driven into the village and taken everything they wanted. About twenty of them had shown up at Martha Kernig's house. They reeked of alcohol, sweat, and death. That little gingerbread house looked promising. Between the store and the apartment, there was all the booty one could possibly hope for. Food, alcohol, clothes, even some jewelry. And then there were Martha, Elsie and Hilde. They had shared them out after some noisy altercation and each group had shut themselves up in a room. The group that had won Martha had chosen the dining room. As the soldiers took turns raping her, she could hear Elsie and Hilde screaming. She had begged them to spare her daughter, at least, since she was just thirteen years old. But the soldiers did not understand German. And even if they had understood, it would not have made any difference. At some point, however, something must have happened. Martha had not seen anything, but she had tried to reconstruct the events in retrospect, after they had left her for dead. They had dragged Hilde into the store and stretched her out on the counter behind which she had served for years. She had always been shy and submissive, but in those last moments of her life, she must have summoned up all the anger she had never expressed. Perhaps while the two rapists were taking a pause, Hilde had managed to take a large pair of dressmaking scissors out of a drawer and kill one of the Russians. The corpse was still there with the blade stuck in his throat and his tongue hanging out. The animals had not even bothered to bury their comrade. They had avenged his death, though. They had killed Hilde and then they had turned their rage on Martha and Elsie. Martha had fainted. When she had come to in the middle of the night, covered in bruises and blood, her teeth knocked out, she had staggered through the house. The rooms were illuminated by the red glow of the fires that were devouring the surrounding buildings. She had found Hilde first and then Elsie. She had held her daughter's lifeless body until the following morning, when a neighbor had finally managed to convince her to join her and the other survivors in the exodus to the west. The Russians let them go. They were clearing Germans out of the whole region. Anyone who did not leave was killed.

The field-kitchen attendant was wearing a uniform that looked like the American one, with a scarlet UNRRA insignia on his sleeve. Since the war had first torn at her ankles like a rabid dog, this was the first military uniform that did not instill fear in her. The man gestured for her to hand him the mess tin. Martha obeyed and he filled it with three generous ladles of thick meat and potato soup with lumps of fat floating in it. Martha came out of the tent and crouched in a corner. She ate voraciously, not because she was hungry, but out of fear that someone might take the tasty, hot soup away from her. As she ate, she heard the confused beginnings of an argument. She did not look up until she had wiped the bottom of the bowl clean with a piece of bread she had kept aside at breakfast. At that point, she got up, put the mess-tin in the haversack she had slung over her shoulder, smoothed her skirt down a few times, and went to see what was going on.

Two British military police officers were yanking at a man who was wearing a patched-up Wehrmacht coat that was far too big for him. That man was trying to explain, mixing up English and German, that he had never been a Nazi. He had been a corporal in the army like everyone else. One day he had received his draft papers and had had to go to war. What else could he have done? The policemen were inflexible, pointing to the scar the suspect had on his cheek.

"It's a war wound. I got it on the eastern front," the man explained.

The policemen shook their heads. The Allies were beating the refugee camps in search of SS officers and National Socialist Party leaders. One way to recognize them were scars from dueling. For centuries, members of German university fraternities had loved to flaunt these badges of honor, which they procured while challenging one another to the *Mensur*, an academic duel in which the candidates essentially proved their courage by standing their ground and stoically enduring injury. Nazis, who had initially disbanded fraternities as possible sources of resistance to their rule, had eagerly embraced the fashion. Now they were regretting it.

"I told you it was shrapnel!"

The man was dragged away by force. Another man in the crowd, perhaps a Pole, cheered.

"Nazi pig!" another man shouted.

Martha nodded. Yes, the Nazis were pigs. They had opened the gates of hell and now they were trying to hide in full view among the victims of their folly.

"Nazi pig!" shouted Martha Kernig summoning all the breath she had.

66

San Ramón, Central Nicaragua, July 24, 1982

W ord had spread swiftly and now a long line of people had formed in front of the tavern. The old Dodge from the dictatorship days repainted in the colors of the Sandinista army had appeared in the late morning, immediately attracting gazes. Military vehicles were often seen passing through the area, owing to the war on the Contras up north on the Honduran border. Usually, however, these vehicles carried soldiers, whereas here, in addition to the sergeant driving, there were three foreigners in civilian clothes in the open-backed jeep, one of whom was a blonde woman with the palest complexion anyone in the village had ever seen, except at the movies for the lucky few who had been to the Salón Nacional in Matagalpa. The foreigners had stopped at the only inn in San Ramón, on the main square, in front of the church.

Before entering, Sergeant Corral had handed a coin to a young boy to keep an eye on the luggage. Not that the three had anything particularly valuable in their bags. The suitcases containing the clothes Anton and Natalya had bought in Western Europe were stowed safely at the hotel in Managua.

When they had finished eating, Anton had offered to take a look at a nasty boil the landlady's son was sporting, a boy of about ten who had stared at them gravely from behind the counter all the way through lunch. Without any drugs, Anton had not been able to do much, but he had managed to make a small incision with a makeshift scalpel to release the pus and stop the infection, and he had prescribed an aloe pack to disinfect the wound and help the healing. The landlady had thanked him profusely and refused their money. At that point, however, the situation had gotten out of hand. The village had no health service and many other villagers wanted that good, generous doctor to examine them. Shlomo and Natalya signaled that they should leave, but a big crowd had gathered outside the inn. There had been shouts. Someone had waved a stick in the air. Sergeant Corral had advised them to comply with their demands, at least for a while. Assisted by the landlady, who acted as his nurse and who seemed very proud of that role, Anton started seeing patients using a bench as an examination table.

Shlomo and Natalya chain-smoked at the back of the room. Shlomo had finished his Lucky Strikes and unceremoniously helped himself to Natalya's Gauloises, tearing off the filter before lighting up. He had already smoked a quarter of her packet, but Natalya did not seem to mind. There were more important preoccupations. They had stopped to stretch their legs and grab a bite, and had planned to set off again right away, but instead they had been stuck in that place for more than two hours.

Anton was treating a little girl accompanied by her grandmother. The old woman had repeatedly touched her granddaughter's throat to indicate to the doctor what the problem was. Anton gestured to the child to open her mouth and she obeyed with a serious expression. The landlady handed him a Soviet-made flashlight, powered by a dynamo activated by pressing a lever in the handle. Shlomo seemed to be the only one who found the object absurdly out of date. The creaking noise the contraption made was driving him crazy. He threw his cigarette butt and put it out with an angry stamp of his foot.

"Are you planning to keep playing Dr. Schweitzer for much longer?" he growled at Epstein, who had his back turned to him. Anton chuckled while continuing to examine his young patient's tonsils.

"Comrade Yakovchenko told you yesterday: your cynical humor is out of place in a socialist country."

"Well, I agree with Libowitz this time," Natalya said, putting her cigarette out on the dirt floor, too. "Let's leave. We've wasted too much time already."

"I've taken the Hippocratic oath," Epstein replied sardonically, still leaning over the child.

"And I've sworn to liquidate Lichtblau," Shlomo snapped. "If we go on like this, he'll die of old age before we get him."

Epstein ignored him and signaled that the little girl could shut her mouth.

"She should go to the hospital. She needs to have her tonsils out," he said in English to the grandmother, sounding out the words carefully. The old woman, however, did not seem to understand.

"That's right, she should go to hospital. You can't do anything for her in this condition," Shlomo interjected. And he grabbed Anton by the arm. The old woman let out a cry.

Shlomo looked around, searching for a solution.

"Pay her," he said to Natalya.

"What?"

"Give her some money, so she can afford to go to a city where there is a hospital."

Natalya did not know what to do. She hated the idea of taking orders from that old Zionist, but his proposal made sense.

"How much should I give her?" Natalya asked, unable to conceal her bewilderment.

Shlomo had no idea. He cast a glance at Sergeant Casimiro Corral, who was looking on in amusement from one of the tables.

"Will ten dollars be enough?" Libowitz asked him.

Corral nodded.

Shlomo pushed Anton toward the door. The old woman let out another shout, drawing the attention of the villagers outside the inn.

Natalya thrust a bill into her hand and the old woman fell silent.

The trio, followed by the sergeant, went outside. They were

immediately surrounded by the crowd, claiming their right to health care. They shouted, threatened, and pleaded. One man reached out and touched Anton, as if he could be cured by mere contact.

"More money!" Shlomo ordered.

Officer Yakovchenko opened her wallet and tossed bills here and there, trying to select only the smallest denominations. She threw what she had: American dollars, Western and Eastern marks, Italian lira, even a London subway ticket. The crowd began to disperse. Some were already competing for money with their neighbors. The four reached the jeep, jumped aboard, and the sergeant started the car.

The landlady waved from the tavern door. Anton, who was sitting in the back of the vehicle along with Shlomo, stood up to reciprocate. "Goodbye," he yelled in order to be heard above the din of the crowd.

"Stop it, you idiot," Natalya said from the front passenger seat.

"Are you jealous?" Anton asked with a cocky grin.

She did not answer and turned away.

The Dodge jerked abruptly forward and Anton fell back on the seat.

"Well, doctors always exert a strong attraction on nurses," Shlomo commented, feigning objectivity.

Anton and Shlomo burst out laughing, at first softly, then more and more loudly. The sergeant did not understand but he laughed with them. The two friends stared into each other's eyes, guessing one another's thoughts. They had never once laughed together.

67

Heilbronn, Germany, US zone of occupation,
October 2, 1945

The people at UNRRA preferred to use the expression "collection center" because they felt the word "camp" might sound sinister. But whatever they called it, it was as close to a home Shlomo had had since he had been deported from his village more than four years earlier. He had arrived there at the end of a long, mostly solitary journey through the ruins of the Third Reich. The first to leave had been Epstein. Shlomo and Zev had tried to convince him that going back to Prague was pointless, but at Poznań station he had jumped onto a southbound train. It was his choice. Then it had been Zev's turn. In Silesia they had bumped into a gang of Galician Jews from a *shtetl* not far from Zev's. They had survived by hiding in the woods, eating berries and roots. They were extremely thin, but alive. They, too, were on their way to the west. They wanted to go to America, where one of them had relatives, or England, or maybe even Australia. Their only certainty was that they were planning to get to a French port on the Atlantic. Shlomo and Zev walked with them for days, sharing food and makeshift lodgings. There was an unmarried woman in the group. Zev made his mind up quickly. Perhaps for him, who was older than Shlomo, and who had had a wife and children before the war, forming a family again was more important than where he was heading. But there was another factor. The fact that the three survivors of the Gardenia Kommando separated without further ado a few weeks after the liberation was not just because they had different plans. There had been an unspoken uneasiness among them since the Baron had shot the Nazi. It was the shame of being still alive, just the three of them, while all the others had met their death. Their fortune was a mystery, a painful issue they could neither avoid nor comprehend. Splitting up had been a way to dodge it. Shlomo had carried on walking along streets crowded with refugees, hunger, and despair. He slept wherever he found shelter, he stole food, when he got the chance, he carried out big or small acts of revenge. But little by little, the excitement he had felt in the early days had dissipated. And the mirage of Palestine had also faded. How was he going to get there? With what ship? With what passport? By the time he reached Heilbronn he was exhausted, and it was not only because he had walked all the way across Germany from east to west.

At the center, at least, he had received new clothes, regular meals, and a place to sleep, though it was only a tent he shared with three others. But despite these obvious improvements, he was living in limbo. The war was over, but peace had not yet begun. Peace was signed by states. Which state did Shlomo Libowitz belong to? Technically, he was a Polish citizen, but there was nothing there for him anymore. And the more time went by, the more gruesome the stories that came out about the new waves of violence Jews were suffering there. The situation was the same in Hungary. Jews who returned to the towns and villages where they had been born were insulted, beaten, or were unable to recover the property that had been taken from them during their imprisonment. It was a paradox but for now, Germany was safer than Poland or any other Eastern European nation for Jews.

Shlomo lit a cigarette butt he fished out of the ashtray under his bunk, inhaled with gusto, then got up and dressed. The sun was high in the sky and the others were already at work. One was a shoemaker in the camp's re-soling unit. The second was teaching mathematics in the refugee school. The third was a mechanic in a nearby workshop. Shlomo, on the other hand, had no occupation, despite all the sermons from the UNRRA. They were all good, solid American Protestants, well-meaning but boring. Shlomo went outside and immediately ran into a Ukrainian. They exchanged distrustful looks and went their separate ways. There were people from about fifteen different nationalities in the camp, from the Baltics to the Danube, and cohabitation was often challenging. Especially with the Ukrainians and Latvians who had shown such enthusiasm for collaborating with the Germans. Shlomo stopped to chat with a Romanian who was busy de-lousing a little girl. He cadged a cigarette off a UNRRA official, a Quaker who inflicted a grueling lecture on Jesus in exchange for tobacco. And he found himself loitering in front of the entrance to the collection center just as the most extraordinary creature Shlomo had ever seen in his life walked through the door.

He was a Jew, but he had the proud confidence of the warrior class. He was a Jew, but he was wearing a uniform. And on that uniform was a blue and white insignia, with a six-pointed star in the middle, the flag of the Jewish national hearth, something that had not been spoken of since the destruction of the Second Temple in 70 AD He was a Jew, but his Yiddish was nonexistent, his mother tongue Hebrew, a language that had slowly faded over the last two thousand years and was now coming back to life in Palestine. And it was there, in Eretz Yisrael, that the Jew in uniform wanted to lead the Jews without uniforms. Life would not be easy, the officer explained. This was not only because the British Empire wanted to keep the Arabs happy and did not want them to go. One could get to Palestine even without a visa, slipping through the controls of Her Majesty's Navy, which patrolled the Mediterranean and sent all the Jews it could get its hands on to Cyprus. Many had already reached Eretz Yisrael and many more would arrive in the coming months and years. But one had to be prepared, because life in Palestine was hard. It was a pioneer's life, a life based on spades and rifles. This was why the movement was setting up special camps. *Hakhsharot* was the word. In these camps, instructors from Eretz Yisrael would teach the future citizens of the Jewish state everything they needed to know, from the new language to how to hit a moving target with a rifle.

"We're setting one up right near here. Who's interested?" Nahum Goldstein asked the small crowd gathered around the jeep from the back seat where he was standing, exuding natural authority. As he spoke, a woman in her mid-twenties went through the crowd taking down names. She wasn't in uniform, but she had the same military bearing as her companion. Shlomo was struck by her serious gaze that was such a contrast to her sweet face.

"I'll come," Shlomo said quietly, looking down at the toes of his shoes.

68

Cordillera de Amerrisque, northern Nicaragua,
July 26, 1982

Finding the 5th *Batallón de lucha irregular* of the Sandinista People's Army turned out to be a tougher task than expected. The appointment they had made by radio when Agent Yakovchenko's group had set off from Managua had been missed because the battalion had had to move suddenly. They had hoped to intercept Huberman's gang, which had been reported in a valley not far away, but their hope had been in vain as always. The 5th had moved but had no way of informing them because the Dodge was not equipped with a two-way radio. "Soviet organization," Shlomo had chuckled softly, though he made sure it was loud enough for Natalya to hear him.

The 5th Battalion commander, however, had left his attendant at the agreed meeting place. Nestor had explained what had happened, they had made room for him in the car, and he had guided them along a narrow road full of hairpin bends and potholes that snaked up the mountain. At one point, however, the Dodge had been unable to go any further because a landslide had eaten a section of the road. Corral had turned back with the jeep, while the others had continued on foot. "Impeccable socialist planning," had been Shlomo's comment. This time, Officer Yakovchenko was unable to stop herself. She had slung insults at him and threatened to throw him into the ravine. Shlomo had let her insult him without reacting. He had no desire to argue and, anyway, maybe she meant it. She was KGB, after all. She may really have had the guts to send him flying off a cliff. If she had, Shlomo wouldn't have stood a chance, as the boy would doubtless have taken the side of the comrade from Moscow and Epstein would have been unlikely to side against his mistress. Shlomo chuckled to himself and wished he had a cigarette. The way things were, cadging a Gauloises from her wasn't an option.

They set off, packs on their backs, and any conversation or argument was extinguished by the rain that accompanied them mercilessly until dusk. Soaked and starving, they settled under a large tree and tried to get some sleep, but only Nestor succeeded. The other three spent the night on the brink of sleep, their senses continually aroused by the damp and the animals, whose cries echoed through the dark foliage throughout the night. As soon as there was enough light to move, they got up, still feeling exhausted, and set off in single file behind Nestor. No one said a word until they reached the 5th Battalion camp. It was still early. The men had only just risen. The orders of sergeants and corporals echoed in the air. Nestor led them through the bivouacs to the commander's tent.

The headquarters in Managua had said they would send reinforcements. When he saw them coming out of the jungle, Peter Jennings thought the Nicaraguan revolution must be in really terrible shape if by reinforcements they meant two old men and a big-assed woman.

Anton Epstein had expected someone completely different. His idea of a Soviet military adviser was an overweight, middle-aged colonel with eyes clouded by vodka. By contrast, a young man somewhere between thirty-five and forty years old was standing there. He was quite tall and his blond mustache gave his face a benevolently cheeky expression.

"Major Peter Jennings," Nestor said, pointing out his commander to the three foreigners. In the boy's serious tone, they sensed his pride in the position he held in the hierarchy of the 5th *Batallón de lucha irregular*, as well as the veneration the boy felt for his superior.

Jennings's chest, which was broad and hairless, was bare. He had an Anglo-Saxon complexion and was stubbornly pale despite the tropical sun. He was shaving in front of a mirror hanging from a branch. He was rinsing his razor in an enamel basin on a small camp table. He reminded Anton of a hero in a Conrad novel, a latter-day Lord Jim, who had come to that primitive forest to fight someone else's war as a challenge to himself and the world.

Behind Major Jennings stood his tent. And inside that tent was a woman. She was no older than twenty-five, with the aquiline nose of the Maya and long raven hair which she was tying into a ponytail with a quick and confident gesture, fastening with an elastic band, and draping carefully over her green uniform. The girl tied the red and black handkerchief with the acronym of the Sandinista Front for National Liberation around her neck and walked out of the tent. Shlomo thought she was beautiful, as beautiful as Rivka had been at her age. She sketched a smile at the newcomers and walked towards the camp kitchen. With the soft breeze, a penetrating aroma of coffee wafted into the clearing. This put Shlomo in a good mood, almost making him forget the exertions of the jungle march and the sleepless night.

Natalya followed the girl who had slipped out of the major's tent with her gaze. She wondered whether this evident show of lax behavior among the ranks of the 5th Battalion depended on the temperament of its commander, or the Sandinistas' lack of ideological rigor. It could be the product of both. Whatever its origin, these goings-on that looked like a cross between a student assembly and the Commune of Paris merited a report to the KGB headquarters in Managua. However, as far as relaxed customs were concerned, Natalya Yakovchenko was well aware that she was not exempt from criticism. Besides, she had not gone there to write reports. She decided to give Major Jennings a chance. Perhaps, behind that irritating facade of bohemian adventurer, there lurked a capable fighter.

Peter Jennings greeted them one by one with a nod as Nestor introduced them to him. They looked like a rather ill-assorted trio. They were not very impressive as individuals, either, especially the woman who stared at him from under her straw-yellow fringe. Why had they sent him these three?

Natalya saw the bafflement in the Englishman's eyes.
"We know where Huberman's hideout is," she said.
Peter Jennings's face broke into a wry, friendly smile.
"Welcome! Please, come and have breakfast with us."

69

Oberursel, Germany, American occupation zone,
January 23, 1946

The room had no windows and stank of smoke. The bare concrete walls contained two chairs, a table and an ashtray. An orderly had emptied out the butts, but there were thick gray whiskers on the blue glass. Colonel Siegel stretched his legs under the table, yawning loudly. He took his metal-rimmed glasses off and ran a hand over his face, as if that gesture might help chase away his fatigue. He had been locked in there for ten hours. Sometimes he felt his condition was not that different from the people he interrogated. He picked up the list. "One more and that's it!" he shouted loud enough for guard on the other side of the thick metal door could hear him.

The soldier put his head through the door.

"Who do you want, Colonel?" he asked.

Siegel scanned the names of those left for him to interrogate.

"Lichtblau. Bring me Herr Obersturmbannführer Hans Lichtblau," he replied with a second yawn. "And a cup of coffee, too."

The coffee arrived immediately. No sugar, a teaspoonful of cream. By now, they knew how he liked it in the kitchen. On the tray there was also a ham sandwich. "Great idea," the colonel said to himself, and polished it off in a couple of bites. Personal initiative was a point of pride in Uncle Sam's armed forces. In the Third Reich, no orderly would ever produce an unsolicited sandwich. The colonel thanked his lucky stars for ending up in the right army, the one that had won the war and had tons of ham sandwiches. He took a sip of coffee. If his father had not emigrated from Frankfurt at the end of the previous century, Robert Siegel would have found himself on the wrong side of the table. Or buried in a mass grave in the steppe. The Krauts had really screwed up this time. Still, he felt some sense of belonging with the Germans and he admired their rigor and culture. The reason he had been assigned to the Joint Intelligence Objectives Agency, and quickly become one of its most valued bloodhounds, was precisely because he knew them well and spoke their language.

He took another sip from his cup, after which he fished Lichtblau's file from the large leather bag hanging from a leg of the table. A group of Italian partisans had stopped him in Bolzano on May 12, 1945. The report said he had a Swiss passport with him, but it had not been included in the dossier. In any case, it had turned out to be false. That was why they had arrested him. They were GAP partisans. Siegel imagined they knew a lot about forged documents after two years of relentless clandestine fighting in the city. He had met a few of them in the winter of 1944, when he had found himself operating behind German lines between Padua and Vicenza. They were smart. A little too far to the left for his taste, but their skills in unconventional warfare were undeniable. The partisans had handed Lichtblau over to the British military police, who imprisoned him in Austria, along with a bunch of other Nazi suspects. The clues were all there: the forged passport, the scar on his eyebrow, the insignia torn off his jacket and coat, the air of belonging to a superior race. The British, however, had considered him a garden-variety SS officer. They had not realized that he was a distinguished member of the Ahnenerbe. In December, Siegel had visited the prison. He and his colleagues were scouring detention centers set up by the Allies on the soil of the defunct Third Reich. It had not been difficult to identify Lichtblau. He had been born and raised in the US. The agency had several photographs, albeit somewhat dated. Siegel had recognized him thanks to a page in his school yearbook. Almost twenty years had gone by, but Hans Lichtblau had not changed much since he had been a student at Lincoln Park High School in Chicago. Nazism had kept him young. Siegel had immediately requested that he be transferred to Oberursel. The British had made a fuss, but had eventually given in.

During the war, Luftwaffe personnel interrogated captured enemy pilots in Oberursel. The Americans had commandeered the building and were turning it into their main intelligence gathering center in Europe. That was where Siegel and his colleagues started screening for candidates. The operation had begun even before the end of the war. As Anglo-American forces penetrated the Reich, one of their tasks was to locate and dismantle Nazi research facilities and then ship everything to the United States. The first significant discovery had occurred on April 13, 1945 in Thuringia, when a battalion of the 1st Infantry Division came across an aircraft laboratory just outside a nondescript town. There was reaction apparatus, V-2 rocket fuel, and a state-of-the-art wind tunnel. Not to mention the lab director, Dr. Adolf Busemann, one of the world's leading experts in the field of aerodynamics. The hunt had begun. The first Luftwaffe scientists headhunted by American agents had been locked in a hotel in the spa town of Bad Kissingen. To keep them on their side, they had plied them with food, alcohol, and cigarettes.

Siegel was not thrilled that Uncle Sam was taking all those Nazis on board. However, as the Nazis would say, orders are orders. Besides, if they didn't enlist them, there was the chance that the Russians would. They could not leave the crème de la crème of German military research in the hands of Stalin. The Reds were not the Joint Intelligence Objectives Agency's only competitors, however. Siegel and his colleagues were combing the length and breadth of Central Europe, seeking out Hitler's scientists. At the same time, there were other American intelligence officers on a similar hunt for war criminals. Often these were the one and the same thing and the outcome could be quite unpredictable. With the same resumé, a man could end up on death row or in a fancy Manhattan apartment. There were one hundred and sixty Nazi scientists in the United States to date and more were to on their way.

The door opened and the guard let Lichtblau in.

Siegel signaled for him to sit down and the prisoner took a seat.

"Cigarette? "

This was the usual opening gambit.

The German took a Camel out of the packet on the table. Siegel rolled the wheel-lighter of the Zippo and lit Lichtblau's cigarette.

"Did you know that it is copied from an Austrian lighter?" Lichtblau asked, nodding at the Zippo.

Siegel knew. Lichtblau was the third Nazi scientist to explain to him that whoever designed the Zippo was inspired by a model from the IMCO company in Vienna. The Krauts always wanted to prove that they were ahead of the game. If they were so far ahead, how come they had lost the war?

Siegel downed a bit more coffee.

"Would you like some too?" he asked.

Lichtblau declined.

Colonel Siegel was surprised by how cagey his interlocutor was being. Usually, these people couldn't wait to show off their wares. Sometimes they would surrender spontaneously and nobody even needed to go and look for them. Take Wernher von Braun, for example: a true prima donna. He hadn't even bothered to feign remorse. He had introduced himself and his partner Dornberger and told them they wanted their baby to end up in the right hands. In the underground industrial complex in Nordhausen where the V-2s were being built, von Braun's team employed slave laborers from the Mittelbau-Dora Lager. Working conditions were appalling. Thousands had died down there. Von Braun lived a few kilometers from the complex in a mansion confiscated years earlier from a wealthy Jewish family. Siegel had wanted to arrest the bastard and hang him without ceremony. But he had been the most brilliant mind in the German missile program.

"Okay," the colonel said, hoping to close the file in a hurry and go to sleep. "What do you have to sell me?"

Lichtblau told him a long, detailed, and at times scary story. Siegel had a degree in engineering and his specialty was interviewing designers in the aircraft industry. He was not convinced. Lichtblau's story might have seemed unintelligible to him for the simple reason that he did not know much about plant chemistry. Or else, the Kraut was deliberately leaving things out. After months screening Nazi scientists for credibility and intentions, Siegel realized they were pathological liars. They lied as easily as they breathed. They lied to others and to themselves. Von Brauna swore he never knew that his workers were dying from hunger and overwork in the Nordhausen tunnels. Lichtblau may not have been lying, but he had almost certainly left out some important details. He may want to keep some things to himself in order to sell them later, perhaps to another buyer. Perhaps. Overall, though, the Obersturmbannführer looked like a pretty solid candidate for the program. Siegel reread the two pages of notes he had taken while Lichtblau was giving his account.

"I have to talk to my superiors," the colonel finally said, "but I think it can be done."

Lichtblau looked pleased.

"What's the time frame?" he asked.

Siegel shrugged.

"It depends. In any case, they could put you to work right away in one of the labs we are setting up here in Europe while you wait for your visa to be issued."

"Visa?" Lichtblau asked, simultaneously astonished and contemptuous. "I am an American citizen."

Siegel looked him straight in the eye.

"You *were* an American citizen. You returned your passport to the Berlin consulate on September 12, 1938, a week before you joined the SS," Siegel retorted, reading from the file open on the table.

Lichtblau did not respond. He held the colonel's gaze with utter indifference, as if what he had said did not concern him.

"And you did the right thing," Siegel added. "If you had not renounced your citizenship, the FBI would now be required to prosecute you for treason."

Lichtblau took another cigarette from the pack without asking.

"Where are you from, colonel?" he asked in German. Up to that point, the conversation had been mostly in English. But if the US government was so keen to stress that he was German, then the man should make an effort to speak to him in his own language.

"I'm from Chicago."

Lichtblau's face took on an expression of philosophical detachment from the set-backs and vagaries of life.

"I've gotten this far only to get caught by a North-Side kraut like me?"

"Actually, I grew up on Taylor Street. My mother was Italian," Siegel answered.

"Ah, the Rome-Berlin Axis."

Any other time, out of courtesy if nothing else, Robert Siegel would have at least pretended to smile at that idiotic joke. But he was tired and his expression was flat. He put the Lichtblau dossier back in his bag and the packet of Camels in his jacket pocket, along with the Zippo.

"We'll see you in a couple of days," he said. Then he got up and left for the hotel.

70

Cordillera de Amerrisque, northern Nicaragua,
July 26, 1982

B efore leaving Managua, the headquarters of the Sandinista Popular Army had given them each a backpack
containing a faded Cuban-made camouflage, a waterproof poncho, a cap, and a pair of combat boots. They had
traveled this far in civilian clothes, but once they reached the
battalion they had changed. Anton had refused to begin with,
but once it had been pointed out to him that his white shirt
would be a perfect target for Huberman's men, he had capitulated. Shlomo felt quite comfortable in the outfit, while Anton
looked miserable. He wandered unhappily around the camp.
He felt more like a prisoner on yard time than a soldier. Natalya
Yakovchenko, on the other hand, was born to wear a uniform.
The more Libowitz looked at her, the more he thought it suited
her. But perhaps, he told himself, it was just a typical Israeli
obsession with women in uniform.

In front of Jennings's tent, the commander of the 5th *Batallón
de lucha irregular* and his officers were in council. They sat in
a circle on the ground, with a big military map of the area in
the middle, along with the material that Shlomo had handed
over to Jennings. The centerpiece was, of course, the map with
Huberman's location marked on it, but there was also a photograph of the fortress. The image was not very sharp and it
only depicted a corner of the structure, a rampart partially covered with vegetation, but it was enough to suggest that the walls
were thick.

Shlomo leaned against the trunk of the tree under which he
was sitting. For once, he was not the one who had to make a
plan and take decisions. He took a sip of the rum that Nestor

had brought him at the end of lunch. Jennings must have told him to take care of the guests. And the boy had obeyed to the letter. The meal had consisted of the usual dish of beans, in true army slop style. The rum was good, though. Shlomo took the cigar that one of the men had given him, a recruit he had helped fill the machine gun ribbons, one tracer for every nine bullets. He peeled off the bottom of the *purito* with a bite, lit it up, and began to smoke with gusto. He was not at all unhappy to be fighting with the Sandinistas.

There were five company commanders. Carla was the only woman. She led the 1st Company and was the deputy commander of the battalion. She had been since before Peter Jennings came along. She had joined the movement when she was fifteen and had been engaged in guerrilla warfare since, except for a six-month stint in a Somozista prison. Carla still bore the marks of that experience on her back, but of all the active members of the 5th, Jennings was the only one who knew.

"The walls are at least three meters thick," Oscar from the 3rd Company was saying. "Our mortars won't even make a dent in them. We're asking for air support. Two assault helicopters would pave the way for us."

Carla shook her head. "Too much confusion," she said. "We shouldn't even be in Honduras. If we bring helicopters with us, can you imagine what kind of hornet's nest we'll be stirring up? Managua will never give us permission."

"But it's Managua asking us to accompany these three when they pick Huberman up, isn't it?" Oscar argued.

"Precisely," Carla replied. "Comrade Yakovchenko is here for Huberman's lab and we don't know what part of the fortress it's in. If we start firing random rockets, we risk blowing everything up and leaving her with a fistful of flies."

Carla's point was unassailable. Jennings and the other officers were silent. The Englishman was chewing on the unlit cigar. The synthetic drug business the KGB agent had told him about was a bit bizarre but it certainly explained a lot. Anyway, apart from the lab issue, there was no way they would get any helicopters. Carla was right. Managua could not afford to tread too heavily on Honduran territory. They didn't want to escalate the conflict. And, anyway, there was no need. The Contras posed no real threat. They had no credibility with the population, there were very few of them, and what's more, they were divided into warring factions.

"We could use this airstrip here," Lucio, the commander of the 4th Company suggested, pointing at a spot on the map Libowitz had given them. "We could bring some cannons with a transport helicopter."

Jennings looked at him, dumbfounded. Lucio was both an experienced fighter and a serious comrade, committed to the cause, but he could be a bit dense.

"Excuse me," he said, trying to be kind. "If we said they won't allow us to use combat helicopters, why should we be allowed to use transport helicopters? "

Lucio looked down, embarrassed. The other officers chortled. Carla made no allowances.

"And how would you get the cannons up to the fortress?" she asked Lucio. "According to the map, it's at least ten kilometers from the airfield."

Lucio buried himself under the visor of his cap.

"This is how we'll do it," Jennings said.

Everyone's eyes fell on him.

"If Libowitz's information is correct, Huberman has no more than a hundred men. We will overwhelm them with numbers. We will attack at dusk. We will create a diversionary action with mortars here." He pointed his finger to the north side of the fortress. "Meanwhile, a team will blow the gate open." His finger moved to the south side. "The team will be led by Lucio, who, among all of us, has more experience with explosives."

Lucio nodded, full of gratitude.

"Any questions?" the Englishman asked.

There were no questions.

"The battalion will move at dawn," Jennings announced before closing the meeting.

Shlomo had been following the summit from under the tree. He was not close enough to hear them. And even if he had been, he would not have understood much. The Spanish he had learned during a couple of operations in Argentina and Paraguay was rather elementary. It was fine for exchanging small talk with Nestor, but not for keeping up with an extended conversation. Even without understanding the words, however, the hierarchies within the command group of the 5th *Batallón de lucha irregular* were fairly easy to read. Jennings was clearly a charismatic leader whose opinion was rarely questioned. The Englishman did not look as if he were getting too full of himself, though. He maintained a certain detachment from his role and the aura that surrounded him. Agent Yakovchenko was right. Peter Jennings was not a mercenary. He was a cross between an adventurer and a professional revolutionary. Shlomo was reminded of some of the volunteers he had met in 1948, during the War of Independence. People had come to fight in Palestine from all over the world. American marines, French and Italian partisans, RAF pilots. They had come because they believed in the cause of Israel though some of them were not even Jewish. But perhaps they had also come because fighting had become a habit for them. After years spent on the battlefields, they could not imagine any other way of life. They combined a detached, professional demeanor with the mischievous twinkle in the eye of a gambler. Just like Major Jennings.

71

Heilbronn, Germany, US occupation zone,
August 7, 1946

They had snuck out in the dark and walked the city's deserted streets. They had been lucky. No one had seen them creep into the UNRRA camp. Luckily for them, the day had been very hot. The Ukrainian had been in front of his tent smoking and enjoying the coolness of the night. He had noticed them coming but had not been alarmed. Why should he have been? Three lads like them.

As soon as they got close enough, the taller one pulled out a revolver.

"Follow us, or I'll kill you like a dog," he said.

The Ukrainian obeyed without saying a word.

Shlomo and his two companions had studied the plan in every detail. They would take him to the glove factory near the bridge over the Neckar. It had been burned down during a bombing raid. No one ever went there. They would execute him and bury him in the ruins. They had dug a grave in the inner courtyard. All they needed was the body.

But in every plan, there is a flaw. The Ukrainian was as big and fast as a boxer. When they had made it into the ruins of the factory, he had spun around sharply and punched Shlomo in the face, knocking him to the ground. He still had his gun but the Ukrainian had jumped him and was pinning him down with one knee. He was so heavy that Shlomo could hardly breathe. The attacker was holding his wrists down. His grip was extremely strong. Shlomo tried to resist, but he could feel his fingers wrapped around the butt of the revolver start to loosen their hold.

Mordechai leaped onto the man's back, trying to wrest him away from Shlomo. The Ukrainian swiped at him with his right hand and the boy, who weighed a mere forty kilos, went flying, ending up on the ground near a smoke-blackened beam a couple of meters away. Yossi was so scared that he did not even try to intervene. Without taking his eyes off Shlomo and the struggling Ukrainian, he backpedaled to the wall and flattened himself against it, as if he hoped the bricks would open up and engulf him.

After freeing himself of Mordechai, the Ukrainian went back to punching Shlomo in the face. Once, twice, three times. Shlomo let go of the revolver. The Ukrainian reached out to pick it up.

"Freeze!"

The Ukrainian turned around.

Rivka Berkovits was pointing a 9mm silenced revolver at him.

The man made a snap decision that the little schoolmarm was not a threat. He had killed a lot of Jews. They yelled, they wept, but they never had the guts to fight. His hand crept towards the revolver lying in the dust.

A puff came out of Rivka's Beretta. The Ukrainian screamed and pulled back his hand. He brought it to his chest and examined it. The bullet had grazed the back. Nothing serious. Much worse had happened to him in the war. He nevertheless tried to dab the wound with his other hand.

"Don't move," Rivka repeated.

The man nodded and stayed on one knee.

Shlomo and Mordechai had gotten up. Shlomo was badly beaten up. One eyebrow was split and his nose was turning purple. Rivka took a wide circle around the Ukrainian man, picked up the revolver, and tucked it into her pants behind her back.

"How did you find us?" Shlomo asked.

"Talia told me everything."

"She's an idiot," Mordechai said.

Rivka gave him a dirty look.

"You three are the idiots. What did you think you were doing?"

"Obtaining justice!" Shlomo said.

"Justice!" Mordechai repeated. "This swine was one of the guards at the Majdanek camp. Yossi recognized him."

Rivka shifted her eyes to the smallest of the three, who had not moved from his corner.

"Are you sure?" she asked him.

"Yes," Yossi replied in a hushed voice. "Last week we went to watch a game at the UNRRA soccer field. He was there in the crowd. I was in Majdanek six months. I'm sure."

Rivka's gaze returned to the Ukrainian.

"Were you with the Hiwis? "

The man did not answer.

"Were you with the Hiwis? "Rivka asked again, stretching out her arm and pointing the gun straight at his forehead.

"Yes, but that was before. There was a war on," the man justified himself in his crude German.

"Let's kill him!" Mordechai yelled.

He went up to Rivka and tried to take the revolver out of her belt.

She slapped him with the back of her hand. Mordechai was about to fight back, but it was enough for Rivka to raise her hand to stop him.

The Ukrainian roared with laughter.

Rivka stared at him. The moonlight filtering through the half-ruined roof flickered. Rivka could not see the man's features clearly, but the stench of sweat was getting stronger. Despite his bluster, the former Majdanek concentration camp guard was afraid.

"Now Mommy's going to ground you little Jews," the Ukrainian said, bursting out laughing again.

A blind, archaic fury took hold of Rivka. She peered into the darkness seeking out the Ukrainian's eyes. Part of her hoped to find them. She knew that if she looked into his eyes, she would not have the courage to shoot. The other part of her was glad the clouds had veiled the moon. The Ukrainian's hoarse voice echoed in the darkness. Rivka did not give him time to finish his sentence.

The three boys stared at her in silence.

"If you make one more mistake, I will throw you out of *hakh-shara* and you can walk to Palestine," Rivka said. "You are not rebels. You are militant Zionists and you must follow directives. If you spot a Nazi, come and tell me or Nahum. Is that clear?"

"Quite clear," Shlomo replied.

"Come on, let's bury him," Rivka ordered.

They threw the body into the pit they had dug the previous day and covered it with bricks and tiles they found in the rubble.

When they were done, Shlomo went back into the room where the Ukrainian had been executed. Rivka followed him. She watched him poking through the dust by the light of a match.

"What are you doing?" she asked.

The boy held his open hand out to her. Illuminated by the weak moonlight, the shell of a 9mm bullet shone in his palm. Shlomo handed the piece of brass to her as if it were a precious jewel.

"In case the US military police come to investigate," he explained.

Rivka took a step toward him. She studied him with her eyes, which were always so serious. For a moment, Shlomo thought she was about to kiss him and he felt weak at the knees. "Does it hurt?" Rivka asked, pointing at his swollen nose.

"Not much," Shlomo lied.

"Anyway, go to the infirmary in the morning and get it checked out."

Shlomo said he would. He liked the fact that she was concerned for him. But he didn't like her big-sister tone. She was only a year older than him.

"Revenge serves no purpose," Rivka said. "Revenge means wanting to restore some kind of moral order. In Europe there is nothing to restore. The best way to take revenge on Europe is to abandon it forever."

"What about that man, then?" Shlomo said, nodding towards the grave in the middle of the courtyard.

The woman shrugged. She could not explain it even to herself.

"I was not in the camps. I saw what the Germans did, though." She paused, searching for words. "We can no longer afford to be weak."

She walked toward the exit. Shlomo followed her with his two companions behind him.

"You shoot well," he said, admiringly.

Rivka did not answer.

The moon had disappeared again.

"The sooner we get out of this immense cemetery, the better," Rivka said in the thick darkness shrouding the ruins.

72

Cordillera de Amerrisque, northern Nicaragua,
July 26, 1982

The afternoon went by preparing for the expedition. The 5th *Batallón de lucha irregular* would set off at dawn the following day as its commander had ordered. The men and women of the battalion cleaned their weapons and filled their haversacks and cartridge belts with ammunition and hand grenades. Lucio and his men checked that the plastic explosives were stored properly. They checked the saddles and harnesses of the donkeys that would be carrying the mortars. Jennings told them to bring two extras, in case Anton and Shlomo were unable to keep up with them. The Israeli looked tough, but he had his doubts about the Czech. He also made sure the three of them were provided with weapons. Nestor and a sergeant from the 2nd Company took care of that. Anton refused point blank. He had never fired a shot in his life. The sergeant told him it was for his own safety, but Anton had refused anyway and in the end they realized there was no point in insisting. Natalya took a semiautomatic Makarov and an AK-47 assault rifle. When it was Shlomo's turn, the sergeant only offered him a semiautomatic. Shlomo told him he wanted a Kalashnikov, too. The sergeant was young and did not mean to sound disrespectful, but it was clear what he thought. Shlomo did not make a fuss. He didn't want an argument, but he had to prove to the sergeant that he was not an old jerk who would shoot himself in the foot as soon as the attack began. Shlomo pulled his rain poncho out of his backpack and laid it on the ground. Then he approached the sergeant and reached out for the AK-47 he had slung over his shoulder. The sergeant let him take it. He was curious to see how it turned out. Shlomo picked up the assault rifle, removed the magazine, checked that the chamber was empty, crouched on the poncho, and began to disassemble the weapon. It was just like a Galil, except for the wooden stock. He had no problems with it. He lined up all the pieces tidily on the waterproof cloth. As soon as he had finished, he reassembled the rifle, calmly and precisely. The whole operation took him less than four minutes. He stood up and handed the AK-47 to the sergeant. The small crowd that had gathered to watch the performance erupted in applause. Nestor shook Shlomo's hand warmly.

"Give Mr. Libowitz an assault rifle," Jennings ordered. According to Yakovchenko, he was some kind of fanatical Mossad killer. No wonder he knew how to disassemble a Kalashnikov. Jennings liked him instinctively, though. Besides, he had learned a long time ago not to take KGB information too seriously. Their analysts had been sure that the tussle in Afghanistan would be over in a few weeks. The Red Army had been mired in that war for more than two years and there was still no real prospect of victory

Night fell suddenly and he found Anton and Shlomo sitting next to a small, nearly-extinguished fire over which Nestor had been making coffee. Peter Jennings emerged from the shadows and sat down next to them.

"May I?" he asked politely.

"Please," Anton replied.

Jennings and Epstein appeared to have nothing in common. But deep down, without their realizing it, they shared their bourgeois origins. A common set of values, norms, and rules they had grown up with, which had been swept away by the turbulent age they were living in. Yet, after all the fighting and abnegation, in the heart of a tropical jungle, the two men were staging a ritual from that other world they had both left behind.

May I?

Please.

"I brought whiskey," Jennings said, producing a bottle with curves like a double-bass and a label that said "Jura." Neither Anton nor Shlomo said a word. Jennings had also brought three glasses.

"It's my last bottle," he said as he opened it. "I was saving it for a special occasion." He poured the whiskey and passed the glasses around.

Shlomo was certainly no expert on Scotch whiskey, but it was delicious. He downed it in one gulp and asked for more.

"I'm glad you like it," Jennings said as he poured him a more generous measure than the first.

Anton found it good, too, but he preferred to savor it. Besides, he didn't want to overdo it. Natalya had invited him to come to her tent later that evening.

Nestor came by and asked if they needed anything. Jennings asked for some water. "Whiskey is more enjoyable if you alternate it with a sip of water," the Englishman explained.

"Is this what it's like in the whole Sandinista army?" Shlomo asked feigning ingenuousness.

Jennings shook his head. "That's really our only perk," he replied, pointing to the Jura bottle.

"Aside from the guerrilla lady warming your bunk," Shlomo thought, but kept the bad thought to himself. Not least because Carla had certainly not been offered to him by the Party. Instead, he asked, "How did you end up fighting in the Sandinista People's Army?"

The major looked vague, as if to say that it was a long and complicated story.

"Let's just say that I have a passion for lost causes," he replied, bursting into a laugh.

"Well," Shlomo quipped, "it looks like you're winning here."

"Yes, we are," Jennings said, turning serious again. "We are winning. But it's not easy." With a broad gesture of his hand, he gestured at the 5th Battalion, sleeping by the fires, or chatting. "These people have been exploited for generations. The

Sandinistas liberated them from the dictatorship of the Somoza family. They have given them hope. But they are peasants, not soldiers. When they first joined up, most of them could barely hold a rifle. Now they are an efficient fighting unit. That's already something."

Anton couldn't stop himself from commenting. "Helping the peasants of Nicaragua to defend their revolution is fine. But you are helping them on Brezhnev's behalf."

He immediately regretted his rude comment, but it was too late by then.

Jennings sketched a smile, signifying that he wasn't offended. But he didn't answer. He took a sip of whiskey and lit a cigar. He did not like Brezhnev much either, although he was careful not to say so. Of course, he realized that it was harder for Epstein to evaluate the situation with any kind of detachment. He was Czechoslovakian.

Mosquitoes buzzed hungrily in the dark. Jennings blew smoke into the air in an attempt he knew full well was illusory to keep them away.

"Sometimes," he said eventually, "to be on the right side, you have to have the courage to fight with the wrong people."

Shlomo found this concept very profound and helped himself to another ration of whiskey.

73

Upper New York Bay, September 22, 1946

L eaning on the parapet of the first-class deck, the man who had once called himself Hans Lichtblau watched as the Statue of Liberty emerged from the morning haze and gradually became real. Farther away, he glimpsed the dark mass of Ellis Island, where generations of Europeans had already arrived before him, seeking a new life in a new world. In his case, it was more accurate to say that he was *returning* to seek a new life, thus disproving the line that there are no second acts in American lives.

Two tugboats ready to help the liner dock were chugging straight towards them. They let out a blast with their sirens in greeting. The transatlantic steamer responded with a long whistle. "Prepare to disembark, prepare to disembark," an attendant on board announced.

The passengers who had come out to admire the giant statue illuminating the world with its torch and, further on, the island of Manhattan with its multitude of skyscrapers, began to throng towards their cabins. But Victor Huberman—as his new identification papers called him—preferred to remain outside. Better to enjoy the view a little longer than to squeeze through the corridors waiting for permission to disembark. The skyscrapers were getting closer. The swarming cars and buses were just coming into view on the streets. Huberman could already feel the relentless rhythm of the big city pulsating around him. The acrid stench of the subway. The clanking of the elevated railway. The heat that on summer days rises from the asphalt and clings to you, taking your breath away. Cities that rise up into to the sky and expand further and further, devouring new acres of land every year. Cities so different from those in Germany, which are immobile, locked inside their medieval walls, burdened with centuries of culture. And yet, Berlin had not been so different from Chicago or New York. Certainly, Weimer-era Berlin hadn't been but, in the end, neither had Adolf Hitler's Berlin. Since the turn of the century, Germany had been the most American country in Europe. Hadn't Berlin been nicknamed Chicago on the Spree? The standardized organization of labor and mass production, as well as the strategies of the Madison Avenue advertising agencies, had been a point of reference for the National Socialist Party. They may never have said so explicitly, but they had been. The Volkswagen, a car that every citizen of the Third Reich could afford, had been inspired by Ford's Model T. The romanticism of steel that Goebbels spoke of was a welding of Henry Ford's technology with Richard Wagner's poetry. The new Siegfried now drove a tank. But it was a troublesome alchemy, an unstable fusion. During the war, the soulless mechanization of the Americans had ended up prevailing over the national-socialist experiment. After all, what else had the war been but a family feud? The Germans of America against the Germans of Europe. Who had led the American armies? Germans, such as Admiral Nimitz and General Eisenhower. The sons of immigrants had won. They had been stronger and richer. It was only fair. It was the law of nature. But the battle was ongoing. New uniforms, new flags, new buzzwords, but the same battle. A no-holds-barred war against the same old enemies. Jews, communists, Negroes, perverts: anyone who might contaminate the purity of Aryan blood. The battle was raging everywhere in America, in the countryside of the South as much as in the metropolises of the North. Victor Huberman was reporting for duty, ready to take his place on the front lines.

"We are about to disembark," the attendant announced again. This time, Huberman accepted the invitation and made his way towards the stairs. The ship was entering the harbor.

He went to his cabin to get his suitcase. Through the porthole, he glimpsed the gigantic suspension bridge over the East River with the silvery latticework of its stays. The man who had once called himself Hans Lichtblau smiled.

He had come home.

74

Department of Olancho, southern Honduras,
July 30, 1982

Three days march through the jungle. Anton had made the journey almost entirely on donkey-back, but it had nevertheless been exhausting clinging to the saddle with its endless, monotonous, rocking, tormented by insects and humidity. Now that they had arrived at their destination, he wondered how he had managed it. They had been lying under the trees for several precious hours, resting up for the attack. The six companies that made up the 5th *Batallón de lucha irregular* had spread out around the fortress in a ring. None of them had encountered any watchmen. Evidently Huberman thought he was safe. The Sandinistas did not usually pursue the Contras into Honduran territory, in fact. The rare times they had trespassed there, it was only for a few kilometers. And Huberman's hideout was pretty far inland.

The 3rd Company had set up mortars in a clearing and deployed observers to log the blasts. Lucio had prepared the Semtex with his sappers. Everything was ready. They just had to wait for sundown. They lay there in silence, savoring the momentary pleasure of stillness.

Sitting at the Mexican-tiled counter in the large kitchen in the northeast bastion, Melissa Blumenthal was mixing a Martini. All her life she had scrupulously adhered to a very simple principle: no alcohol before sundown. That day, according to official data from the weather service in Tegucigalpa, the sun was due to set over southern Honduras at 6:18 P.M. At 6:15 P.M., Melissa started prepping. She sliced the lemon peel, being careful not to cut too deeply in order to separate the peel from the pith. In Paris, a waiter at the Ritz bar had once told her that Martinis should be served with an olive before a meal and with a twist of lemon after, to aid digestion. She liked it better with lemon, however, not only because of the fragrance of the essential oils, but also because she found the twist more elegant. From an aesthetic point of view, the thin wisp was objectively superior to a little green ball watered down in the bottom of the glass. Not to mention that olives occupied a certain volume in the glass and reduced the gin. Melissa was willing to accept an olive only when, on the whim of the moment, she followed the unorthodox school of Harry's Bar and served Martinis in a tumbler. The olive suited the cylindrical shape. There was a contrast between the verticality of the container and the circularity of the contents, which she found pleasing to the eye. She did not feel in the mood for eccentricity that afternoon, however, and intended to use the traditional martini cocktail glasses.

Melissa looked happily at the two yellow spirals she had fashioned from a fragrant Amalfi lemon. In the greenhouse, Victor was growing a tree especially for their aperitifs. Melissa left the rinds on the counter, next to the vermouth bottle, and got up to fetch the rest. Ice, gin, mixer and, of course, the glasses. She heard a noise that at first, she was unable to identify but that intuitively alarmed her. A dull thud, immediately followed by others.

As established by the plan of attack, at 6:20 P.M. Lieutenant Alvaro Camino, battery commander, gave the order to open fire. The four 120mm mortars began to target the northern sector of the fortress. The first salvo fell short, on a patch of trees a few hundred meters from the wall. Over the radio, observers on the edge of the forest signaled to extend their range.

Melissa decided to leave her Martini for a moment and went to the window to see what was going on. She didn't see a thing.

She did not even have time to look out. A maelstrom of fire and stones blasted her.

At 6:25 P.M., on the south side of the fort, a team from the 4th Company, led by Lieutenant Lucio Fuentes, crawled up to the gate and began applying plastic explosive charges to it. From beyond the walls came the echoes of mortar fire, along with the frantic shouts from the garrison. Judging from the yells, there was panic inside. The other members of the Company were hiding in the bush, weapons leveled, ready to cover Lucio and his team. When an Indian peered over the walls, Corporal Alfonsina Cardenal, the best sniper in the battalion, shot him in the forehead.

The laboratory had been set up in the fortress dungeon. From underground, Huberman did not notice the attack until a mortar shell hit the main generator, plunging him into darkness.

When he came out into the courtyard, there was chaos. Screams. Rubble and shrapnel flying everywhere, mowing down whatever crossed its path. Men running for cover. Others firing blindly into the jungle where the shelling appeared to be coming from. The beginnings of a fire in a warehouse.

Carlos was running toward him.

"La señora!" he shouted. "La señora has been hit! In the kitchen!" The bodyguard kept saying the same thing but Huberman didn't seem to understand. The world he had built with years of sweat and toil was about to implode around him. With trembling fingers, Huberman popped a tablet into his mouth. His mouth was so dry he could hardly swallow it. Within seconds, the tremor had vanished and his mind had come back into focus. The señora had been hit. Melissa was fifteen years younger than him and Victor had always assumed he would die first. The fact that she could disappear from his life like that, without warning, was inconceivable. But at that moment, there were many things that were hard to conceive. A whistle went through the air. Huberman threw himself to the ground and covered his head with his hands. The grenade exploded in the center of the courtyard, causing no apparent damage.

"Sons of bitches," Huberman muttered between his teeth, as he got up.

"Is it the Colombians?" Carlos asked.

Another shell pierced the darkening sky. Huberman strained to listen. Mortars. The negligible effects they produced were a clear indication. The Colombians were not so cheap that they would walk for days through the jungle with mortars on their backs. They were more likely to arrive in grand style, aboard assault helicopters. Only those shitty little Sandinistas would come all this way with fucking mortars. They wouldn't even leave a scratch on the walls.

"It's the Reds," Huberman said. "I'm going to go see Melissa. You, find someone to start the secondary generator and then go get Guillermo."

"Right away," Carlos replied, and disappeared in a cloud of dust raised by an explosion.

Huberman ran to the northeast bastion. He took the steps two at a time. When he reached the kitchen, which Melissa had furnished personally in her impeccable taste, ordering everything from the best stores in Mexico City and Los Angeles, Victor saw her lying on the floor under a crack in the wall, where there had previously been a window. Dr. Wasserman was bending over her.

The cook came up to him. She was in tears.

"She opened the window," she sobbed in despair.

Huberman ignored her and carried on.

Wasserman made a clumsy attempt to stop him from seeing her, but he was aware that he had no right to do so. He tried without much conviction. Huberman knew this.

In place of Melissa's beautiful face there was a bloody pulp, a revolting mass of flesh, with what may have been an eye here, a jaw there, a lock of burnt hair in the middle. They had been together for eighteen years. They had traveled, they had made love, they had experimented with every kind of narcotic substance—natural or synthetic—and above all, they had talked. The thing he would miss most about her, he already knew, was her conversation. Melissa was never dull. Victor did not necessarily agree with her, but what Melissa had to say always interested him. Huberman wanted to kiss her one last time, but there was nothing left to kiss. He bowed his forehead to her chest. A grenade crashed into the side of the bastion. It did not even rattle the wall. Those two-penny mortars could just about kill a woman at the window, a woman who had had more class and intelligence in her toenail than all the Sandinistas in the world put together. But no matter how cheap the Sandinistas were, they could not really be so idiotic as to think they could knock down twenty-foot-thick stone walls with mortars. That was when Huberman realized, but by then it was too late.

Crouching behind a rock, a few hundred meters from the stronghold, Lucio set off the charges.

The gateway shattered in a deafening roar.

Jennings sprang to his feet. Nestor was beside him.

"Attack!" the major yelled and launched himself into the breach.

The 5th *Batallón de lucha irregular* followed him without hesitation.

75

Eastern Mediterranean, October 12, 1947

The legionnaires from Fort Saint-Nicolas had loaded the ship at the prefect's request because the Maghrebi dockworkers in Marseilles had refused to work for the Zionists. One morning, two French army trucks had arrived at the dock. Men with thick necks wearing white *képi* had climbed out and immediately set about loading crates into the hold. It was rumored that former Nazis had been enrolled in their ranks, but there were no incidents to speak of. If anything, the soldiers were rather kind. There was a disabled girl who was unable to use the footbridge and one of the legionnaires had lifted her as delicately as if she had been a crystal chandelier, hoisted her onto his back, and without any apparent effort carried her aboard amid applause. At the end of the day, the old Italian merchant ship renamed *Hannah Szenes* in honor of the young fighter shot by Hungarian fascists in 1944, was ready to set sail.

There had been a heated debate on what to call the ship. Some had wanted a biblical name but the idea had not met with much enthusiasm. Berihah leaders were almost all atheist socialists. They preferred to celebrate the heroes and heroines of the 20th century rather than the rulers of the ancient kingdom of Judea. Hannah Szenes had been a brave woman who had shaken off centuries of diaspora shame, a model of the new kind of Jew that Zionism was forging. Those in the Irgun had been even bolder. They had named a ship *Ben Hecht*, after the Hollywood screenwriter who had paid for it. Not that the California aura had protected it from misfortune. The *Ben Hecht* had been intercepted by the Royal Navy and all its passengers interned in Cyprus. The Third Reich had been reduced to rubble, but there were still governments that wanted to lock Jews in camps surrounded by barbed wire. The wind was changing, however. The British Mandate in Palestine was coming to an end and, every day, more and more Jews were landing in Eretz Yisrael.

Shlomo had tried to imagine what life was like for a Hollywood writer, but he had failed. He liked the idea that, as well as the hatred, there were so many in the world willing to help his people, even among the *goyim*, even among the British *goyim*. In addition to refugees from all over Europe, two volunteers were also traveling on the Hannah Szenes. One was Canadian, a Jew from Montréal of Russian origin, who had been a fighter pilot during the war and whose skills were particularly valuable to the fledgling armed forces of the nascent Jewish state. The other volunteer, who had taken part in the Normandy landings, was from Liverpool. He was not Jewish, but he had participated in the liberation of the Bergen-Belsen concentration camp. Both were going to Palestine to risk their lives of their own volition.

The cargo stowed in the *Hannah Sze*nes was as varied in origin as the passengers. Some of the weapons were new, purchased in France. There were residues from the Wehrmacht purchased in Czechoslovakia. And there were pistols and rifles shipped from the Jewish Mafia in New York. The longshoremen there had had no objections. On the contrary. They were Irish, and they had been delighted to contribute to dismantling the British empire. Other weapons had taken even more circuitous and bizarre routes, passing through Nicaragua, where the Somoza family took a percentage on any goods that transited there.

The ship's captain was a Finn. He had said he was sympathetic to the Zionist cause but had nonetheless extorted a high fee. So far, it looked like Berihah had made a good investment, as the Finn had managed to avoid the British ships and was close to their destination. However, the last leg of the journey was the most dangerous. Which is why they had doubled the number of watchmen.

When Shlomo got off the quarterdeck at the end of his watch, he handed the binoculars to Yossi, who had come to relieve him, and warned him to be on his guard.

"Don't fall asleep like you did yesterday."

The boy flushed with shame and shook his head.

Shlomo went off to look for Rivka. Their evening assignation was still far off, but every minute he spent with her was precious. He had begun courting her in Heilbronn. A city girl like her didn't even recognize the clumsy peasant's attempts at courtship. It was the first time he had felt any desire for a woman since he had left the Lager, and the desire had been growing. At first, the girl had protected herself by erecting an insurmountable wall. Rivka was older than him and she was a leading light in the *hakhshara* hierarchy. Who did he think he was? At the same time, however, Rivka Berkovits was a *sabra* and she admired stubbornness. She had watched the Polish laborer bang his head against the wall for weeks and at a certain point she had given in. Shlomo had strong hands. She liked it when they touched her.

The ship was so crowded that getting around was not easy. Men, women, and children thronged the decks, concentrating on the most diverse activities of daily life. After all those precarious, itinerant years, no one seemed particularly uncomfortable in the midst of all that promiscuity. Or maybe the reason no one complained about the conditions of the journey had nothing to do with the past. Maybe it was the opposite. It had to do with the future. The *Hannah Szenes* was taking them to a place where fear, poverty, and exile would end and where they would finally be a nation. Shlomo dodged two old men sitting on coiled ropes playing backgammon in the middle of the deck, scolded a group of kids who were playing chase and bumping into everything and everyone, and skirted the crowd listening to Mr. Shapiro's daily account of the Kielce pogrom. Shlomo had heard it three times and every time the man had added more and more imaginative details. And yet, as much as the narrator was good at inventing and embellishing, the core of the tale was absolutely authentic. Authentic and unbelievable.

July 4, 1946. The war had been over for over a year. Most of the exterminations had taken place in Poland. Of the three million Jews living in the country in 1939, only 400,000 had survived. Evidently, for many Poles there were still too many. That day the *pogromchik* killed 42 Jews. Mr. Shapiro had been lucky. He had only had a few stones thrown at him. The accusations were as old as the pogroms. Rumors that Jews had kidnapped Catholic children to spill their blood in one of their evil secret ceremonies had spread around town.

Shlomo's eyes met Mr. Shapiro's. The badly-shaven cheeks and deep wrinkles on his face made him look older than he was. He spoke quietly and his audience milled around him to listen.

"Regina Fisz's son was barely three weeks old. He was mercilessly slaughtered along with his mother."

From the small crowd around Shapiro came the subdued moans of wounded animals.

Rivka had been right. The best way to get revenge on Europe was to abandon it forever.

Shlomo slid down the ladder that led into the ship's belly. The metal handrail was sticky and smelled of salt, like almost everything else on the *Hannah Szenes*. He found Rivka in the engine room.

The crew members had been recruited by the captain, who had offered them the usual conditions. But this was by no means a typical trip. When the sailors had found out how much their captain was being paid, they had immediately demanded a raise. Rivka had been put in charge of conducting the negotiations. Being a socialist put her in a difficult position. The crew was well within their rights to ask. But as a Berihah director, she could not afford to be soft.

"I'll say it again," the huge Greek stoker acting as a union delegate, was saying. "We are not willing to go below ten percent." Apart from sandals and a handkerchief knotted around his forehead, he was wearing only a pair of shorts. His chest and arms were covered in tattoos: a sailboat, an anchor, a pair of big-breasted sea nymphs, and several girls' or perhaps ships' names.

Hands stuffed into her trouser pockets, Rivka squared the half-naked giant, not at all intimidated.

"No way, comrade. We can go up to a maximum of eight percent."

"Nine," the Greek answered.

Rivka took a few seconds to think.

"Okay, nine percent, but only if we reach Palestine. If they capture us, you'll have to settle for eight."

The giant held out his hand.

Just as they were sealing the deal, they heard the high whistle of the ship's siren.

"Ship in sight! Ship in sight!" the second officer shouted over the tannoy.

The commander took over instantly.

"Sailors to their stations. All engines ahead!"

The stoker descended to his realm of soot, heat, and yells.

As Rivka hurried up the ladder, she collided with Shlomo descending. They climbed back on deck together. Crewmembers were running to and fro. Passengers were leaning over the bulwarks, scanning the sea in every direction. Everybody seemed to spot a British patrol vessel. To the southwest, there was indeed a silhouette of a ship, its funnels leaving a thin dark streak in its wake. The *Hannah Szenes* increased her speed, but the other vessel was keeping up. Gradually, the outline became clearer. Anyone without a specific task was leaning out watching the approaching ship. No one dared speak.

Suddenly, Yossi yelled in jubilation.

"It's a Turkish merchant ship!"

All eyes on deck shifted to the quarterdeck, where the puny

boy with binoculars around his neck was waving triumphantly, more from pride at being the messenger than relief at their narrow escape.

The ship was shaken by chorus of exultation. Shlomo and Rivka hugged. When they let go, she saw that Shlomo's eyes were moist.

Why are you crying?" she asked as she stroked his face.

"Maybe we'll make it," Shlomo murmured."

"Aren't you happy?" Rivka asked in astonishment.

Shlomo didn't answer. She peered into those somber, watchful eyes.

"Is it because of your father?" Rivka ventured.

Shlomo's eyes lit up like a child's when a magician pulls a stream of colorful handkerchiefs from his breast pocket. She could read his mind. Nothing like this had ever happened to Shlomo. It was exciting, but frightening, too.

"Maybe he would have wanted to come with us," Shlomo said, staring at the toes of his shoes and speaking so quietly she could hardly hear him. "It's not America, but he might have liked it anyway."

Rivka pulled him close.

"But he *is* here. All the six million who were murdered in Europe are here with us."

Shlomo shook his head.

"I let him die."

"What could you have done?"

"I could have died with him."

Rivka took his face in her hands and looked at him.

"Dying doesn't help anyone."

At dusk, they ate on the deck. A little Hasidic Jew of seven or eight years old stared curiously and enviously at their can of corned beef. Rivka realized the child would never have an experience as simple as eating corned beef. Unless, by scandalizing his own family, he decided to ignore the Law. She looked

at the boy and hoped that in the course of his life he would find
the strength and intelligence to rebel against archaic traditions
that no longer had any reason to exist in the modern world.

At nightfall, the two lovers found refuge in a lifeboat, taking
great care not to be noticed. In that wooden shell, under the
tarpaulin that covered the boat and protected them from the
cold of the sea and the gaze of the world, their bodies sought
each other out. Shlomo had never felt more alive than when he
was alone with Rivka.

The romanticism was interrupted for a moment as he slipped
on a condom. Even though he was becoming more adept at
handling them, Shlomo hated the things. He had never used
them before. In the village, he had heard about them from an
older friend who had done his military service in Warsaw. But
he had described them as a way to protect yourself against disease. Rivka, on the other hand, saw them as a way to avoid
pregnancy. And she was unwilling to compromise. It was that
or nothing. It was good even with a condom. In the middle of
the night, Shlomo threw the used condom out of the lifeboat as
a gesture of victory. The box he had bought in Marseilles was
finished. He hoped he would find more in Palestine.

At dawn, Rivka and Shlomo exchanged one last long kiss
and clambered out of the lifeboat.

At the bow, the outline of a low, sandy coastline stood out
sharply under a cloudless sky.

"We're back," someone behind them said.

Shlomo turned around. It was Mr. Shapiro.

"Yes, we are back," a Hungarian Jew echoed.

Shlomo was aware that the phrase didn't make sense, but
he somehow felt that the land that was opening up before him
belonged to him and that he belonged to it.

We are back.

76

A t 6:32 P.M., when he heard the Semtex charges explode, Lieutenant Alvaro Camino ordered a ceasefire. "Let's move," he said.

According to Major Jennings's plan, once the others had broken into the stronghold, Camino's team was to stop targeting the walls, abandon the mortars in the clearing, and go join the rest of the battalion.

Camino turned around to pick up the AK-47 he had left on the ground and saw one of his men lying face down on the ground with an arrow lodged in the base of his neck.

"What the . . . ? "

The question hung in the air. The lieutenant felt a stab of pain in his chest. He looked down and realized that he, too, had been pierced by an arrow. It had penetrated deep into his flesh. It was long and light, and the feathers at the bottom of the shaft swayed in the wind. In disbelief, he looked up to find a bare-chested Indian warrior, covered in necklaces and war paint, who struck him on the head with a club. The lieutenant crashed to the ground.

The warrior pulled out a dagger and quickly and accurately slashed his jugular. A tremor ran through Camino's legs and a last gasp escaped from his mouth.

In the clearing, more warriors were finishing off the other mortar servants with hatchets and knives. The men in the unit were overwhelmed within seconds, in absolute silence. The Indians were carrying rifles and machine guns on their shoulders, but they had not fired a single shot.

Once they had eliminated all the enemies, the warriors

sprinted towards the fortress. They ran through the trees over-taking one another. It might have looked like a game, except for the blood glinting on the blades hanging from their belts.

At the edge of the bush, they ran into the three observers who had been directing the mortar fire. Without pausing, or giving them time to grasp what was happening, they surprised them like a swarm of wasps, knocking them down with clubs and axes in a whirlwind spray of blood.

Jennings and his men launched themselves into the gap opened by the explosives. They found themselves a dense cloud of dust, firing at whatever shadows stood before them. There was no defender fire. One Sandinista ended up skewered on the pointed stakes at the bottom of a trap door next to the entrance but, apart from him, the 5th Battalion only suffered a couple of injuries. They quickly took control of the southern part of the fortress.

"It went smoothly," Jennings said.

"Too smoothly," Carla replied.

The Englishman agreed. Like her, he was wary of operations that were too easy.

Anton, Shlomo, and Natalya had been placed in the second wave, along with the 4th Company.

"Let's go," Shlomo shouted to his old friend. "We're missing the best part!"

Anton slowly emerged from behind the tree where he had been hiding since the beginning of the attack. Leaving the safety of that trunk terrified him.

"Remember our agreement," Natalya growled at Shlomo. They had agreed that Lichtblau should be kept alive until he had answered all the questions that she deemed necessary.

"Fear not, Comrade Yakovchenko, I have a good memory."

Shlomo turned back to Anton.

"Come on! Can't you hear that they've almost stopped firing?"

Anton followed Shlomo, Natalya, and the 4th Company soldiers as if he were in a dream.

Carlos had slipped into the tunnel that linked the fortress dungeons to the village. But he had not even reached halfway, when he ran into Guillermo Rocas, followed by a hundred of his men. As soon as the first shots had echoed in the valley, the village had raised the alarm. The shaman had distributed the pills and given the ritual blessing, after which the warriors had left. Most of them had entered the tunnel leading to the fortress, while a detachment of a dozen or so men had proceeded to the surface, running into the mortar battery.

By the time Rocas's group reached the fortress, the Sandinistas had almost taken the entire fortress under their control. Only one small unit in the northeast bastion was resisting under the leadership of Dr. Wasserman, and another in the warehouses, commanded by Lichtblau. The warriors leaped out of the tunnel like fire ants and the fighting flared up again furiously.

"Now it all adds up," said Jennings to himself, who had installed his command in a small tower above the gate. He replaced the magazine of the machine gun and shot a volley.

Anton, Shlomo, and Natalya had barricaded themselves in the workshop, along with portion of 6th Company. When they had gone in, it sounded like the fighting was coming to an end, but it had suddenly revived. Hiding behind a truck under repair, Shlomo calmly took aim and fired his AK-47. Officer Yakovchenko struggled to imitate him but could not conceal her agitation. Anton was not ashamed to show that he was petrified. Nevertheless, at one point he looked up over the parapet and saw him.

They had almost run out of ammunition in the warehouses and there were only four of them left, two wounded.

If Guillermo Rocas had not arrived with reinforcements, they would have been forced to surrender within minutes. Rocas's arrival changed everything. Huberman, followed by the other three, came out into the open to go and join the reinforcements. He ran into the middle of the courtyard. He could not get the image of Melissa's face smashed to a pulp out of his mind. He stopped short and leveled his assault rifle, looking for a target.

Anton saw him, despite the storm that was enveloping everything and dulling his senses. Everything should have conspired against seeing that detail. The terror that gripped him in a vice. The deafening noises. The shadows cast by the setting sun. Yet, he saw those eyes. The body was completely different. He remembered him when he was fit and young, while now it was an old man he was looking at. And the clothes were different. No longer a black uniform with silver insignia but an odd outfit that Anton could only describe as hippy. But those eyes of ice were unmistakably his. He would have recognized them anywhere.

"There!" Anton shouted, pointing to something in the middle of the courtyard.

Shlomo saw it too and instinctively raised his rifle. Natalya grabbed the barrel and pushed it down.

Huberman reached Rocas's group. By now his men had all come out of the tunnel and were scattering around the yard and on the walls, forcing the Sandinistas, who at that point were outnumbered, onto the defensive.

Entering the fortress, the tail of 6th Company had been halted by enemy fire. They had thrown themselves to the ground and were engaging the enemy from there. When the clutch of Indians that had taken out the mortar unit appeared behind them, they found themselves in the middle of the crossfire and were wiped out.

Seeing the reinforcements triumphantly enter the stronghold

over a carpet of corpses, Rocas's men started whooping with delight. The whole fortress echoed with their joy.

Jennings hurled a grenade at the enemy reinforcements right below him. The battle was becoming chaotic and fragmented. He could only lead the few men within reach of his voice or his gestures. He could only trust in the numerical superiority of the 5th Battalion and the tenacity of his soldiers. Ultimately, this was always the case. Once the fray began, commanders had limited opportunities to actually command. They can devise a plan, try to foresee what they can, but once the battle was on, chance played a decisive role. Jennings signaled to Corporal Cardenal to take out the heavy machine gun on top of one of the ramparts.

Alfonsina pointed the sniper rifle, studied the target through her telescopic sights, and pulled the trigger.

The man at the machine gun slumped over his own weapon.

Huberman ran into the dungeon, heading for the lab. The battle could still go either way, but if he were on the losing side, he did not intend to leave the fruit of his research in the hands of the communists.

Shlomo was about to rush out of the machine shop. Natalya held him by the arm. Bullets were spraying furiously from every corner of the yard, like hail during a summer storm. The Israeli hung back behind the truck.

As when summer storms pass the peak of greatest violence, the battle soon began to diminish in intensity. The 5th had held on. The Sandinistas had not panicked and had fought the enemy for every inch of the fortress. Their numerical superiority had made a difference. The northeastern bastion had been captured. Little by little, Rocas's men were driven from the walls and courtyard. Eventually, only a handful of fighters remained barricaded in the warehouses where Huberman had been hiding before.

"Now!" Natalya yelled.

The trio exited the machine room. By now there were almost no gunshots. All the shooting was concentrated around the storerooms. They quickly crossed the courtyard and reached the entrance to the dungeons.

From the ceiling, halogen lamps gave out a dim, yellowish light. The three of them proceeded cautiously down the tunnel. They reached a fork and split up, Shlomo to the left, Anton and Natalya to the right. Natalya went first, her Kalashnikov leveled in front of her. Anton walked behind her. The burrow proceeded straight for a hundred meters, then made a sharp bend. When they turned the corner, they found themselves in a large, brightly lit room. At the back of the room, Victor Huberman was hunched over a lab bench. He was stuffing test tubes and containers inside a haversack. Next to the microscope was a Walther P38.

Natalya did not notice the gun. She only had eyes for Huberman. She did not know what she had expected, but this was certainly not it. A saffron Indian cotton shirt, hair pulled back into a long ponytail, necklaces. The Nazi scientist they had been hunting was some kind of shaman. Natalya turned to Anton, as if to ask, "Is that really him?"

She did not have time to get an answer. From the back of the room, Huberman had started shooting. He emptied his magazine, grabbed his bag, and ran through the door behind him.

Natalya doubled over. The room was growing dark. She couldn't breathe and she fell to the floor.

She felt Anton taking her hand.

She tried to speak but her thoughts were confused. Her lips parted only to let out a sigh.

Anton stroked her face. Tears welled in his eyes without his noticing it. He heard footsteps and turned around. It was Shlomo.

"Are you hurt?"

Anton shook his head. "Where did he go?" Shlomo asked.

Anton pointed to the door at the back. His eyes were begging him to get their revenge.

Shlomo nodded and started running toward the door.

Anton clutched Natalya's lifeless body to himself and stayed there for several minutes. At one point, however, he began to hear a ticking sound. He laid Natalya down on the floor and began to inspect the room. That noise scared him. It didn't take him long. On the counter was a bundle of dynamite, connected to what looked like an alarm clock with colored wires.

Epstein was terrified, but he stayed put. The instinct to get out as soon as possible clashed with his desire to get Natalya out. He could not leave her there. He had to bury her, at least. But he would never be able to drag her body away. He went back to check the timer. He couldn't read it. He had no idea how much time he had. He rushed out of the room. He turned the corner and continued down the tunnel. When he had almost reached the courtyard, he heard the explosion.

Anton leaned against the wall of the burrow. He was breathing with difficulty. Once again, he found himself among the survivors without having done anything to deserve it. He covered his face with his hands. In his nostrils he smelled disinfectant. The nauseating smell that stagnated in the room where, thirty-seven years earlier, he had found the bodies of eight murdered children.

77

Prague, May 15, 1948

A ll the front pages were reserved for them, the Jews of Palestine. Sitting in the café opposite the Faculty of Medicine at Charles IV University, Anton Epstein was reading the account of the historic day in Tel Aviv. At the Museum of Art, under the leadership of David Ben Gurion, the Jewish People's Council had ratified the proclamation declaring the establishment of the nascent State of Israel to the world. The Soviet Union was preparing to recognize it. Anton knew that the USSR had not always been benevolent toward Jews, and in particular toward Zionists. Perhaps, he reasoned, they were changing course intentionally to make life difficult for the British. The proclamation coincided with the end of the British mandate in Palestine. Now it would be more difficult for the British to play Arabs and Jews against one another. But whatever the reason, Anton was happy with the new line. The idea that somewhere a state for Jews existed was ultimately reassuring.

On page three, there was an in-depth piece that reconstructed the history of the relationship between Czechoslovakia and the Zionist movement, which the Czech government had always supported. In 1927, President Masaryk had traveled to Palestine, where Jews had welcomed him enthusiastically. Israel was not even on the horizon. A state visit like that had filled with pride 230,000 Jewish settlers trying to build a nation amid the growing hatred of the Arabs and the traps set by the British. That bond had not been severed by the war. As soon as news of the declaration had reached Europe, the mayor of Prague had sent a telegram of congratulations to his counterpart in Tel Aviv. The article didn't mention it, but their mutual sympathy had made Czechoslovakia the Zionists' most important supplier of arms. The first contract had been signed on December 1, 1947, forty-eight hours after the UN resolution calling for the partition of Palestine into two states: one for Jews and the other for Arabs. Beginning in February 1948, the airport at Žatec, near Prague, had been made available to the Haganah, the paramilitary organization of Ben Gurion's Labor Party. Decommissioned transport planes filled with rifles, machine guns, and munitions flew from Žatec, as well as Spitfire and Avia S-199 fighters, which were the first nucleus of the Israeli air force. Their destination was the Ekron airbase in the Negev desert.

There was nothing else of interest in the newspaper. Anton folded it, put it into his leather briefcase, and walked out of the café. He had an appointment with Anna. They planned to go together to buy some wine and something special for dinner. That evening they were celebrating with some friends her first commission: a large canvas for the conference room of the transport ministry. Locomotives and red flags. Not that Anna was particularly inspired by the subject, but it was still an important recognition for a young artist at the beginning of her career. Besides, she would be paid well for it. Mr. and Mrs. Epstein had been brought up with bourgeois expectations, but the wealth of the prewar era was a thing of the past. The war had taken almost everything away and the people's government of the new Czechoslovakia had taken the rest. Neither had any regrets, however. Anton and Anna believed in the future of their country.

A warm sun, heralding summer, shone over the old town. Anton was content and took long strides as he clutched his briefcase under his arm. The world finally seemed to be back on the right track. Shlomo Libowitz came to his mind. It had been a long time since he had thought about him. He hoped that he had managed to reach the Promised Land.

High above him, against the clear sky, flew a large four-engine plane. Anton had no idea but it was a cargo plane for the Haganah fighters. Anton also had no idea that before long, the love affair between the Czechoslovak Republic and the Jews would come to an end. In September, Il'ja Ėrenburg would publish an article in Pravda harshly attacking Zionism, a signal of yet another change of course imposed by Stalin. In the years that followed, in the USSR as well as in the other countries in the socialist bloc, the many trials of spies, deviationists, and traitors of various ideological persuasions featured Jews. In Czechoslovakia, one of the most prominent victims of this wave of repression would be Foreign Minister Vladimír Clementis, the main architect of arms sales to Israel.

Pro-Zionist, pro-Yugoslav cosmopolitan Jew.

78

Department of Olancho, southern Honduras,
July 30, 1982

Shlomo was running down the tunnel. He heard the explosion behind him but he did not even turn around. He kept running. He had chased Lichtblau halfway around the world, had had him in his sights, and let him get away. It was all down to that KGB bitch.

He paused for a moment to catch his breath and felt ashamed of the thought. Not only because Natalya Yakovchenko was dead, but also because he knew that she had only prevented him from shooting Lichtblau because she had a mission to accomplish, just as he did. Except that for Shlomo the mission was much more important. It was not any old assignment that any old agent of any old organization might be given. It was something for which Shlomo Libowitz had been waiting for thirty-seven years. For thirty-seven years he had been convinced that if only he could find Lichtblau, strangle him, and watch his eyes pop out and his face turn blue as he took his last breath, then the ghosts of the Łódź Ghetto, the Soldau Lager, and the castle would be laid to rest. For thirty-seven years, Shlomo Libowitz had waited for that mission. At last, the time had come. However, just before the Group gave him the assignment, Eli had been killed in Lebanon. That death—the closest and most painful—would not be exorcised by the cyanotic face of an old Nazi. That death was a different matter altogether. But it was still part of the same picture. Rivka said that History had hoodwinked the Jews. They had been the victims of bellicosity twice over: first, the Germans' and then their own, which should have protected them, but which was killing them from inside.

He resumed running, his rifle tightly clutched in his fist. He ran into the tunnel, looking for the exit. It felt like he had been in there forever. Thirty-seven years. Three less than Moses in the desert of Sinai. The thought made him want to laugh, but he suppressed the desire because it would have slowed him down. Moses and Aaron had reached the Promised Land. Or was it only Aaron who had gotten there? Shlomo couldn't remember. Screw the Pentateuch, he had a war criminal to bring to human justice. He sped up and finally saw the exit.

Huberman had thought it prudent to stay away from the village. Guillermo Rocas's warriors were fighting to defend his kingdom and he was abandoning the battlefield. What did those savages know about a scientist's duty to his research anyway? In any case, no one had noticed him, except for a woman washing at the stream with her child. He had merely nodded a greeting and carried on. He began to make his way into the jungle. Burdened by the weight of his backpack, it was hard going. He did not have a machete. At a certain point, the vegetation became less dense and he was able to increase his pace. It was getting dark, but he counted on being able to find the hut where the shaman supervized ancient rituals. Huberman had been there several times to try the magic mushroom. There were always supplies in the hut as visits to the land of the spirits could last several days. He would be able to wait there until the Sandinistas left. They would not stay long on Honduran territory.

Shlomo came out into the open sweating and panting. He looked around. There was a woman washing clothes in a stream. A little farther on, a child, knee-deep in water, was playing with a small wooden dugout. Shlomo approached her. Leisi stiffened, called to her son and held him close. Shlomo tried to appear as unthreatening as possible and slung his rifle over his shoulder.

"Where did he go?" he asked in a casual tone that he knew was absurd.

The woman did not answer.

"Lichtblau . . . Huberman. Where did he go?" The tone was beginning to be less friendly.

Still no answer.

Shlomo could no longer control himself. Lichtblau was there somewhere. The bitch had to give him a clue or he would lose him. With a sudden jerk, Shlomo took the gun out of its holster and placed the muzzle of the weapon against the woman's forehead. The child burst into tears. Shlomo Libowitz had done some things in his life he was not very proud of, but he had never done anything like this, and part of him was ashamed of it. His father Baruch would have been ashamed. So would Rivka. But they were not there. They were not charged with catching Lichtblau. He hoped that the woman would give in. He asked again.

"Where? Where?" he yelled in her face.

The woman pointed toward a spot in the bush, shaking like a leaf.

Shlomo lowered his rifle. The woman didn't move. She was holding onto her son, who was racked with sobs, stroking his head and whispering words of comfort to him, all the while staring at the stranger with a mixture of fear and hatred. Shlomo took a few steps in the direction indicated by the woman, but then turned back and eyeballed her harshly.

"If you have lied, I'll burn your house down. "

Huberman made his way into the jungle. It was not far now. He was certain. He clambered over the giant roots of a very tall tree. He stopped for a moment to rest. He crushed a mosquito that had landed on his cheek, adjusted the shoulder straps of his backpack, and set off again. There was a bit of an incline, which was a good sign. The hut was at the top of a rise. He lengthened his stride and suddenly landed up in a squelchy puddle.

He tried to get out but the mud was gripping his calves. He thrashed around but the more frenzied he grew, the more the thick slime dragged him down. A little farther on, through the luxuriant foliage, Huberman thought he could see the outline of the hut. He let out a scream of angry desperation.

Shlomo was making slow progress, not only because he was tired and the vegetation dense, but also because at every step he was seized with doubt about which direction to take. Every so often he found, or thought he found, signs of Lichtblau's passage. A footprint. A broken branch. They were faint traces, which grew fainter as it got darker. All of a sudden, a yell echoed. And then a voice cursing fate. In German. Shlomo Libowitz followed it.

By the time he reached the pool, Lichtblau had already sunk as far as his chest in the quicksand. His arms were still thrashing in the air, desperately looking for something to hold on to. He was so busy trying to free himself that he did not notice his pursuer. Shlomo stood stock still, observing the scene. He wanted to enjoy the moment to the fullest and to make sure that everything took place as it should, so that every single detail would be lodged in his memory. But as he decided to move one step closer to his prey, he realized that his legs could hardly bear his weight. He leaned against a tree. His heart was thumping wildly. He was afraid that, having come so far, he would not make it. His target was a few meters away, immobilized. He was impossible to miss. Shlomo clenched the butt of the gun tightly in his palm, as if to convince himself he could kill him. But was it really Obersturmbannführer Hans Lichtblau? In the shadows of the jungle, Shlomo strained to get a better look. The snow-white ponytail told one story. But the voice that kept cursing the world was the one he remembered. He moved away from the tree and this time managed to get closer. Lichtblau was there in front of him. Shlomo leveled his rifle and took aim. He had been waiting thirty-seven years for this moment. *You cannot do anything for him now but one day you will avenge him.* Was this what the red triangle prisoner had meant in the Soldau concentration camp yard? That everything would come to an end in a pool of quicksand in Central America? Was this really it? He stood with his weapon leveled for a few seconds, his finger tight on the trigger, and finally lowered his arm.

"Do you remember me?" he asked.

Huberman looked up and stared at him in utter wonder. He thought it was a vision. Or perhaps the whole thing was a dream. The Sandinista attack. Melissa's death. The treacherous mud. And now an old Jew dressed as a warrior. A palpable, almost didactic representation of the Jewish-Bolshevik conspiracy. Hooked nose, protruding lips, and a Kalashnikov on his shoulder. This could not be true. It must be a hallucination.

"I must have reached the hut," Huberman thought, "and the magic mushroom has given me the worst trip of my life. "

He had to breathe deep and try to relax. Soon, everything would disappear.

"Orange juice," he said. "In such cases you need a lot of orange juice."

Shlomo looked at him blankly.

"Do you remember me?" he asked again.

"Should I?" Lichtblau answered coldly. If that grotesque hallucination wanted small talk, fine, he would engage in small talk.

"Maybe not," Shlomo conceded. "To you, we were just lab rats. But I was the one who brought you the guinea pigs. I was your trained monkey. There's a chance you might even remember me."

The hallucination spoke German that reeked of Yiddish. Huberman studied the man's face in the dim light filtering through the trees. The face reminded him of something. From what recess of his psyche had he slipped out?

"There was another one, too," Huberman said, mostly to himself because he could not help finding the idea of talking to that caricature absurd. The faces were beginning to come back to him. "Yes, the medical student."

"He's here, too," Shlomo countered. "He's back at the fortress."

The hallucination had brought a friend along. This was hilarious. Huberman burst out laughing.

Ever since he had left Haifa a month earlier, Shlomo had been fantasizing about how he would kill Lichtblau. He had shot him. He had strangled him. Stabbed him. Hanged him. Thrown him off a cliff. He had even handcuffed him, locked him in a car parked in a garage, and then gassed him with exhaust fumes. But he could never have imagined a situation like this. What would Sara have wanted? Something gorier, probably. In truth, nothing would have sufficed for Sara, not even a scalp with congealed blood. What about Baruch? What would he have wanted? Shlomo had no answer to that question, which he had asked himself many times. He looked at the weapon he was wielding. Was it revenge even if he didn't shoot him? Technically, if he didn't shoot, he would not be the one to eliminate the target. His death would be accidental, almost by chance. Chance had played a significant role from the beginning. Surviving captivity had been chance. And it had been chance that his persecutor had reappeared shortly after Eli's death. Had Obersturmbannführer Hans Lichtblau a.k.a. Victor Huberman's number finally been called?

The mud had now reached his neck, but the man who had once been called Hans Lichtblau did not despair. He still had a voice.

"Jew Libowitz, cut off a branch and stretch it toward me," he commanded. "Quick!"

Shlomo smiled. Now he knew what to do. He stuck his pistol

back into the holster, sat at the foot of a tree leaning his back comfortably against the trunk, and lit a cigar. Lichtblau looked like he was trying to speak but in vain. Shlomo just sat there quietly, smoking, and watching the Nazi vanish into the mud down to the last strand of hair.

"*Untermensch*!" Huberman wanted to shout when he saw that Shlomo, instead of following his orders, was squatting on the sandbank. He tried to speak, but his mouth filled with mud. His spontaneous reaction was to spit it out but he couldn't. Then he tried to help himself with his hands, but they did not respond. The quicksand had him in its primordial grip. That thick ooze filled his throat and nostrils. Huberman screwed up his eyes and made one last desperate attempt to breathe. All he managed to produce was a bubble that rippled the surface of the mud pool.

In the uncertain shadows of his passing, perhaps Hans Lichtblau looked for the glittering helmets of the Valkyries, but no warrior deity came down from heaven to lead him to Valhalla. His body was sucked to the bottom of that foul-smelling pool and his spirit perished along with the flesh.

79

Galilea, Palestine, May 18, 1948

The old man watched impassively as soldiers placed mines around his house: four peeling walls and a mint plant in the window. He considered whether to take that away too but the pot was too heavy and he gave up. His neighbors had almost all fled long ago. Many because they had been afraid, both of the fighting and of what might happen next. The month before, in the village of Deir Yassin, west of Jerusalem, Jews had murdered more than a hundred civilians in cold blood, including women and children. Some, however, had left with the belief that they would return soon. They would be away for the few weeks it would take for the armies of the Arab states to throw the Zionists back into the sea. There were also those who thought that without Arab manpower, the Jews would never survive and their economy would collapse. The old man knew that this was all nonsense. Over the years, he had seen the numbers increase. The settlements expand. Crops thrive where they had never grown. Roads paved. The Jews didn't need anyone else. And as far as the Arab states were concerned, the Syrians he had seen transiting towards Safed had not seemed very organized to him. To the extent that the Jews had routed them. Rumor had it that the Arab Legion, commanded by British officers, was fighting well. But it was in the south, with the Jordanians. In any case, the old man had not moved from his home. His children had been born there. His wife had died there. And he would die there, too. At least, that was what he had thought before the soldiers came into the village. When he saw them, the urge to die had left him. He had picked up his most precious possessions and left the sappers to their precise and definitive work.

An airplane with the Star of David on its wings sped by at low altitude and disappeared over the hills. The Jews even had aviation. Those who thought the Arab states could beat them were deluded.

The old man threw his bag on his shoulders and joined the column marching toward the Syrian lines. There were old men like him. There were women with large bundles on their heads holding their children's hands. There were boys whose eyes were ablaze with humiliation and hatred. Soldiers guarded them from a distance. When he heard the explosion, the old man tried hard not to turn around so as not to give the Jews the satisfaction, but he could not stop himself. At first, he saw only a large cloud of dust. Then, as the cloud dissipated in the air, a pile of rubble appeared where his house had once been. The old man fell to his knees and burst into tears. Tears ran down his wrinkled cheeks, like rain on sun-cracked earth.

One of the soldiers, a young, stocky man with strong hands, pulled him up, helped him put the bag back on his back, and waved him on with the others.

"What a shitty job," said Marc.

Dov shrugged.

"Think of all the Germans destroyed," he replied.

"I've never seen a *shtetl*. And neither have you, for that matter. But I see this village here, and what we are doing. I don't like it at all."

Marc was from Bordeaux. Dov, on the other hand, was a *Sabra*, born and raised on a kibbutz. They were walking side by side, rifles leveled, checking that civilians were getting out of the houses and not obstructing the bomb squad.

Shlomo Libowitz walked a meter ahead of them. He took no part in the conversation. With Marc, there were certain issues he could not even begin to discuss. The Frenchman was a good fighter. He had been in the Resistance, and Shlomo had great respect for that. But he was filled with doubt. A classic

Diaspora Jew. He reminded him of Anton Epstein. Shlomo wondered where the young student had ended up.

He went into a house. A filthy hovel, buzzing with flies. Inside, a woman was throwing her possessions onto a cloth spread out on the floor. In a corner, a child stared at him fearfully. Shlomo lowered his rifle and stood in the doorway. The woman did not dignify him with a glance and went on packing, if one could call it that. When she was finished, she pulled the corners of the cloth together into a bundle and tied a knot. Then she took her son by the hand. Shlomo took a step to one side and she left the house, still without looking at him.

Marc may be a classic Diaspora Jew filled with doubt, but theirs was a shitty job for sure.

Shlomo returned to the street and joined his two companions. They were still arguing.

"Well, if you feel that way, you could have stayed in France," the *sabra* said.

This time it was Marc who shrugged. His whole family had been exterminated in the camps. Palestine was the only place he could go.

"Don't we have a right to have a homeland, too?" Dov insisted.

"Of course," Marc replied with conviction. "But if we have to kick people out of their homes in order to have a homeland then it would have been fairer to take Bavaria."

A spontaneous laugh erupted in Shlomo's throat. Take Bavaria. It was the wackiest of Marc's wacky ideas, but he had a point. Now that would have felt good. Kicking all those German asses out of their neat little houses. Unfortunately, it hadn't been on the agenda.

An Avia S-199 flew by at a low pass. Shlomo followed it with his gaze toward the front line. The outline of that aircraft always made him uneasy. It was in fact a Messerschmitt 109. Avia, the biggest Czechoslovak aircraft industry, had produced many exemplars for the Luftwaffe during the war. Now, the Czechs had resumed building it with a new name. The fighter gained altitude and disappeared over the hills. It must be a reconnaissance flight. They had captured Safed after fierce house-to-house fighting against Syrians and Iraqis, who had been forced to fall back. But perhaps they were regrouping.

"The UN proposed an absolutely equal partition plan," Dov resumed. "We accepted it. The Arabs didn't. They want Palestine all to themselves. What do you think we should do?"

Shlomo muttered his assent.

"Defend ourselves by any means available," Marc retorted. "The Arabs understand only the language of force, and their leaders are inept and corrupt."

Dov listened to him with the superior look of someone who has turned the argument around.

"But still," Marc remarked, "the fact remains that pointing a rifle in the face of an unarmed civilian, throwing him out of his house, and maybe even blowing it up, is the stuff of fascists."

"The fascists would have killed them!" the *sabra* snapped indignantly.

"Well, we did that in Deir Yassin," the Jew from the Diaspora said.

"It was the Irgun people in Deir Yassin."

"That's what Ben Gurion says. But two squads of our armored cars took part in the battle, as well as a machine-gun section."

Shlomo quickened his pace and left his comrades behind. The discussion was completely useless. They were fighting a war, a war for their survival. And in war, sometimes you have to do terrible things.

He stopped a hundred meters past the last houses in the village. The Arabs were marching in a line. A column of about thirty people. Suddenly, the air was shaken by a roar. Out of all the Arabs, only one old man turned around, who fell to his knees and began to sob. Shlomo slung his rifle over his shoulder and reached for him. He pulled the old man up, helped him put the bag back on his back, and motioned for him to go on with the others. The man obeyed without uttering a word.

Shlomo stood there, watching the Arabs walk toward their fate. Behind him, TNT charges exploded at regular intervals. Gradually, the Arabs became small dark shapes in the plain and finally disappeared, swallowed by the landscape.

80

Cordillera de Amerrisque, northern Nicaragua,
August 5, 1982

C orporal Martinez sat at the infirmary table and Duarte loosened his bandage. Anton leaned over to check the stitches that zigzagged from his elbow almost to his shoulder along the gash that the shrapnel had opened in the flesh. He ran an alcohol-soaked swab over it and told Duarte to apply a clean bandage.

Since the battle, and throughout the return trip, Anton had been tending to the wounded. As a doctor, he had considered it his duty. Not to mention that that commitment had helped him take his mind off Natalya. Now that the battalion had returned to Nicaraguan territory, Dr. Epstein had taken over responsibility for the small field hospital of the 5th *Batallón de lucha irregular*, assisted by Duarte, a nurse seconded from a clinic in Managua who had represented the entirety of the medical staff of the unit until then.

Anton stepped out of the tent and lit one of Natalya's Gauloises. It was a sunny day and the 3rd Company was preparing to go on patrol under Major Jennings's leadership. The district command had reported a possible infiltration of the Contras just to the north. The rest of the battalion, under Carla's command, would intervene if necessary. Fervent preparations were taking place throughout the camp. Every time someone passed the infirmary, they greeted the new medical officer with extreme respect.

Shlomo had been sorry to return the Kalashnikov. It was a good weapon. Not as good as the Galil but it was reliable. And it was the weapon he had used to storm Lichtblau's fortress. The

Sandinistas would have gladly let him keep it, but there was the problem of how to take it on board. He might have made it as far as Mexico City on the Aerolíneas Nicaragüenses flight, but he would never get on an El Al plane with it. He was reminded of the Shin Bet officer who had questioned him at Tel Aviv airport. It would be fun to be stopped at check-in with a disassembled AK-47 in his suitcase. As a souvenir, Shlomo had had to make do with a box of cigars and a bottle of rum, which had been delivered to him the previous evening by Jennings, with the gratitude of the entire battalion. Without Shlomo Libowitz's help, they might never have succeeded in eliminating Huberman's crew.

By the time Shlomo had returned to the fortress, the battle was already over. Guillermo Rocas's warriors had fought for their fugitive king to the last man. Only in the northeastern bastion had they been able to take prisoners: a few Indians and Dr. Wasserman. Jennings had always hated firing squads, but after Anton had illustrated the German's résumé, the major had no qualms about putting him against the wall on the spot. The following morning, they had buried the dead. They had set fire to the coca plantation and what remained of the fort, and they had departed amid the cries of birds circling in the smoke from the fires. The column had proceeded without incident. Neither the Contras nor the Honduran army had attempted to intercept it. They had crossed the border on the afternoon of August 2. Headquarters had congratulated them on the success of the operation. KGB headquarters was less pleased, but this was more of an issue for the Sandinista People's Army than it was for the 5th *Batallón de lucha irregular*.

Sergeant Corral had arrived to take them back. The Dodge was parked beside the battalion's trucks. Shlomo threw his haversack into the car and went to look for Anton. He found him smoking in front of the infirmary tent at the foot of a bare hill. He asked for a Gauloises, tore the filter off, and lit up.

"Have you packed?"

"I'm not going," Anton said. His tone was awkward, almost conspicuous.

"Are you joining the international brigades?" Shlomo asked, following the question with a laugh.

"They don't have a doctor."

"Don't you want to go back to your country?"

"A doctor has no country."

"There was a time when you would have said that a communist has no country."

Anton made a vague gesture, signifying that there was not much difference after all. The thought had burrowed like a worm into his mind since the day of the battle. Maybe there, in the middle of the jungle, Dr. Epstein might recover his belief in humanity.

All of a sudden, Shlomo threw his arms around him.

"Next year in Jerusalem," he whispered.

Anton pulled his head back and stared into Shlomo's eyes. There was no trace of irony.

"Next year in Jerusalem," he said, with emotion.

Epstein loosened himself from the embrace, looked at his friend one last time, then turned and started up the hill. Halfway up, Nestor waited with two donkeys. One carried boxes of medical supplies. The other had a leather saddle for the doctor. Further up, on the crest of the hill, 3rd Company was ready to go. At the head of the unit, he could see the silhouette of Peter Jennings, black beret and cigar between his teeth.

"Move along, Comrade Epstein!" the Englishman shouted cheerfully. "The revolution is like a bicycle: if it stands still, it falls over."

The men set off. Heading toward the car, Shlomo heard them singing. Months later, as he and Rivka sat in front of the television set in their living room watching in dismay as images of the bodies of men, women, and children lay on top of each other, piled at the foot of walls covered with bullet holes in the rubble of a refugee camp, Shlomo would remember their singing, and for a moment wish he had decided to stay down there with them.

Central and Eastern Europe between 1941 and 1944

Baltic Sea

Lithuania

• Königsberg

East Prussia

White Rutenia

Danzig-West Prussia

Białystok District

Kulmof (Chełmno)

Treblinka

Berlin •

Wartheland

• Warsaw

Litzmannstadt (Łódź)

Volinia

General Government

Praha •

Protectorate of Bohemia and Moravia

Slovakia

Romania

Vienna •

Hungary

——— Germanic Reich border